LIVE THEATRE AND DRAMATIC LITERATURE IN THE MEDIEVAL ARAB WORLD

To Raija-Kaarina

'I remember thee, the kindness of thy youth,
the love of thine espousals,
when thou wentest after me in the wilderness,
in a land that was not sown.'

Jeremiah, II. 2

LIVE THEATRE AND DRAMATIC LITERATURE IN THE MEDIEVAL ARAB WORLD

SHMUEL MOREH

EDINBURGH UNIVERSITY PRESS

Edinburgh University Press
22 George Square, Edinburgh

Typeset in Linotron Baskerville
by Koinonia Ltd, Bury, and
printed in Great Britain by
Page Bros Ltd, Norwich

British Cataloguing in Publication Data
Moreh, Shmuel
Live theatre and dramatic literature in the
medieval Arab world.
I. Title
792.0956

ISBN 0 7486 0292 5

Contents

Scheme of Transliteration

أ	'a, ; 'u, ـئـ 'i		ط		ṭ
آ		'	ظ		ẓ
ـا	، آ or ى	ā	ع		'a
ب		b	غ		gh
ت		t	ف		f
ث		th	ق		q
ـة	in construct	t	ك		k
ج		j	ل		l
ح		ḥ	م		m
خ		kh	ن		n
د		d	ه		h
ذ		dh	و	long	ū
ر		r	و	in diphthong	w
ز		z	ي	long	ī
س		s	ي	in diphthong	y
ش		sh	ـُ		u
ص		ṣ	ـَ		a
ض		ḍ	ـِ		i

Notes:

1. The definite article *al-* is used before solar and lunar letters.
2. ة at the end of words and names is not transliterated, e.g. مدة *(mudda).*
3. A *shadda* is represented by doubling the relevant letter.
4. Arabic words or letters transcribed into Latin characters are shown in italics.
5. Titles of books and articles in the *Encyclopaedia of Islam* (hereafter *E.I.*) are given according to their transliteration, such as *Naḳā'iḍ*, instead of *Naqā'iḍ* and *maḳāma* instead of *maqāma*.

Preface

The present work is the outcome of my interest in the question whether the theatre of Ya'qūb Ṣanū' (James Sanua – Abū Naḍḍāra) (1839–1912), the father of modern Egyptian theatre, was purely European in origin or on the contrary partly rooted in an old Egyptian tradition of popular theatre. In a preliminary paper on the subject delivered at the XIX Orientalists' Congress held in Paris in 1973, I tried to show that the *muḥabbaẓūn* , or itinerant actors, mentioned by E. W. Lane in his *Manners and Customs of the Modern Egyptians,* were active already in the seventeenth century. In this book I have extended the field of inquiry to medieval Islam and have come to the conclusion that, contrary to what is generally assumed by both Arab scholars[1] and western Orientalists, there was a profane and live theatre in the pre-modern Arab world. The Arabs continued the tradition of the Near Eastern popular theatre and they developed this tradition before, and later alongside, the medieval shadow plays,[2] marionettes and *ta'ziya* passion plays.[3]

This book will thus help to trace the roots of the modern Syrian and Egyptian theatres as established respectively by Mārūn Naqqāsh (1817–55) in Beirut in 1848, and Ya'qūb Ṣanū' in Cairo in 1870.

Fortunately, it was possible to find some Persian and Turkish drawings in Islamic art books which illustrate various types of Islamic actors and entertainers mentioned in this book. I found it useful to add these plates here as there are no such paintings known to me by Arab painters.

My thanks are due to Professor Metin And of Ankara University for his kind help and for sending me illustrations of actors and entertainers from his book *Osmanli Şenliklerinde Türk Sanatlari* (Ankara, 1982), and for permission to publish them.

The research was made possible by scholarships from the CNRS, Paris, and DAAD, Bonn, to work in the Bibliothèque Nationale, Paris (summer, 1977), and at the Orientalisches Seminar at Bonn

University (summer, 1979, 1983), as well as the Universities of Berlin, Frankfurt and Tübingen. To both foundations, the CNRS and DAAD, as well as to the universities mentioned, my thanks are due.

I am also grateful to Professor Ch. Pellat (Sorbonne) and especially to the late Professor Dr. O. Spies, as well as to Professor Dr. S. Wild of Bonn University, who gave me valuable help during my stay in France and Germany. I would also like to acknowledge my indebtedness to Professors H. Gaube, F. Steppat, Dr. H. Kellerman, and R. Sellheim for their kind assistance during my stay in Germany; and to Professor J. Sadan of Tel-Aviv University who supplied me with several passages on shadow plays and other quotations from manuscripts of great value to my research.

Much of the research was completed during the summer and autumn of 1982. I was a Visiting Fellow at Clare College, University of Cambridge, England, where I worked at the Cambridge University Library, the Library of the School of Oriental and African Studies, London University, and the British Library in London; I was also Visiting Professor at the Department of Asian and African Studies at Helsinki University, Finland. My thanks are due to the following: Dr. Patricia Crone of Oxford University for her kind assistance in supplying me with copies of many articles concerned with Chapter 1 of this book; Dr. S. Brock of Oxford University for much help with Syriac material; Mr. D. Cowan of London University for his help on translating some Arabic passages, the late Professor Jussi Aro, the former Head of the Department of Asian and African Studies at Helsinki University, for his kind help with Syriac, Latin and Greek passages; Mr. H. Halén for his help in translating passages from Turkish, Persian and Russian and to Professor H. Palva, both of the same department; Mrs. Mirjam Avissar for her help in German and Latin material and to Ms. Aviva Butt; the authorities of U.C.L.A. where I spent my sabbatical year during 1986–7 to complete this research; and especially Professor H. Davidson, Head of the Department of Near Eastern Languages and Cultures; Professor Georges Sabagh, Director of Gustave E. von Grunebaum Center for Near Eastern Studies; Prof. Lev Hakak, Dr. Elizer Chammou, and Ms. Jane Bitar of U.C.L.A.; and my colleagues at the Hebrew University, Professor A. Arazi, Director of the Concordance of Ancient Arabic Poetry, for the great help which the Concordance rendered to this research, Professors D. Ayalon, J. Blau, Dr. S. Hopkins, Dr. M. Lecker, Sh. Shaked, P. Shinar and Miss Lubna Safadi; The Hebrew University authorities and the Faculty of Humanities; as well as many other scholars and librarians whose names I am unable to mention for lack of space. I would also like to thank Marina Hausler of Bonn University, my friend Mr. Victor Ozair of Los Angeles, Mr.

and Mrs. Henry Welby, and Dr. Davide S. Sala of London; and further Professor Ch. Pellat, of Paris, Dr. P. C. Sadgrove and Dr. Patricia Crone for reading the typescript of the entire book and for their valuable remarks; Dr. Crone in particular made numerous suggestions for improvement in respect of both contents and presentation. I am also indebted to Dr. Carole Hillenbrand, the editor of the Islamic Surveys series.

Finally, my thanks go to my wife Raija-Kaarina and my children Maya and Avi for their help and patience while I was writing this book.

S.M

Notes

1. Arab writers who emphasised that Arabs did not know theatre before the nineteenth century are: Muḥammad ʿAbd al-Raḥīm ʿAnbar, *Al-Masraḥiyya bayn al-Naẓariyya wa-'l-Taṭbīq* (Cairo, 1966), pp. 26–31; Muḥammad ʿAzīza, *al-Islām wa-'l-Masraḥ* (Cairo, 1971); ʿUmar al-Dasūqī, *al-Masraḥiyya, Nash'atuhā wa-Uṣūluhā* (Cairo, 1957), pp. 14–18; Tawfīq al-Ḥakīm, *al-Malik Awdīb* [*Oedipus Rex*] (Cairo, 1944), pp. 14–29; id., *Qālabunā 'l-Masraḥī* (Cairo 1949); Muḥammad Ghunaymī Hilāl, *al-Adab al-Muqāran* (Cairo, 1962), pp. 169–72; Idwār Ḥunayn, 'Shawqī wa-'l-Masraḥ', *al-Mashriq*, XXXII, (1934), pp. 563–77; Ṭaha Ḥusayn, *Fī 'l-Adab al-Jāhilī* (Cairo, 1927), pp. 354–9; id., *Ḥadīth al-Arbiʿā'* (Cairo, 1937), vol. II, pp. 15; Muḥammad Mandūr, *al-Masraḥ* (Cairo, 1963); id, *al-Adab wa-Funūnuh* (Cairo, 1963), pp. 69–72; id., *Masraḥiyyāt Shawqī* (Cairo, 1955), pp. 1–7; id., *al-Thaqāfah wa-Ajhizatuhā* (Cairo, 1962), pp. 56–9; Aḥmad al-Shāyib, *Uṣūl an-Naqd al-Adabī* (Cairo, 1946), p. 313; Muṣṭafā al-Shakʿa, *Min Funūn al-Adab al-ʿArabī* (Cairo 1957), pp. 1–4. A contrary view was expressed by Muḥammad Kamāl al-Dīn, in *al-ʿArab wa-'l-Masraḥ* (Cairo, 1975), and Muḥammad Ḥusayn al-Aʿrajī, *Fann al-Tamthīl ʿinda al-ʿArab* (Baghdad, 1978). ʿAlī ʿUqla ʿArsān, *al-Ẓawāhir al-Masraḥiyya ʿind al-ʿArab* (Damascus, 1985), 3rd edn., and ʿUmar M. al-Ṭālib, *Malāmiḥ al-Masraḥiyya al-ʿArabiyya al-Islāmiyya* (al-Maghrib, 1987). A good summary of both views is given by M. M. Badawī, *Early Arabic Drama* (Cambridge, 1988), pp. 2–6.
2. See my article, 'The Shadow Play (*Khayāl al-Ẓill*) in the Light of Arabic Literature', in *Journal of Arabic Literature* XVIII (1987), p. 46, and my article 'Live Theatre in Medieval Islam', in *Studies in Islamic History and Civilization in Honour of Professor David Ayalon*, (Jerusalem, 1986), pp. 565–611.
3. See P. J. Chelkowski (ed.), *Ta'ziyeh, Ritual and Drama in Iran* (New York, 1979); Badawī, *Early Arabic Drama*, pp. 8–10; ʿAzīza, *al-Islam wa- 'l-Masraḥ*; and 'Islam Folklorunda Muharrem ve Taziye', in *Türk Folkloru Arastirmalari Yilligi*, III, 1976, pp. 1–38.

I Introduction

1

The Near Eastern Background

I

A theatrical tradition of foreign origin has twice been implanted in the eastern Mediterranean. First, Hellenistic theatre arrived in the wake of the Greek and Roman conquests of the Near East (331 B.C.E. onwards). The ruins of several Hellenistic and Roman theatres in Mesopotamia, Syria, Lebanon, Jordan, Israel, Egypt and North Africa testify to the considerable role which theatre played in the religious, political and cultural life of Hellenistic pagans and to a certain extent also in that of Jews and Christians. Next, from the beginning of the nineteenth century, the theatres and opera houses of Europe attracted the attention and admiration of Arab scholars,[1] who tried to imitate them in the hope that they would be adopted as a means of cultural, social and literary reform, which in its turn would bring about a renaissance of the Arab world. But what was the situation in between? Was the Near East entirely devoid of theatre (or at least live theatre, as opposed to shadow plays) in the two millennia between the spread of Hellenism and the impact of modern Europe? In what follows I shall argue that it was not; on the contrary, the Muslim world had a well-established tradition of live theatre, if only at a popular level. In many respects the popular theatre of the Muslim world represents a continuation of that attested for the pre-Islamic Near East; it is thus in the pre-Islamic Near East that we must start. We may begin by considering the evidence for theatrical performances among the Jews.

There is no evidence for drama of any kind in the Bible.[2] However, the Jerusalem Talmud {compiled c. 400 C.E.) and the Babylonian Talmud (compiled c. 500 C.E.) are both familiar with the Hellenistic theatre, as well as the circus and stadium:[3] they refer to the theatre by terms such as *tiaṭron, batei, teaṭraoth, teaṭraioth,* and so on, calling the circus *batei kirkasaoth* and the like.[4] In both these and other works the rabbis display a hostile attitude to the theatre, which they considered one of the main symbols of Greco–Roman paganism: 'one should not go to theatres or circuses because entertainments are arranged there in honour of the idols', as the Babylonian Talmud says.[5] In *Midrash Rabba* it is emphasised that the people of Israel never attended *batei teaṭraoth* or *batei kirkasaoth*, but rather kept away from them out of fear of God,[6] as well they might: the same work contains a description of a 'comedy' played by Greek actors ridiculing Jewish rites, especially the Jewish observance of the Sabbath.[7]

The Babylonian Talmud also forbids entertainments which do not directly involve honouring idols, such as visiting stadiums (areas for gladiatorial contests) and 'camps' (the Roman *castra*) or witnessing the performances of sorcerers, enchanters, clowns, mimics, buffoons and so on (the names of whom are given in corrupted Latin terms). Attendance is construed as transgression of the precept implied in Psalms I: 1–2, that one should not sit in the seat of the scornful, but rather delight in the law of the Lord; and it is asserted that 'those things cause one to neglect the Torah'.[8] Finally, Israelites were prohibited from building roads or theatres using stones brought from the statue of Mercurius.[9]

There is no evidence at all for Jewish attempts at the theatrical genre until Ezekiel, the Jewish poet of Alexandria and 'writer of tragedies', who probably died during the first century B.C.[10] His drama *Exagoge* (Exodus) was written in Greek in the style of the Septuagint. Only 269 verses have been preserved, but it clearly related the history of Moses and the exodus of the 'chosen seed' from Egypt according to the Bible, with some additions probably taken from the *Aggada*. Apparently its purpose (and possibly that of the genre in general) was to strengthen the Jewish faith by reminding the audience of the miracles of their history, as well as to discourage Jews from visiting pagan theatres.

This drama was written in five acts with no unity of time or place.[11] It starts with Moses encountering Zipporah and her sisters and saving them from the evil shepherds near the well. In later acts it shifts to the palace of Reuel, the ruler of Midian, to Moses on Mount Horeb conversing with God, and to Pharaoh's palace. In the final act Moses is seen in the Sinai desert after having crossed the Red Sea with the tribes of Israel. The difficulty of changed locations was solved by painting 'some pieces of landscape on the revolving *periaktoi* [which] would inform the audience that the country scene were set in different places each time, and some symbols also painted on the *periaktoi* would differentiate the palace of Madiam from that of Egypt'.[12] In answer to the question whether this tragedy was performed before a Jewish audience, Sifakis observes that 'a Jewish audience and theatre is not unlikely, say, in Alexandria, since a Jewish amphitheatre is known in Berenice (Benghazi)'.[13]

By then Jewish actors were well known in Rome: thus Aliturus, who was one of the favourites of the emperor Nero (54–68 C.E.), the actress Faustina (first century C.E.), and the actor Menophilus (first century C.E.).[14]

Greek was the spoken language in the Hellenised cities of Palestine, such as Caesarea, and theatres, circuses and amphitheatres were the main places for popular entertainment. In the Jerusalem Talmud the story of the mime Pantokakus is related with some details which show that Jewish women were also employed in the theatre, though such employment was considered sinful. Pantokakus, after being asked to pray for rain, reveals his profession to Rabbi Abbahu: 'This man [meaning himself] commits five sins every day; he adorns the theatre, engages *hetaerae* [sc. musicians and dancers], brings their clothes to the bath-house, claps hands and dances before them and clashes cymbals before them.' Patokakus's only good deed, which made him worthy of offering the prayer for rain and being answered by God, was that he sold his last belongings in order to save an innocent woman from working in the theatre.[15] A second episode in the Midrash shows that in Palestine Jewish women should not attend the theatre or circus. Naomi warns Ruth that in case of her conversion to Judaism she would not be able to attend such performances.[16]

According to the Midrash, Joseph 'went into the house to cast up his master's accounts' while 'all flocked to see the day of the Nile Festival, a day of theatrical performances'.[17] The rabbis were thus aware that theatrical performances were given in Egypt on the day of the Nile festival, a day which was celebrated by the Copts and later also by the Muslims until the nineteenth century. Medieval Muslim scholars likewise saw this festival as a direct continuation of Pharaonic celebrations.[18]

In the Talmud some rabbis permit visiting the stadiums for humanitarian reasons: 'it is permitted to go to the stadiums because by shouting one may save [the victim from the wild animals]. One is also permitted to go to a camp for the purpose of maintaining order in the country, provided that one does not conspire [with the Romans]... One should not go to the stadiums because they are "the seat of the scornful", but Rabbi Nathan permits it for two reasons: first, because by shouting one may save [the victim], second, because one might be able to give evidence [of death] for the wife [of a victim] and so enable her to remarry'.[19]

All in all, it is clear that the Jews were familiar with theatrical performances even if they were not supposed to attend them.

The early Christians would appear to have been no less hostile to the theatre than were the rabbis. From the second century C.E. onwards, theatre was the object of numerous diatribes in both Greek and Syriac, such as those of Aristides, Justin, Tertullian (second century C.E.)[20] and Theodore of Mopsuestia (fourth century C.E.); the latter roundly condemned the theatre, the circus and the race-course along with athletic contests, water organs and dances as so many means whereby Satan led the souls of men to perdition.[21]

Play-acting was one of the occupations which the convert had to abjure before he could be admitted to instruction.[22] Converts duly abandon their theatrical profession in a story told by Palladius, Bishop of Hellenopolis whose *Paradise of the Holy Fathers* was composed in Greek in 420 C.E. and translated into Syriac in the sixth or seventh century. Serapion was sold to 'comic actors' in a 'city of heathens' and suffered humiliation until 'he had taught them and made them Christians, and had freed them from following the business of the theatre'; when both the leader of the actors, his wife and the actors themselves had been baptized, they all abandoned their occupation to live a God-fearing life.[23]

In fact, there were also pagans who were wary of the theatre. Thus the emperor Julian (355–63 C.E.), who organised a pagan priesthood in the provinces of the Roman empire, instructed its members to avoid licentious theatrical performances and prohibited priests from entering theatres and having actors or charioteers as friends. He also forbade priests and even sons of priests to attend hunting shows with dogs performed inside a theatre.[24]

Such attitudes notwithstanding, the theatre continued to flourish.[25] In fourth-century Antioch 'there were a number of different types of entertainment – classical tragedy and comedy, pantomime, mime and dancing, some of which seem to have been somewhat of the order of ballet'.[26] Libanius was primarily concerned to keep 'the theatre prosperous and protect it from attacks by Christian interests, though he did ... recognize the political dangers that arose from the activities of some of the theatrical companies and from the political employment of the applause and acclamation of the organized theatrical claques'.[27] On the other hand, Chrysostom, a compatriot of Libanius, endeavoured to persuade the Antiochenes to keep away from theatrical entertainment on the grounds that it was licentious and corrupted 'the individual and, directing men's thoughts constantly to these subjects, would make them discontented with their family life'. He did not, however, have great success in his efforts.[28]

A no less vehement critic of the theatre was Jacob of Serugh, the zealous bishop of Batnan (the chief town of Serugh). He died on 29

November 521 C.E., a century before Muḥammad's *hijra*. His homilies against the theatre testify to the great interest of both Christians and pagans in Greek dramas, which were still being played in the Byzantine cities of the sixth century.[29]

Jacob of Serugh condemns the themes, dances and music of the theatre as derived from pagan mythology, which he deems ludicrous and immoral. He incidentally reveals some details about the theatre of his day, for example that actors would don false breasts in order to appear as women: he contrasts this procedure with that of Moses, who was 'girt with truth' and who did not 'bind the sandal on his foot, and the plate of metal, that he may strike upon it; but he loosens his sandals, that he may go down and tread the Egyptians under foot'.[30] He also alludes to many dramas based on Greek mythological themes, such as Kronos devouring his own sons and mutilating Uranus, or Zeus in various guises committing 'fornication with many women and immorality with men', carrying off Ganymede as an eagle, assuming the form of a bird to commit adultery with Leda, that of a bull to commit fornication with Europa, and beguiling Danae in a shower of gold.[31] Other paragraphs allude to the legend of Hermes winning the affection of Ikarius's daughter Penelope and transforming himself into a goat to give birth to the god Pan; to the myths of Herakles, Artemis and the adultery of Ares and Aphrodite; to the legend of Apollo and Daphne; and to the birth of Aphrodite from foam.

The Christians who frequented the theatre argued that they were baptised Christians confessing one Lord who knew the mimes to be false and that they attended only in order to laugh; but Jacob brushes aside such justifications with the declaration that 'the mimer of the spectacles meditates on the stories of the gods; who can bathe in mud without being soiled?' Nobody could, because the miming of lying tales is a 'teaching which destroys the mind'.[32]

Jacob's dicussion shows that some Christians remained hostile to classical theatre, although others had become fond of it. It reveals considerable knowledge of the classical lore and indicates that the cultural barrier between Christians and pagans was less sharp than that between pagans and Jews. But it also provides the last evidence for the continuation of classical theatre in the Christian Near East.

It seems that during the first centuries of Christianity, while the Church Fathers were attacking the theatre, the pagans used the institution to ridicule Christian rites and ceremonies, as they did with Jewish tradition too.[33] Such evidence is supplied by two sources, a Coptic martyrdom and a Syriac play. The Coptic martyrdom of Saint Mercurius (Marqūryūs) describes the martyrdom of an actor who died in the reign of Julian the Apostate (360–3) as follows:

> The eighteenth day of the month of Tūt [September 15]: we celebrate the feast of Saint Mercurius. He was an actor (*khayālī*). At first he was not a Christian. When Constance (Qusṭus), the son of the emperor Constantine (Qusṭanṭīn), died, the infidel Julian (Yūliānūs), who killed Saint Mercurius, succeeded him. This infidel was the nephew of the emperor Constantine; he revived idol worship, and many were martyred at his hands. On the occasion of his birthday he gathered musicians (*malāhī*) and actors *(mukhāyilūn)* to play. This saint was among them. The obstinate emperor ordered them to play a parody imitating (*yuḥākī*) Christians. He acted a comic play imitating them (*aḥkā bihim*). When he began to imitate the sacred baptism making the sign of the holy cross upon the water in the name of the Father, the Son and the Holy Ghost, the Lord enlightened his mind and he saw the grace of the Divinity descending upon the water and the light covering it. He immediately took off his clothes and plunged into [the water] three times. Then he got out of the water, put on his clothes and confessed that he was a Christian ... Then the emperor ordered that he be beheaded....[34]
>
> (The Arabic terminology of this passage will be dealt with in Chapter 2)

The Syriac play is a tragedy written a century later, in the fifth century. It is known as *The History of the Mimes of Oxyrhynchus* and seems to have been translated from the Greek. J. Link, who translated it in part, was unable to fix the exact dates of either the composition or the translation. Some names of apparently historical figures do appear, but not all can be identified. Judging from the style of the Syriac translation, however, the play seems to have been translated after the time of Simeon the Stylite (d. 459 C.E.). The colophon of the Syriac manuscript states that the play was copied in Alkosh (near Mosul) by the deacon Isho' Bar Isaiah, a fact which shows that there was interest in drama in Mesopotamia too.[35]

The plot of the play is a miraculous incident in which pagan mimers and dancers gather to perform a comic play ridiculing Christian rites, only to convert to Christianity in the end. Initially the actors make a mock church, cross and altar, and appoint a bishop and other churchmen. They begin to recite the Psalms and the Gospel. But when the actor who plays the bishop sits down to preach the Gospel and give the blessing, his heart is filled with the faith, as are the hearts of the six actors who play listeners, and also some of the 'audience' in the play. He is asked to baptise them. They are dressed in white and kiss the cross. They then change the play to a Christian one. The six actors who have accepted Christianity try to persuade the others to convert. The reflection of the light from the cross shines on the head of the baptized actors, a miracle which convinces the others. Some still refuse to accept the new religion, but in the end all are converted and become martyrs.[36]

Evidently, this text suggests that despite their general hostility to the theatre, the Christians had themselves come to make use of it. It also testifies to the survival of drama in the Near East, at least as a literary form.

From the sixth century onwards, however, there is no further evidence for live theatre as a high art, only for games, mimes and other lowbrow performances. Thus we hear of *mimoi* who played on a platform in the sixth century at the time of the emperor Mauricius;[37] and in the city of Emesa, a monk who disapproved of the theatre prevented an actor from following his profession and forbade association with prostitutes and actors,[38] We even hear of children play-acting. Of the future Athanasius of Alexandria we are told that 'he used to play (*yal'ab*) with other children and to say to them, "I am your bishop (*usquf*)". He would appoint some of them priests and others sextons. Once Saint Alexander (Alkhsandrus), the Patriarch of Alexandria, saw him (playing) and told him, "you will be a bishop in reality". And it happened as he said'.[39] We also have evidence of six century mimes playing in the courtyards of churches. Thus John of Ephesus tells a story, set between 537 and 541 C.E., of 'certain great and holy persons, children of eminent men of Antioch, who despited the world and all that is in it and lived a holy life in it in poverty of spirit in an assumed garb'. The relevant passage goes as follows:

> When I was in the city of Amida nine years ago, and was constantly devoting myself to reciting the service and to vigil in the holy church, I used to see a young man of handsome appearance as in the garb of a mime-actor, and with him moreover a young girl whose beauty cannot be portrayed and whose appearance was comely and marvellous accompanied him in the garb of a courtesan, and they used to go about the city in that assumed garb in order to deceive the spectators, lest anyone should perceive and know what they were, and they used constantly to perform drolleries and buffooneries, being constantly in the courts of the church like strangers, jesting at the clergymen and everyone, and being boxed on their heads by everyone as mime-actors, while at all hours of the day a large number of people surrounded them, chiefly on account of their marvellous appearance, and the comeliness of their faces, joking and playing with them, and giving them slaps on their heads.[40]

The importance of this story lies not only in its account of actors performing drolleries and buffooneries in the courtyards of churches, but also in the detail that the actors were slapped on their heads while performing, a custom which seems to have continued in the medieval Muslim world; in Arabic such actors were called *ṣafāʿina* (slap-takers or slapstick actors).[41]

Besides theatre proper, there were pagan festivals such as the Greek spring festival[42] and the orgiastic nocturnal festival, the *Maiumas*, which recurred every three years.[43] The pagan spring festival of May 496 was described by Joshua the Stylite in his *Chronicle*.[44] There is a striking similarity between the manner in which this festival was celebrated and that attested for the later Coptic festival of Nawrūz or Nayrūs (as the Copts were to call their New Year, using a Persian term), which was celebrated on March 21 every year (in the month of Tūt).[45] Joshua the Stylite's description of the *Maiumas* festival is also similar to the descriptions of Nawrūz by Muslim historians such as al-Masʿūdī [46] and al-Maqrīzī.[47] All three speak of the kindling of large numbers of lamps along river banks, in the main streets in public and private buildings and in the markets. Dancers (*orkhestai*) performed in the pagan festival, while masked actors (*samāja*), singers and musicians performed in the Coptic festival in both the Byzantine and the Islamic eras (the documentation being particularly rich for the Fatimid period). Both festivals were celebrated for seven days 'with singing and shouting and lewd behaviour', as Joshua the Stylite puts it; and both were viewed with suspicion by the authorities: the pagan spring festival was prohibited by edict of the emperor Anastasius in 502 C.E., while Justinian I (527–65) prohibited all pagan festivals and theatrical performances;[48] and Muslim rulers would prohibit the celebration of Nawrūz and other Coptic feasts from time to time.[49]

The Muslim scholar Ibn al-Ḥājj (d. 737/1336) vehemently criticised popular Muslim behaviour in Egypt and North Africa, which he regarded as heretical (*bidaʿ*); and he denounced the Nayrūz and the Nile festivals, both celebrated by Copts and Muslims alike, as Pharaonic customs:

> This feast [sc. Nayrūz] is similar to that which they celebrate on the day of the Nile. These two feasts are characteristics of Pharaoh which remained among his people, who are the Copts, and spread from them to the Muslims.[50]

It was not however only from the Byzantine world that Muslim authors discerned continuity. Thus the anonymous author of *Kitāb al-Tāj fī Akhlāq al-Mulūk* (attributed to al-Jāḥiẓ, d. 255/868f) has it that the Arabs adopted three classes of court companions (*nudamāʾ*) from the Persians, that is singers (*mughannūn*), jesters (*muḍḥikūn*) and buffoons *(ahl al-hazl wa-'l-biṭāla)*.[51] Though this author is concerned with practices at court rather than the popular level, there is also a striking similarity between the *kawsaj* (a man devoid of hair on the sides of his face) in the celebration of *yawm Hurmuz* by the Persians and the *amīr al-Nawrūz* in the Nawrūz celebrations of the Copts.[52] Ibn al-Ḥājj and the anonymous author of *Kitāb al-Tāj* were undoubtedly right in their assumption of a carry-over from both Byzantine and Persian civilizations to the Islamic world.

II

There is only scant evidence for Arab awareness of theatrical performances in the Byzantine empire on the eve of Islam. The most important evidence is supplied by Ḥassān b. Thābit (d. 54/674?), Muḥammad's poet and defender who was active in both the Jāhiliyya and Islam. During the pagan period Ḥassān used to frequent the courts of the Christian Arab kings of the Ghassanids in Syria and the Manādhira in Ḥīra, bordering on the Byzantine and Persian empires respectively. In one poem he adduces the *mayāmis Ghazza* as an example of something feeble (*wāfir* meter): *mayāmisu Ghazzatin wa-rimāḥu ghābin//khifāfun lā taqūmu bihā 'l-yadāni* ('the *mayāmis* of Gaza and the reed spears from the forest of lances// light, lending the hands no force').[53] What then are these *mayāmis*? The commentators on Ḥassān's *Dīwān* inform us that '*mīmas* is the singular of *mayāmis*; he is a person who is ridiculed (*wa-huwa 'lladhī yuskhar minhu*) It is not derived from *mūmisa*, for *mūmisa* is a prostitute and its plural is *mawāmis*'.[54] If this is correct, Ḥassān was referring to mimes. Though the parallel Hebrew expression *meyumase 'Azza* has been explained with reference to the Maiumas, the orgiastic festival mentioned above,[55] the commentators are probably right. When David ben Abraham al-Fāsī (tenth century) speaks of the mime (Greek *mimos*) in his *Kitāb Jāmi' al-Alfāẓ* he calls the mimic *mutamaymis*, using a similar construction. The mimic throws sparks of fire, spears and other tools of death, revealing the actors performance in al-Fāsī's time: *ka-'l-mutalāhī 'l-mutamaymis alladhī yarmī 'l-sharār wa-'l-sihām wa-sā'ir ālāt al-mawt*, 'like the *mimos* who entertains by throwing sparks of fire, spears and other instruments of death'.[56] Horovitz was also of the opinion that Ḥassān b. Thābit used the term *mayāmis* in its Greek sense, though he opted for *mimesis* rather than *mimoi*.[57]

Some further evidence is supplied by the poet Jarīr (33?–110/653?–728) who, in one of his poems, speaks of 'Christians playing in the morning of a feast'.[58] It is by no means unlikely that 'playing' here is to be understood in the sense of giving a theatrical performance. The feast referred to was probably *Sha'ānīn*,[59] which Arab Christians used to celebrate by carrying palm leaves and censers to the church, chanting hymns and performing a prayer near the gate of the church; and this ritual may have been one among several types of semi-theatrical performances once held in the courtyards of Syria. According to Sebastian Brock:

> Although religious drama never developed among the Oriental churches in the way that it did in the medieval West, there were several semi-dramatic elements inherent in their liturgies: in particular in some of the religious poetry, which contains dialogues. One of these, a dialogue between the Penitent Thief and the Cherub (Luke 23: 42–3) is actually mimed on Easter Monday in some churches in Iraq ... How old this is there is no means of telling, though the poem itself could be fifth-century – and is in any case pre-Islamic ... There is no evidence for any of the other dialogues being mimed, though ... the parable of the Wise and the Foolish Virgins is re-enacted in some form by the deacons some time in the Holy Week. (The dialogue poems used on Palm Sunday are between Church and Zion/Synagogue).[60]

In his article 'Syriac Dialogue Poems' Brock adds that

> Syriac is rather rich in dialogue poems where the participants are usually biblical figures; best known of these, perhaps, is Ephrem's *memra* on the Sinful Woman, a piece which ... influenced (in translation) the early development of Greek and Latin liturgical drama. Among the many extant Syriac dialogue poems the *soghyatha* form a distinct group whose chief characteristic is the allocation of alternate stanzas to each speaker; this particular form of stylized dialogue in fact has its origin in another genre, the ancient Mesopotamian precedence dispute (prose or verse), a genre which was subsequently to travel, by way of the Arabic *munāẓara*, to medieval Europe.[61]

In view of this information, it is tempting to read Jarīr's line as an allusion to actual enactments of such dialogues. Alternatively, it refers to a procession such as that on Palm Sunday.

Further evidence is provided by the story of 'Amr b. al-'Āṣ (d. 42/663) related by al-Kindī and al-Maqrīzī. Both say that 'Amr used to frequent Egypt with his merchandise in the Jāhiliyya. Once he happened to visit Alexandria during a feast which the Egyptians used to celebrate in a *mal'ab* (theatre or amphitheatre) with plays, or, as al-Kindī puts it, 'a feast during which they assemble and play' (*yajtami'ūna fīhi wa-yal'abūna*). After the play the princes would gather to throw a ball; it was predicted that the person in whose lap the ball fell would become the ruler of Egypt, and in that year the ball duly fell into 'Amr's lap:[62]

This theatre (*mal'ab*) would be attended by thousands of

> people. There would not be anyone [among the spectators] who could not see [the spectacle] opposite them. If a letter was read, all of them would hear it, and if any kind of play was played (*aw lu'iba lawnun min anwā' al-li'b*), they would all see it. They did not infringe on the rights of other spectators though some would sit in higher and others in lower rows.[63]

Whether this story is true or not, it suggests that some Arabs attended Byzantine theatres. It was perhaps also in a theatre that Ḥassān b. Thābit watched a mime's performance.

After the final victory of Islam in the time of the third caliph 'Uthmān b. 'Affān (24–35/644–55) we hear of a Jewish magician and player from one of the villages of Kūfa near Jisr Bābil. Al-Mas'ūdī gives his name as Baṭrūnī, while other sources call him Bustānī, name well attested for Jewish families in Babylonia.[64] He is said to have performed 'buffoonery' (*a'mālan min al-sukhriyya*), which can mean miming, as is clear from the definition of *mīmas* by the commentators of the poetry of Ḥassān b. Thābit as 'a man who is ridiculed' (*huwa 'lladhī yuskharu minhu*).[65] That the Jew was not only a magician, but also an actor or mime is corroborated by al-Mas'ūdī's statement that he performed 'various kinds of magic, illusion tricks and acts of buffoonery' (*ya'malu anwā'an min al-siḥr wa-'l-khayālāt wa-a'mālan min al-sukhriyya*) before al-Walīd b. 'Uqba, the governor of Iraq in 35/655. The full version of al-Mas'ūdī's account is as follows:

> Among these things was the deed of al-Walīd b. 'Uqba in the mosque of Kūfa. He heard of a Jew called Baṭrūnī, an inhabitant of one of the villages of Kūfa near Jisr Bābil called Zurāra, who performed various kinds of magic, illusion tricks and acts of buffoonery. Al-Walīd b. 'Uqba fetched him. The man showed him various kinds of appearances (*takhyīl*) in the mosque. He represented to him at night a huge Yemenite king (*qayl*) on a horse galloping in the courtyard of the mosque. Then the Jew was metamorphosed into a she-camel walking on a rope. Then he showed him the figure of a donkey, which he entered via its mouth and left via its behind. He also beheaded a man and separated his body from his head; then he turned the sword on him, whereupon the man got up [alive].[66] A group of people from Kūfa attended the [performance], among them Jundab b. Ka'b al-Azdī. Jundab sought the refuge of God from the work of the devil and from acts which distance (man) from the Merciful. He understood that this was a kind of magic and illusion (*takhyīl*). He unsheathed his sword and struck the Jew a blow which caused his head to roll from his body, saying 'the truth has come, and falsehood has vanished away; surely falsehood is ever certain

> to vanish'.[67] It is also said that this happened in daytime and that Jundab went to the market, approached one of the swordmakers and took a sword, whereupon he went in and beheaded the Jew saying, 'if you speak the truth, then resurrect yourself'.[68]

In the pre-Islamic past people used to 'visit stadiums ... and witness there (the performances of) sorcerers and enchanters', as the Babylonian Talmud says. The story of Baṭrūnī shows that popular performers of this kind were still plying their trade after the Arab conquests.

The conclusion of Stefan Wild in his article 'A Juggler's Programme in Medieval Islam' is relevant here:

> Like other and more important parts of the Islamic cultural heritage, the juggler's repertoire shows two layers of tradition, one superimposed upon the other. One layer is openly Hellenistic, goes back to translated works and schools of translation, and can be dated with relative certainty to the early Abbasid period ... There is another layer ... which is historically much more difficult to assess ... It was transmitted directly, not by books, but by jugglers, who visited and performed in the centers of the Oriental Hellenistic world: Alexandria, Jerusalem, Emesa and so on. If this is true, the cups and balls would be a case parallel to the Greek farces, which must have been played all over the Hellenistic world and which have surely influenced what was to become the Arabic shadow play – another form of popular entertainment which has been neglected by official Arabic literature. And the juggler has always been the brother of the actor, the mimos.[69]

To this conclusion I would add that Hellenistic jugglery and farces influenced the live theatre of the medieval Islamic world as well.

To sum up, although Judaism, Christianity, and as we shall see in the following chapters Islam, rejected the dramatic traditions of the Greeks, Romans, Turks and Persians, nevertheless it is possible to observe evidence of the survival of ancient seasonal fertility rites and myths of these nations in their dramatic performance a long time after Islam. These cultures used drama to celebrate death and resurrection in rituals of agricultural festivals pertaining to the vegetation and seasonal cycle, and in rites derived from shamanism which are 'not related to the calender and are not seasonal in nature',[70] as in some aspects of central Asian cultures.

By the eve of Islam, the original meanings of the pagan religious dramas among the Greeks, Romans, Turks and Persians had been long forgotten. Instead, these dramatic ceremonies came to be understood as commemorating some legendary or historical event and became seasonal folk theatre. These dramas which became secular entertainment tended towards parody and mockery of the former customs and rituals.[71] This change is obvious in the Persian and Central Asian dramatic elements contained in the Muslim world, mainly the *kurraj*, the *samāja* and the performance of *Amīr al-Nawrūz*, as we will see in the following chapters.

Notes

1. Rifā'a Rāfi' al-Ṭahṭāwī, *Takhlīṣ al-Ibrīz fī Talkhīṣ Bārīz*, (Cairo, 1958), pp. 165–70; 'Alī Mubārak, *'Alam al-Dīn*, (Alexandria, 1299/1882), vol. II, pp. 397–440; Aḥmad Fāris Shidyāq, *al-Wāsiṭa fī Ma'rifat Aḥwāl Māliṭa wa-Kashf al-Mukhabbā 'an Funūn Urubbā* (Constantinople, 1299/1881f), pp. 305–12.
2. *Encyclopedia Judaica* (hereafter *EJ*), s.v. 'Theatre'.
3. M. Jastrow, *A Dictionary of the Targumim* (New York, 1950), vol. II, p. 1663.
4. *Talmud Yerushalmi, Masseketh Horayoth*, fol. 18b; *Talmud Babli, 'Abodah Zarah*, letter *gimel*, fol. 18b, and *Masseketh Megillah*, fol. 6a. Cf. also Nathan me-Romi, *Sefer ha-Arukh* (*Aruch Completum*), (Vienna, 1926), vol. VI, p. 190, col. 1.
5. *Talmud Babli, 'Abodah Zarah*, fol. 18b = *The Babylonian Talmud, Seder Nezikin, 'Abodah Zarah*, (London, 1935), p. 95.
6. *Midrash Rabba*, letter *gimel*.
7. Ibid., letters *yud-zayn*.
8. *Talmud Babli, 'Abodah Zarah*, fol. 18b = p. 94.
9. Ibid., fol. 42a = p. 208.
10. *EJ*, s.v. 'Ezekial the Poet'; J. Wieneke (ed.), *Ezechielis Judaici Poetae Alexandrini Fabulae Quae Inscribitur Exagoge Fragmenta* (Münster, 1931); G. M. Sifakis, *Studies in the History of Hellenistic Drama* (London, 1967), pp. 122f, 135; H. Jacobson, *The Exagoge of Ezechiel* (Cambridge, 1983).
11. Sifakis, *Studies*, p. 123.
12. Ibid., p. 135.
13. Ibid., p. 123.
14. *EJ*, s.v. 'Theater', col. 1050.
15. *Talmud Yerushalmi, Taanith*, I, 4, fol. 64a; cf. S. Liebermann, *Greek in Jewish Palestine: Studies in the Life and Manners of Jewish Palestine in the II–IV Centuries CE* (New York, 1942), pp. 31f.
16. *Midrash Rabba* (Jerusalem, 1965), vol. IV, ch. 2, p. 9, no. 23; cf. also *EJ*, vol. XV, col. 1050.
17. *Midrash Rabba*, vol. I, ch. 87, p. 187, no. 7.
18. See for example Ibn al-Ḥājj, *al-Madkhal al-Shar' al-Sharif* (Cairo, 1929), vol. II, pp. 49–51.
19. *Talmud Babli, 'Abodah Zarah*, fol. 18b = pp. 94f.
20. C. Moss, 'Jacob of Serugh's Homilies on the Spectacles of the Theatre', *Le Muséon* XLVIII pp. 92–5; Tertullian, *Apology, De Spectaculis* (London, 1931), pp. 230–301.
21. M. L. W. Laistner, *Christianity and Pagan Culture in the Later Roman Empire* (Cornell, 1951), p. 7.

22. Ibid., p. 33; cf. W. Riedel and W. E. Crum (eds and trs), *The Canons of Athanasius of Alexandria* (Oxford, 1904), Arabic text, pp. 23f.
23. Palladius, *The Paradise of the Holy Fathers* (Oxford, 1934), vol. I, pp. 248–50.
24. J. B. Segal, *Edessa, 'The Blessed City'* (Oxford, 1970), p. 164; cf. G. Downey, *A History of Antioch in Syria from Seleucus to the Arab Conquest* (Princeton, 1961), p. 440.
25. Cf. P. Brown, *The World of Late Antiquity* (London, 1971), p. 38: plate no. 28 ('Watching a circus race. Crowded scenes such as this, though condemned by Christian bishops, show that the town life of the Mediterranean survived ... up to the sixth century'); cf. ibid., p. 180, plate no. 180 ('A Greek tragedy being performed at Constantinople in the sixth century').
26. Downey, *Antioch*, p. 443.
27. Ibid., p. 444.
28, B. H. Vandenberghe, 'Saint Chrysostome et les Spectacles', *Zeitschrift für Religions und Geistesgeschichte* VII (1955), pp. 34–46; cf. Downey, *Antioch*, p. 444.
29. Moss, 'Jacob of Serugh', pp. 87–112; cf. Segal, *Edessa, 'The Blessed City'*, p. 165.
30. Moss, 'Jacob of Serugh', p. 104.
31. Ibid., pp. 110f.
32. Ibid., pp. 105, 109.
33. J. Link, *Die Geschichte der Schauspieler nach einem syrischen Manuskript der königlichen bibliothek in Berlin* (Berlin, 1904), pp. 15–18; cf. above, n. 7.
34. R. Basset (ed. and tr.), *Le Syntaxe Arabe Jacobite (Mois de Tout et de Babeh)* (Paris, 1907), vol. I, pp. 279f.
35. Link, *Schauspieler*, p. 9.
36. Ibid, pp. 10–30, where the play is summarised.
37. Ryden (ed.) *Das Leben des heiligen Narren Symeon, von Leontius von Neapolis* (Uppsala, 1963), pp. 150f.
38. Ibid., p. 150, ll. 7–9.
39. A. Scher (ed. and tr.), *Histoire Nestorienne (Chronique de Séert)*, part I, (Paris, 1908), vol. IV, p. 252; cf. Īrīs Ḥabīb al-Miṣrī, *Qiṣṣat al-Kanīsa al-Qibṭiyya* (Cairo, 1953), pp. 190f.
40. John of Ephesus, *Lives of the Eastern Saints* (Paris, 1924), vol. XIX, pp. 166f; cf. J. B. Segal, 'Mesopotamian Committees from Julian to the Rise of Islam', *Proceedings of the British Academy*, XLI (1955), p. 116.
41. Cf. below, Chapter 4, pp. 82–3, n. 17.
42. Segal, *Edessa*, p. 106.
43. Downey, *Antioch*, p. 444.
44. Joshua the Stylite, *Chronicle* (Cambridge, 1882), pp. 24f, 42 (Syriac), 20f, 35 (English).
45. On the Nawrūz, see J. Richardson, *Dictionary : Persian, Arabic and English* (London, 1806), p. lix; I. Lassy, *The Muḥarram Mysteries among the Azarbeijan Turks of Caucasia* (Helsinki, 1916); J. Patel, 'The Navroz, its History and its Significance', *Journal of the K. R.*

Cama Institute (Bombay), XXXI (1937), pp. 1–51; M. Boyce, *A History of Zoroastrianism* (Leiden and Cologne, 1975–82), vol. I, pp. 224, 245; vol. II, pp. 108–10.

46. al-Mas'ūdī, *Murūj al-Dhahab*, (Paris, 1861–77), vol. III, pp. 413f.
47. al-Maqrīzī, *al-Mawā'iẓ wa-'l-I'tibār fī Dhikr al-Khiṭaṭ wa-'l-Āthār* (Būlāq, 1270/1854), vol. I, pp. 468, 493f; ed. G. Wiet, (Cairo, 1922–4), vol. IV, pp. 224ff.
48. Downey, *Antioch*, p. 531 and Segal, *Edessa*, p. 163. None the less, in 692 the Council of Trent reiterated the canon prohibiting a priest to attend the hippodrome which was first enunciated by the Councils of Laodicea (340–80), cf. C. Andresen, 'Altkristlicher Kritik am Tanz – ein Ausschnitt aus dem Kampf der alten Kirche gegen heidnische Sitten' in H. Frohnes and W. Knorr (eds), *Die Alte Kirche* (Munich, 1974), p. 371, n. 89; J. D. Mansi (ed.), *Sacrorum Conciliorum ... Collectio* (Graz, 1960), vol. XI, p. 953.
49. al-Maqrīzī, *Khiṭaṭ*, vol. I, pp. 468f; Ibn Taghrī Birdī, *al-Nujūm al-Zāhira* (Cairo, n.d.), vol. III, p. 87; vol. II, 30–2; cf. S. 'A. F. 'Āshūr, *al-Mujtama' al-Miṣrī fī 'Aṣr Salāṭīn al-Mamālīk* (Cairo, 1962), p. 201; Ibn Iyās, *Badā'i' al-Zuhūr*, (Wiesbaden, 1974), vol. I, part 2, pp. 363–5.
50. Ibn al-Ḥājj, *Madkhal*, vol. II, p. 49.
51. al-Jāḥiẓ (attrib.), *Kitāb al-Tāj fī Akhlāq al-Mulūk* (Beirut, 1970), p. 31. On the subject of entertaining in pre-Islamic Persia, see A. Christensen, *L'Iran sous les Sassanides* (Copenhagen, 1944), pp. 371, 402ff, 482ff.
52. Cf. al-Qazwīnī, *Kosmographie* (Wiesbaden, 1967), vol. II, p. 82 (on *yawm Hurmuz*); Ibn Iyās, *Badā'i'*, vol. I, part ii, pp. 363ff (under Sha'bān, year 787 AH); E. W. Lane, *An Arab–English Lexicon* (London 1869–93), s.v. '*ksj*' (on the *kawsaj*); cf. also below Chapter 3, p. 48.
53. F. Schulthess, 'Über den Dichter al Nağāši und einiger Zeitgenossen', *Zeitschrift der Deutschen Morgenländisches Gesellschaft* LIV (1900), p. 432; Ḥassān b. Thābit, *Dīwān* (London and Leiden, 1910), p. 193; (London, 1971), vol. I, p. 360 (no. 190: 3); vol. II, p. 256. Cf. also J. Horovitz, *Spuren griechischer Mimen im Orient* (Cairo, 1905), pp. 77–88.
54. Schulthess, 'Über den Dichter', p. 432. One of the commentators invokes 'Abd Allāh b. al-Zubayr (d. 65/684) as the authority for this view.
55. Y. Kutscher, *Millim ve-Toldoteihen* (Jerusalem, 1965), pp. 4f, with reference to *Mikhilta d'Rabbi Ishmael*, ed. H. S. Horovitz (Jerusalem, 1960), p. 80. Cf. Downey, *Antioch*, pp. 444f, n. 177.
56. Ibn Janāḥ, *The Book of Hebrew Roots* (Oxford), 1875), col. 793, l. 16, where Neubauer quotes David ben Abraham al-Fāsī, *Kitāb Jāmi' al-Alfāẓ* (New Haven, 1936–45), vol. I, p. 154, 1. 26. In vol. II, p. 553, 1. 36, *la'ag we-qeles* (Ps. 44.14), is translated into *lahw wa-maymasa* (entertainment and *mimos*); cf. R. P. A. Dozy, *Supplément aux Dictionnaires Arabes* (Leiden, 1967), vol. II, p. 631.
57. Horovitz, *Spuren*, p. 88.

58. Jarīr, *Dīwān* (Cairo, 1935), p. 120, l. 8. On the Caliph al-Ma'mūn's participation in a Sha'ānīn celebration in a monastery, see al-Shābushtī, *Diyārāt*, pp. 177f.
59. On the *Sha'ānīn*, see al-Maqrīzī, *Khiṭaṭ*, vol. IV, part 2, pp. 225f; cf. also Severus b. al-Muqaffa', *History of the Patriarchs of the Coptic Church of Alexandria* (Paris, 1907 and 1910), vol. I, p. 506.
60. S. Brock, letter of 6/11/1982. Cf. W. A. Wigram, *The Assyrians and their Neighbours* (London, 1929), p. 198; cf. also J. Mateos, *Lelya-Sapra* (Rome, 1959), p. 239n. More is known about Byzantine theatre, though religious drama is not securely attested till after the Iconoclast controversy (cf. G. La Piana, 'The Byzantine Theatre', *Speculum* XI (1936); H. G. Beck, *Geschichte der byzantinischen Volksliteratur* (Munich, 1971), pp. 111–13; R. J. Schork, 'Dramatic Dimensions in Byzantine Hymns', *Studia Patristica* VIII (1966), pp. 271–9. (My thanks to Dr. S. Brock for his valuable information and assistance.)
61. S. Brock, 'Syriac Dialogue Poems: Marginalia to a Recent Edition', *Le Muséon* XCVII (1984), p. 31.
62. al-Kindī, *The Governors and Judges of Egypt* (Leiden, 1912), p. 7; al-Maqrīzī, *Khiṭaṭ*, vol. I, part 1, p. 134.
63. Thus al-Maqrīzī.
64. al-Mas'ūdī, *Murūj*, vol. IV, pp. 266f; al-Balādhurī, *Ansāb al-Ashrāf* (Jerusalem, 1936), vol. V, pp. 31f; Ibn Durayd, *Kitāb al-Ishtiqāq* (Göttingen, 1854), pp. 290f; Ibn 'Abd al-Barr al-Qurṭubī, *al-Istī'āb fī Ma'rifat al-Aṣḥāb* (Cairo, 1380/1960), vol. I, pp. 258f., no. 343; Ibn Ḥajar al-'Asqalānī, *al-Iṣāba fī Tamyīz al-Ṣaḥāba* (Cairo, 1383/1970), vol. I, pp. 511ff., s.v. 'Jundab b. Ka'b'.
65. See n. 53.
66. On such illusion tricks see anon., *Kitāb yusammā 'l-Muntakhab fī-Fawāyid wa-Ḥikāyāt wa-La'ib*, MS Cambridge University Library, Qq. 164, fol. 66a. See also S. Wild, 'A Juggler's Programme in Medieval Islam', in R. Matran (ed.), *La Signification du Bas Moyen Âge dans l'Histoire et la Culture du Monde Arabe* (Aix-en-Provence, n.d.).
67. Qur'an, 17:83.
68. al-Mas'ūdī, *Murūj*, vol. IV, pp. 266f. The term *takhyīl* is also attested in the sense of 'appearances' or 'illusion tricks' in Ibn 'Abdūn 'Risāla fī 'l-Qaḍā' wa-'l-Ḥisba' in É. Lévi-Provençal (ed.), *Thalāth Rasā'il Andalusiyya fī Adab al-Ḥisba wa-'l-Muḥtasib* (Cairo, 1955), p. 113 (*kadhalika yamna'u ahl al-takhyīl alladhī yuẓhiru annahu yaf'alu shay'an min ghayri fi'lihi wa-yukhayyilu bihi, mithl al-nawārīj wa-qalb al-'ayn wa-mā ashbāha dhālika, wa-huwa min bāb al-siḥr*).
69. Wild, 'Juggler's Programme', p. 355.
70. See Metin And, *Culture, Performance and Communication in Turkey* (Tokyo, 1987), pp. 78f.
71. Ibid., pp. 35–47.

II Actors and Entertainers

2

La''ābūn, Mukhannathūn and Players of *Kurraj*

La''ābūn

On the eve of Islam impersonators, clowns and buffoons had replaced the classical theatre in the Near Eastern provinces of the Roman empire. As regards the cradle of Islam, Mecca and Medina, however, neither the Qur'an nor the vast *Ḥadīth* literature mentions any theatrical plays, be they indigenous or of Greek, Roman or Christian derivation. *Ḥadīth* conveys only a vague impression of the different types of entertainment familiar to the early Muslims.[1] The verbal noun *li'b* (also *la'b, la'ib*) occurs mostly in traditions on children playing with dolls, animals or each other and statements on dice and chess; but as will be seen, there are also some in which it is used of entertainers playing musical instruments, dancing or simulating duels.[2]

The attitude to entertainment in *Ḥadīth* is hostile. Muḥammad is said to have issued a ban on entertainment (*al-nahy 'an al-muzāḥ*) on the grounds that it was a deviation from worship, leading to immoral behaviour, and a transgression of God's will.[3] One tradition on the 'prohibition of the pursuit of the comical' (*al-nahy min ta'āṭī mā yuḍḥik*)[4] bases itself on Muḥammad's warning against lies told for the sake of making people laugh: 'Woe to him who relates and tells lies in order to make people laugh; woe to him, woe to him; woe to him who acts in jest.'[5] Another has Muḥammad state that 'every amusement with which a man enjoys himself is futile except for using his bow, training his horse and caressing his wife' (*kullu lahwin yalhu bihi 'l-rajul fa-huwa bāṭil illā ramyahu bi-qawsihi wa-ta'dībahu li-farasihi wa-mulā'abatahu ahlahu*).[6] The scholars were unanimously agreed on the authenticity of this tradition, which was taken to mean that everything in a man's life should be aimed at religious benefit in this world and the hereafter: the bow and the horse were intended for *jihād*, while the caresses were for the procreation of Muslim children.[7] Hence strict scholars rejected the literal meaning of a tradition in which Muḥammad appears to be endorsing entertainment, by allowing 'Ā'isha to watch a performance by Ethiopians (*li'b al-Ḥabasha*). They argued that the performance was in fact training for war (*al-tadrīb 'alā 'l-ḥarb*) and that the play or dance (*li'b*) was not a play in the sense of being aimed at entertainment, but only in the sense that the performer 'intended to stab his partner without really doing it, but merely deluding him, as if he were doing it'.[8] Such arguments were also used against Ṣūfīs who allowed music, singing and dancing in their sessions and who invoked the tradition on the Ethiopians in their favour; the *'ulamā'* reiterated that the Ethiopians did not dance 'with singing, kicking of feet and gesturing, as do the Ṣūfīs and *Mukhannathūn* [literally effeminate men, here entertainers]; rather, they were training with weapons for war'.[9] But the tradition clearly does envisage the Ethiopians as entertainers, and it is also as such that they appear in Ibn Abī 'l-Ḥadīd (d. 655/1257), according to whom they were *aṣḥāb al-dirkila* who used to play and dance (*yal'abūn, yarquṣūn*); the term *ḍirkila* is explained as 'an Ethiopian play which includes dancing' (*la'ba li-'l-Ḥabash fīhā riqṣ*), which is interesting in that it shows that by the thirteenth century at least a clear distinction was made between plays and dancing.[10]

As the case of the Ethiopians shows, liberal *'ulamā'* and defenders of the Ṣūfī use of singing and dancing could also find ammunition in *Ḥadīth.*[11] They listed traditions in their favour under the heading 'permission to jest' (*al-tarkhīṣ bi-'l-muzāḥ*), and many *adab* books also contain chapters on the legality of jesting (in which the authors use the opportunity to tell their own jokes and impudent anecdotes).[12] The tradition on the Ethiopians is the most commonly cited evidence;[13] but we also hear much of two slave girls who played the tambourine (*duff*) in the presence of 'Ā'isha and Muḥammad, who allowed them to continue despite Abū Bakr's scolding, on the grounds that it was a feast day.[14] The tradition on 'Ā'isha playing with dolls (*banāt*) before her marriage to Muḥammad is also much cited:[15] we are told that he himself encouraged her to play with them. Another tradition has it that a dark-skinned woman (Suwaydā') used to visit 'Ā'isha to play (or dance) in her presence and make her laugh (*tal'abu bayna yadayhā wa-tuḍḥikuhā*);[16] sometimes Muḥammad would watch and laugh too, and it is said that he honoured Suwaydā' after her death by praying over her because 'she was eager to make me laugh.'[17] The phrase *tal'abu bayna yadayhā* hardly means that 'she danced before her', though the commentators explain *li'b* as *raqṣ* and *zafan* (dancing);[18] it is more likely to mean that she mimed, the term *li'b* here having the same meaning as in the expression *li'b al-Ḥabasha.*

It should be noted that the *Ḥabasha* are only called *la''ābūn* in a few transmissions,[19] clearly with reference to their simulation of duels with spears and shields. Elsewhere, *la''āb* is a player simulating duels on a hobbyhorse called *kurraj.* Thus al-Bukhārī (d. 257/870) cites a tradition to the effect that there was a *la''āb* among the *Muhājirūn.* This tradition, which concerns an incident witnessed by 'Umar b. al-Khaṭṭāb, does not specify what kind of *la''āb* was involved, but al-Suhaylī has it that 'Umar b. al-Khaṭṭāb 'saw a player (*lā'ib*) playing (*yal'ab*) with a hobbyhorse (*kurraj*), so he said: "if I had not seen this (*kurraj*) played with in the time of the Prophet, I would have expelled him from al-Medina"'.[20] It is therefore reasonable to suppose that the *la''āb* witnessed by 'Umar in the incident cited by al-Bukhārī was a player on a hobbyhorse (*kurraj*), a play borrowed by Arabs from the Persians.

Although these traditions only provide rudimentary evidence of dancing, singing and miming for comical purposes, they use what was to become the basic terminology of later centuries, *li'b* and *la''āb.* After the conquests the root *l'b* is commonly used in connection with theatrical performances. Thus Surāqa b. Mirdās (d. 80/699) speaks of the Jewish juggler and comedian Baṭrūnī or Bustānī as a 'performing magician', *sāḥir lā'ib,*[21] Al-Ṭabarī speaks of *la''ābūn* performing at the court of Khusraw II (591–628),[22] and of *la''ābūn* among the musicians, singers and players in the company of the Abbasic caliph al-Amīn (d. 193-809).[23] Ibn Abī 'l-Ḥadīd quotes 'Ikrima as saying that Ibn 'Abbās (d. 68/687) sent him to invite *la''ābūn* when his children were circumcised: they performed for a fee of four dirhams.[24]

It seems that in al-Fāsī's Lexicon, from the second half of the tenth century, the Islamic phrase *lahw wa-la'ib* (entertainment and play)[25] became known as *lahw wa-maymasa* (entertainment and mimicry) among non-Muslims. Thus one may assume that *maymasa* had become a usual term among non-Muslims, especially in view of the fact that the Greek term *mimos* was adapted into Syriac as *mimsa.*

Ibn 'Asākir (d. 572/1176), in an anecdote concerning 'Abd Allāh b. Aḥmad b. Bashīr b. Dhakwān (173/789–242/856), says that a man came from al-Ḥurjula, a village near Damascus, to look for *la''ābūn* in order to invite them to perform at his brother's wedding. He was told that the ruler (*sulṭān*) had forbade them to perform, so that he could only invite a certain type of religious singers called *al-mughabbirūn*[26] (singers of ascetic songs). He then asked a frivolous ṣūfī where he could find such singers, The ṣūfī, who wanted to make fun of him, pointed to the scholar 'Abd Allāh Ibn Dhakwān. The villager complained to the latter that he could not find *mukannathūn* for his brother's wedding, thus using this term as a synonym for the term *la''ābūn.* Ibn Dhakwān, who enjoyed the joke, pointed to another scholar in the mosque as being the master (*ra'īs*) of the *mughabbirūn,* and stated that if the scholar agreed to go to the wedding he would also come. The fact that the *laʿʿābūn* or *mukhannathūm* were forbidden to perform and that the *mughabbirūn*, who sang ascetic songs, were allowed to sing at weddings indicates that the performance of the former was considered by the ruler as immoral, and that these performers were led by a master.

However, Ibn al-Nadīm (d. 377/987)[27] and al-Bīrūnī (d. 440/1048),[28] when speaking of the Indians and their religious dramas, used the term *talāʿub* (acting) and *liʿb* for the Indian drama, and Ibn al-Nadīm used the term *raqṣ* (dance) as a synonym for the term *laʿb*. In Andalusia the eleventh-century philologist Abū 'l-Qāsim al-Iflīlī is said to have produced a play called 'The Play of the Jew' (*Laʿbat al-Yahūdī*);[29] and Pedro de Alcala lists the term *laʿʿāb*, fem. *laʿʿāba*, in the sense of actor, buffoon and mimer in his *Vocabulista Aravigo en Letra Castellana*, published in Granada 1505.[30]

Translators from Syriac and Coptic rendered the Greek term *theatron* as *malʿab* (pl. *malāʿib*), only rarely transcribing it as *ṭiyāṭir* (corresponding to the Hebrew *teaṭron* and Syriac *te'aṭron*). Thus the Arabic translation of the *Canons of Athanasius of Alexandria*, probably made in the thirteenth century,[31] uses the term *malʿab* twice in the following passages: 'If it be found that the son of a priest hath gone to the theatre (*malʿab*), the priest shall be put forth a week, because he hath not trained his son aright';[32] 'none of the Children of the Church shall go into the theatre (*malʿab*) or into places of assembly (*maḥfal*) or any places of the heathen.'[33]

In the Canon of the Synod of Antioch, priests are forbidden from attending players, acting in wedding feasts: 'Priests should not attend entertainment or musicians (*lahw wa-maghānī*), not even those who play the lute (*ʿūd*), or who dance (*yarquṣ*) or play with dice ... and not even actors (*mukhāyilīn*) at a wedding feast, [but rather] he has to hurry and leave before they enter'.[34]

Arab historians and geographers likewise used the term *malʿab* to describe the ruins of classical theatres. Thus al-Ḥimyarī metnions a *dār malʿab* and other antiquities in the vicinity of Murviedro in Spain;[35] al-Idrīsī notes a *ṭiyāṭir* unparalleled in this world among the ruins of Carthage (Qarṭājannā), adding that 'it is said that this building was a *malʿab* and a *mujtamaʿ* (meeting place)'.[36] Al-Maqrīzī was extremely well informed about the *malʿab* which ʿAmr b. al-Āṣ had supposedly attended in Alexandria, as discussed above.[37] The function of such theatres was clearly well known to Arab scholars.[38]

The term *malʿab* continued to be used in the sense of 'theatre' in Muslim Spain until the very end.[39] In the Muslim East, it was still current in the nineteenth century. Thus the Egyptian historian ʿAbd al-Raḥmān al-Jabartī described the opening of the Comédie

Française in Cairo on 29 December, 1800 as follows:[40]

> On that day the place which they estabished at al-Azbakiyya by the site known as Bāb al-Hawā' was completed. It is the place called *al-kumidī* in their language; it is a place in which they gather every ten nights to watch plays (*malā'ib*) which are performed (*yal'abūhā*) for the purpose of amusement and entertainment for four hours each night in their language.

Al-Ṭahṭāwī (1801–73) similarly uses the root *l'b* in his account of the theatre he had attended during his studies in Paris. He describes it as a place in which imitation (*taqlīd*) of any sort of event is performed (*yul'ab fīhā*), calling the acting *la'b*, the play *la'ba*, the actor and actress *lā'ib* and *lā'iba*.[41] He apologises for the fact that he does not know an Arabic term for 'spectacles' and 'theatres' (both of which terms he transliterates into Arabic) and suggests the term *khayālī* for 'theatre', noting that the Turks call it *kumidya*.[42] Ya'qūb Ṣanū' (1839–1912), on the other hand, adopted the Italian term for theatre (transcribed as *al-tiyātrū*) and used the terms *li'b* for acting, *li''īb* and *li''ība* for actor and actress, and *riwāya* for play.[43] In North Africa the term *la'ba* is used to denote a shadow play.[44]

Mukhannathūn

In Abū 'l-Faraj al-Iṣfahānī's version of the play of the caliph al-Amīn with the *kurraj*, the expression *al-la''ābūn yal'būn* (the players playing) used by al-Ṭabarī is replaced by *al-mukhannathūn yuzammirūn wa-yaḍribūn* (the *makhannathūn* blowing flutes and drumming).[45] Apparently the terms *la''ābūn* and *mukhannathūn* could be used synonymously. The commentators on the *Naqā'iḍ* of Jarīr and al-Farazdaq likewise speak of *mukhannathūn* in the sense of actors: *al-kurraj la'ba yal'abuhā 'l-mukhannathūn*, 'the hobby-horse is a play played by *mukhannathūn*', they say.[46] The best-known meaning of *mukhannathūn* is 'effeminate person', 'homosexual', or 'male prostitute', but it is also attested in the sense of 'actor' in the Arabic translation of the Syro–Roman law book. This text, translated from Greek into Syriac at the end of the seventh or the beginning of the eighth century,[47] and from Syriac into Arabic before 1408 C.E., enumerates the professions of those who are excluded from succession in the Syriac version, as follows:

> The following are infamous, both men and women, and cannot be made heirs: those who serve in the *teaṭron*, *ippika* (hippodrome), or the *stadium* or *mimoi*, and in addition prostitutes, charioteers (*enoikoi*), *ludiarii*, and those, men or women, who are accused of adultery.[48]

The Arabic translation renders 'infamous' as *mukhannathūn* and translates 'those who serve in the teatron' as *man yuṣayyiru nafsahu shuhra* ('he who makes a display of himself'); *ippika* (hippodrome) as *jalabāt* (also *ḥalabāt*) (horse race-track); *stadium* as *mawāḍ' al-ṣirā'* (places of wrestling); and *mimoi* as *muḍḥikūn.*[48] All those who serve in the theatre including *muḍḥikūn* (to whom I shall return in Chapter 4) are thus included in the classification *mukhannathūn.*

Moreover, in the Syriac dictionary *Thesaurus Syriacus* the Greek term *mimos* is given in Syriac as *mīmas* and *mīmsā* with their Arabic meaning as *al-mukhannath al-muḥākī al-maskharī* (the imitating comedian mimic), as well as *mukhannath, muḥākī, al-muḍḥik.*[50] Hence al-Shābushtī (d. 388/998) could use the verb *takhannatha* in the sense of 'joined the art of actors, jokers and jesters' in his account of 'Abbāda al-Mukhannath:[51]

> 'Abbāda was one of the most jesting and miming of men[52] and most amiable and ready-witted with jokes. His father was a cook of al-Ma'mūn's (r. 813–33) ... then his father died. So he joined the actors and jesters (*takhannatha*) and became a byword in dissipation and dissolution. He was praised (for his talents) (*wuṣifa*) in front of al-Ma'mūn, he jested and made jokes, mimed (*ḥākā*) and gestured. Al-Ma'mūn liked him and said, 'Take him to Zubayda so that she will see him and laugh'.[53]

Of another entertainer, al-Mukhannath al-Baghdādī al-Dallāl, we are told that he was a good flautist who had female singers; he was a rich man and fond of beardless young men (*murdān*), on whom he used to spend great sums of money; he was killed in 415/1024 by his lover in a gaming house.[54]

In *al-Rawḍ al-Unuf* by 'Abd-Raḥmān al-Suhaylī (d. 581/1185) it is related that there were four effeminate men (*mukhannathūn*) in the time of Muḥammad. They did not practise homosexuality, but they spoke in a soft voice and dyed their hands and feet and toyed or danced (*li'ban ka-li'bihinna*) like women.[55] Some of these effeminate men used to play (*yal'ab*) with the *kurraj* (a wooden mare or horse).[56] There are also some traditions in which Muḥammad curses effeminate men and orders their expulsion from Medina. When other types of entertainment developed, these *Ḥadīths* were applied to them. Ibn al-Ḥājj (d. 737/1336) has a chapter in his *Madkhal* dealing with the heresy (*bid'a*) of decorating boys who had learned the Qur'ān by heart as brides with silken dresses and golden necklaces, and roving with them in processions. The author comments: 'It is mentioned that the Prophet has cursed men who imitate women.'[57]

In *Dhayl Zahr al-Ādāb* there is an anecdote which may shed light on the way in which *mukhannathūn* performed their repertoire and their improvisiation in order to avoid punishment.

> A son of 'Isā b. Ja'far invited a troup of *mukhannathūn*, and they performed their plays and dances (*fa-ja'alū yal'abūn wa-yarquṣūn*). Only one *mukhannath* remained idle. When he was

> asked to perform he apologised, saying that he had no repertoire. The host got angry and said: 'You son of a bitch, then why have you come here? Servant, bring me a bowl full of dung and another full of embers.' When they were brought he told the *mukhannath*: 'By God you must eat the contents of one of these bowls, otherwise I will beat you to death.' The *mukhannath* begged to be allowed to pray first. When the host observed that the *mukhannath* was prolonging his prayer he said: 'You son of a bitch, how long do you pray? You have prayed more than twenty prostrations.' The *mukhannath* answered: 'O sire, I am praying to God to transform me into an ostrich to enable me to eat embers, or into a pig to enable me to eat dung, but God has not yet answered my prayers. So allow me please to pray and invoke him, perhaps He will comply with my prayers.'[58]

It seems therefore, that in cases in which a *mukhannath* has to escape punishment or in which his repertoire was not pleasing, he improvised a short dramatic scene to please his masters. In fact, the playing and dancing of *mukhannathūn* such as 'Abbāda al-Mukhannath also involved short dramatic scenes,[59] as we shall see later on.

Players of *Kurraj*

The *kurraj* to which *Ḥadīth* refers would seem to have been a Persian game.[60] Arab lexicographers unanimously confirm that the term *kurraj* is a Persian word meaning colt, donkey or mule,[61] which suggests that the acting was of Persian origin too. At all events, the definition of the *kurraj* given by Arab lexicographers is 'a foal of wood with which one plays,' or in other words a hobby-horse. It should not be confused with the hobby-horses used by children, which were of course known too. For example, Ibn Shuhayd al-Andalusī (382/922–426/1035) relates that when he was five years old his 'horses were then selections of reeds, and the shields were peels of wood' (*wa-'l-khayl idh-dhāka nukhabun min qaṣab wa-'l-daraq qushūr min khashab*).[62]

However, in most cases in which Arabic sources mention *kurraj*, the purpose of its usage is unclear. This is because there is no description of the plays or dramas acted by the performers, and no attempt was made to indicate the purpose of the play or its significance. Therefore, only through analogy with central Asian Shamanic and seasonal fertility rituals is it possible to venture a conjecture to explain the content and significance of such plays.

In ancient Persia and Central Asia, the hobby-horse was used in various dramatic rituals in Shamanic rites, as well as in seasonal fertility rites 'to help establish contact with spirits'.[63]

However, a story found in one of the Arab sources dealing with the use of the *qaṣaba*[64] (a horse-headed reed, or simply a stick-horse) tells of the besieged Persian king Bahram Gour who put a reed between his legs and galloped about with a crown of sweet basil on his head, together with his 200 maids, singing, shouting and dancing.[65] This seems to have been a mock-play imitating a Shaman rite to defeat the besieging enemies. Seeing him in this manner, the viziers were disappointed in their king and decided to dethrone him. The reaction of the viziers might indicate that they did not believe in the power of such Shamanic rites to expel the besieging enemies.

With the rise of Islam, the earliest information concerning the use of the *kurraj* is the tradition cited by al-Bukhārī which states that it was found in the Prophet Muḥammad's camp after a raid (*ghazwa*).[66] Among the Muhājirūn (emigrants) in the camp there was *la''āb* (a hobby-horse player), who kicked an Anṣārī man on the hip (*kasa'a*), which resulted in both men calling for their people to help fight against the other. That the Prophet did not raise any objections against the use of the *kurraj* might indicate that he did not find the *la''āb*'s play a pagan or magical rite. However, it is impossible to know whether the player was performing a mock-battle, imitating some scenes of the Prophet's raid, or celebrating the Prophet's victory.

Only al-Fākihī in *Akhbār Makka* gives the term *kurrak*, describing it as a play which was practised in every feast in various quarters in Mekka from the pre-Islamic period up to 252/866, adding that in Iraq it was wrongly called *kurra* (see al-Fākihi, 1858–61). On the other hand, in volume VIII of his *Murūj* (pp. 101f.) al-Mas'ūdi speaks of a dance called *al-Ibl wa-'l-kurra* (the camel and the hobby-horse), played in the time of al-Mu'tamid (870–93).

The fact that actors of the *kurraj* were given degrading names such as *mukhannath*, might indicate that they did not perform any magical or ritual dramatic dance. The *mukhannaths* were active in Medina at the time of the Prophet and they are also mentioned in the time of 'Umar's caliphate, when he reputedly said that he would have expelled them from Medina if he had not seen comparable entertainment in the time of the Prophet himself.[67] The association between *kurraj* and *mukhannath* was so strong that during later periods effeminate men came to be known as *kurrajīs*.[68] In this case there is no possibility of any analogy between the *kurraj* and al-Burāq, the mount on which the prophet Muḥammad made his ascension to the seven heavens.

The *Naqā'iḍ* of Jarīr and al-Farazdaq shed more light on the *kurraj* during the Umayyad period,, especially on its appearance and player representation. However, there are no details of the contents of the plays or their significance.

In *al-Aghānī* there is a story concerning v. 62 of poem no. 64 by Jarīr, according to which the governor of Iraq, al-Ḥajjāj (41/661–96/714) ordered Jarīr (33(?)/653(?)–114/732) and al-Farazdaq (d. 110/738) to come to him at his palace in Baṣra dressed in the attire of their pre-Islamic ancestors.[69] Apparently there was an ancient custom for Arab poets to sometimes dress in an unusual manner,[70] to enable them to communicate with their muse (*jinn*) of the valley of 'Abqar. However, in the particular case of Jarīr and al-Farazdaq, the dressing up in their ancestor's attire had a different purpose. Al-Farazdaq dressed in silk brocade (the *Naqā'iḍ* adds that he also put on a bracelet), while Jarīr came with forty horsemen. He was clad in armour, carried a sword and spear and borrowed a noble horse. Presumably, this was a vestige of a dramatic ritual attempting to communicate with the world of the ancestors, in which curses against a rival's ancestors might bear magical significance.

On seeing al-Farazdaq in his silken garments Jarīr mocked him by comparing him to a laughing stock clad in the two ornamental belts and small bells of a *kurraj*, while he describes himself as a warrior clad in arms among his wives, and asking them to put on their ornaments and to perfume themselves, yielding to him sexually (*ṭawīl* metre):

Labistu adātī wa-Farazdaqu lu'batun//
'alayhi wishāḥā kurrajin wa-jalājiluh
A'iddū ma' al-ḥalyi 'l-mlāba fa-innamā//
Jarīrun lakum ba'lun wa-antum ḥalā'iluh
Wa-a'ṭū kamā a'ṭat 'awānun ḥalīlahā//
aqarrat li-ba'lin ba'da ba'lin turāsiluh[70]

(I have put on my arms while al-Farazdaq is a laughing-stock//
dressed in the two ornamented belts and bells of a kurrah
Prepare perfume with the ornaments;
Jarīr is your husband and you are his wives.
And yield to him, like a middle-aged wife yields to her husband//
after she had asked marriage from various men.)

What seems to be a dramatic ritual of communication with the ancestors is described by Jarīr as a *kurraj* performance. Jarīr describes himself as a warrier clad in his arms, while his opponent is a laughing-stock (*lu'ba*) ornamented with two belts and bells of the player of the *kurraj* plays. Thus Jarīr on his horse represents the male or the husband, while al-Farazdaq with his *kurraj* is the female or the wife. This is evident not only from the above mentioned verses, but also in verse 11, poem no. 97 (*kāmil* metre):

Amsā 'l-Farazdaqu fī jalājil kurrajin//
ba'da al-Ukhayṭal zawjatan li-Jarīri[72]
(Al-Farazdaq with his bells of *kurraj* became
after the small Akhṭal a wife to Jarīr.)

The duties of a wife were to perfume and ornament herself when receiving the warrior husband. The comparison of a *kurraj* player to a woman possibly indicates that wives received victorious men or entertained their husbands with the *kurraj*. But the kind of dramatic performance this involved is very difficult to tell. Yet according to the commentators of the *Naqā'iḍ* we have here a dramatic scene (*ḥikāya*) performed with the *kurraj*.

In another verse Jarīr mocks al-Farazdaq for his silk dress being like the dress of the *kurraj* player, who amuses himself with degraded plays of heaving (*nazw*) like a horse, while Jarīr on his horse is the real defender of his tribe against any calamity.[73] Moreover, in poem no. 42, verses 9–11, Jarīr describes al-Farazdaq (with his bells of *kurraj* and moustache, which resembles a monkey) as a masked actor wearing a fur like a monkey.[74] All these verses are considered by the commentators of the *Naqā'iḍ* as various types of plays (*ḥikāyāt*) performed by the *mukhannathūn* with the *kurraj*.

The compiler of the *Naqā'iḍ Jarīr wa-'l-Farazdaq*, Abū 'Ubayda (d. 207/822), and his three transmitters, Muḥammad Ibn Ḥabīb (d. 245/859), al-Sukkarī (d. 275/888) and Muḥammad Ibn 'Abbās al-Yazīdī (d. 310/922),[75] glossed the term *kurraj* first as *al-khayāl alladhī yal'ab bihi al-mukhannathūn*[76] (the wooden figure of a horse with which *mukhannathūn* play), and next as *la'ba yal'abuhā 'l-mukhannathūn*[77] (a play played by *mukhannathūn*). The third time the term appears it is given in the form *kurraq*, which is a rhyme exigency for *kurraj*, and defined as *al-kurraj alladhī yal'ab bihi al-mukhannathūn fī ḥikāyātihim* (the *kurraj* with which *mukhannathūn* play in their impersonations).[78]

During the Abbasid period in Baghdad the *kurraj* was played by a caliph. Both al-Ṭabarī and Abū 'l-Faraj al-Iṣfahānī relate that the caliph al-Amīn (d. 198/813) ordered two singers to join other singers in a courtyard full of big lit candles 'and behold Muḥammad [the caliph al-Amīn] is in the *kurraj* [sic. underneath the robe] and the house is full of servant girls and attendants, and behold the singers, musicians and players (*la''ābūn*) (according to *Aghānī*: *mukhannathūn*) are playing (*yal'abūn*), while Muḥammad is in their midst dancing (Ṭabarī: *yarquṣ*, Iṣfahānī; *yartakiḍ*) in the *kurraj*'. al-Amīn continued to rove the courtyard while the servants and players recited over and over again a short love poem until dawn.[79]

Unlike the commentators of the *Naqā'iḍ*, al-Ṭabarī and al-Iṣfahānī do not mention if al-Amīn performs any *ḥikāya*. This leaves us to wonder why a caliph would dance the whole night listening over and over again to the music accompanying a love song. This can possibly be explained as an attempt by al-Amīn to enter into a delirious and ecstatic state through the song of love, and that the riding of a *kurraj* was a symbol for such spiritual sublimation. This interpretation is strengthened by the warning of the guards to the two famous singers to beware of discordance, probably since such discordance might cause a shock to the caliph in his ecstatic trance.[80] Such a trance brought about through dancing, singing and music enabled the caliph to continue his play with the *kurraj* all night without feeling tired or bored.

M. Gaudefroy–Demombynes attempted to find a connection between the caliph al-Amīn with his *kurraj* among his singing maids, and the winged horse among the dolls of 'Ā'isha.[81] However he does not explain the significance of each kind of play. In contrast, Amnon Shiloah in his study of the *kurraj* concluded that it is 'an artistic dance performed by qualified dancers', and that it is 'une sorte de ballet avec une élément choréographique …'.[82] However, in *Ḥadīth* the *kurraj* was played by a single player (*la''āb*) and/or *mukhannath*,[83] as well as by common people. It was only in the Abbasid period that it was played in a developed manner with dancers, singers , players and music, a time when the arts of entertainment developed in general. According to Ibn Khaldūn, the *kurraj* is equipment for dancing and playing (*raqṣ*, which implies acting too) consisting of 'decorated (*musarraja*) wooden figures of horses attached to robes (*aqbiya*) such as women wear. [The dancers or actors] thereby give the appearance of having mounted horses. They attack and withdraw and compete in skill [with weapons]'. Ibn Khaldūn adds more details of the way in which *kurraj* players would entertain at parties and during festivals in Baghdad and elsewhere. The dance was accompanied by poems and song and to the music of tambourines and flutes. Women also used to simulate cavalry duels accompanied by music, and it became a popular play and game during parties, wedding, festivals and leisure.[84] This is suggestive of an element of acting out a mock-battle or contest.

However, according to Metin And 'elements of combat or contest are a survival of fertility rites in which the contestants of opposed forces symbolize a struggle between the powers of life and death, summer and winter, light and darkness, the old king and the new king, father and son, the Old Year and the New Year. The fight itself may be mimetic battle between groups, or more often between individuals'.[85] This seems to be substantiated by Jarīr's reference to himself as a warrior received by his wives with ornaments and perfume, as in a rite of fertility. In fact, the commentators on the

Naqā'iḍ called entertainment involving hobby-horses *ḥikāyāt* (imitations).[86] The *ḥikāya* or *khayāl* mentioned by al-Musabbiḥī, and copied by al-Maqrīzī in the context of Egyptian festivals, may also have been performances with hobby-horses in the streets and markets of Cairo, serving as mock-guards to various processions. Thus al-Musabbiḥī's description of processions in Fatimid Cairo uses the term *afrās al-khayāl* (lit. mare or horse of acting – hobby-horse) as a synonym of both *ḥikāya* and *khayāl*, instead of the more usual term *kurraj*, in connection with the events of Dhū '-Ḥijja (415/1024):

> On Wednesday, the long dining table (*simāṭ*) made of sugar and the palaces (of sugar) were carried through the great street. People gathered in the streets to look at it. They crossed the street with it led by forerunners, *afrās al-khayāl*, the Farḥiyya Sudanese drummers ... Sheikh Najīb al-Dawla 'Alī b. Aḥmad al-Jarjarā'ī paid its expenses. Its parts and statues numbered 157 pieces, the number of its large palaces made of sugar was seven.[87]

It seems that the players of such wooden mares (*afrās al-khayāl*), called *raqqāṣūn* (dancers), served also as guards who punish offenders.[88]

Among the events of the year 441/1049–50 in Baghdad, the bricks for building a new gate in al-Karkh were paraded with drums, flutes and entertainers with hobby-horses, (*makhānīth ma'ahum ālāt al-ḥikāya*). It is interesting to note here that Maimonides who was of Andalusian origin and served as a physician to the Ayyubid court in Egypt used a similar term for hobby-horse, i.e. *faras al-'ūd* (horse-headed stick) with which *yal'abūna bihi fī 'l-khayāl* (they perform *khayāl*): *faras al-'ūd yarkab 'alayhi 'l-mulhiyīn (sic) yal'abūn bihi fī 'l-khayāl , wa-huwa mashhūr 'ind ahli 'l-la'ib* ('the horse-headed stick which the entertainers (*mulhiyīn*) ride upon and play with when performing *khayāl*. It is well known among entertainers (*ahl al-la'ib*)'.[89] However, in another place in his *Mishna Commentary*, Maimonides used instead of *ahl al-la'ib* (entertainers) the words *al-zamara wa-'l-khayyālīn* (the players of wind instruments and actors): *faras al-'ūd alladhī yal'ab bihi al-zamara wa-huwa mashūr 'inda ahl al-la'ib wa-'l-khayālīn* (sic)/('the horse-headed stick, with which the players of wind instruments (*zamara*) and actors play and it is well known among entertainers.')[90] Maimonides used these terms for players of *kurraj*, instead of al-Musabbiḥī' term al-*raqqaṣūn*, al-Ṭabarī's term *la''ābūn*, and al-Iṣfahānī's term *mukhannathūn*.. This variety of terms denoting the players of *kurraj*, caused confusion among scholars of theatre in the Arab world. However, Maimonides term *ahl al-la'ib* includes entertainers such as *mukhāyilūn* or *khayāliyyūn*.

It seems that Maimonides' term *faras al-'ūd* is synonymous to the

Figure 1 A *simāṭ* (dining-table) procession, with food and candy figures of various types and animals (*tamāthīl*). (After Metin And, *Osmali Şenliklerinde Türk Sanatlari* (Ankara, 1982). Courtesy of Professor Metin And.)

much older term *qaṣaba* (reed). The latter term is sometimes called *qaṣaba Fārisiyya* (Persian reed), and is described as 'a reed with a hunk of cotton wrapped in a rag on its head'[91] in the shape of a horse head. The *qaṣaba* was in mode during the Abbasid period among ṣūfī mendicants who pretended to be fools, mainly among those scholars who wished to avoid being appointed as judges or shunned work in the service of rulers. Some of these ṣūfīs even smeared their faces with black, hung garlands of bones around their necks in the manner of Central Asian shamans, and galloped upon a *qaṣaba* while preaching both to rulers and the common people.[92] During the reign of the caliph al-Mahdī (755–85), one of these ṣūfīs, who seems to have been influenced by actors, developed an original way of preaching by performing a play while riding on a *qaṣaba*, the content of which will be discussed in Chapter 5 below. What is interesting about this performance is that the ṣūfī imitates riding a horse by putting a reed between his legs (*yarkabu qaṣabatan*) and then gallops to the top of a hill followed by multitudes of men, women and children.[93] This strange scene could involve traces of Central Asian shamanism which influenced Islamic Sufism. It is possible to suggest that the riding of the *ṣūfi* on a *qaṣaba* enabled him like 'a shaman to fly through the air to reach heaven'.[94] Thus it is possible to assume that the ṣūfī, by riding upon a stick-horse in his play and climbing a hill, is simulating a flight to heaven. Furthermore, the involvement of men, women and children in the play might symbolise resurrection. The trial of the Muslim caliphs symbolises the day of judgement, as we will see below (Chapter 5).[95] This assumption is confirmed by the fact that the ṣūfī Buhlūl al-Majnūn al-Kūfī (d. 183/799) 'one day went to the cemetery galloping upon a reed which he used as his horse, with a whip in his hand'. When he was asked by a sufi scholar where is he going he answered that he is going 'to be inspected by God …'.[96]

Another dramatic scene involving the riding of a 'stick-horse' is described by the frivolous comedian and buffoon (*musākhir*) poet and *maqāma* writer, Ibn Sūdūn al-Bashbaghāwī (d. 868/1464). In Ibn Sūdūn's *al-Maqāma al-Jīziyya*, it is possible to observe various elements of fertility rituals symbolising both 'death and resurrection on one hand and the abduction and recovery of a girl (or her reunion with her mother) on the other'.[97] In this *maqāma* there are three characters. One is a young man wearing a headgear of coloured paper, with a wax figure of an ostrich on its top and a rope tied up to his sideburns. He limps as he walks, plays upon his *rebab*, and acts as if toxicated with *ḥashīsh*. The second character is his mother, an old woman, her hair covered with a net and a bell around her neck, riding a palm-leaf stalk (*jarīda*) (like the *ṣufi* actor riding upon a reed) and driving it by whips of a cow's tail. On the left of the old woman is her daughter, a naked baby girl holding a rope with a sea shell and hollowed fish bones in her right hand, while in her left hand she holds a lit candle, with a reed flute in her mouth.[98]

It is possible to assume that such a scene is taken from a dramatic shamanic rite of Central Asia since many of the props used are vestiges of Central Asian shamanism. These include the stick-horse, the whip, the sea shells, the candle, the headgear with a figure of a bird, the bodily defect of the young man, the old woman as a symbol for the old year, the naked baby girl symbolising probably the abducted daughter or the new year.[99] This conjecture is further substantiated by the fact that many thousands of white slaves were brought from Central Asia, especially of Turkish origin, to the Abbasid courts in Iraq and to the Mamluk courts in Egypt. Besides, Ibn Sūdūn admits that troops of 'Ajam came to Egypt and he imitated some of their repertoires.[100]

It should be noted that the *kurraj* is also attested for Muslim Andalusia. Al-Shaqundī (d. after 1229) in his *Risāla fī Faḍl al-Andalus* enumerates the various arts and tools of entertainment in Seville, using the term *kurrayj* for the more usual *kurraj*:

> *wa-sami'ta mā fī hādha al-baladi min aṣnāf adawāt al-ṭarab ka-'l-khiyāl wa-'l-kurrayj wa-'l-'ūd wa-'l-rūṭah wa-'l-rabāb wa-'l-qānūn ... wa-mā kāna bi-Ubbadata min aṣnāf al-malāhī wa-'l-rawāqiṣ al-mashhūrāt bi-ḥusni 'l-inṭibā' wa-'l-ṣan'ati, fa-innahunna aḥadhaqu khalqi Allāh ta'ālā bi-'lli'b bi-'l-suyūf wa-ikhrāj al-qarāwī wa-'l-murābiṭ wa-'l-mutawajjih.*
>
> And you have heard about the means of entertainment in this country, such as the figures of the *khiyāl* [here shadow play?], hobbyhorse, lute, rūṭa (rotta), rebab and *qānūn* ... among its glories is what is found in Ubeda, namely different sorts of musicians and dancing girls famous for the excellence of their talent and their art, for these women are truly the most skilful of God's creatures at sword play, juggling, staging the live play of the 'Villager', sleights of hand, and acting with masks (*mutawajjih*, corresponding to acting with *samāja*, to which I shall come back).[101]

In Andalusia, too, the *kurraj* was played in the palaces of caliphs and grandees. In 367/977, Ibn Martīn, the commander of al-Mu'tamid, was surprised in his palace in Cordoba by his enemies when he was entertained by *kurraj ('dhukira annahu kāna sā'ata-'idhin yul'abu bayna yadayhi bi-'l-kurraj')*.[102]

However, during the twelfth century the 500 young slaves who roved the court in the palace of Ibn Jarīr (the vizier of the Almohades) on wooden horses with lances, seems to have been involved in military training.[103]

Figure 2 Two actors of *kurraj* (hobby-horse) players (note the players' feet), with ram-holder, statues, fortress-constructions. (After Metin And, *Osmanli Şenliklerinde Türk Sanatlari* (Ankara, 1982) Courtesy of Professor Metin And.)

Therefore, it is possible to conclude that the use of the *kurraj* and *qaṣaba* throughout the Islamic period might be a vestige of pre-Islamic dramatic rites practised not only in Arabia, but mainly in Persia and Central Asia.

The descriptions of *kurraj* given by al-Iṣfahānī and Ibn Khaldūn as well as the various illustrations of Islamic hobby-horse show clearly that the player was hidden behind the drapery of the *kurraj*, which had no wheels or legs to support riding players. Hence it cannot have been a saddled wooden horse on which the players ride, as one of the meanings of the word *musarraja*, used by Ibn Khaldun, would suggest.[104] The second meaning of the word *musarraja* is 'decorated', and Jarīr described the *kurraj* as decorated with ornamented belts and bells. So too does Ibn Khaldūn himself.

No author, however, mentions any dialogue in connection with the *kurraj*, only singing and dancing; and no activities other than 'attack and withdrawal and competing in skill (with weapons)', seems to have been represented. But if the *khayyālūn* (actors) used to perform on a hobby-horse, as it is attested my Maimonides, then it is possible to assume that the actors' repertoire involved not only dancing and singing, but also dialogue and plot as in the case of the ṣūfī's play.

Notes

1. On theatrical elements in the Jāhiliyya, see M. Y. Najm, 'Ṣuwar min al-Tamthīl fī 'l-Ḥaḍāra al-'Arabiyya', *Āfāq 'Arabiyya* III, no. 3, Nov. 1977, pp. 59–63. On other kinds of entertainment, see N. D. Asad, *al-Qiyān wa-'l-Ghinā' fī 'l-'Aṣr al-Jāhili* (Cairo, 1969); M. And, *Near Eastern Rituals and Performances.* (Paris, 1989); Ullman, *WKAS*, vol. II, pp. 779ff.
2. Cf. A. J. Wensinck *et al.* (eds), *Concordance et Indices de la Tradition Musulmane* (Leiden, 1967), s.v. 'li'b'; of. also svv. '*lahw*', '*ḍiḥk*'.
3. Ibn Ḥajar al-Haythamī (d. 973/1565), *Kitāb Kaff al-Ru'ā' 'an Muḥarramāt al-Lahw wa'l-Samā'*, printed in the margin of Ibn Ḥajar al-Haythamī, *Kitāb al-Zawājir 'an Iqtirāf al-Kabā'ir* (Cairo, 1322), vol. I, pp. 1–22; anon., *al-Risāla fī Bayān* (see Bibliography for full title), MS Staatsbibliothek Berlin, shelf no. We. 1811, fols 89a–101b. There are several manuscripts on the question of the legality of dance and music in Berlin, cf. W. Ahlwardt, *Die Handschriften-Verzeichnisse der Königlischen Bibliothek zu Berlin, Verzeichniss der arabischen Handschriften* (Berlin, 1893), vol. V, pp. 57–72, nos. 553–63. See also Ibn al-Jawzī, *Talbīs Iblīs*, ed. K. D. 'Alī (Beirut, 1368/1948f), pp. 192ff, 222ff.
4. Ibn Ḥanbal, *al-Musnad* (Cairo, 1313/1895f), vol. I, pp. 434, 454, 465.
5. Ibid. vol. V, pp. 3ff; cf. also vol. III, p. 38; al-Rāghib al-Iṣfahānī, *Muḥāḍarāt al-Udabā' wa-Muḥāwarāt al-Shu'arā' al-Bulaghā'* (Cairo, 1287/1870f.), vol. I, p.. 177

6. Ibn Ḥajar al-Haythamī, *Kaff al-Ruʿā' ʿan Muḥarramāt al-Lahw wa-'l-Samā'*, in the margin of *Kitāb al-Zawājir* ... (Cairo, 1322/1904), vol. I, pp. 40, 155f, 163f; ʿAdb al-Ra'ūf al-Mināwī, *Kitāb al-Taysīr bi-Sharḥ al-Jāmiʿ al-Ṣaghīr* (Cairo, 1286/1869), vol. II, p. 214, where swimming is added to the other activities.
7. Ibn Ḥajar al-ʿAsqalānī, *Fatḥ al-Bārī bi-Sharḥ Ṣaḥīḥ al-Bukhārī* (Cairo, 1325/1907), vol. VI, p. 60; Ibn Ḥajar al-Haythamī, *Kaff*, vol. I, pp. 49f; anon., *Risāla fī Bayān*, fols 90b–91a.
8. Cf. the references given in the preceding note; Muslim, *Ṣaḥīḥ*, ed. M. F. ʿAbd al-Bāqī (Cairo, 1955), vol. II, pp. 299–304.
9. Ibn Ḥajar al-Haythamī, *Kaff*, vol. I, pp. 50f; cf. Ibn al-Ḥājj, *Madkhal*, vol. II, pp. 5f.
10. Ibn Abī 'l-Ḥadīd, *Sharḥ Nahj al-Balāgha* (Cairo, 1959), vol. VI, pp. 330–2.
11. Cf. Ibn Ḥajar al-Haythamī, *Kaff*, pp. 44, 79, 88; ʿAbd al-Wahhāb al-Dakdakjī, *Rafʿ al-Mushkilāt fī Ḥukm Ibāḥat al-Ālāt bi-'l-Naghamāt al-Ṭayyibāt*, MS Staatsbibliothek Berlin, shelf no. We. 1811, fols 1a–29a (he defends the *samā*ʿ of the Ṣūfīs at fols 5a–b); Muḥammad b. Aḥmad al-Tūnisī (d. 882/1477), *Kitāb Faraḥ al-Asmāʿ bi-Rukhaṣ al-Samā*ʿ. Staatsbibliothek Berlin, shelf no. We. 1505.
12. See for instance Ibn ʿAbd Rabbih, *al-ʿIqd al-Farīd* (Cairo, 1368/1949), vol. IV, p. 381; al-Ibshīhī, *al-Mustaṭraf min kull Fann Mustaẓraf* (Cairo, 1379/1960), vol. II, pp. 231f; al-Nuwayrī, *Nihāyat al- Arab* (Cairo, 1923–84), vol. IV, pp. 160f; Rosenthal, *Humor in Early Islam* (Leiden, 1965), pp. 1–16. For an interesting survey of humorous literature in Islam, see also Muḥammad Qarah ʿAlī, *al-Ḍāḥikūn* (Beirut, 1980); Abū 'l-Barakāt Muḥammad al-Ghazzī, *al-Marāḥ fī 'l-Muzāḥ*, MS Staatsbibliothek Berlin, shelf no. We 1764, (Damascus 1340/1930); Ibn al-Ḥājj, *Madhkal*, vol. I, pp. 205f; Aḥmad al-Tīfāshī, *Kitāb Nuzhat al-Albāb fīmā lā yūjad fī Kitāb*, MS Bibliothèque Nationale, arabe 3055, fol. 3a; Ibn Abī 'l-Ḥadīd, *Sharḥ*, vol. VI, pp. 330–2.
13. Ibn Ḥanbal, *Musnad*, vol. IV, pp. 85, 166, 186, 242; cf. also vol. III, p. 152; al-Ibshībī, *Mustaṭraf*, vol. II, p. 147; Ibn Abī 'l-Ḥadīd, *Sharḥ*, vol. VI, pp. 330–2.
14. al-Ibshībī, *Mustaṭraf*, vol. II, p. 147; Ibn Ḥajar al-Haythamī, *Kaff*, vol. I, pp. 76–7; anon. *Risāla fī Bayān*, fol. 92a; Muslim, *Ṣaḥīḥ*, vol. II, p. 607ff, n. 892.
15. al-Ibshīhī, *Mustaṭraf*, vol. II, p. 232; cf. Ibn Ḥanbal, *Musnad*, vol. VI, pp. 84, 166.
16. Ibn ʿAbd Rabbih, *ʿIqd*, vol. VI, p. 381; Ibn ʿĀṣim al-Qaysī al-Andalusī, *Ḥadā'iq al-Azhār fī Mustaḥsan al-Ajwiba wa-'l-Afkār*, MS British Library 1378, fols 33a–34b. In Abū 'l-Fidā, *Tārīkh* (Cairo n.d.), vol. XIII, p. 200 (year 656 AH) the verb *talʿabu* is used as a synonym of *tarquṣu*. In al-Ghazzī, *al-Marāḥ* p. 18, ʿĀ'isha smeared Sawda with food made of flour.
17. Ibn ʿAbd Rabbih, *ʿIqd*, vol. VI, p. 381.
18. Ibn Ḥanbal, *Musnad*, vol. III, p. 152.
19. Ibid; Ibn Yūsuf al-Mizzī, *Tuḥfat al-Ashrāf fī Maʿrifat al-Aṭrāf* (Bom-

bay, 1400/1980), vol. XI, p. 487; Muslim, *Ṣaḥīḥ*, vol. II, p. 610; Ibn Ḥanbal, *Musnad*, vol. IV, p. 242.
20. al-Bukhārī, *al-Ṣaḥīḥ*, ed. and tr. M. M. Khan (Gujranwala, 1971), vol. IV, ch. 8, no. 720; 'Adb al-Raḥmān al-Suhaylī, *al-Rawḍ al-Unuf*, ed. 'A. R. al-Wakīl (Cairo, 1967–70), vol. VIII, p. 247. See below n. 6.
21. S. M. Ḥusain, 'The Poems of Surāqa b. Mirdās al-Bāriqī, an Umayyad Poet', *Journal of the Royal Asiatic Society* (1936), p. 620, v. 15.
22. al-Ṭabarī, *Annales* (Leiden, 1879–1901), ser. I, p. 1011. For a *la''āba* playing cymbals, see al-Jawālīqī, *al-Mu'arrab* , (Leipzig 1867), p. 101: *ḍarbu yad al-la''ābati 'l-ṭawsūsā* .
23. al-Ṭabarī, *Annales*, ser. II, p. 971f.
24. Ibn Abī 'l-Ḥadīd, *Sharḥ* , vol. IV, p. 335.
25. See above, Chapter 1, n. 56.
26. See Ibn 'Asākir, *Tārīkh Madīnat Dimashq* (Dimashq, 1982), vol. XX, pp. 299–300, and Ibn 'Asākir, *Tahdhīb Tārīkh Dimashq al-Kabīr* (Dimashq, 1351/1932–3), vol. VII, p. 276. The term *mughabbirūn* appears in *Tārīkh Madīnāt Dimashq* as *mu'abbirūn*. On *mughabbirūn*, see Ibn Manẓūr, *Lisān al-'Arab* (Beirut, 1955–6), vol. V, p. 5, col. 1, and Ibn Khaldūn, *al-Muqaddima* (Paris, 1858), vol. I, pt. 2, p. 359.
27. See Ibn al-Nadīm, *al-Fihrist* , Cairo edn., p. 348.
28. See al-Bīrūnī, *Taḥqīq mā li-l-Hind min Maqūla Maqbūla fī 'Aql aw Mardhūla* (Hyderabad Abād al-Dakan, 1958), pp. 488ff.
29. Ibn Bassām al-Shantarīnī, *al-Dhakhīra fī Maḥāsin Ahl al-Jazīra* (Beirut, 1979), vol. I, p. 242; cf. also below, Ch.7, n. 65.
30. Pedro de Alcala, *Vocabulista Aravigo en Letra Castellana* (Granada, 1505), p. Jii. I should like to thank the authorities of Bibliothéque Nationale, Paris, for allowing me to use their rare copy of this dictionary. See also R. Dozy, *Supplément aux Dictionnaires Arabes* , vol. II, p. 535, col. 1.
31. *Canons of Athanasius,* introduction; cf. also Abū 'l-Fidā, *Historia Anteislamica Arabica* (Leipzig, 1831), pp. 106f.
32. *Canons of Athanasius* , p. 40 (Arabic) = 48 (English).
33. Ibid., p. 23 (Arabic) - 30 (English).
34. 'Erste Abteilung: Texte und Übersetzungen *al-Ṭibb al-Rūḥānī* , der Nomoksnon Mikhā'īls von Malig', in *Oriens Christianus* (1907), vol. VII, pp. 116–18 (Arabic) = 117–19 (German).
35. al-Ḥimyarī *Ṣifat Jazīrat al-'Arab* (Cairo, 1937), p. 181 no. 171.
36. al-Idrīsī, *Description de l'Afrique et de l'Espagne* , ed. R. P. A. Dozy and M. J. de Goeje (Amsterdam, 1969), pp. 112f.
37. See Ch. 1, n. 79.
38. Cf. also *Defter der Abū Muṣṭafā* , v. Jahre 1860 (MS Staatsbibliothek Berlin, Nachlass Wetzstein, no. 31–43), in which a certain Darwīsh Rajab al-Ḥakīm describes a *mal'ab* he had seen during his journeys along the following lines: it is a crescent-shaped court like a semi-circle, with ten steps; each step is higher and wider than the former; during feasts, vacations and festivals the nobles

and grandees would sit on the steps, the higher ranks on the higher steps; in the middle the guilds would play, for example those of snake charmers or acrobats.

39. Alcala, *Vocabulista*, p. ii.
40. al-Jabartī, *'Ajā'ib al-Āthār fī 'l-Tarājim wa-'l-Akhbār* (Būlāq, 1297/ 1879f), vol. III, p. 142. On Arabic theatrical terms see Atia Abul-Naga, *Recherche sur les Termes de Théâtre et leur Traduction en Arabe Moderne* (Alger, SNED, n.d.)
41. al-Ṭahṭāwī *Talkhīṣ*, p. 166.
42. Ibid., p. 167.
43. M. Y. Najm (ed.), *al-Masraḥ al-'Arabī, Dirāsāt wa-Nuṣūṣ, Ya'qūb Sannū' [sic] (Abū Naḍḍāra)* (Beirut, 1963, pp. 193, 195, 201.
44. K. Levy, *'Lā'bät Elḥôtä*, 'ein Tunesisches Schattenspiel', in *Studien zur Geschichte und Kultur des Nahen und Fernen Ostens* (Leiden, 1935), pp. 119–24.
45. Abū 'l-Faraj al-Iṣfahānī, *Kitāb al-Aghānī* (Cairo, 1927 –74), vol. XVIII, p. 71; cf. above, n. 23. In a *hijā'* by Abū 'l-Faraj al-Iṣfahānī, he describes his satirised enemy's walk as *'mukhannath yal'abu bi-'l-shīzi'* (an entertainer playing with castanets). See Yāqūt, *Mu'jam al-Udabā'* (Cairo, 1936–8), vol. XIII, p. 109. This is an example of using *yal'ab* for playing music.
46. A. A. Bevan (ed.), *The Nakā'iḍ of Jarīr and al-Farazdaḳ* (Leiden, 1905–9), vol. II, p. 624.
47. Cf. P. Crone, *Roman, Provincial and Islamic Law* (Cambridge, 1987), p. 12.
48. K. G. Bruns and E. Sachau (eds and trs), *Syrisch–römisches Rechtsbuch aus dem fünften Jahrhundert* (Leipzig, 1880; repr. 1961), pp. 7 42 (Syriac), 47 (German).
49. Bruns and Sachau, *Rechtsbuch*, pp. 71f. On *shuhra*, see also n. 50 and below, Chapter 4, notes 71 and 73; on the *ḥalaba*, see Ibn 'Abd Rabbih, *'Iqd*, vol. I, pp. 206f; Ibn Iyās, *Badā'i'*, vol. I, part 2, p. 380; Ibn Taghrī Birdī, *Ḥawādith al-Duhūr* (Berkeley and Los Angeles, 1930f), vol. XXVII pp. 597f. On *ṣirā'*, see id. *al-Nujūm al-Zāhira fī Mulūk Miṣr wa-'l-Qāhira*, MS Bibliothéque Nationale, Arabe 1783, fols 157a; cf. also al-Qazwīnī, *Kosmographie* (Göttingen, 1848), vol. I., p. 128. On the *muḍḥik*, see Chapter 4.
50. See R. Payne Smith, *Thesaurus Syriacus* (Oxford, 1879–1901), vol. II, col. 2093, and in col. 4370 *teaṭron* is given in Arabic according to Bar Bahlūl (active 963 C.E.) as *shuhra, manẓar, mawḍi' al-ḥalba* and *mal'ab*.
51. On this person see Ibn Shākir al-Kutubī, *Fawāt al-Wafayāt*, (Būlāq, 1283/1866f), vol. I, pp. 201f; the edn I. 'Abbās (Beirut, 1974). vol. II, pp. 153f, n. 210; al-Iṣfahānī, *Aghānī*, vol. XX, p. 255; Ibn al-Athīr, *al-Kāmil fī 'l-Tā'rīkh* (Leiden, 1851–76), vol. VII, pp. 36f; al-Shābushtī, *Kitāb al-Diyārāt* (Baghdad, 1966), pp. 185–90.
52. *Min aṭyabi 'l-nās*. For the synonymity of *muṭāyaba* and *muḥākāt*, see al-Tha'ālibī, *Yatīmat al-Dahr* (Cairo, 1399/1979), vol. II, p. 377; al-Tanūkī, *Nishwār al-Muḥādara* (Beirut, 1971), vol. I, pp. 4, 185, 265; cf. also Ch. 3, n. 63. In Payne, *Thesaurus Syriacus*, col. 2093, in

Syriac *mimsutha* (mimesis), it is given in Arabic as *takhnīth*.

53. al-Shābushtī, *Diyārāt*, p. 185.
54. Cf. Ch. 3 n. 48 and 50 and Nuwayrī, *Nihāya*, vol. Iv, p. 25–33. See also al-Musabbiḥī, *Akhbār Miṣr* (Cairo, 1978), vol. 40, part 1, p. 104. For a *mukhannath* who was a pimp of five women, see ibid., p. 68; for another who was a passive homosexual, see Ibn 'Āṣim al-Andalusī, *Hadā'iq al-Azhār.* fols 46a–48a.
55. al-Suhaylī, *Rawḍ*, vol. VII, p. 274; Wensinck, *Concordance*, s.v. *'lahw'*. For a *mukhannath* in Medina in the time of 'Umar, II, see al-Iṣfahānī, *Aghānī*, vol. VI, p. 337.
56. al-Suhaylī, *Rawḍ*, vol. VII, p. 274.
57. Ibn al-Ḥājj, *Madkhal*, vol. II, pp. 52f; cf. vol. I, p. 146.
58. See al-Ḥusrī al-Qayrawānī, *Dhayl Zahr al-Ādāb* (Cairo, 1353/1934), p. 195.
59. See below, p. 00.
60. On the *kurraj*, see M. Gaudefroy-Demombynes, 'Sur le Cheval-jupon et *al-Kurraj* ' in *Mélanges offerts à William Marçais* (Paris, 1950), pp. 155–60; A. Shiloah, 'Réflexions sur la Danse Artistique Musulmane au Moyen Âge', *Cahiers de Civilisations Médiévale V* (1962), pp. 463–74. Cf. also al-Suhaylī, *Rawḍ*, vol. VII, p. 274. For an illustration, see Figure 2 of this book, p. 00.
61. Lane, *Lexicon*, s.v. '*kurraj* '; Ibn Manẓūr, *Lisān al-'Arab,* vol. II, p. 352; Abū 'l-Ḥasan 'Alī b. Ismā'īl al-Andalusī Ibn Sīda al-Marsī, *Kitāb al-Mukhaṣṣaṣ* (Būlāq, 1320/1902f), p. 19; Shihāb al-Dīn Aḥmad al-Khafājī, *Kitāb Shifā' al-Ghalīl* (Cairo, 1325/1907), p. 170. Cf. also M. Ullmann, *Wörterbuch der klassischen arabischen Sprache* (Wiesbaden, 1970), vol. I, p. 120, col. 2; F. Steingass, *A Comprehensive Persian-English Dictionary* (London, 1947), p. 1026. The lexicographers insist that this word was arabised as *kurraj*,the original term being *kurra*; but though it is indeed *kurra* in New Persian, the Arabic word reproduces Middle Persian *kurrag.* (I am indebted to Professor S. Shaked for this information).
62. Ibn Bassām, *al-Dhakhīra*, vol. I, part i, p. 19.
63. And, *Culture*, p. 23.
64. See Gaudefroy-Demombynes, 'Sur le Cheval-jupon,' p. 160, where he translated *qaṣaba* into *cheval*.
65. al-Jāḥiẓ (attrib.), *al-Tāj*, pp. 178f.
66. al-Bukhārī, *al-Ṣaḥīḥ* vol. IV, ch. 1, no. 720. See n. 20 above.
67. Cf. n. 55 above.
68. Cf. the editorial note to al-Suhaylī *Rawḍ*, vol. VII, p. 274.
69. Abū 'l-Faraj, *Aghānī*, vol. VIII, pp. 76f.
70. Cf. al-Shābushtī, *Diyārāt*, p. 199 and n. 9 thereto; C. E. Bosworth, *The Medieval Islamic Underworld* (Leiden, 1976), vol. II, pp. 14 (v. 59), 198.
71. Bevan, *Nakā'id*, vol. I, p. 320; vol. II, pp. 624, 650.
72. Ibid., vol. II, p. 936.
73. Ibid., vol. II, p. 844.
74. Ibid., vol. I, p. 246.
75. Ibid., Introduction, p.

76. Ibid., vol. I, p. 246. The word *khayāl* in Jarīr's poetry in the sense of 'scare-crow'; apparently any figure in the shape of a man, horse or other was called *khayāl*, cf. ibid., vol. III, p. 362 (and cf. also p. 461; Ibn Manẓūr, *Lisān al- 'Arab*, vol. XI, p. 230). On *khayāl* as a human figure at night, see the tradition in Ibn 'Asākir, *Ta-'rīkh Madīnat Dimashq*, vol. XXI 1981, p. 423; *in ra'ayta khayālan fī 'l-layl fa-lā takun ajban al-khayālayn.*
77. Bevan, *Nakā'iḍ* vol. I, p. 624.
78. Ibid., vol. II, p. 844.
79. al-Ṭabarī, *Annales*, ser. III, pp. 971f (year 198 A.H.); al-Iṣfahānī, *Aghānī*, vol. XVIII, pp. 71f (where *kirḥ* should be emended to *kurraj*).
80. Cf. M. And, *Culture*, p. 21.
81. M. Gaudefroy-Demombynes, 'Sur le Cheval-jupon,' p. 159.
82. Shiloah, 'Reflections,' p. 474.
83. al-Suhaylī, *Rawḍ* vol. VII, p. 247.
84. Ibn Khaldūn, *Muqaddima*, vol. I, part ii, pp. 360f; tr. R. Rosenthal (New York, 1958), vol. II, pp. 404f.
85. And, *Culture*, p. 79.
86. Cf. n. 78 above.
87. al-Musabbiḥī, *Akhbār Miṣr*, vol. XL, part i, pp. 79f; cf. al-Maqrīzī, *Khiṭaṭ*, vol. II, p. 100; Ibn Taghrī Birdī, *Nujūm*, vol. IX, p. 215, vol. X, p. 48. For an illustration of a *simāṭ* procession see Figure 1.
88. al-Musabbiḥī, *Akhbār Miṣr*, vol. XL, pp. 79f. See also Ch. 3, n. 43. See also Ibn al-Jawzī, *al-Muntaẓam*, vol. VIII, p. 141.
89. Maimonides, *Commentaire de Maimonide sur la Mischnah, Seder Tohorot* ed. J. Derenbourg (Berlin,1887), vol. I, p. 135, 27; cf. I. Friedlaender, *Arabisch-Deutsches Lexikon zum Sprachgebrauch des Maimonides* (Frankfurt a. M., 1902), p. 40. In Tanḥum ben Yosef Ha-Yerushalmi's (d. 1291) dictionary of Maimonides Mishna Commentary entitled *al-Murshid al-Kāfī* (MS National Library, Jerusalem, shelf n. 8^0 1203, vol. II, f. 107a), the entry *rkf* gives the term *markof*. This term is defined as in the case of Maimonides, but with minor changes: *wa-huwa faras al-'ūd alladhī yal'ab bihi al-zumarā wa-'l-mukhayilīn (sic) fa-huwa idhan ismun mushtarakun fī ālāt al-malhā kamā ra'ayta* (the horse-headed stick, with which the flutists and actors play. It is then a common term for entertainment props, as you have seen). However, Tanhum changes Maimonides term *khayālīn* into *mukhāyilīn* , i.e. the usual term used by Muslim scholars in the Eastern part of the Muslim World. My thanks to Dr. Hadassa Shay for referring me to this dictionary, of which she is preparing a scientific edition.
90. Maimonides, *Commentaire* vol. I, p. 142, 1. 1, and Friedlaender, *Lexikon*, p. 40.
91. al-Naysābūrī, *Uqalā' al-Majānīn*, (Najaf, 1387/1968), p. 87.
92. Ibid., pp. 40f, 76ff. On the relations between shamanism and ecstasy, mysticism, mental illness and masks, see M. Eliade, *Shamanism, Archaic Techniques of Ecstasy* (Princeton, 1974), pp. 5–7, 26–7, 67, 151ff.

93. Ibn 'Abd Rabbih, *al-'Iqd,* vol. IV, pp. 152ff.
94. And, *Culture*, p. 25; Eliade, *Shamanism,* pp. 151–467.
95. See p. 91 below.
96. al-Yāfi'ī al-Yamanī, *Kitāb Rawḍ al-Rayāḥīn fī Ḥikāyāt al-Ṣāliḥīn* (Cairo, 1297/1880), p. 50, no. 33. Cf. U. Marzolph, *Der Weise Narr Buhlūl* (Wiesbaden, 1983), p. 48, n. 85.
97. Cf. And, *Culture*, p. 24.
98. Ibn Sūdūn, *Kitāb Nuzhat al-Nufūs wa-Muḍḥik al-'Abūs* (Cairo, 1280/1863f) pp. 158ff. Cf. Eliade, *Shamanism*, p. 157f; 'The headgear of a shaman is made of feathers and imitates a bird.'
99. Cf. And, *Culture*, p. 83.
100. Ibn Sūdūn, *Nuzhat al-Nufūs*, p. 4.
101. al-Shaqundī, *Risāla fī Faḍl al-Andalus wa-Ahlihā,* in S. -D. al-Munajjid (ed.), *Faḍā'il al-Andalus wa-Ahlihā li-Ibn Ḥazm wa-Ibn Sa'īd wa- l-Shaqundī* (Beirut, 1968), pp. 52, 56; cf. also M. Kurd 'Alī, 'Ḥāḍir al-Andalus wa-Ghābiruhā,' *Majallat al-Majma' al-'Ilmī al-'Arabī*, 1922, Damascus II, p. 235. I shall return to this passage in Chapter 7.
102. R. Dozy (ed.) *Historia Abbadidarum* (Leiden, 1846), vol. I, p. 324, 2; cf. also H. Peres, *La Poésie Andalouse en Arabe Classique au XIe Siécle* (Paris, 1937), pp. 344f.
103. M. Gaudefroy-Demombynes, 'Sur le Cheval-jupon,' p. 160.
104. See above n. 84, and Figure 2 in this book.

3

Samāja and *Muharrijūn*

Samāja

Arab lexicographers define *samāja* as 'foul, unseemly, or ugly'.[1] But in literary and historical works it has another meaning beside ugliness, that is 'a masked actor' or 'mask worn by such an actor'.

In the *Naqā'iḍ* there is rare evidence which connects the *kurraj* with the *samāja*, provided most probably by the third commentator, Abū 'Abdallāh Muḥammad b. al-'Abbās al-Yazīdī (d. 310/922), who is mentioned as the commentator on poem no. 42, v. 6. Verses 8–11 of this poem runs as follows, (*wāfir* metre):[2]

٨ لَقَدْ أَمْسَى البَعِيثُ بِدَارِ ذُلٍّ   وَمَا أَمْسَى الفَرَزْدَقُ بِالخِيَارِ
٩ جَلَاجِلُ كُرَّجٍ وَسِبَالُ قِرْدٍ   وَزَنْدٌ مِنْ قُفَيْرَةَ غَيْرُ وَارِ
١٠ عَرَفْنَا مِنْ قُفَيْرَةَ حَاجِبَيْهَا   وَجَدًّا فِي أَنَامِلِهَا القِصَارِ
١١ تَدَافَعْنَا فَقَالَ بَنُو تَمِيمٍ   كَأَنَّ القِرْدَ طُوِّحَ مِنْ طَمَارِ

8. Al-Ba'īth is disgraced and al-Farazdaq has no better choice.
9. [Small] bells of *kurraj* , moustaches of a monkey, // and fire drill of Qufayra [al-Farazdaq's mother] which can't strike fire.
10. We are well acquainted with the brows of Qufayra // and the shortening of her diminutive fingers.
11. We pushed one another, and Banū Tamīm said: // 'it looks as if the monkey has been thrown from a high place.'

The commentator glosses the 'small bells of *kurraj*' of l. 9 with the explanation that 'he (Jarīr) is mocking him (al-Farazdaq). He (Jarīr) means that he is a *samāja*'. Presumably Jarīr is referring to al-Farazdaq dressed up in a silken garment and a bracelet and riding on a mule (as described in the previous section): he is calling him an actor dressed up as a monkey wearing a moustache and riding a *kurraj*, adding that later this monkey fell off his horse. If this explanation of these verses is correct, it throws new light on the passage in the *Aghānī* concerning the Umayyad caliph al-Walīd b. Yazīd (125/743-44) which interested Ettinghausen:[3]

> When al-Walīd b. Yazīd became caliph he was devoted to singing, drinking and hunting. Singers were brought to him from Medina and other places. He sent for Ash'ab, who was brought to him, and he clothed him with trousers of monkey skin with a tail and told him: 'Dance and sing a poem that will please me. If you do, I will give you one thousand dirhams.' Ash'ab sang, and al-Walīd was pleased and gave him one thousand dirhams.[4]

Ettinghausen saw this passage as evidence of the entertainment portrayed in a painting in the Umayyad palace of Quṣayr 'Amra which shows 'a seated bear playing a stringed instrument to the tune of which a monkey, standing on his hind legs, claps his front paws' ... The music-making bear leaves little doubt that one faces here again a dressed up ensemble of human entertainers.[5] Ettinghausen observes that this custom was a pre-Islamic one:

> Further evidence establishes the fact that the dressing up as animals, and particularly as monkeys, is much older in the Near East than the thirteenth century. If we start with the earliest evidence, we can point to a bronze lamp in the Musee du Louvre which is related to those from the Eastern Roman Empire; it was, however, found by R. Ghirshman in Susa and seems to date from the Parthian period. On the lid of the cover for the oil intake is the fully sculptured figure of a monkey ... The way in which this figure sits, carries its head, and is seen reading a scroll – all this points to a masked actor rather than an animal. If this should be the case, and it seems most likely that it is, the custom must have existed many centuries before the Muslim period. Also, a connection with late antique popular spectacles suggest itself at once[6]

In fact, the custom of wearing masks of animals or demonic features, as well as whitening the face with lime or flour or blackening it with soot or ashes, was an integral part of dramatic rituals among many nations, including the Arabs.[7] In Arabia, 'procession, combats and masquerades' were used in rain rituals (*istisqā'*) during the pre-Islamic period.[8] Clearly, the commentator on the *Naqā'iḍ* was also familiar with such masked actors: he knew them under the name of *samāja* . It is not clear whether the term *samāja* was used in the time of Jarīr and al-Farazdaq themselves or only in that of the commentators. But even so, this is the earliest passage known to me in which the term *samāja* stands for an actor. (It is also the only example before the nineteenth century of small bells and monkeys associated with such actors.)

The term *samāja* recurs in al-Ṭabarī's account of the fall of al-Afshīn (killed in 226/841). 'In his [al-Afshīn's] house was found a room in which there was a wooden statue of a man (*timthāl insān*) dressed with many ornaments and jewels. On its ears were two white stones interlaced with gold .... From his house were taken *ṣuwar al-samāja* and other things, statues (*aṣnām*) and other things ... magic religious books.'[9] In fact, al-Ṭabarī's account of the fall of the Afshīn may shed light on the Central Asian pagan cults and cultures among the Turks during the Abbasid caliphate. The Afshīn, who is deemed to have been 'one of the major bearers of Inner-Asian culture and artistic influences',[10] was accused of reviving pre-Islamic religions in Turkistan and of allowing his subjects to address him as 'god of gods', thus transgressing Islamic monotheism. In fact, such a title reveals that 'the cult of deified ancestors was the main religious concept prevalent in the area of Ushrūsana'.[11] Emel Esin arrived at the conclusion that 'al-Ṭabarī's account appears to confirm the historical, numismatic and iconographic data', and describes red hair masks, totemic figures and paintings of grotesque figures found in Ushrūsana.[12] These masks and totemic figures might be similar to *ṣuwar al-samāja* and the *aṣnām* mentioned by al-Ṭabarī. The fact that al-Mu'taṣim killed al-Afshīn and at the same time allowed entertainers to use such masks to celebrate the Nayrūz may indicate that in the Abbasid court such masked celebrations in the Nayrūz were a parody of Persian and Turkish ritual dramas.

Samāja in the sense of comic masks and/or masked actors are attested for Iraq and Egypt from the ninth to the eleventh centuries in the context of Nayrūz celebrations by Muslims and Copts in the times of the Abbasid caliphs al-Mu'taṣim (218–27/833–42), al-Mutawakkil (232–47/847–62), al-Mu'taḍid (279–89/892–902), Ibn al-Mu'tazz (247–96/861–908) and the Fatimid caliphs al-Mu'izz (341–65/952–75), and al-Ẓāhir (1020–35), under whom *samāja* actors are mentioned for the last time.

Thus during the reign of al-Mu'taṣim, Nayrūz was celebrated with *samāja* actors playing with dancing *ṣafā'ina* (slap-takers or slapstick comedians). Abū'-Faraj al-Iṣfahānī in his *Maqātil al-Ṭālibiyyīn* gives us a hint of the attitude of pious Muslims to such performances. Dealing with Muḥammad b. al-Qāsim, the descendant of 'Alī who was brought as a prisoner to al-Mu'taṣim on a Nayrūz day in 219/834, the narrator says:

> The *samāja* actors (*aṣḥāb al-samāja*) were playing (*yal'abūn*) before al-Mu'taṣim, and the *ṣafā'ina* [slapstick comedians; in the text: *Farāghina*] were dancing. When Muḥammad [b. al-Qāsim] saw them, he wept and exclaimed: 'O God! you know that I am eager to change this [matter] and to denounce it....' The *ṣafā'ina* began to attack the common people and to throw dirt and carrion (*al-qadhar wa- 'l-mayta*)[13] at them, to the laughter of al-Mu'taṣim, while Muḥammad b. al-Qāsim was glorifying God and asking God's forgiveness, moving his lips and

> cursing them. Al-Muʿtaṣim was sitting in his palace in al-Shammāsiyya, looking at them while Muḥammad was standing. When al-Muʿtaṣim finished playing, they brought Muḥammad b. al-Qāsim to him....[14]

In fact, it is not clear from the above paragraph what kind of playing the *samāja* did, how the *ṣafāʾina* danced, or why they threw dirt and meat at the common people. What is clear is that pious Muslims were against celebrating the Nayrūz in this fashion, and also that there was now a distinction between the *laʿb* (play) of the *samāja* and the *raqṣ* (dancing) of the *ṣafāʾina*, though previously these two terms had been synonymous.

The author of *Kitāb al-Diyārāt*, ʿAlī b. Muḥammad al-Shābushtī (d. 388/998), gives a more detailed description of the *samāja* players wearing ugly masks (*samāja*) of various shapes, celebrating the Nayrūz in the presence of al-Mutawakkil, the son of al-Muʿtaṣim:

> On a Nawrūz day Isḥāq [b. Ibrāhîm] came to al-Mutawakkil, while the *samāja* were in front of him. Al-Mutawakkil, was wearing a garment of heavy embroidery. The *samāja* were very numerous and they approached him to pick up the dirhams which were being scattered to them, and even pulled the flaps of his garment. When Isḥāq saw that, he went away with anger saying: 'Fie! Our guarding the empire is no use when such waste is going on.' Al-Mutawakkil saw him going out. He said (to his servants): 'Woe to you, bring Abū al-Ḥasan back. He has gone out angry.' So the attendants and servants went after him. He came in talking very harshly to Waṣīf and Zurāfa, and came to al-Mutawakkil. He asked: 'Why are you angry? Why did you go out?' He answered: 'O Commander of the Faithful, perhaps you imagine that this kingdom does not have as many enemies as loyal subjects. You sit in a place in which such dogs are insulting you. They pulled the flaps of your garment and each of them is disguised by a revolting mask (*wa-kull wāḥidin minhum mutanakkirūn bi-ṣūratin munkara*). One can't be sure that there is not among them an enemy who is willing to lay down his life out of religious zeal, with evil intention, to attack you. How can such a man give up his intention, even if you were to get rid of all your enemies?' Al-Mutawakkil said: 'O Abū ʿ l-Ḥusayn, don't be angry! You will never see me doing such a thing again!' Then a gallery was built for al-Mutawwakil so that he looked down upon *ṣamāja*'s (performance).[15]

The Abbasid poet and prince, ʿAbd Allāh b. al-Muʿtazz, who ruled only one day, gives us more details about the way in which the *samāja* perform their acts with masks in the following verses on *samājat al-Nayrūz* (*munsariḥ*) metre):[16]

فَاشْرَبْ غَدَاةَ النَّيْرُوزِ صَافِيَةً   أَيَّامُهَا فِي السُّرُورِ سَاعَاتُ
قَدْ ظَهَرَ الجِنُّ فِي النَّهَارِ لَنَا   مِنْهُمْ صُفُوفٌ وَدَسْتَبَنْدَاتُ
تَمِيلُ فِي رَقْصِهِمْ قُدُودُهُمُ   كَمَا تَثَنَّتْ فِي الرِّيحِ سَرْوَاتُ
وَرُكِّبَ القُبْحُ فَوْقَ حُسْنِهِمِ   فَفِي سَمَاجَاتِهِمْ مَلاحَاتُ

Drink clear (wine) early on the morning of the Nayrūz//
The Days of (this feast) are so happy that they are but hours.
The demons appeared to us during the day//
Some are (arranged in) lines and some are dancing holding hand in hand.
In their dancing their bodies sway//
As the cypresses sway in the wind.
Ugliness was installed [by masks] upon their beauty,//
and in the ugliness [of their comical masks] there is prettiness.

In Ibn al-Muʿtazz' verses the *samāja* look like demons with their masks, and they dance swaying their bodies holding hands or in rows, but there is no indication of any imitation in their play.

In the *Kitāb al-Dhakhāʾir wa-'l-Tuḥaf* of Ibn al-Zubayr (wrote ca. 440/1048), *samāja*, here clearly in the sense of masks, are once more associated with *al-ṣafāʿina* (slapstick comedians):

> Qaṭr al-Nadā (the wife of al-Muʿtaḍid) made *samajāt* for Nayrūz which cost thirteen thousand dinars, and thirty servant girls were produced from the palace to perform a dance with the *farāʿina* (sic = *ṣafāʿina*).[18]

In Egypt the *samājāt* are not mentioned as performing in the rulers' courts but rather in the streets and markets of Cairo during the Nayrūz and other feasts, together with other types of mimes, as well as elephants and giraffes, sugar statues, music, songs and dancing.[19] Most of the Fatimid caliphs encouraged such celebrations, but some of the Mamluk sultans, especially Barqūq (784–93/1382–89), prohibited them because of the immorality they entailed: people drank wine, frolicked in the water and wine, threw each others' turbans around and slapped each other with leather mats and slippers. All these deeds were considered violations of Islamic law.[20] The historian Ibn Zūlāq's description of a Nayrūz celebration in the year 364/974–5 is quoted by al-Maqrīzī in his *Khiṭaṭ*, and here too we meet *samāja* in the sense of masks:

> A mention of al-Nawrūz ... Ibn Zūlāq said: 'In this year al-Muʿizz li-Dīn Allāh prohibited lighting fires in the streets on the eve of the Nawrūz, and splashing water on the day of Nawrūz.' He said concerning the year 364/975: 'There was a lot of playing with water and lighting fires. The market people

Figure 3 Masked actors (*samājāt*) performing grotesque dance (below) The Album of Ahmed I, 1603-17. (After Metin And, *Osmali Şenliklerinde Türk Sanatlari* (Ankara, 1982). Courtesy of Professor Metin And.)

roved [the streets] and made (statues of) elephants (*fiyala*) and set out to Cairo with their plays. They played for three days and displayed comic masks (*samājāt*) and (wore their) jewels (*ḥuliy*)[21] in the markets ... The entertainers (*mu'annathūn* = effeminate men) and lewd women (*fāsiqāt*) would assemble near al-Lu'lu'a palace so as to be seen by the caliph, with musical instruments in their hands. Clamour arose, wine was drunk, and people splashed each other with water and wine.'[22]

In his *Sulūk* al-Maqrīzī adds that on the second of Shawwāl (592/1196) people took to throwing eggs and slapping each other on the neck with leather mats, in addition to their customary practice of splashing each other with dirty water or wine. Later on they added neck-slapping with slippers and turban-throwing in the markets and alleys. Processions of *samājāt* (actors with comic masks) played in the street, with comical figures, statues, and *khayāl* (itinerant actors) to amuse people.[23] Such processions were known in pre-Islamic Persia and other ancient nations who celebrated the vernal equinox.[24]

The performance of Amīr al-Nayrūz in carnival processions of the 'Feast of Fools' in Medieval Islam resembles what Arab historians called *rukūb al-kawsaj* (the procession of the thin-bearded), which in ancient Persia was a festival called *Kosa nishin* (the ride of the thin-bearded). In this festival a play of 'temporary king' or 'false Amir', which symbolises the expulsion of winter or the driving out of the old year, is acted.[25] Arab historians described the pre-Islamic *kawsaj* in Persia as:

> an old beardless one-eyed figure, representing the departing winter, mounted on an ass (or a cow) or a mule, with a crow in one hand, and a scourge and fan in the other. In this manner he paraded the streets, followed by all ranks of people, from the royal family to the beggar.. Amongst many frolics which the populace played with the old man, they sprinkled him alternatively with hot and cold water; whilst he, crying out *gurma, gurma* (i.e. *gurma*, 'heat') ... sometimes fanned himself, and sometimes lashed his tormentors. He had the privilege of going into every shop, and into every house; where the least delay in presenting him with a piece of money, gave him a right to seize the effects of every trader, and to bespatter the clothes even of the greatest nobles with a mixture of ink, red earth, and water, which he carried in a pot by his side. But all were prepared for *kousa* at their doors; and their offerings were made the moment of his approach ... From the first to the second hour of prayer, the amount of the receipts was the property of the old man; and here his pageant ended. He

> then suddenly disappeared: for after this time, the first person he met in the streets might severely beat him with impunity.[26]

However, the Nayrūz (Arabicised version of the Persian Nawrūz), with its lighting of fires, splashing of water, knocking on doors, and celebration with the *samāja* retained pre-Islamic rituals and symbols which the Muslims found hard to explain. Some Arab historians held that 'the burning of fire is for dissolving the rottenness in the air which the winter left in it, and the splashing of water the following day is to purify the bodies from the smoke of the fire which was lit on the former night', while other said that 'it is to celebrate the rain which fell after seven years of drought in the time of Firuz b. Yazdajird'.[27] In fact, the original meaning of these rituals was long forgotten, for the fires and candles of Nayrūz were part of an old ritual in which light was used to scare the evil spirits and to keep them at a distance, for light was a symbol of security and happiness, while water was a symbol of purity and prosperity.[28] The ugly masks, the noise and the music which were integral parts of these processions were also means to keep evil spirits at a distance, because evil spirits are not attracted to ugly things.[29]

It should be noted that *samāja* also means comic masks (synonymously with *wajh al-maskhara*) in Ibn Sīnā's (429/1037) commentary on Aristotle's *Poetica.*[30]

> والقوموذيا يراد بها المحاكاة التي هي شديدة الترذيل ، وليس بكل ما هو شرّ ، ولكن بالجنس من الشرّ الذي يستفحش ، ويكون المقصود به الاستهزاء والاستخفاف . وكان قوموذيا نوعًا من الاستهزاء . والهزل هو حكايةُ صَغار واستعداد سَماجة من غير غضب يقترن به ، ومن غير ألم بدني يحلّ بالمحكي ، وأنت ترى ذلك في هيئة وجه المسخرة عندما يُغَيّر سِحْنَتَه لِيُطَنّز به ، في اجتماع ثلاثة اوصاف فيها : القبح لأنّه يحتاج الى تغَيّر عن الهيئة الطبيعيّة الى السَماجة .

Ibn Sīnā's passage (possibly based on the translation of Yaḥyā b. 'Adī) (d. 252/866) is a rendition of the following passage in Aristotle:

> Comedy represents the worse types of men, worse, however, not in the sense that it embraces any and every kind of badness, but in the sense that the ridiculous is a species of ugliness or badness. For the ridiculous consists in some form of error or ugliness that is not painful or injurious, the *comic mask* for example, is distorted and ugly, but causes no pain.[31]

If *wajh al-maskhara* means comic mask, then Ibn Sīnā's last sentence *al-qubḥ li-annahu yaḥtāju ilā taghayyurin 'an al-hay' al-ṭabī'iyya ilā samāja* means, most probably, 'ugliness, because (the comedian) needs a comic mask (*samāja*) to change his natural appearance'. In Andalusia the mask was called *wajh mu'ār* and *wajh 'ayra,* and masked actor was *mutawajjih*.[32]

How did the *samāja* actors act? Clearly, they dressed up, using masks and other forms of disguises (such as the trousers of monkey skin used by Ash'ab, the monkey attire with which Jarīr credits al-Farazdaq or the 'demonic' appearances in Ibn al-Mu'tazz). In fact, the *safā'ina* with whom they are often associated also dressed up: thus al-Maqrīzī compares an official changing of turbans and attires every time he changes office to the behaviour of *al-ṣafā'ina min al-mukhāyilīn* (slap-takers from among the itinerant actors).[33]

Samāja actors might however also use make-up rather than masks, as emerges from an anecdote in the *Baṣā'ir wa-'l-Dhakhā'ir* of Abū Ḥayyān al-Tawḥīdī (d.c. 400/1010):

> 'Abū 'l-'Alā al-Minqarī joined the funeral of Aḥmad b. Yūsuf the secretary. He wept for a long time and got kohl (in his eyes). The kohl flowed upon his cheeks. A woman looked at him and exclaimed: 'May your eyes become sore. By God, you are like a dripping kitchen. What is this *samāja*.'[34]

Apparently, *samāja* actors and related entertainers would imitate both human beings and animals. Thus a passage in the *Kitāb al-Imtā' wa-'l-Mu'ānasa* by Abū Ḥayyān al-Tawḥīdī says, with reference to al-Ṣāḥib b. 'Abbād (d. 385/995), that:

> *Fatarāhu … yatahālak wa-yatamālak, wa-yataqābal wa-yatamāyal, wa-yuḥākī 'l-mūmisāt wa-yakhruju fī aṣḥāb al-samājāt …*
>
> You find him … staggering, then gaining control of himself. Sitting straight, then swinging, and impersonating prostitutes, and you find him acting in the manner of masked actors (*aṣḥāb al-samājāt*).[35]

At all events, *samāja* actors are also associated with animals in the stories of al-Farazdaq and Ash'ab.

The description of *samāja* by Arab scholars and poets fit the paintings and drawings collected and described by Ettinghausen, though he himself did not know of any literary references to persons fully or partly dressed up as animals. He describes one figure which is 'dressed in ordinary human fashion, but carries the head mask of an animal. It is hardly possible to identify the type of animal depicted … but rather a genus with a protruding muzzle or snout of a more general, terrifying nature'.[36] This description brings to mind Ibn al-Mu'tazz's verses on the *samājat al-Nayrūz*[37] as 'demons' (*jinn*) which have 'appeared to us during the day', or the guard of al-Mutawakkil who said: 'each of them is disguised with revolting mask'.[38] The 'exaggerated movements and gestures' of the masked actors which Ettinghausen spoke of remind us of Ibn al-Mu'tazz's description of the *samāja*: 'in their dancing their bodies sway as the cypresses sway in the wind'.[39]

In general, *samāja* actors were associated with *ḥikāyāt*, impersonations, and it is as such that they appear in al-Maqrīzī quoting the Egyptian historian al-Musabbiḥī (d. 1029), who described the carnival accompanying the pilgrimage of Muslims and Copts to the prison of Joseph in 1024f:[40]

> وأقام [أمير المؤمنين الظاهر لإعزا ز دين ا للّه ابو الحسن على بن الحاكم بأمر اللّه] هناك يومين وليلتين الى أن عاد الرمادية الخارجون الى السجن بالتماثيل والمضاحك والحكايات والسماجات فضحك منهم واستظرفهم وعاد الى قصره يوم الاربعاء لثلاث عشرة خلت منه . وأقام اهل الاسواق نحو الاسبوعين يطوفون الشوارع بالخيال والسماجات والتماثيل ويطلعون الى ا لقاهرة بذ لك ليشاهد هم اميرالمؤمنين ويعودون ومعهم سجل وقد كتب لهم ان لا يعارض احد منهم في ذهابه وعوده . وكان دخولهم من سجن يوسف يوم السبت لأربع عشرة بقيت من جمادى الاولى وشقوا الشوارع بالحكايات والسماجات والتماثيل ، فتعطل الناس في ذلك اليوم عن اشغا لهم ومعايشهم .
>
> (The Commander of the Faithful, ʿAlī b. al-Ḥākim bi-Amr Allāh) stayed there for two days and two nights until the performing actors (*al-ramādiyya al-khārijūn*) returned to the Prison (of Joseph) with (sugar and candy) statues, comic figures, *ḥikāyāt* and *samājāt.* He was amused by them and enjoyed them. He returned to his palace on Wednesday the 13th of the month (Jumādā I, 415/1024). For two weeks the people of the market continued to rove the streets with *khayāl, samājāt* (masked actors), and [sugar] statues (*tamāthīl*), and going up to Cairo with that so that the Commander of the Faithful would see them. They returned with a scroll to the effect that none of them was to be prevented from coming and going. They entered the Prison of Joseph on Saturday, fourteen days [from the end] of Jumādā I. They passed through the streets with *ḥikāyāt, samājāt* (masked actors), and *tamāthīl* (sugar statues). That day, the people stopped work and did not engage in earning their living.

The *samāja* are here associated with *khayāl* (impersonating), a word used synonymously with *ḥikāya* (miming or imitating). The actors performing these *ḥikāyāt* and *khayāl,* here called *ramādiyya,* are thus identical with the *ṣafāʿina min al-mukhāyilīn* (slapstick comedians from among the [itinerant] actors).[41]

As for the term *tamāthīl* al-Musabbiḥī says that they are statues of sugar decorating the *simāṭ* (dining table) ordered by the Fāṭimid Commander of the Faithful and by his officials for their dependents. Such a *simāṭ* contains between 152–7 statues or figures (*tamāthīl*), as well as decorations and seven palaces of sugar,[42] food, sweets, baked foods, and roasted meat in large dishes and bowls. The *simāṭ* is carried through the streets preceded by a pageant of drummers, horn blowers, masked actors (*samāja*) and *ḥikāyāt* or *khayāl* (probably here itinerant actors impersonating on hobby-horses, called *afrās al-khayāl* by al-Musabbiḥī).[43] However, there is no indication of the size of these statues and their shapes, although al-Maqrīzī does note that they were of a comic nature (*maḍāḥik*).

We may note in passing that in the Abbasid period, dolls rather than *tamāthīl* used to celebrate Nayrūz and other festivals. Al-Tanūkhī (328–84/939-94) in his *Nishwār al-Muḥāḍara* describes a doll with which the Nawrūz in the time of al-Muʿtaḍid was celebrated. This doll is called *Dūbārka*,[44] and it is described as follows:

> The *dūbārka*: It is a foreign term and the name of dolls as big as children; the inhabitants of Baghdad used to put them on the roof during the nights of al-Muʿtaḍid's Nawrūz. They used to play with them and decorate them with beautiful attire of luxurious clothes and jewelry, decorating them as it is done with brides. Before them drums were beaten and flutes were blown, and fires were lit.[45]

It seems that such statues or dolls were used in other celebrations in Damascus even during the eighteenth century on the occasion of the birthday of Sultan Salīm III. The ruler of Damascus then, ʿUthmān Pāshā. 'proclaimed ... that whoever has a doll (*luʿba*), even if it would be of clay or wood, or who has knowledge of any kind of magic (*sīmyāʾ*) which is called *malāʿib* (should come to him) and he would receive a great reward'.[46] Such dolls were also used in Iraq in the procession of Muslim brides, accompanied by music, till the beginning of the twentieth century.[47]

Muharrijūn

After the eleventh century Arab historians no longer use the term *samāja* except when copying from older chronicles or dealing with former centuries. The last Arab historians to use it appear to be Ibn Zūlāq (d. 387/997), al-Shābushtī (d. 388/998) and al-Musabbiḥī (d. 420/1029); when al-Ibshīhī (d. 850/1446) spoke of the *samājāt* of Qaṭr al-Nadā mentioned by Ibn al-Zubayr, he turned them into *shammāmāt*.[48] Yet masked actors clearly persisted.[49] They are depicted in paintings from the thirteenth century onwards.[50] We do not know by what name they were known between the eleventh and the nineteenth century, but by the nineteenth century some of them were known as *muharrijūn*, singular *muharrij*. It seems that this is one of few Arabic theatrical terms which passed to some European languages. According to Wetzstein, the term *muharrij* was brought by the Umayyads to Spain.[51] On the other hand, Dozy and Engelmann think that the Spanish term *moharrache* or *homarrache* are from the Arabic *muharrij* and are synonym to *mascara*, and that both terms, i.e. *mascara* and *moharrache* have both the meaning of buffoon and a masquerade.[52] This is confirmed by Alcala who gave

Figure 4 *Mukhāyilūn* (actors) and *samājāt* (masked actors) performing Persian *Kösa* type folk play according to Muḥammad-ī Haravī (d.c. 1590), courtesy of L. A. Mayer Memorial Institute for Islamic Art, Jerusalem. Similar to that in Leningrad State Library (R. Ettinghausen, 'The Dance with Zoomorphic Masks', plate no. III). (After Metin And, *Osmali Şenliklerinde Türk Sanatlari* (Ankara, 1982). Courtesy of Professor Metin And.)

the meaning of *moharrache* as *guêchi moîr* which might be the Arabic term *wajh muʿār* (false face = mask) and not *mughayyir al-wajh* (lit. changer of face) as M. Müller thinks.[53]

A figure wearing a conical cap with bells and the tail of an animal[54] is also depicted in a painting by Muḥammad-ī Haravī (d.c. 1590), described by Ettinghausen as follows:

> Here, within a landscape, three figures, completely dressed up as goats, gambol in animal fashion; only the human hands and feet, as well as the peculiar stance of the figures and the fact that two of them carry clappers or castanets, indicate that these are not real animals ... at the top three additional figures perform very exaggerated steps accompanied by equally exaggerated gestures. It seems also significant that one of the high conical caps worn by these dancers is decorated with bells, which are also applied to the cap of a third type of dancer ... The latter's headgear is also adorned with the tail of an animal which is made to flutter by means of bizarre gestures ... The music for these performers is provided by four men in the lower right foreground who play the tambourine, a panpipe, and two types of drum.[55]

Moreover, European travellers mentioned such masked actors in the Muslim world in general, as well as the Holy Land and the Levant, from the sixteenth century onward without mentioning their Arabic names. S. Gerlach who visited Istanbul between 1574–6 describes a play performed by Jewish actors (originally refugees from Spain), performing with masks.[56] The missionary F. Eugene Roger in his description of Ramaḍān celebrations during the first half of the seventeenth century in the Holy Land mentions both buffoons and masked actors: 'Les maisons ou l'on boit le *Quaoué* (= le café), sont toutes pleines de monde, ou se trouvent des bouffons, mascarades, pantalons et joueurs d'instruments.'[57] Although Wetzstein says that such masked actors are called in Syria *muharrijūn*, Dozy and Engelmann think that the French terms *mascarades* here must be the Arabic term *maskhara*. The French traveller of the seventeenth century, Thévenot mentions that in the Levant there were masked entertainers: 'Puis suivent quelques gens habillés en mascarades.' Dozy and Engelmann quote M. Mahn's opinion that the Italians were the first European nation to adopt this Arabic term from the Sicilian Arabic in the sense of Bouffon and baladin.[58]

Although the *muharrij* is not associated with actors dressed up as animals in *al-ʿĀshiq wa-'l-Maʿshūq*, such actors were common at least in nineteenth-century Damascus, and they too were known as *muharrijūn*, as Wetzstein informs us:

> there is in Damascus a class of people representing various

crafts who perform at night at large assemblies (wine and women are held secret because of the *'assa* (night guard)). At these parties they have music at first; then the *ḥakawātī* (storyteller) presents short witty declamations *shi'r muḍḥik* (funny poems); then come the *muharrijūn*, always in groups of 3 or 4; if there are only two of them they choose one from the assembly to perform with them. Usually they perform *faṣl al-nāqa* (the play of the she-camel), where a bedouin hires (*yakrī*) the *nāqa*; then *faṣl al-faḍis* (the play of the carcass) (one is enveloped in a cloth and sold to the gypsies as a carcass, *fāḍīs*), and *faṣl al-dubb* (the play of the bear); also a *faṣl al-ḥāris* (door sentinel). The *dubb* (bear) wears a turned fur-coat and another one fights with him; the *dubb* is beaten hard at this occasion.[59]

Such plays involving actors dressed as bears, monkeys and other animals were played in nineteenth-century Egypt too. Sa'īd al-Bustānī's novel criticising Egyptian society, *Riwāyat Dhāt al-Khidr* (1874), mentions an actor called 'Alī Kākā who used to appear in the shape of various animals on the Prophet's birthday. Such a performance is described by the author as *tamthīl* and *hazl* (acting and jest):

> (Dhāt al-Khidr) saw a large crowd of people behind the circle of tents (of the *Mawlid*'s square, where the Prophet's Birthday was celebrated). They were staring at a man, stretching their necks in order to see him. He was playing in their midst, in such a way that good taste would reject it and a chaste soul would shun it. The man is called 'Alī Kākā. He acts in his play with different forms and shapes. Once in the form of a bear and once in the form of a monkey.[60]

Fortunately, Prüfer adds some details on the performance of 'Alī Kākā:

> A similar figure in the streets of Cairo is the well-known ... fun-maker 'Alī Kākā, who appears occasionally at *Mūlids* (birth festivals), and at the fair held every week on the open square below the Citadel. He is the prototype of the coarse, half-idiotic, clownish peasant who, to the music of two flutes and a *darabukka* (earthenware drum), performs ape-like, obscene dances and makes absurd jokes. He goes barefoot, and wears a bent tail of stiffened cotton, in one hand he holds a long peasant's stick (*nabbūt*) and in the other a so-called *farqilla*, a kind of long, thick, noisy, but harmless whip of twisted cotton, with which he constantly lashes his musicians, and even his audience.[61]

Prüfer's description of 'Alī Kākā's performance with his tail, his ape or bear-like dances, and his band of musicians reminds us of

Figure 5 A pageant with three coaches shaped as shops of blacksmith, weaver and confectioner. On the left two men carrying figures of animals (*tamāthīl*). The pageant is led by drummers and trumpeters round the Hippodrome of Istanbul. (After Metin And, *Osmali Şenliklerinde Türk Sanatlari* (Ankara, 1982), plate no. 131. Courtesy of Professor Metin And.)

Ettinghausen's Figure 1 depicting entertainers dancing to the accompaniment of flutes and earthenware drum.[62]

According to Wetzstein, the *muharrijūn* would dress as bears and perform a *faṣl*, a short one-act comical play involving both dialogue and action.[63] Al-Bustānī and Prüfer described their performance as 'ape-like, obscene dances and absurd jokes'. Acts which involved dialogue are also evident from Ettinghausen's article. In Figure 5 (about the third decade of the seventeenth century), a drawing from the period of Shāh 'Abbās (1557–1628) shows actors dressed up as billy goats, two of them carrying clappers. 'Only one of these figures, the one on the left, is actually seen dancing, while the other two, one of them standing, the other sitting, seem to be involved in declamatory speech-making .... (There are) two more non-masked performers who are wearing the broad *kulah* ending in an animal tail.'[64] These actors are accompanied by a band of five musicians. No dialogue is attested for the *samāja*, except for the poetry declaimed by Ash'ab and al-Farazdaq. Such actors with goat masks are considered by Metin And as performing ritual '*kösa* type folk plays,'[65] which involves dialogue. However, the *muharrijūn* witnessed by Wetzstein were clearly actors of a different type.

These findings show that in Arabic the terms *maskhara* and *muharrij* are synonymous, and that they mean both 'buffoon' and 'a man with mask' and it seems that both terms were adopted in European languages in both senses also.

Notes

1. Lane, *Lexicon* s.v; cf. also Dozy, *Supplément*, vol. II, p. 680: ('figures grotesques'); Ch. F. Seybold (ed.), *Glossarium Latino-Arabicum* (Berlin, 1900), p. 345: 'obscenitas' (*samāja*).
2. Bevan, *Nakā'iḍ*, vol. I, p. 246.
3. R. Ettinghausen 'The Dance with Zoomorphic Masks', in G. Makdisī (ed.), *Arabic Studies in Honor of Hamilton A. R. Gibb* (Leiden, 1965), p. 219.
4. al-Iṣfahānī, *Aghānī*, vol. VII, p. 46.
5. Ettinghausen, 'Dance', p. 219.
6. Ettinghausen, 'Dance', pp. 218f.
7. M. And *Culture*, pp. 24, 33, 36, 40, 42, 86, 88. cf. Eliade, *Shamanism.*
8. M. And *Culture*, p. 53, and Ibn Sa'ad, *al-Ṭabaqāt al-Kubrā*, ed. Z. M. Manṣūr (al-Medina, 1408/1987–8), Suppl. Vol. pp. 194–5.
9. al-Ṭabarī, *Annales*, ser. III, p. 1318. De Goeje in his Glossarium (p. ccxcvii) at the end of al-Ṭabarī's history translated the term *ṣuwar al-samāja* as *imagines obscenae* (obscene images), which is a literal translation but which does not fit with other attestations of the term. Cf. M. M. Ahsan, *Social Life under the Abbasids 786–902* (London and New York, 1979), p. 270 (where *ṣuwar al-samāja* is translated as 'figures', 'masks').
10. E. Esin, 'The Cultural Background of Afshīn Ḥaider of Ushrūsana

in the Light of Recent Numismatic and Iconographic Data', in A. Dietrich (ed.), *Akten des VII. Kongresses für Arabistik und Islamwissenchaft* (Göttingen, 1976), p. 126. (I owe this reference to Dr. P. Crone.)

11. Ibid., p. 142.
12. Ibid., plate VIII.
13. Cf. Boyce, *Zoroastrianism*, vol. I, p. 224; cf. pp. 150f, 171, 197, 245, 321; cf. also al-Musabbiḥī, *Akhbār Miṣr*, p. 46, where he speaks of the slaughtering of cattle during Nayrūz.
14. Abū 'l-Faraj al-Iṣfahānī, *Maqātil al-Ṭalibiyyīn* (Cairo, 1949), pp. 385f.
15. al-Shābushtī, *Diyārāt*, pp. 39f.
16. 'Abdallāh b. al-Mu'tazz, *Dîwān* (Istanbul, 1945), part IV, pp. 617f; Muḥammad b. Yaḥyā al-Ṣulī, *Ash'ār Awlād al-Khulafā'*, ed. J. Heyworth-Dunne (Cairo, 1936), p. 249 (who has *ḥissihim* for *ḥusnihim*). See Figures 3 and 4.
17. On *dastaband*, see Ibn Manẓūr, *Lisān al-'Arab*, vol. III, p. 173, s.v. '*fanzaja*'; al-Nuwayrī, *Nihāya*, vol. IV, p. 144; D. S. Rice, 'Deacon or Drink', *Arabica* V (1958), p. 27. On the *dastaband mākhūri* dance, see Khayr al-Dīn al-Ziriklī, *Rasā'il Ikhwān al-Ṣafā* (Cairo, 1928), pp. 170, 175.
18. Rashīd b. al-Zubayr, *Kitāb al-Dhakhā'ir wa-'l-Tuḥaf* (Kuwait, 1959), p. 39; cf. p. 220; cf. also al-Ibshīhī *Mustaṭraf*, vol. II, p. 54; al-Tīfāshī, *Nuzha*, fols 1a–3a; Ibn al-Nadīm, *The Fihrist of al-Nadīm, a Tenth century Survey of Muslim Culture*, New York and London, 1970, vol. II, p. 735; Rosenthal, *Humor*, pp. 6f, n.5; al-Tanūkhī, *Nishwār*, vol. I, p. 102. There is a unique description of *ṣafā'ina* in *Alf Layla wa-layla*, ed. Muḥammad Qiṭṭa 'Adawī, (Būlāq, 1279-80/1862-3), vol. I, pp. 254–8 (Night 31). Cf. also ibid., vol. II, p. 218; and the reference given below, n. 62. Cf. Ibn 'Abd Rabbih, *al-'Iqd al-Farīd*, vol. VIII, pp. 104ff.
19. On processions with elephants, see al-Maqrīzī, *Khiṭaṭ*, ed. Wiet, vol. IV, p. 245; id., *Khiṭaṭ*, ed. Būlāq, vol. I, pp. 289, 493; on processions with giraffes, see al-Maqrīzī, *Khiṭaṭ*, ed. Būlāq, vol. II, p. 289; al-Maqrīzī, *al-Sulūk* (Cairo 1936), vol. I, part ii, p. 626; al-Musabbiḥī, *Akhbār Miṣr*, p. 65; Ibn al-Ḥājj, *Madkhal*, vol. II, p. 332. Masked actors performed in Nawrūz celebrations in Mazandarān (northern Iran) as late as 1944 (see M. Sutūdah, 'Namāyish-i 'Arūsī dar Jangal', *Yadigar* I, 1324/1945, pp. 43. I owe this reference to Dr. M. Unamid of UCLA who also supplied me with a copy and an English translation).
20. Cf. Ibn Zūlāq, *Tārikh Miṣr wa-Faḍā'iluhā* MSS Bibliothèque Nationale, arabe 1820, fols 58b, 74b–75a; 1817, fols 48a, 58a–b; Ibn Iyās, *Badā'i'*, vol. I, part i, p. 363 (*wa-min al-ḥawādith anna 'l-sulṭān [al-Ẓāhir Barqūq] rasama bi-ibṭāl mā kāna yu'malu fī yawm al-Nayrūz, wa-huwa yawm al-sana al-qibṭiyya, fa-kāna yu'malu fī dhālika 'l-yawm bi-'l-diyār al-miṣriyya min qadīm al-zamān fī ayyām al-aqbāt*).
21. According to K. Inostrantsev, 'K upominaniyu *khayāl* 'a v arabskoy literature' ('On the occurrence of *khayāl* in Arabic Literature'),

Zapiski Vostochogo Otdel. Imp. Russk. Archeol. Obscestva XVIII (St. Petersburg, 1907), p. 165, the word *ḥuliy* should be read as *khayāl*. But there is no textual basis for this emendation (all manuscripts and published editions have *ḥuliy*), nor is it necessary. Ibn al-Ḥājj, *Madkhal*, vol. II, p. 332, says that even boys used to dress up in expensive garments decorated with jewelry and gold during such celebrations: *wa-yuḥallūnahu bi - 'l-qalā'id min al-dhahab wa-ghayrih ma'a qalā'id al-'anbar ka'annahu 'arūs tujlā*. Even horses were decorated with golden masks (*wajh min al-dhahab*). See also the description of a wedding procession in J. B. Wetzstein (ed.), *Die Liebenden von Amasia, ein Damascener Schattenspiel* (Leipzig, 1906), p. 78: *wa-muzawwaqīn bi-awā'ī ẓirāf wa-mushakkalīn bi-'l-almās wa-ḥuliy al-ḥarīm*, 'They were embellished with fine garments and decorated with diamonds and the jewelries of women'. (I would like to thank Ms. Hedda Wetzstein, West Berlin, for presenting me with a copy of this shadow-play, copied and edited by her grandfather.) Hence it cannot be said that Ibn Zūlāq (d. 388/988) provides us with the oldest attestation of *khayāl* in Arabic literature, as Inostrantsev claims. (My thanks are due to Ms. Pirkko Soikkeli, Helsinki, and Prof. M. Zand, Jerusalem, for translating this article from Russian for me.)

22. al-Maqrīzī, *Khiṭaṭ*, ed. Wiet, vol. IV, pp. 245f.
23. al-Maqrīzī, *al-Sulūk*, vol. I, part i, pp. 136f.
24. Ibn Iyās, *Badā'i'*, vol. I, part ii, p. 363 (year 787 A.H.); cf. Ibn al-Ḥājj, *Madkhal*, vol. II, pp. 51–3.
25. And, *Culture*, pp. 19f, 85ff.
26. Richardson, *Dictionary*, vol. I, pp. LIXff; cf. al-Qazwīnī, *Kosmographie*, vol. II, p. 82; Maḥmūd Shukrī al-Ālūsī, *Bulūgh al-Arab fī Ma'rifat Aḥwāl al-'Arab* (Baghdad, 1314/1896f), vol. I, p. 393; Anastās al-Kirmilī, 'Al-Marfa', Aṣluh wa-Shuyū'uh 'inda 'l-Umam', *al-Mashriq* IX (1 March, 1906), no. 5, pp. 198f.
27. al-Ālūsī, *Bulūgh al-Arab*, vol. I, p. 386.
28. Lassy, *Muḥarram Mysteries*, pp. 156f, 197f, 200, 2223; And, *Culture*, pp. 19f, 35, 85.
29. Lassy, *Muḥarran Mysteries*, p. 201; M. And, *Culture*, p. 23.
30. 'Abd al-Rāḥmān Badawī, *Fann al-Shi'r ma'a 'l-Tarjama al-'Arabiyya al-Qadīma wa-Shurūḥ al-Fārābī wa-Ibn Sīnā wa-Ibn Rushd* (Beirut, 1973), p. 174. On performing with masks (*wujūh*), see Chapter 3, no. 13, n.68 and no. 14, n.71
31. Badawī, *Fann*, p. 95 (cf. also Ibn Rushd's term *wajh al-mustahzī'*, ibid., p. 208); cf. T. S. Dorsch (tr.), *Classical Literary Criticism. Aristotle on the Art of Poetry* (London, 1965), p. 37. On the possibility that Ibn Sīnā used Yaḥyā b. 'Adī's translation, see Badawī's introduction to Aristotle, *Fann*, pp. 50-4.
32. Dozy, *Supplément*, vol. II, p. 785, quoting Pedro de Alcala; and R. Dozy and W. H. Engelmann, *Glossaire des Mots Espagnols et Portugais Dérivés de l'Arab*, (Amsterdam, 1915), pp. 308f. Cf. also Ch. 2, n.94 and this chapter, n.53.
33. al-Maqrīzī, *Sulūk*, ed. 'Āshūr, vol. IV, part i, pp. 670f.

34. Abū Ḥayyān al-Tawḥīdī, *al-Baṣā'ir wa-'l-Dhakhā'ir* ed. I. Kaylānī (Damascus, 1964), vol. II, p. 647.
35. Abū Ḥayyān al-Tawḥīdī, *Kitāb al-Imtā' wa- 'l-Mu'ānasa* (Cairo, 1939; repr. Beirut, 1953), vol. I, p. 59.
36. Ettinghausen, 'Dance', p. 211; cf. Figures 3 and 4 of this book.
37. Ettinghausen, 'Dance', p. 217.
38. Ibid., pp. 218f.
39. Cf. above, n.16.
40. al-Maqrīzī, *Khiṭaṭ*, ed. Wiet, vol. IV, p. 245; this passage is scattered in several passages in al-Musabbiḥī, *Akhbār Miṣr*, pp. 39, 41–3.
41. The term *al-ramādiyya al-khārijūn* (which is missing from al-Musabbiḥî's version), is translated here as 'performing actors' because the term *kharaja fī 'l-ḥikāya* or *'l-khayāl* means 'he performed a play', and the expression should be understood as '*al-ramādiyya al-Khārijūn ... bi-'l-ḥikāyāt wa-'l-samājāt*'. It seems that the actors are called here *ramādiyya* because performers used to paint their faces with ashes (*ramād*) or soot, see And, *Culture*, pp. 23, 33, 80; and my 'The Meaning of the Term *Kharja* of the Arabic Andalusian *Muwashshaḥ*', in Y. Ben-Abou (ed.), *Litterae Judaeorum in Terra Hispanica* (Jerusalem, 1991).
42. Cf. below, Ch. 5, section on *ḥikāya*. See also Figure 1.
43. al-Musabbiḥī, *Akhbār Miṣr*, pp. 78f. On *simāt*, see also Ibn Taghrī Birdī, *al-Nujūm al-Zahira*, (Cairo, n.d.) vol. IV, pp. 87f; al-Maqrīzī, *Khiṭaṭ*, ed. Wiet, vol. I, p. 387. See also Ch. 2, n. 88.
44. It resembles the *qudhurjug (kudurğuk)* mentioned by Th. Menzel, *Meddāḥ Schattentheater und Orta Ojunu* (Prague, 1941), p. 9; cf. C. Brockelmann, *Mitteltürkischer Wortschatz* (Leipzig, 1938), p. 63.
45. al-Tanūkhī, *Nishwār*, vol. II, pp. 222f.
46, al-Budayrī, *Ḥawādith Dimashq al-Yawmiyya*, ed. M. S. al-Qāsimī (Cairo, 1959), pp. 233f.
47. See 'Abd al-Ḥamīd al-'Alawjī, *Min Turāthinā 'l-Sha'bī* (Baghdad, 1966), pp. 98f.
48. See n. 18 above.
49. Cf. And, *Theatre*, pp. 24ff, for their persistence in Turkey.
50. Ettinghausen, 'Dance', p. 219.
51. J. G. Wetzstein, 'Sprachliches aus den Zeltlagern der syrischen Wüste', *ZDMG* XXII (1868), p. 132, n. 1.
52. Dozy and Engelmann, *Glossaire*, p. 509.
53. Dozy and Engelmann, *Glossaire*, p. 507.
54. Cf. Wetzstein, *Liebenden*, p. 70. On the *muharrij*, see Dozy and Engelmann, *Glossaire*, p. 308.
55. Ettinghausen, 'Dance', p. 212. Plates nos. III and IV of Iranian 'entertainers' with goats' masks given by Ettinghausen in this article, are considered by And (*Culture*, pp. 87f.) as similar to '*kösa* type folk plays in Anatolia ... they combine the rite for the Year End ceremony with the pastoral ceremonies for the fecundity of cattle'. Cf. Figure 4 in this book.
56. S. Gerlach, *Tage-buch* (Frankfurt a. M., 1674), p. 157. My thanks to

Prof. M. And for sending me a copy of this passage. For the activities of the Spanish Jewish actors from Spain and Italy in the Ottoman Empire see And, *Culture*, pp. 50f.

57. F. E. Roger, *La Terre Sainte* (Paris, 1646), p. 229, also quoted by Dozy and Engelmann, *Glossaire*, p. 506.
58. Thévenot, *Voyage au Levant* (Paris, 1665), vol. I, p. 279, cf. Dozy and Englemann, *Glossaire*, p. 506.
59. Wetzstein, *Liebenden*, pp. 132f. On *muharrijūn* in Egypt, see Qara 'Alī, *Ḍāḥikūn*, p. 171.
60. Sa'īd al-Bustānī, *Riwāyat Dhāt al-Khidr*, 2nd ed. (Alexandria, 1904), pp. 147f.
61. C. Prüfer, 'Drama (Arabic)', in *Encyclopaedia of Religion and Ethics* (New York, 1914), vol. IV, pp. 872ff.
62. Ettinghausen, 'Dance', pp. 212f.
63. Wetzstein, *Liebenden*, pp. 132f. n.68.
64. Ettinghausen, 'Dance', p. 216.
65. And, *Culture*, pp. 87f.

4

Jesters, Buffoons and Participants in Pageantry

Jesters *(Mudḥikūn)*

Jesters are said to have been familiar to the Muslim world since the time of Muḥammad.[1] Over the centuries, court jesters developed from their ranks, that is to say jesters who would not merely entertain the ruler, but also ridicule his rivals and even criticise the ruler himself,[2] being granted special dispensation because of their wit and, in some cases, unusual physical features (such as disablement).[3] It is difficult to distinguish the jester from the impersonator and teller of anecdotes (*ḥākiya*) since the jester would also imitate and impersonate; but an attempt will nonetheless be made.

As mentioned already, *Ḥadīth* takes a dim view of jesters,[4] but even so there are traditions in which the Prophet is amused by a jester by the name of Nuʿaymān, whose mock sale of the freedman Suwayd into slavery made him 'laugh ... for a year'.[5] 'Ā'isha, too, is said to have been entertained by (female) jesters at times; one of them, who 'used to visit the families of Quraysh and make their women laugh' was received as a guest by another female jester in Medina, an incident on which the Prophet is said to have commented that 'each kind finds its own'.[6]

During the Umayyad period the Ḥijāz, especially Medina, became a centre for singing and entertainment,[7] and Ḥijāzī jesters would appear to have been highly thought of: according to Ibn al-Jawzī, the three things the caliph al-Walīd II (d. 127/744) wanted to know on encountering a simple bedouin from Medina were whether he knew the Qur'an by heart, collected *Ḥadīth* or bedouin poems and stories, or had acquired a store of anecdotes from the Ḥijāzis and their jesters (*aḥādīth ahl al-Ḥijāz wa-maḍāḥīkihā*).[8]

There are numerous stories in Arabic literature about caliphs and witty men confronted with bedouin, villagers and other simpletons, listening to their naive stories of visits to urban centres and making fun of them.[9]. Apparently jesters had a repertoire of such anecdotes from all over the world. Professional jesters could however become the target of jokes themselves. A *muḍḥik* living in Medina in the Umayyad period, for example, was the victim of a successful plot to ridicule him when his host of the latter's singing girl added a laxative to his wine.[10]

The caliph Yazīd II (d. 724) was the first Umayyad caliph to allow his boon companions (*nudamā'*; singular *nadīm*) to sit with him and to laugh and jest in his presence. In the *Kitāb al-Tāj* by pseudo-Jāḥiẓ it is reported that Yazīd was the first caliph to be abused to his face in scurrilous jest (*wa-huwa awwal man shutima fī wajhihi min al-khulafā' 'alā jihat al-hazl wa-'l-sukhf*).[11] In the Abbasid period, al-Mahdi (d. 169/785) was the first caliph to mix with his companions and comedians, whilst al-Mutawakkil (d. 218/861) encouraged his boon companions to jest, mime and behave scurrilously.[12]

Of course, in some cases the *muḍḥik* was just a jester, not an actor in our sense of the word. The jester Alī b. al-Junayd al-Iskāfī, was chosen by the caliph al-Mu'taṣim (d. 227/842) as his boon-companion (*nadīm*), because he was 'amazing in his appearance and talk' (*kāna 'ajība'l-ṣūra wa-'l-ḥadīth*).[13] When he was asked to be boon-companion to caliph al-Mu'taṣim and to prepare himself accordingly, he rejected the required conditions. He said he could not use a false head or even buy a new beard. When the caliph asked why he had refused to be his companion, Ibn al-Junayd, who seems to have been a *ḍarrāṭ* (fart maker) by profession, answered: 'Your frivolous messenger came to me with the conditions [laid down] for Ḥassān the Cup-bearer (*al-sāqī*) and Khālawayh the impersonator (*al-ḥākī*) and said to me "Don't spit and don't sneeze." ... If you agree that I keep company with you, I do so on condition that if I have to break wind noiselessly or fart with noise, I will do that openly [in your presence]; otherwise, we shall have nothing to do with each other.' Hearing these conditions al-Mu'taṣim laughed 'until he scratched up the ground with his legs and could not bear laughing any more' and agreed to them. When they were on a mule, Ibn al-Junayd, the jester, told al-Mu'taṣim that he would like to call Ibn Ḥammād (the chamberlain). Al-Mu'taṣim ordered to bring him forth. Ibn al-Junayd told Ibn Ḥammād: 'Come, I would like to tell you a secret.' When he came near him he released a noiseless wind, stretched his sleeve and said 'I feel something creeping into my sleeve, can you please see what it is.' Ibn Ḥammād put his head in the sleeve and smelt (the bad smell) of a lavatory, and said: 'I don't find any thing, but I did not know that there is a lavatory in your clothes.' Al-Mu'taṣim covered his mouth by his sleeves and laughed without control. Then Ibn al-Junayd began to release wind one after the other and told Ibn Ḥammād: 'You advised me [when you offered me the job of a companion to al-Mu'taṣim] not to cough, not to spit and not to blow my nose [in his presence]; I haven't done that, but

I defecate on you.' He continued to break wind while al-Muʿtaṣim kept putting out his head out of the mule-borne sedan (in which he was with al-Junayd). Then Ibn al-Junayd said to al-Muʿtaṣim: 'I finished this game and I would like another one.' Al-Muʿtaṣim shouted when he could not bear laughing anymore: 'Woe unto you! O, servant, let me down to the ground. I will die immediately.'[14]

Jesters, boon companions, slapstick comedians, singers, musicians and other entertainers at court all received wages (*arzāq*) as well as money thrown to them when they performed (*nuqūṭ*). It is said that when the caliph al-Mutawakkil was assassinated in 247/861, his expenses were audited and found to include payments to 'slapstick clowns (*ṣafāʿina*), jesters (*muḍḥikūn*), ram and cock holders (*kabbāshūn wa-dayyākūn*), trainers of fighting dogs (*aṣḥāb kilāb al-hirāsh*) and fart-makers (*ḍarrāṭūn*) coming to five hundred thousand dirhams'.[15]

In the same period scholars became interested in entertainers and composed books about them. Thus Ibn al-Nadīm discusses comedians such as al-Kutanjī, Abū'l- ʿAnbas, Abū'l-ʿIbar, Juḥā, and Ashʿab in his *Fihrist*,[16] the third chapter of which has a section on 'boon companions (*nudamāʾ*), associates (*julasāʾ*), men of letters (*udabāʾ*), singers (*mughannūn*), buffoons (*ṣafādima*), slapstick clowns (*ṣafāʿina*) and jesters (*muḍḥikūn*).'[17] Ibn al-Nadīm mentions that al-Kutanjī wrote several books,[18] including a *Compendium of Foolish Things and the Origin of Follies* (*Kitāb Jāmiʿ al-Ḥamāqāt wa-Aṣl al-Raqāʿāt*), *Witticisms and Fools* (*Kitāb al-Mulaḥ wa-'l-Muḥammaqīn*), *Slapstick Comedians* (*al-Ṣafāʿina*) and *al-Makhraqa* (on charlatanry, juggling, or a wreath used in dancing).[19] He adds that 'he succeeded Abū 'l-ʿIbar as jester after the latter's death'. But for details of how they actually jested we must turn to the eleventh-century author al-Ḥuṣrī al-Qayrawānī. According to him, they would say the opposite of what they meant and act out deeds that were the reverse of their intentions, a method known from the later Arabic shadow play as well.[20] For example, when Abū 'l-ʿIbar al-Hāshimī (d. 250/864) was young and studied the art of comedy (*hazl*) under a master jester along with other boys, they would say 'good evening' in the morning and 'good morning' in the evening; and if told to walk forward, they would walk backwards.[21] Abū 'l-ʿIbar used the same technique of contrariness in correspondence with his friends, and sometimes in his dramatic performances. He also used it in the way he dressed for comic purposes. Once he appeared before al-Mutawakkil with a slipper (*khuff*) on his head, two tall hats (*qalansuwas*) on his feet, trousers (*sirwāl*) worn as a shirt and a shirt worn as trousers; and when the caliph addressed him, he replied in opposites, making the caliph laugh.[22] We may take it from the description of his training in *hazl* that he was taught to improvise jokes as well.

Among the few anecdotes we have about him there is only one long one, which is about his miserly behaviour towards the female singer Baṣbaṣ, with whom he was in love. Although it contains long dialogues between Abū 'l-'Ibar and his beloved Basbas, and between other characters too, there is no indication that it was performed as a play.[23]

As for al-Kutanjī, Abū 'l-'Ibar's successor as jester and boon companion to al-Mutawakkil, he was considered to be the caliph's fool of the class *ahl al-ḥamāqāt* or *al-muḥammaqūn* (fools or people pretending to be fools).[24] Al-Ābī describes the way in which such jesters performed their task, the wages they received, their character and the fondness of some caliphs for them, mentioning that when al-Kutanjī died al-Mutawakkil mourned him and wondered who would enliven him and comfort him in his grief. He was told that al-Kutanjī had two witty sons, had them brought before him, admired them and bestowed their father's wages on the elder son, nominating a lower wage for the younger. The younger one, however, argued that 'this is against custom'. The caliph asked, 'what custom?', to which the younger son replied: 'we excel, as did our father before us, in foolishness (*ḥamāqa*). It is customary for wise people, when one of their numbers dies, to appoint the oldest son in his place; but among fools the youngest should be appointed to his father's place; I am indeed more foolish than my brother'. The caliph asked what proof he had. He replied: 'a lot. The most recent is that last year my father went on pilgrimage to Mecca; when the time of his return drew near, my brother travelled … to Kūfa [south of Baghdad] whereas I travelled to Hulwān [north-east of Baghdad] because I missed him more … and my father was very pleased with my deed'. The caliph agreed that he was indeed a greater fool than his brother and ordered him to be made head of fools in his brother's place.[25]

A jester of the same group, Abū 'l-'Anbas Muḥammad b. Isḥāq al-Ṣaymarī, was a real actor too, for he described himself as a *ṣaf'ān*, slapstick comedian: 'My brother and I were twins. We both issued from Ṣaymara on the same day at the same time. We both entered Surra-man ra'ā at one and the same time. He has become a judge and I have become a *ṣaf'ān*. How then can astrology be held to be true?'[26]

An anecdote related by al-Ḥuṣrī al-Qayrawānī throws some light on the word-play in which a *ṣaf'ān* might engage:[27]

> Abdallāh b. al-Marzubān said to Ibn Manāra, 'I would like to jest *(ab'ath)* with Abū 'l-'Aynā' [Muḥammad b. al-Qāsim al-Hāshimī, d. 283/896]. But he said, "you can't compete with him". Ibn al-Marzubān insisted, however. When Abū 'l-'Aynā' sat down, Ibn al-Marzubān said, "Abū 'Abdallāh, why have you

put on a *jubba'a*?" He asked, "what is a *jubba'a*?" Ibn al-Marzubān replied, "something between a *jubba* [an outer garment] and a *durrā'a* [an outer garment of another kind]". Abū-'Aynā' swiftly retorted, "because you are a *ṣafdīm*. Ibn al-Marzubān asked, "what is a *safdīm*?" He replied, "someone between a *saf'ān* [slapstick comedian] and a *nadīm* [boon companion]"

Bar Hebraeus (d. 1286) translated most of al-Ābī's anecdotes on Abū 'l-'Ibar al-Hāshimī, Abū 'l-'Anbas al-Ṣaymarī and Muzabbid al-Madanī in his *Laughable Stories.*[28] He omitted the jesters' names, however, attributing the jokes to anonymous 'comedians' (*qōmiqē*) and 'actors' (*mīmasē*), thereby conveying the impression that he was transmitting pre-Islamic, or at any rate non-Islamic, tradition. But in fact the 'comedians' and 'actors' were ninth-century Muslin jesters.[29]

The repertoire of these jesters did not consist only of clever responses;[30] they also recited absurd compositions of the sort known in modern European literature as Dadaism. According to al-Ṣūlī, Abū 'l-'Ibar used to get up early in the morning to sit on the Bridge of Baghdad with an inkpot and scroll in hand; he would record everything he heard from passers-by, such as sailors and donkey-drivers, until he had filled both sides of the scroll. Then he would tear the scroll into two halves and stick one on the back of the other, thereby creating a composition of which it would be said that 'nothing in the world was more foolish than it.'[31]

But jesters could also be comedians (*ahl al-hazl*) who imitated other people's accents, attire and behaviour, and who would improvize in single actor plays during which they would tell jokes and exchange sharp retorts with their audiences. There were three well-known comedians of this type, two of them connected with famous rulers and the third an itinerant performer. All three were famous for their ability to mime and jest (*muḥākāt wa-muṭāyaba*). The first, Ḥusayn b. Sha'ra, was a singer known as 'the Jester of al-Mutawakkil' (*muḍhik al-Mutawakkil*).[32] His favourite subject was Ahmad b. Ṭūlūn. This pleased Ibn al-Mudabbir, his patron who was a rival of Ibn Ṭūlūn's. When Ibn Ṭūlūn heard that Ibn Sha'ra was ridiculing his gravity and manner of speech (*akhraja ḥikāyatahu fī tazammutihi wa-kalāmihi*), he called him and warned him not to do it again. But Ibn Sha'ra went straight to Ibn al-Mudabbir, informed him of Ibn Ṭūlūn's censure, entered the wardrobe, selected the type of turban and attire that Ibn Ṭūlūn wore, came back and began to imitate Ibn Ṭūlūn to Ibn al-Mudabbir. He imitated his way of sitting and speaking, repeating the very words with which he had been rebuked to the delight of his patron. Later, however, Ibn Ṭūlūn found an excuse to punish him. Allegedly, a flowerpot from the roof of Ibn Sha'ra's house (or one of them – he is described as a rich man with much property) fell on Ibn Ṭūlūn's horse, whereupon Ibn Ṭūlūn had him flogged and the house demolished.[33]

The second comedian who used to impersonate other people was the frivolous poet Abū 'l-Ward, the jester of the Buyid vizier al-Muhallibī. According to al-Tha'ālibī he 'was one of the wonders of the world in respect of jesting and impersonation (*kāna min 'ajā' ib al-dunyā fī 'l-muṭāyaba wa l-muḥākāt*)'. He used to impersonate the characters in so perfect a way that his audience would admire him to the point that 'the one bereaved of child would laugh'. His favourite personality for imitation was the writer Abū Isḥāq al-Ṣābī (313–84/925–94).[34]

The third comedian was Ibn al-Maghāzilī who presented his wide repertoire in marketplaces and courtyards during the reign of al-Mu'taḍid (d. 289/902), a period in which theatrical performances of *samāja* (masked actors), *ṣafā'ina* (slapstick comedians), *ḥākiya* (impersonators), and *muḍḥikūn* (jesters) flourished. Al-Mas'ūdī describes Ibn al-Maghāzilī as 'an itinerant storyteller' (*rajul yatakallam 'alā 'l-ṭarīq*) who told stories, anecdotes and produced comic imitations (*al-akhbār wa-'l-nawādir wa-'l-maḍāḥīk*) to his audience who would form a circle around him (*ḥalqa*). One day in the reign of al-Mu'taḍid he was standing by the Private Gate (*Bāb al-Khāṣṣa*), jesting and telling anecdotes (*yuḍḥik wa-yunādir*). One of al-Mu'taḍid's eunuchs attended and was in the circle of his audience. When he saw the eunuch, he started imitating eunuchs (*akhadhtu fī ḥikāyat al-khadam*). The eunuch told the caliph about Ibn al-Maghāzilī's skill in telling anecdotes and impersonating (*yuḍḥik wa-yuḥākī*), and so he was commanded to perform in the caliph's presence. He then imitated a bedouin, grammarians, entertainers (*mukhannathūn*), judges, Zuṭṭīs, a Nabatean, a Sindī, a Zanjī, a eunuch, a Turk and so forth, mixing his impersonations with anecdotes and jokes. Al-Mas'ūdī's version of Ibn al-Maghāzilī's repertoire goes as follows:

> Once in Baghdad there was a storyteller (*rajul yatakallam 'alā 'l-tarīq*), a man who used to stand in the street and tell people sundry stories, anecdotes and funny jokes. He was known by the name of Ibn al-Maghāzilī. He was extremely accomplished and anyone who saw him and heard him talk could not help laughing. Ibn al-Maghāzilī [once] said: 'One day, during the reign of the caliph al-Mu'taḍid, I was standing by the Private Gate (*Bāb al-Khāṣṣa*), jesting and telling anecdotes. One of al-Mu'taḍid's eunuchs was amongst my audience circle. I started imitating the eunuchs (*akhadhtu fī ḥikāyat al-khadam*). The eunuch liked my imitation (*ḥikāyatī*), and adored my humorous anecdotes. He left, but soon came back, took my hand and said: "When I left your circle, I entered and stood in front of

> al-Muʿtaḍid, the Commander of the Faithful. [Suddenly] I thought of you and the anecdotes you had told and [burst out] laughing. The Commander of the Faithful saw me and reproached me for that and said: "What has happened to you? Woe unto you." I said: "O Commander of the Faithful, at the Gate there is a man known as Ibn al-Maghāzilī, who jests and imitates (*yuḥākī*) a bedouin, a Najdī, a Nabatean, a Zuṭṭī, a Zanjī, a Sindī, a Turk, a Meccan, and a eunuch, and on top of that, tells anecdotes which would make even a woman bereaved of child laugh."[35]

When Ibn al-Maghāzilī appeared before al-Muʿtaḍid, he was told by the latter: 'I have heard that you perform imitations and jest (*balaghanī annaka taḥkī wa-tuḍḥik*). For al-Muʿtaḍid, he also imitated a grammarian (*naḥwī*), an entertainer (*mukhannath*) and a judge (*qāḍī*). Yet, Barbier de Maynard in his translation of al-Masʿūdī's *Murūj al-Dhahab* failed to note that *rajul yuḥākī* means 'a man who imitates' and translated it into French as *conteur*, rendering *ḥikāya* as *histoire*.[36]

Evidently, the three above comedians, who were all described as *muḍḥikūn*, combined the telling of anecdotes with imitation of mannerisms and idiosyncrasies of speech. Only Ibn Shaʿra is explicitly said to have used special attire, as he did in order to impersonate Ibn Ṭūlūn. Abū 'l-ʿIbar dressed only as a clown.

Ibn Shaʿra and Abū 'l-ʿIbar served in the court of al-Mutawakkil, received wages (*arzāq*) from the caliph's treasury and were well off;[37] but Ibn al-Maghāzilī was a poor itinerant comedian, who performed in the marketplace. It was only late in his career that he was spotted by a eunuch and asked to perform before the caliph al-Muʿtaḍid.

One comedian performed in a hospital. Thus Umayya b. ʿAbd al-ʿAzīz al-Andalusī (d. 528/1133?) heard of a comedian giving lunatics 'psychological treatment' during his stay in Egypt:

> Amongst the nicest things I ever heard is that in Egypt of late there was a man who used to dwell in a lunatic asylum (*māristān*). He was summoned for the patients exactly as was the doctor. He would go in to see the patient, tell him funny stories and amusing legends, and he would perform imitations with comical masks for him (*wa-yukhriju lahu wujūhan muḍḥika*). He was gentle with his comic turns, good at it and very able.[38]

However, not every *muḍḥik* was an impersonator. Some of them were only jesters, in so far as one can tell. During the Mamluk period some sultans, such as Sultan al-Malik al-Ashraf Barsbāy (d. 842/1433), had a special jester with the title of 'The Sultan's Jester' (*muḍḥik al-sulṭān*);[39] there was another comedian described as one of *Nāẓir al-Khawāṣṣ* jesters.[40] The former served in Sultan Baybars' kitchen, the latter was appointed chief physician. Al-Maqrīzī relates some details about the way in which a favorite young jester worked in the kitchen of Sultan al Malik al-Nāṣir Ibn Qalawūn (d. 742/134) and was free to say whatever he chose by way of scurrilous jokes (*sukhf*).[41] However, once when he criticised the soldiers of *al-rawk al-Nāṣirī* (the survey of the public land ordered by *al-Nāṣir Muḥammad*), he was severely punished for jesting. The story goes that the sultan was seated with his senior amirs, resting in a garden, and the jester started a new joke to amuse the sultan. He portrayed a soldier of *al-rawk al-Nāṣirī* as riding a shabby horse, his saddle-bag behind him and his spear on his shoulder. The sultan, who did not permit any criticism of his land surveying project or of his soldiers, became furious and ordered him to be tied to the water-wheel until he was on the verge of death.[42] This incident (which was related by both al-Maqrīzī and Ibn Taghrī Birdī) shows that jesters used openly to express people's criticism and points of view to the sultan. Even some Mamluk amirs, such as Amīr Aḥmad Shād al-Sharāb, used to jest and play the buffoon to ridicule the sultan's opponents, to warn the sultan of plots against him, or to inform him of rumors amongst the common people. Such jesting often played an important role in the destiny of sultans.[43]

In fifteenth century Damascus, jesters (*muḍḥikūn*) are mentioned not only in the presence of the rulers, but also as in attendance at festivities of rich merchants, and even amongst the riffraff in market-places. Comedians and jugglers (*aṣḥāb al-malāʿib*) used to assemble in the Taḥt al-Qalʿa quarter, together with story-tellers (*ḥakawiyya wa-musāmirūn*) and were to be found elsewhere as well.[44] In 999/1590–91 the *muḍḥikūn* are mentioned in *al-Tadhkira al-Ayyūbiyya* as a type of entertainer different from *arbāb al-khayāl* (itinerant actors and/or shadow players):

> *wa-'stamarrat al-ṭubūl wa-arbāb al-malāhī wa-'l-maghānī wa-'l-ṭuruqiyya wa-'l-muḍḥikūn naḥwa sabʿati ayyāmin wāridīn min awwal al-nahār ilā ākhirih. wa-fī 'l-layl arbāb al-khayāl wa-'l-mushaʿbidhīn wa-sā'ir aṣnāf al-malāhī yastamirrūn min awwal al-layl ilā ākhirih ...*
>
> The drums, musicians, singers, *ṭuruqiyya* (banū Sāsān – beggars),[45] and comedians went on [performing] for seven days, from the start of the day until the finish of the day; and itinerant actors and shadow players, jugglers and all other types of musicians, from sunset to the finish of night.[46]

Arab historians do not often give detailed description of jesters or their performances, probably because such performances were already well known to their contemporary readers. Only on the rare occasion of an extraordinary event did they deign to do so, as in the case of al-Nāṣir's *muḍḥik*. On the other hand, European travellers give their readers a clear picture of Arab jesters, from their own point of view, in their descriptions of Arab society. One such description is by a British traveller, Alexander Russell, who gives an account of an impersonation performed in the middle of the eighteenth century in his *Natural History of Aleppo*:

> The natives, rather frugal in the general economy of their family, are on certain occasions, profusely liberal. Their feasts have every appearance of plenty, and hospitality. The master of the house deputes his sons, or one or two of his kinsmen, to assist the servants, in attendance on the guests. A band of music, placed in the court yard, plays almost incessantly; the fountains are all set a spouting; the attendants deck their Turbans with flowers; and the company, drest in their best apparel, assume an air of festivity and cheerfulness ...
>
> A set of Buffoons commonly attend at all great entertainments. These are composed of some of the musicians, and of others who for hire, assume the character of professed jesters. Some of them are good mimicks, taking off the ridiculous singularities of persons who happen to be well known and sometimes, in an extempore interlude, making burlesque allusions to persons present in the company: but their wit borders too near on the obscene, and, though the natives appear to be highly entertained, the mummery soon becomes insipid to a stranger.
>
> There is hardly a man of rank who has not a jester among his dependants, with whom he may divert himself at pleasure, and who, being invested with the liberty of saying whatever he chooses, often exercises his privilege with tolerable humour, both on his patron and the company. The Bashaw's Chauses (attendance at the gate) occasionally assume the character of buffoons, and perform interludes for the entertainment of their master.[47]

Buffoons *(Maskhara)*.

The Arabic word for buffoon was *maskhara* (pl. *masākhir* or *masākhira*), a term which originally meant a laughing-stock. According to Dozy and Engelmann, in Arabic the word *maskhara* only acquired the meaning of buffoon from the twelfth century onwards, and it was used later on in Spanish as *mascara*, in French as *masque* and in Italian as *masschera*.[48] But it is in fact attested in Arabic as buffoon much earlier. In *Ḥikāyat Abī 'l-Qāsim al-Baghdādī*, composed about 400/1010, Abū 'l-Qāsim tells guests who would like him to relate anecdotes that he is not a *maskhara* to be laughed at: 'One [guest] would say, "Abū 'l-Qāsim, please tell us some of those anecdotes (*ḥikāyāt*) you would entertain us with your stories (*aḥādīth*)". Abū 'l-Qāsim would reply, "you like mimicry (*musākhara*), sir! You want somebody to make fun of (*taḍḥaku 'alayhi*); you buffoon lover (*maskhara dūst*). No sir! Look for somebody else to make fun of!"[49] The term *maskhara* is also used in the sense of buffoon in *Alf Layla wa-Layla*[50] and in Mamluk historiography.[51]

In Abū 'l-Qāsim's passage a buffoon is a *ḥākiya*, a teller of anecdotes, and Ibn Sīnā's translation of Aristotle's *wajh al-maskhara* could be taken to suggest that he wore a mask.[52] The thirteenth-century historian Ibn al-Ṭiqṭaqā says that the last Abbasid caliph in Baghdad, al-Musta'ṣim, used to waste his time watching *maskhara*, which could likewise be taken to mean that *maskhara* were masked actors, on a par with the *samājāt* mentioned at the 'Abbasid court in earlier sources.[54] Richardson cites the term *maskhara* as 'a buffoon, fool, jester ... a man in masquerade'.[55] Dozy and Engleman confirm that in European languages it means a buffoon as well as a masked actor, as in the case of Arabic.[56] Al-Maqrīzī distinguishes *masākhir* from *mukhāyilūn* (itinerant actors) in his account of the year 755/1349;[57] most probably to denote that the *masākhir* were masked actors. On the other hand Ibn al-Ukhuwwa (d. 729/1329) defines the *maskhara* as 'a person who makes himself a laughing stock by his speech or clothing' (*wa-man ja'ala nafsahu maskharatan yuḍḥaku bihi fī kalāmihi aw libāsihi*) without making any mention of masks.[58] Ibn Taghrī Birdī's account of the disgrace of a vizier in Buyid Baghdad also implies that a *maskhara* might dress up in clownish costume, but that he would wear a mask.[59]

One of the most famous *musākhir* was the popular poet 'Alī b. Sūdūn al-Bashbaghāwī (d. 868/1464), whose *Dīwān* contains humorous, satirical and foolish poems and *maqāmāt* dealing with everyday life and children's behaviour, some of which were adapted for shadow plays. He was reputed to have been the first to revive the shadow play in Egypt[60] after its extinction at the hands of the Mamluk sultan al-Ẓāhir Jaqmaq, who had forced shadow players to sign an undertaking not to perform anymore after burning their figures in 855/1452.[61] But Ibn Sūdūn's *Dīwān* gives no indication that he was a shadow player, the only reference to shadow plays in it being a verse on the vicissitudes of time ('Time does not continue in the same state, hence they have likened it to a shadow play that is presented').[62] Nor is there any suggestion that he was a live actor. Some of his *maqāmāt* are dramatical, however, and one of them describes a pantomime performed in an *īwān*. The *maqāma* is narrated by an imaginary *rāwī* by the name of Ibn Suftaja ('Son of the Bill of Exchange'), who tells of how he wanted to be dressed like his sister after watching the latter's wedding ceremony. His mother agrees, and when the curtain is removed, he appears in his sister's wedding clothes, complete with her hair-style and make-up, and proceeds to imitate her coquettish gait, affectionate gestures and facial expressions to the accompaniment of tambourines, flutes of various kinds, songs and the trilling cries of joy of the women. There is also a grotesque scene in his *Dīwān* under the heading of *al-Tuḥaf al-ʿAjība* (the wondrous unique works of art). It involves three characters, an old woman who rides on the stalk of a palm-leaf, whipping it with a cow's tail, a young man playing with *rebab* and a baby girl who blows through a whistle with fishbones and candle in her hands.[63] Whether this fantasy is taken from a scene played by Ibn Sūdūn himself is hard to say. It is clear, however, that his buffoonery (*tamaskhur*) consisted in reciting funny poems and *maqāmāt* in public places, where his audience would form a circle (*ḥalqa*) around him:

> It is said ... that he practised as a buffoon and a jester (*taʿāṭā 'l-tamaskhur*) with the villains in the open space of Taḥta 'l-Qalʿa in Damascus. His father was a judge and looked for him in Damascus. Once he saw his father standing in the circle formed by his audience he recited humorous verses: "My father hoped to see me as the judge of the city/ let those who have children be admonished."[64]

His buffoonery is well illustrated in a poem composed in imitation (*muʿāraḍa*) of a famous piece known as the 'Burlesque Ode' (*al-Qaṣīda al-Sukhriyya*); it begins with the following lines:

> 'Wonder, O wonder / a red cow with a tail
> Milk in its udder / appears for people when they milk it
> When it is cursed, it shows no anger,
> While people get angry when they are cursed.[65]

According to Ibn Sūdūn's contemporary, the historian al-Badrī (d. 817/1443), the open space of Taḥta 'l-Qalʿa in Damascus was the main square where entertainers were gathered:

> As for the open space called Taḥta 'l-Qalʿa, one can hardly see the actual ground there because of the enormous number of people, both peddlars of food and petty traders (*mutaʿayyishīn*) and those receiving charitable allowances (*waẓāʾifiyya*). Interspersed among them one finds those who make up the circles of Ṣūfī devotees (*arbāb al-ḥalaq*), casters of horoscopes (*faʾlātiyya*), jesters (*muḍḥikūn*), jugglers (*aṣḥāb al-malāʿib*), reciters of stories and tales (*al-ḥakawiyya wa-'l-musāmirūn*) and indeed everything in which the ear delights, which rejoices the eye and which the soul can desire – all these folk continuing their activities morning and evening, without end, but above all in the evenings ... [66]

Al-Qazwīnī gives a similar description of places of entertainment in

Damascus.[67] The squares and orchards in which entertainers would perform were called *amākin al-muftarajāt*, places of entertainment, by some Mamluk historians.[68]

In a culture in which exposure to public mockery was the ultimate disgrace, it is not surprising that those who earned a living by making fools of themselves had a bad name. *Shuhra*, conspicuousness or notoriety, was associated with dishonour. An actor was someone who 'made a display of himself' (*man yuṣayyiru nafsahu shuhra*), and all entertainers were infamous (*mukhannathūn*), as the fourteenth-century translator of the Syro-Roman law book put it.[69] In tenth-century Bukhāra a baker who had helped the brothers of Naṣr b. Aḥmad (914–43) escape from prison was publicly disgraced, prior to his execution, by being paraded through the streets in the company of entertainers (*shuhira bi-Bukhāra wa-bayna yadayhi al-mukhannathūn*).[70] In eleventh-century Iraq a vizier destined for execution was paraded through the streets on a camel wearing the conical cap of a clown and with a leather garland around his neck 'like a buffoon'.[71] Elsewhere we learn that convicted criminals were dressed in *thawb shuhra* and paraded through the streets on donkeys;[72] and it was likewise *thawb shuhra* that actors wore. Thus the fourteenth-century Ibn al-Ḥājj identifies as garments of *shuhra* the costume of the actor playing 'Prince of Nawruz' during the New Year celebrations in Egypt. His account, to which there are parallels in al-Maqrīzī and Ibn Iyās, goes as follows:

> Look (O reader), may God have mercy on both of us, at this shameful deed which they (Copts and Muslims) perform on this day (*al-Nayrūz*). They choose somebody among them, and they violate tradition, I mean in changing his appearance and countenance, so they are included in what the saying of (Muḥammad), may God bless him and grant him salvation, intended: 'God's curse upon women and men who change the creation of God', or however Muḥammad said it. They would change his countenance with lime or flour, and stick a beard of fur and the like on him. Then they would dress him in a red or yellow dress, making him a laughing-stock (*li-yushhirūhu*). It was mentioned in the *Ḥadīth*: 'He who puts on a garment of luxury/ostentation (*thawb shuhra*), God will dress him on the day of resurrection a dress of disgrace and humilation, then He will put it in flames (of Hell).' Then they put on his head a long conical cap (*ṭurṭūr*), and make him ride on an ugly donkey, surrounding him with green palm branches, and bunches of dates, putting in his hand something which is similar to a ledger, as if he is accounting with people for what he would like to charge them of forbidden

> and illegal charges. They rove with him by the doors of the alleys and streets of the city, and by most of the shops and houses in the markets, and collect whatever they collect in a manner which is no less than oppression, extortion and tyranny, spending (the money they collect) unlawfully .... Although some would agree to this, by way of amusement and jest, yet it is censured by the law of Islam. For the condition of jest and amusement (in Islamic law) is that it is based on truth, while their jest is rarely without falsehood and the utterance of atrocities .... They justify (their behavior) on the pretext that it is the *Nayrūz* feast and they argue that on this day there is no objection (to any kind of behaviour), and no authority is imposed.[73]

Of special importance to the study of the term *shuhra* as a theatrical performance, is Maimonides' usage of the Hebrew word *sebakha* (in Arabic: *shabaka*) (net), which he connects to the term *ishtihār.* Accordingly, the hobby-horse actress, while going from one house to another in the same street, wears a net upon her hair, while wearing a shirt of fine fabric but of hideous (*mushawwah*) shape, for comic purposes, in her theatrical performance (*wa-'l-gharaḍ an takūn hadhih 'al-sebakha' li-'l-li'b fī 'l-khayāl*) (see Maimonides, *Commentaire*, vol. I, pp. 195, 221). It is possible to conclude that the term *thawb shuhra*, in the medieval Islamic world also denotes an actor's costume.

Participants in Pageantry

Another way of representing everyday-life in a quasi-theatrical form, was through pageantry. At the celebrations of weddings and circumcisions of sons of caliphs, sultans and other grandees there were pageants with various sorts of spectacles, mainly by artisans demonstrating their trades on coaches driven by horses. Thus in 480/1087, on the occasion of the birth of the son of al-Muqtadī, there was a procession of statues of camphor and coaches displaying 'sailors with a ship on wheels, millers working with stone hand-mill, etc.'[74] When the sultan al-Malik al-Nāṣir Muḥammad b. Qalāwūn entered Cairo, the city was decorated, Arab singers sang, and all the streets from Bāb al-Naṣr to Bāb al-Silsila and the citadel, were decorated with small fortresses; at Bāb al-Naṣr the governor (*wālī*) of Cairo made a fortress full of various types of plays, serious and funny, and 'people vied with each other in making sumptuous decorations ... and they set up fortress-shaped constructions ...'[75]

In fifteenth-century Damascus the circumcision of the son of a mere linen weaver was celebrated with a great procession of fully armed men, magnificently attired, and harnessed horses. The son toured the streets with them, weaving with a loom carried by two riding animals accompanied by flautists, drummers, singers and actors (*mukhāyila*).[76] For the eighteenth century, al-Budayrī's short history of Damascus describes a parade in which horsemen played games such as imitating the 'brave men of the bedouin' (*wa-'umila mawkib ... wa-fīhi min al-malā'ib al-gharība min tamthīl shuj'ān al-'Arab wa-ghayr dhālika*).[77] Presumably the 'brave men of the bedouin' were imitated by battle simulation.

According to 'Abdallāh al-Nadīm (1843–96), an Egyptian journalist and playwright, such pieces were theatrical plays performed by actors called *khalbūṣ al-'Arab* (bedouin's clown). These actors would perform plays representing bedouin battles and incidents relating to their encampments and departures.[78]

In Mamluk Egypt the parade of the *maḥmal* provided the occasion for the development of a new performance by the Royal Mamluks. The comedians among them, known as *'afārīt al-maḥmal*, 'the demons of the *maḥmal*', belonged to their disreputable elements (*awbāsh al-mamālīk al-sulṭāniyya*). They used to exchange their clothes for comic or ugly costumes and to ride horses decorated with bells in order to amuse people. Eventually they began to molest people, collecting money for their performances from shops and the houses of amirs in a manner reminiscent of the followers of the *Amīr al-Nayrūz*; and by 871/1467 they had become so troublesome that the sultan ordered their performances to be cancelled. Apparently these Mamluks were inspired by some comedians who use to amuse people during the setting out of the *maḥmal* by disguising themselves, but, we are told, 'when the Mamluks adopted it, they developed it step by step' (*fa-lammā ṣārat al-mamālīk taf'aluh intaqalū min shay' ilā shay'*), or in other words they rapidly developed some sort of comical play.[79]

In the events of the year 1174/1760–1 there is another description of pageants, this time in Damascus in celebration of the birth of the prince who was to become the Sultan Salīm III:

> 'Uthmān Pāshā (sent) the town crier to announce that 'whoever has a doll even if it is of clay or wood, or any one who knows any kind of *sīmā* (magic) which is called *malā'ib* (jugglery), he would get great reward' ... The parades roved (the streets) with all sorts of jugglery (*malā'ib*). They displayed all the professions of the artisans and walked in several wonderous processions. Some were with weapons and equipments, and magnificent shields, others with various precious dresses. In short it was so much decor (*zīnā*) that we did not hear that something similar to it has ever been seen.[80]

Al-Jabartī (1168–1242/1754–1826) described several pageants of guilds in his chronicle *'Ajā'ib al-Āthār*.[81] In one case (year 1229/1813) he spoke of more than 70 carriages. In another procession he counted 91 carriages in the morning and 108 in the evening; this was on the occasion of the wedding of Ismā'īl Pāshā, the son of Muḥammad 'Alī Pāshā:

> The acrobat of the rope stretched his rope, with its beginning opposite the palace of the Pāshā up to the peak of the minaret in Ḥārat (quarter) al-Fawwāla ... Another Syrian acrobat was on the other side ... On Saturday, the day of the beginning of the celebrations ... all sorts of jugglers (*arbāb al-malā'ib*),[82] *mughazlikīn* (singers), acrobats (*junbādhiyya*), itinerant actors or strolling players (*ḥababziyya*), snake charmers and slight-of-hand performers (*ḥuwāt*), monkey-keepers (trainers) (*qarrādiyya*), dancers (*raqqāsīn*), male dancers called *barāmka*, and other sorts and types ... The magicians and acrobats played on the ropes. At the same time, the Christians also celebrated ... It happened to be Christmas, they made swings and *malā'ib* (jugglery). During that time tradesmen and artisans were ordered to prepare carriages shaped in and representing their professions and crafts, in order to join the procession of the bride. Every guild of a profession and craft endeavoured to decorate and embellish their representations. They vied and competed with one another and boasted. Every one whose devil induced him to invent something did it and went to the appointed man (for the preparation of the carriages) and was given a paper to that effect. This (preparation) was not confined to certain people or appointed number, but according to their arbitrariness, and requirement of one another. The head of a guild would impose on its members taxes and money which he collected from them and spent on the carriage, and its requirements of wood, ropes, donkeys, horses or men which would pull them and for what they would hire or borrow for decoration of the carriage such as *muzakrashāt* (silk embroidered with gold thread), *muqaṣṣabāt* (embroideries with gold and silver), and *ṭal'iyyāt*, and the tools of their profession which distinguish it from others. (The carriage) would become in its shape as a shop and the seller sitting in it, such as the confectioner and the containers of candies and sugers in front of him, and surrounded by vessels of sugar coated almonds, and funnels of sugar hung around him ... completing ninety-one carriages ... In front of each carriage the representatives of its guild and profession walking behind the drums and flutes. They were decorated and most of their magnificent dresses were borrowed (from other people) ....[83]

Such procession was accompanied by night with *shunnuk* (salvo of firearms) and *ḥarrāqāt* (fireworks). Al-Jabartī adds that in the evening of the same day another wedding was celebrated and the number of carriages was increased by fifteen carriages, among them one representative of a glass factory.[84]

Notes

1. al-Ghazālī, *Iḥyā' 'Ulūm al-Dīn* (Cairo, 1352/1933), vol. II, p. 325; al-Ṭabarsī, *Makārim al-Akhlāq* (Cairo, 1304/1886), p. 9; Wensinck, *Concordance*, s.v. '*ḍiḥk*'.
2. Rosenthal, *Humor*, pp. 1ff; cf. also J. Sadan, *al-Adab al-'Arabī al-Hāzil* (Tel Aviv, 1983).
3. G. Widengren, 'Harlekintracht und Mönchskutte, Clownhut und Derwischmütze. Eine gesellschafts-, religions- und trachtgeschichtliche Studie', *Orientalia Suecana* II Uppsala, 1953, p. 105.
4. See the references given above, Ch. 2. n. 5.
5. Ibn Ḥanbal, *Musnad*, vol. VI, p. 316; Ibn 'Abd Rabbih, '*Iqd*, vol. VI, p. 381.
6. al-Shaykh al-Maghribī, 'al-Thaqāla wa 'l-Thuqalā', *Majallat al-Majma' al-'Ilmī bi-Dimashq* XII (1932), p. 469; cf. Muslim, *Ṣaḥīḥ*, vol. IV, p. 2031.
7. Asad, *al-Qiyān wa-'l-Ghinā' fī 'l-Aṣr al-Jāhilī*, pp. 58ff.
8. Ibn al-Jawzī, *Akhbār al-Ḥamqā wa-'l-Mughaffalīn* (Damascus, 1345/1926), pp. 16f. On the synonyms of *muḍḥik*, such as *baṭṭāl*, *aḥmaq*, *mughaffal*, see Rosenthal, *Humor*, p. 7n.
9. See J. Sadan, 'The Nomad versus Sedentary Framework', *Fabula* XV (Göttingen, 1974), pp. 59–86; id., 'Vin - Fait de Civilisation' in *Studies in Memory of Gaston Wiet*, ed. M. Rosen-Ayalon (Jerusalem, 1977), pp. 129–60; al-Ibshīhī, *Mustaṭraf*, vol. II, pp. 233ff; Ibn 'Abd Rabbih, '*Iqd*, vol. II, pp. 300–4.
10. Ibn 'Abd Rabbih, '*Iqd*, vol. VI, pp. 393–5; al-Ibshīhī, *Mustaṭraf*, vol. II, pp. 158f.
11. al-Jāḥiẓ (attrib.), *Tāj*, pp. 38f.
12. Ibid., pp. 40f (al-Mahdī); al-Mas'ūdī, *Murūj*, vol. VII, p. 191.
13. On this man, see al-Mas'ūdī, *Murūj*, vol. VII, pp. 107–11; Ibn 'Āṣim al-Andalusī, *Hadā'iq*, fols 54a–b; Sadan, *Adab*, pp. 44f.
14. al-Mas'ūdī, *Murūj*, vol. VII, pp. 109ff.
15. al-Rashīd b. al-Zubayr, *Dhakhā'ir*, p. 220. See also al-Ḥusayn b. Ḥajjāj, *Dīwān*, MS British Library, vo. II, Add. 7588, fol. 149a, where the singer and actress Bint al-Ṭuyūrī is described as a *ḍarrāṭa*: *wa-lā samā'un illā bi-ṭablin taḍruṭu fīhi Bintu 'l-Ṭuyūrī: Bint al-Ṭuyūrī kānat mughanniya ṣaf'āna ḍarrāṭa.* On a man of the same profession see al-Bayhaqī, *al-Maḥāsin wa-'l-Masāwī*, vol. II, pp. 410f. On the other hand 'Alī b. 'Isā, al-Muqtadir's vizier stopped paying wages to the *ṣafā'ina*, Ibn al-Athīr, *Kāmil*, vol. VIII, p. 165.
16. Ibn al-Nadīm, *Fihrist*, vol. I, p. 334; vol. II, p. 735. On Ash'ab, see Nuwayrī, *Nihāya*, vol. IV, pp. 34–46; Rosenthal, *Humor*, pp. 17–35.
17. Ibn al-Nadīm, *Fihrist*, vol. I, p. 334. For the word *ṣafādima* (sq. *ṣafdīm*), see below, n. 27.
18. Ibn al-Nadīm, *Fihrist*, p. 218; p. 336.

19. Cf. Rosenthal, *Humor*, pp. 67, n. 2: 'charlatans (*mukharriqah*?, leg.: *mukharrifah*?'. I am inclined to accept Rosenthal's suggestion that it might be *mukharrifa*, tellers of fictional stories (cf. ibid., p. 143).
20. See for example Muḥammad 'Azīza, *Formes Traditionelles du Spectacles*, p. 52.
21. al-Ḥusrī al-Qayrawānī, *Jam' al-Jawāhir* (Cairo, 1353/1934, p. 81; id., *Dhayl*, p. 66; cf. also Bar Hebraeus, *The Laughable Stories* (London, 1897); al-Ābī, *Nathr al-Durr* (Tunis, 1983), vol. VII, p. 202, no. 13.
22. al-Ḥuṣrī, *Dhayl*, p. 66; cf. id., *Jam'*, p. 81; al-Ābī, *Nathr*, vol. III, pp. 232–46.
23. Ibid., pp. 239–41.
24. Cf. al-Naysābūrī, *'Uqalā' al-Majānīn*, p. 35, where al-Naysābūrī relates that some people pretended to be fool in order to get rich. Among them is the poet 'Alī b. Ṣalūt al-Qaṣrī, who succeeded in his profession even among kings and notables, only after he 'pretended to be a fool and became a jester'. (*thumma taḥammaqa wa-akhadha fī 'l-hazl*).
25. Ibid., vol. VII, pp. 235f.
26. al-Ābī, *Nathr*, vol. VII, p. 203, n. 3.
27. al-Ḥuṣrī, *Dhayl*, p. 183.
28. Bar Hebraeus, *Laughable Stories*, pp. 129–39; cf. al-Ābī, *Nathr*, vol. III, pp. 232–46 (Muzabbid); vol. VII, pp. 200–02 (Abū 'l-'Ibar) and 203f (Abū 'l-'Anbas). On al-Ābī's influence on him, see U. Marzolph, 'Die Quellen der ergötzlichen Erzählungen des Bar Hebraeus', *Oriens Christianus* LXXVIII (1984), p. 218, and LXXIX (1985), pp. 81–125. On the three jesters, see Rosenthal, *Humor*, pp. 12n, 13n and 14n.
29. Bar Hebraeus *Laughable Stories* are not simply reminiscent of *adab* literature (as noted by J. B. Segal, 'Ibn al-'Ibri' in EI[2]); they are actually derived from it.
30. al-Ḥuṣrī, *Dhayl*, p. 66; id., *Jam'*, pp. 81f.
31. Al-Ṣūlī, *Ash'ār*, p. 328.
32. Aḥmad b. Yūsuf Ibn al-Dāya, *Kitāb al-Mukāfa'a wa-Ḥusn al-'Uqbā* (Cairo, 1940), pp. 86f.
33. Ibn al-Dāya, *Kitāb al-Mukāfa'a*, pp. 86f; 'Abdallah al-Madīnī al-Balawī, *Sīrat Aḥmad b. Ṭūlūn* (Damascus, 1358/1939), pp.. 148f.
34. al-Tha'ālibī, *Yatīma*, vol. II, p. 377. On *muṭāyaba* (jest), see also al-Tanūkhī, *Nishwār*, vol. I, pp. 185, 265, 306 (nos 95, 142, 166); Ibn al-Nadīm, *Fihrist*, p. 218 (mistranslated by Dodge, *Fihrist*, p. 336).
35. al-Mas'ūdī, *Murūj*, vol. VIII, pp. 161–6; cf. al-Tanūkhī, *Nishwār*, vol. I, pp. 2–5, on the anecdotes of *al-mutakallimīn 'alā-'l-ṭuruq … wa-aṣḥāb al-nādira wa-'l-muḍḥikīn wa-'l-raqqāṣīn wa-'l-mukhannathīn*.
36. al-Mas'ūdī, *Murūj*, vol. VIII, p. 161 of the French translation; cf. also C. Pellat, 'Ḥikāya' in EI[2]. The story of Ibn al-Maghāzilī is also told in (Anon.) *Durrat al-Zayn wa-Qurrat al-'Ayn*, MS Bibliothèque Nationale, arabe 3440, fol. 40a; al-Ibshīhī, *Mustaṭraf*, vol. II, p. 247 (where it is summarised and set in the time of Hārūn al-Rashīd); and *Alf Layla wa-Layla* (Būlāq, 1279/1862), vol. II, p. 285 (where

the comedian's name has turned into Ibn al-Qāribī). Cf. also Horovitz, *Spuren*, pp. 19–21.

37. Similarly 'Alī b. al-Junayd al-Iskāfī, who was employed by al-Mu'taṣim (cf. Ch. 4, n. 15).
38. Abū 'l-Ṣalt Umayya b. 'Abd al-'Azīz, *al-Risāla al-Miṣriyya*, in 'Abd al-Salām Hārūn (ed.), *Nawādir al-Makhṭūṭāt* (Cairo, 1951), p. 34.
39. al-Maqrīzī, *Sulūk*, vol. IV, part ii, pp. 973, 1071f.
40. Ibn Taghrī Birdī, *Nujūm*, MS, fols 84b–85a; ed. Popper, vol. VII, p. 164 (year 852 AH); cf. vol. VII, p. xxv, where Popper thinks it unlikely that Nāẓir al-Khawāṣṣ should have had buffoons of this kind and suggests that Ibn Taghrī Birdī used the term in a non-technical sense of joker or (derisively) companion.
41. al-Maqrīzī, *Khiṭaṭ*, ed. Wiet, vol. II, p. 31 (*kāna min jumlat ṣibyān maṭbakhihi rajul muḍḥik yahzilu fī ḥaḍrat al-sulṭān fa-yaḍḥaku minhu wa-ya'jab minhu wa-lā yata'arraḍ fīmā yaqūlu min al-sukhf*). On other types of comedians, see Ibn Iyās, *Badā'i'*, vol. II, pp. 165, 202; vol. III, p. 289; vol. IV, pp. 255 (a comedian who played the role of *'ifrīt al-maḥmal*), 481–2.
42. al-Maqrīzī, *Khiṭaṭ*, ed. Wiet, vol. II, p. 31.
43. Ibn Taghrī Birdī, *Nujūm*, vol. X, pp. 158, 191; ed. Popper, vol. VII, p. 164 and the glossary thereto at p. xxv, on Aḥmad b. Shaykh al-Malik al-Muẓaffar.
44. Abdallāh b. Muḥammad al-Badrī, *Nuzhat al-Anām fī Maḥāsin al-Shām* (Cairo, 1341'1922f), p. 63; cf. also al-Qazwīnī, *Kosmographie*, p. 128.
45. Cf. anon., *Kitāb Raqā'iq al-Ḥulal fī Daqā'iq al-Ḥiyal*, MS Bibliothèque Nationale, arabe 3552, fol. 5b: *fī ḥiyali banī Sāsān wa-hum al-ṭuruqiyya.*
46. Sharaf al-Dīn Ibn Ayyūb, *al-Tadhkira al-Ayyūbiyya*, MS, al-Maktaba al-Ẓāhiriyya, Damascus, fol. 359b–360a.
47. A. Russell, *The Natural History of Aleppo* (London, 1974), vol. I, pp. 156f.
48. Dozy and Engelmann, *Glossaire*, p. 505.
49. A. Mez (ed.), *Abul'kāsim, ein baghdāder Sittenbild*, von Muḥammad ibn aḥmad abulmuṭahhar alazdī (Heidelberg, 1902), p. 71.
50. *Alf Layla wa-layla*, Būlāq, vol. I, p. 75; ed. Muḥammad Qiṭṭa 'Adawī, vol. II, p. 135; vol. IV, pp. 685, 709; ed. M. Habicht (Breslau, 1824–43), vol. IV, p. 358, vol. IX, p. 366; vol. XI, p. 79.
51. Ibn Taghrī Birdī, *Nujūm*, MS, fols 85a, 155b, cf. 158a; cf. also al-Maqrīzī, *Sulūk*, vol. I, part ii, p. 294; al-Qazwīnī, *Kosmographie*, p. 128; al-Maqqarī, *Nafḥ al-Ṭīb fī Ghusn al-Andalus al-Raṭīb* (Beirut, 1962), vol. II, p. 298.
52. Cf. above, Ch. 3. n. 30.
53. Ibn al-Ṭiqṭaqā, *al-Fakhrī* (Paris, 1895), p. 448.
54. See above, section on *samāja.*
55. J. Richardson, *Dictionary*, p. 929, col. 1.
56. Dozy and Engelmann, *Glossaire*, p. 506.
57. al-Maqrīzī, *Sulūk*, vol. III, part iii, p. 919.
58. Muḥammad b. Muḥammad al-Qurashī, known as Ibn al-Ukhuwwa,

Kitāb Ma'ālim al-Qurbā fī Aḥkām al-Ḥisba, ed. M. M. Sha'bān and S. A. 'I. al-Muṭī'ī (Cairo, 1976), p. 314.

59. Ibn Taghrī Birdī, *Nujūm*, ed. Popper, vol. II, pp. 172, 176; cf. Ibn al-Athīr, *Kāmil*, vol. IX, p. 644: al-Basāsīrī had the vizier Abū 'l-Qāsim b. Maslama arrested and paraded through the streets wearing a high conical cap, a woolen cloak and necklaces around his neck 'like a buffoon' (*muskhara*); subsequently he was dressed in the skin of an ox and had its horns placed on his head (like a *samāja*, one might add, though this comparison is not actually made).
60. Ibn al-'Imād, *Shadharāt al-Dhahab fī Akhbār man Dhahab* (Cairo, 1351/1932), vol. VII, pp. 307f.
61. Ibn Iyās, *Tārīkh Ibn Iyās al-Kabīr*, MS Bibliothèque Nationale, arabe 1823, fol. 210b; id., *Badā'i'*, vol. I, part i, p. 363.
62. Ibn Sūdūn, *Nuzhat al-Nufūs*, pp. 84ff. On the significance of this *maqāma* see p. 34 above.
63. Ibn Sūdūn, *Nuzhat al-Nufūs*, pp. 157ff.
64. Ibn al-'Imād, *Shadharāt*, vol. VII, p. 308.
65. Ibn Sūdūn, *Nuzhat al-Nufūs*, p. 50; On the structure and rhythm of Ibn Sūdūn's *zajals*, see M. Q. al-Baqlī, *al-Awzān al-Mūsīqiyya fī Azjāl Ibn Sūdūn* (Cairo, 1976).
66. Badrī, *Nuzhat al-Anām*, p. 63; the translation is by Bosworth (*Underworld*, vol. I, p. 108). Cf. al-Maqrīzī, *Khiṭaṭ*, ed. Wiet, vol. II, p. 30, on the Bayn al-Qaṣrayn quarter in Cairo: 'in this quarter many circles were formed for the recitation of romances, historical tales and poetry and for the performance of all sorts of plays and entertainment by the buffoons (*wa-'l-tafannun fī anwā' al-li'b wa-'l-lahw min arbāb al-masākhir*). They form a gathering of people impossible to count'.
67. al-Qazwīnī, *Kosmographie*, vol. II, p. 128; Cf. the wording in Ibn 'Abd Rabbih, *'Iqd*, vol. VI, p. 152.
68. Ibn Iyās, *Badā'i'*, vol. I, part i, p. 365; part ii, p. 364; id., *Tārīkh*, MS, fol. 352b.
69. See above, p. 25. On Dhū 'l-shuhra Abū Dajāna al-Anṣārī, see al-Ibshīhī, *Mustaṭraf*, vol. II, p. 34.
70. Ibn Ẓāfir, *Akhbar al-Duwal al-Munqati'a*, MS Ambrosiana, Milan, codex arab. 96, fol. 125a. (I owe this reference to Mr. L. Treadwell.)
71. See above, n. 59. In Payne, *Thesaurus Syriacus*, vol. II, col. 4370, *theatron* is given in Arabic as *shuhra* (notoriety) as well as *manẓar* (spectacle), *ḥalba* (arena), *maydān* (open place), and *mal'ab.*
72. Shams al-Dīn Muḥammad Ibn Ṭulūn, *Mufākahat al-Khullān fī Ḥawādith al-Zamān* (Cairo, 1381/1962), vol. I, pp. 172f.
73. Ibn al-Ḥājj, *Madkhal*, vol. II, pp. 52f. Cf. And, *Culture*, pp. 20f, 85ff. On *shuhra* in the sense of theatre see n. 71 above.
74. Ibn al-Jawzī, *al-Muntaẓam fī Tārikh al-Mulūk wa-'l-Umam* (Hyderabad al-Dakan, 1359/1940), vol. IX, p. 38. On the Mutawakkil's celebration of the 'Shādhgulāh' (the day of great rejoicing with roses) see al-Shābushtī, *Diyārāt*, p. 160. For an

illustration of such procession see Figure 5 in this book, p. 58.
75. Ibn Taghrī Birdī, *Nujūm*, Cairo, vol. VIII, pp. 165f; al-Maqrīzī, *Sulūk*, vol. I, part iii, pp. 701, 938f.
76. Ibn Ṭūlūn, *Mufākahat al-Khullān*, vol. II, p. 105.
77. al-Budayrī, *Ḥawādith*, pp. 38f.
78. 'Abd Allāh al-Nadīm, *Sulāfat al-Nadīm* (Cairo, 1901), vol. II, p. 63. (My thanks to Dr. Carol Bardenstein for referring me to this book.) On such performances in Arab epic romance, see Fārūq Khūrshīd, *al-Siyar al-Sha'biyya* (Cairo, 1978), pp. 47–9.
79. Ibn Taghrī Birdī, *Ḥawādith*, vol. VII, pp. 535–9.
80. al-Budayrī, *Ḥawādith*, pp. 233f; cf. also pp. 38f.
81. al-Jabartī, *'Ajā'ib*, vol. II, p. 244; And, *Theatre*, p. 24 describing a playlet representing various trades; And, *Culture*, pp. 131–57.
82. On *arbāb al-malā'ib* see H. A. R. Gibb and H. Bowen, *Islamic Society and the West*, vol. I (London 1950–7), part i, p. 277n; G. Baer, *Egyptian Guilds in Modern Times* (Jerusalem, 1964), pp. 9, 43. For a description of entertainers, see E. W. Lane, *The Manners and Customs of the Modern Egyptians* (London, 1954), pp. 172, 180, 384–9, 395, 507, 509.
83. al-Jabartī, *'Ajā'ib*, vol. IV, pp. 198–201. For other descriptions, see ibid., vol. I, pp. 99–100, 220f, 252; vol. III, pp. 70, 142, 225. See Figure 5, p. 58. See the term *ṭal'iyyāt* (*houppes ou franges servant d-ornement*); see Fagnan, *Additions aux dictionnaires arabes*, p. 105.
84. al-Jabartī, *'Ajā'ib*, vol. IV, p. 201. On such processions and guild pageantry in the Ottoman Empire, see And, *Culture*, pp. 151ff.

III Medieval Theatre

5

Ḥikāya

Impersonation and Plays

Arabic lexicographers define *ḥikāya* as meaning imitation, impersonation and aping, as well as a story or tale.[1] The original meaning of the word is imitation,[2] and in early Arabic literature it is sometimes used in the sense of performing an actual play. It seems that the term *ḥākī* (imitator) was a well-known one in the time of the Prophet Muḥammad. Al-Ḥakam b. Abī al-ʿĀṣ was called al-Ḥākī because he imitated the Prophet's manner of walk.[3]

There is a well-known account of mimics in the early Islamic world in the *Bayān* of al-Jāḥiẓ (d. 255/868f):[4]

> We find that the impersonator (*ḥākiya*) is able to imitate (*yaḥkī*) precisely the pronunciation of the natives of the Yemen with all the special accents of that area. This is equally true of imitation (*ḥikāya*) of the Khurasanian, the Ahwazian, the Negro, the Sindi and others. You may, in fact, find that he seems to be more natural than they. When he imitates the speech of the stammerer, it seems that he has become the ultimate stammerer, as if all the peculiarities of every stammerer ever born have been rolled into one. When he imitates the blind man, copying the distinctive features of his face, eyes and limbs, you realise that even in a thousand blind men you would never find one who has all of these combined traits. It is as if he has synthesised the peculiar features of all blind men in one complete character.

Al-Jāḥiẓ, who also remarks on the ability of such persons to mimic animal cries, was clearly taking about professional performers, probably of the type who performed in market places. Other accounts, however, refer to ordinary people mimicking each other, and here the mimicry is invariably parody, the intention being to tease or humiliate the person mimicked. One example is found in al-Shābushtī:[5]

> Ibrāhīm [b. Muḥammad b. al-Mudabbir, d. 297/892] invited a

group of singers; among whom were Jaḥẓa and Qāsim b. Zarzar and his uncle Abū Muḥammad b. Ḥamdūn. Ibrāhīm started imitating (*yuḥākī*) one singer after another. His uncle advised him, 'Don't imitate Jaḥẓa, you should avoid him'. But he refused to listen and imitated him. Jaḥẓa looked around for something to write on until he found a piece of paper and wrote,

I witnessed the *ḥikāya* of a singer / he imitated (*ḥākā*) an old woman singing.

He also imitated an intelligent man approaching her / giving her a long thick one as she wished.

His uncle said, 'Didn't I tell you not to go near a scorpion?'

There is also an amusing example in al-Musabbiḥī's account of a procession of the Fatimid caliph al-Ẓāhir in 1024:[6]

On Thursday the twentieth of the month (Muḥarram 415/1024) Shams al-Mulk refused to attend to his duties and stayed at home. It is related that ... the Persian Junior Sharīf ... was riding after the Commander of the Faithful mimicking (*yaḥkī*) Shams al-Mulk. He twisted his head, shook his turban, pointed to his nose as if blowing it and throwing mucus on Shams al-Dawla's face ...

This *ḥikāya* so offended Shams al-Mulk that al-Ẓāhir had much trouble conciliating him. He might have derived comfort from a story told by al-Sha'rānī (d. 973/1565f), in which the mimic comes to a bad end:[7]

When [Shaykh Aḥmad al-Saṭīḥa] was riding a horse, his servant used to hug him as if he were a child. He used to wear a high *ṭurṭūr* [conical cap] of leather with a neckband under his chin and a red *jubba* [long outer garment] ... Somebody mimicked him (*ḥakā bihi*) by making a *ṭurṭūr* and riding on a horse ... in a servant's lap. [But he fell and broke his neck.]

That *ḥikāya* means imitation in all of these examples is obvious, and it was because it had this meaning (rather than the later one of story) that it was used to translate Greek dramatical terms. Thus Abū Bishr Mattā b. Yūnis al-Qunnā'ī (d. 329/940), the translator of Aristotle's *Poetics,* rendered *mimesis* as *al-tashbīh wa-'l-muḥākāt* or *al-tashhīh wa-'l-ḥikāya,*[8] Ibn Sīnā uses the word *muḥākāt* in his definition of tragedy;[9] and the 'actors of tragedy' in Hippocrates' *Nomos* are translated as *aṣḥāb al-ḥikāya* in Ibn Abī Uṣaybi'a (d. 668/1270).[10] But *ḥākā* and related forms are not often found in the sense of imitating after the eleventh century. Two examples are found in non-Muslim sources. Thus Maimonides (d. 601/1204) refers to a small shield good for nothing except *li-'l-mithāl wa-'l-muḥākāt,* 'theatrical performances and plays';[11] and *yuḥākī* and *aḥkā bi* appear in the sense of play-acting in the Coptic martyrdom discussed in the previous chapter, the hero of which was an actor (*khayālī* and the text of which was translated into Arabic in the fourteenth century).[12] But given that the *aṣḥāb al-ḥikāya* mentioned by Ibn Abī Uṣaybiʿa must be derived from an earlier translation, the only Muslim attestation to have come to light so far seems to be the passage in the sixteenth-century al-Shaʿrānī cited above; and though other examples may well turn up, it is clear that the eleventh century onwards the usual word for mimicry and theatrical performances was *khayāl* (or *khiyāl*). Apparently, *ḥikāya* could no longer be used in this sense. According to Pellat, it was only by the fourteenth century that *ḥikāya* had finally come to mean tale or story, but in fact the semantic shift would seem to have been accomplished some three centuries earlier.[13]

There is nothing in the examples given so far to indicate that impersonation might be combined with any kind of plot, but other attestations make it clear that *ḥikāyāt* sometimes amounted to actual plays, or more precisely scenes or sketches, which might be based on written texts. The commentator on the *Naqāʾiḍ* who spoke of the *mukhannathūn* using hobby-horses in their *ḥikāyāt* presumably had in mind short sketches in which *mukhannathūn* imitated galloping horsemen, though whether such scenes were accompanied by words cannot be said.[14] *Ḥikāya* also means a sketch in an anecdote told now of Jarīr (d. 114/732) and now of Diʿbil (d. 246/960). According to Ibrāhīm b. ʿAwn (d. 322/934), a *mukhannath* threatened Jarīr that if he satirised him, he would 'produce' his mother in a *ḥikāya (in hajānī akhrajtu ummahu fī 'l-ḥikāya)*;[15] according to al-Shābushtī (d. 388/998), ʿAbbāda al-Mukhannath told Diʿbil that if he satirised him, he would 'produce' his mother in a *khayāl* (*la-ukhrijanna unmak fī 'l-khayāl)*;[16] and, according to Ibn ʿĀṣim al-Qaysī (d. 830/1426), a *mukhannath* threatened Diʿbil to 'produce' his mother in a *laʿba* (*la-ukhrijanna ummak fī 'l-laʿba)*.[17] In all three cases the threat is that a mother will be impersonated in a sketch of a satirical kind. For a description of such a sketch we may turn to Ibn al-Athīr, who tells us that the entertainer ʿAbbāda al-Mukhannath used to impersonate ʿAlī at the court of the Abbasid caliph al-Mutawakkil (d. 247/861):[18]

> al-Mutawakkil was full of hatred of ʿAlī b. Abī Tālib, upon him be peace, and his family ... Among his boon companions was ʿAbbāda al-Mukhannath. ʿAbbāda used to tie on his belly a pillow under his clothes, take off his headgear although he was bald, and dance before al-Mutawakkil while the singers would sing, 'The bald one with the paunch is coming, the caliph of the Muslims!' He would impersonate (*yaḥki*) ʿAli, upon him be peace, to the roaring [laughter] of al-Mutawakkil while the latter was drinking [wine]. Once ʿAbbāda engaged in this

performance while al-Muntaṣir [al-Mutawakkil's son and successor] was present. Al-Muntaṣir made a threatening gesture and 'Abbāda fell silent and went quiet out of fear of him. Al-Mutawakkil asked, 'What happened to you?' He got up and told him. Al-Muntaṣir said, 'Commander of the Faithful! What this dog[19] is impersonating (*yaḥkīhi*) and ridiculing is your cousin, the elder of your family and your pride. If you wish, you should slander him, but don't let this dog and his like do so along with you'. Al-Mutawakkil then gave orders to the singers: 'sing, all of you, "The boy protected his cousin / the head of the boy is in his mother's vulva"'. This was one of the reasons why al-Muntaṣir regarded the killing of al-Mutawakkil as lawful.

'Abbāda's display was one of silent mimcry; unlike the imitators admired by al-Jāḥiẓ, he mimicked appearance and behaviour to the exclusion of speech, and there does not appear to have been any dialogue at all. The sketch was none the less accompanied by words in the form of verses sung by the singers (or chorus, as one might say), and these must have been prepared in advance. To this extent the sketch could be said to have been based on a written text.

A *ḥikāya* of a similar type is described by Abū 'l-Faraj al-Iṣfahānī in his *Aghānī*, where we are told that the singer 'Alluwayh composed a sketch mocking a judge by the name of al-Khalanjī. The story goes as follows:[20]

Al-Khalanjī the judge whose name was 'Abd Allāh, was the nephew of 'Alluwayh the singer. He was haughty and arrogant. During the reign of al-Amīn [193–8/809–13] he was appointed judge of the Sharqiyya quarter [in Baghdad]. He used to seat himself by a pillar of the mosque reclining against it motionless. When the litigants approached him, he would lean towards them with his entire body, not reclining, in order to come between them. Then he would return to his previous position. One of the witty buffoons took a slip of paper, such as those papers on which legal proceedings are written, and fastened it with glue to the place where his turban rested [on the pillar], and covered it over with the same glue. When the parties in opposition approached the judge and he leaned towards them with his entire body, as he was wont to do, the turban stuck fast [to the pillar] and stayed hanging [there] and his head was uncovered. Al-Khalanjsī got up angrily, perceiving that a trick had been played on him. He covered his head with the shawl of his garb, and departed, leaving the turban in place, until one of his servants went and fetched it. A certain poet of that epoch composed some verses [ridiculing him] ... These verses and the story became widely known in Baghadad. 'Alluwayh composed a play (*ḥikāya*) which he handed over to

> the dancers (*zaffānūn*) and actors (*mukhannathūn*), and they presented him in it (*akhrajūhu fīhā*). ʿAlluwayh was odious to al-Khalanjī because of a dispute between them, and in this way he was able to disgrace him. As a result al-Khalanjī tendered his resignation from the jurisdiction in Baghdad and asked to be appointed to one of the distant areas, so he was appointed to the city of Damascus or Ḥimṣ.

Here we are explicitly told that the *ḥikāya* was based on a written text. Given that it was composed by a singer, it was presumably versified, and it was sung, danced and enacted by *zaffānūn* and *mukhannathūn*, on a par with the words in ʿAbbāda's sketch, though the precise division of labour is here left unspecified. The subject matter was once more satirical. Ridiculing judges and scholars seems to have been popular with actors and jesters throughout the Arab world.[21]

A very different type of play is described in the *ʿIqd al-Farīd* of Ibn ʿAbd Rabbih (d. 328/940).[22] It was not satirical; it involved no music or dancing or impersonation by *mukhannathūn*, indeed very little impersonation altogether; yet it was a more dramatic piece than the *ḥikāyāt* described so far by virtue of the fact that its subject was a trial. Ibn ʿAbd Rabbih's account of it is one of the longest descriptions of a play to be found in pre-modern Arabic literature; the play itself is one of the earliest, being dated to the time of the Abbasid caliph al-Mahdī (158–69/775–85).

The great importance of this play is its similarity to al-Jāḥiẓ's *Risāla fī Banī Umayya* [23] in content, style, order of events and the wording in several sentences. The comparison between the play of the Ṣūfī and al-Jāḥiẓ's *risāla* leaves but little doubt that the play formed the nucleus of this *risāla*. The fact that al-Jāḥiẓ *Risāla fī Ṣināʿat al-Quwwād* is the first *risāla* known to us in an apparently drama form, and that in his *al-Bayān wa'-l-Tabyīn* spoke about the talents of the *ḥākiya*, confirm our opinion that several plays of the *ḥikāya* and *khayāl* type, and not only popular stories,[24] formed the nucleus of several *rasāʾil* and *maqāmāt*.

Because of the importance of this play, the text was reproduced in Appendix I. It may be translated as follows:

> al-ʿUtbī said, I heard Abū ʿAbd al-Raḥmān Bishr say that in the reign of al-Mahdī there was a mystic (*rajul ṣūfī*) who was intelligent, learned and god-fearing, but who pretended to be a fool (*taḥammaqa*) in order to find a way of fulfilling the command to enjoin what is right and prohibit what is disapproved (*al-amr bi-'l-maʿrūf wa-'l-nahy ʿan al-munkar*) (Qur. 3:104, 110; 9:68, 72, 113). He used to ride on a reed two days a week, on Mondays and Thursdays. When he rode on those two days, no apprentices obeyed or were controlled by their masters. He

would go out (*yakhruju*) with men, women and boys, climb a hill and call out at the top of his voice, 'What have the prophets and messengers done? Are they not in the highest Heaven?' They [the audience] would say, 'Yes'. He would say, 'Bring Abū Bakr al-Siddīq', so a young boy (*ghulām*) would be taken and seated before him. He would say, 'May God reward you for your behaviour towards the subjects. You acted justly and fairly. You succeeded Muḥammad, may God bless him and grant him peace, and you joined together the rope of the faith after it had become unravelled in dispute, and you inclined to the firmest bond and the best trust. Let him go to the highest Heaven!' Then he would call, 'Bring 'Umar', so a young man would be seated in front of him. He would say, 'May God reward you for your services to Islam, Abū Ḥafṣ. You made the conquests, enlarged the spoils of war and followed the path of the upright. You acted justly towards the subjects and distributed [the spoils] equally. Take him to the highest Heaven! beside Abū Bakr.' Then he would say, 'Bring 'Uthmān', so a young man would be brought and seated in front of him. He would say to him, 'You mixed [good and bad] in those six years,[25] but God, exalted is He, says, 'They mixed a good deed with with another evil. It may be that God will turn towards them' (Qur. 9:103). Perhaps there is foregiveness from God'. Then he would say, 'take him to his two friends in the highest Heaven'. Then he would say, 'Bring 'Alī b. Abī Ṭālib', and a young boy would be seated in front of him. He would say, 'May God reward you for your services to the *umma*, Abū 'l-Ḥasan, for you are the legatee and friend of the Prophet (*al-waṣiy wa-waliy 'l-nabī*). You spread justice and were abstemious in this world, withdrawing from the spoils of was instead of fighting for them with tooth and nail. You are the father of blessed progeny and the husband of a pure and upright woman. Take him to the highest Heaven of Paradise'. Then he would say, 'Bring Mu'āwiya', so a boy would be seated before him and he would say to him, 'You are the killer of 'Ammār b. Yāsir, Khuzayma b. Thābit Dhū'l-Shahādatayn and Ḥujr b. al-Adbar al-Kindī,[26] whose face was worn out by worship. You are the one who transformed the caliphate into kingship, who monopolised the spoils, gave judgement in accordance with whims and asked the assistance of transgressors. You were the first to change the *sunna* of the Prophet, may God bless him and grant him peace, to violate his rulings and to practise tyranny. Take him and place him with the transgressors'. Then he would say, 'Bring Yazīd', so a young man would be seated before him. He would say to him, 'You pimp, you are the one who killed the people of the Ḥarra and

> laid Medina open to the troops for three days, thereby violating the sanctuary of the Prophet, may God bless him and grant him peace. You harboured the godless and thereby made yourself deserving of being cursed by the Prophet, may God bless him and grant him peace. You recited the pagan verse, 'I wish that my elders had seen the fear of the Khazraj at Badr when the arrows fell'. You killed Ḥusayn and carried off the daughters of the Prophet as captives [riding pillion] on the camel-bags. Take him to the lowest Hell!'. He would continue to mention ruler after ruler until he reached 'Umar b. 'Abd al-'Azīz, then he would say, 'Bring 'Umar', and a young boy would be brought and be seated before him. He would say, 'May God reward you for your services to Islam, for you revived justice after it had died and softened the merciless hearts; through you the pillar of the faith has been restored after dissension and hypocrisy. Take him and let him join the righteous'. Then he would enumerate the subsequent caliphs until he reached the dynasty of the Abbasids, whereupon he would fall silent. He would be told, 'This is al-'Abbās, the Commander of the Faithful'. He would reply, 'We have got to the Abbasids; do their reckoning collectively and throw all of them into Hell'.

Ibn 'Abd Rabbih gives the contents of this play in his chapter on 'bilious and mad men' because its Ṣūfī author and actor pretended to be a fool. Foolishness was diligently cultivated by many entertainers in the Abbasid period, as has been seen; but unlike Abū 'l-'Ibar and other buffoons at the Abbasid court, the Ṣūfī played the fool in order to fulfil a religious injunction, riding on a reed rather than a horse[27] and engaging in the despised activity of play-acting in order to humiliate himself (though there was nothing humble about the role he took in the play itself). He thus belonged in the tradition of the saintly fools described by John of Ephesus whose methods were perpetuated by the Malāmatīs.[28] His play was a truly Islamic one, both in its purpose (to enjoin good and prohibit evil) and in its subject-matter (a review of the early caliphs).[29] Indeed, one might call it a 'morality play'.

The imaginary trial seems to have been enacted almost entirely through monologue and to have involved very little action. Apart from the Ṣūfī himself, all the actors were young boys whose role was limited to sitting in front of the judge. But apparently there was some audience participation. It must have been the audience that protested at the judge's silence when Abū 'l-'Abbās was brought in (the only alternative being Abū 'l-'Abbās himself); and it was presumably the audience that brought the 'caliphs' in when they were summoned by the judge and took them out again after they had been sentenced (the judge's orders are given in the second person plural). The stage was a hill, and the play was performed twice a week before large audiences of men, women and children (or at least boys), all of whom would abandon their daily tasks in order to attend. According to the narrator Abū 'Abd al-Raḥmān Bishr (d. 218/833),[30] the play had a great impact on the audience, but whether others took up this style of performance is not stated.

Ibn 'Abd Rabbih does not identify the play as a *ḥikāya*, but one assumes that this is what he would have called it, no other term being available at the time. Nor does he say that it was based on a written text, but the Ṣūfī must have memorized his part: the play was performed regularly, apparently without much variation. The young boys may well have been professional, or at least regular, actors too. Ibn 'Abd Rabbih could be admittedly be taken to say that they were picked at random from the audience: 'a young boy would be taken and placed in front of him (*fa-ukhidha ghulām fa-ujlisa bayna yadayhi*), as he says some six times with slight stylistic variations, thereby conveying the impression that the boys were chosen by the audience. But this should hardly be taken literally. The same impression is conveyed by Ibn al-Ḥājj's description of the Amīr al-Nayrūz discussed in the previous chapter: 'They would choose someone from among them ... they would change his countenance with lime and flour and stick a beard of fur or the like on him. Then they would dress him in a red or yellow garment ... they would put a long conical cap (*ṭurṭūr*) on his head and made him ride an ugly donkey, surrounding him with green palm branches and bunches of dates and putting something in his hand that looked like a ledger'.[31] But the same impression is also conveyed by al-Ṭahṭāwī's description of French theatre in the 1820s: 'If they want to play the Shāh of the Persians, for example, they will dress an actor in the garb of the king of the Persians, bring him [to the stage] and make him sit on a chair, and so on.[32] Yet French actors were not chosen, dressed or given a role by the audience. In all three cases the authors would thus appear to be using a literary convention.

Ḥikāyat Abī 'l-Qāsim al-Baghdādī

The fact that the ninth century *Ḥikāyat al-Khalanjī* was composed as a play to be performed by live actors suggests that the same may be true of another *ḥikāya* which is actually extant in full, that is *Ḥikāyat Abī al-Qāsim al-Baghdādī*..

The *Ḥikāyat Abī 'l-Qāsim al-Baghdādī* was composed by Muḥammad b. Aḥmad Abū 'l-Muṭahhar al-Azdī and published by Adam Mez under the title *Ein baghdader Sittenbild*. Mez deduced from some dates mentioned in the *Ḥikāya* that it was composed about 400/ 1009–10.[33] On the other hand, 'Abbūd al-Shāljī, who republished this *Ḥikāya* under the title of *Al-Risāla al-Baghdādiyya*, attributed it to Abū Ḥayyān 'Alī b. Muḥammad al-Tawḥīdī (d. 414/1023), and not to Abū al-Muṭahhar al-Azdī as the manuscript states. Al-Shāljī, who used the MS of this *Ḥikāya* kept at the British Library, argued that it was composed by al-Tawḥīdī in 371/981–2.[34] But this is unlikely to be correct.

The author states in his introduction that his *Ḥikāya* is a compilation of works by several authors and poets, both old and contemporary. Most of the poetic citations are from the scurrilous work of Ibn al-Ḥajjāj (d. 391/1001),[35] while the longest prose passage cited is from al-Tawḥīdī's *al-Imtā' wa'l-Mu'ānasa.*[36] Yet these citations are not copied word for word, as they would have been if copied from a written text or by the author himself; rather they are scrambled. Names of persons and singers cited by al-Tawḥīdī are mixed up.[37] Thus curses by Dajāja al-Mukhannath cited by al-Tawḥīdī in *al-Imta' wa-'l-Mu'ānasa* are mixed up with the dialogue of *shuṭṭār* cited by al-Ābī in *Nathr al-Durr.*[38] Similarly, Ibn al-Ḥajjāāj's verses satirising 'Isā b. Marwān al-Kātib al-Naṣrānī are mixed up with verses by Ibn al-Nājim Sa'īd b. al-Ḥusayn al-Sam'ī (d. 341/942) that appear in a totally different order in al-Tha'ālibī's in *Yatīmat al-Dahr.*[39] This changing around of verses, prose paragraphs and names presumably occurred because the author cited from memory and not from a written text, an assumption corroborated by the author's own statement in his introduction: 'This is the literature I have acquired from other writers, with which I adorn myself, which I claim for myself and (then) relate, along with treatises and verses of my own composition.'[40] It is thus unlikely that the author of the *Ḥikāya* is al-Tawḥīdī as al-Shāljī suggested.

The plot of the *ḥikāya* is simple. Abū 'l-Qāsim enters the house of a person of rank for a party, pretending to be a pious man and wearing a garment (*ṭaylasān*) to go with the pretense. On meeting notable persons, he recites the Qur'an and scolds those who smile with reference to the fact that Ḥusayn was killed at Karbalā', reciting some verses on his martyrdom. He continues in this vein until somebody tells him not to worry: here everyone drinks and fornicates. Only then does he start his performance. He begins by asking the host who the guests might be, and, on learning the answer, responds by uttering insulting remarks on the name and the profession. His remarks are full of ugly, dirty, morbid and pessimistic ideas and jokes, with a strong inclination towards obscenity, scatology and exceedingly vulgar language. When he is reprimanded for these remarks, he responds by uttering more revolting abuse and nasty verses, provoking anger in some of those present, and causing others to join in. Whereas other people's remarks are short, Abū 'l-Qāsim's are long and decorated with verses. If anyone laughs at him, he gets furious and emits a barrage of rude answers and blasphemies against the Qur'ān, the Prophet and all the sacred things of Islam,[41] boasting about his blasphemies in a manner reminiscent of Amīr Wiṣāl in Ibn Dāniyāl's shadow-play *Ṭayf al-Khayāl*.[42] When Iṣfahān is mentioned, he starts comparing it with Baghdad,[43] praising the latter as Paradise and denigrating Iṣfahān as an inferior city in the well-known style of *mufākhara* and *munāẓara*. He dwells on this subject for a long time, comparing the quarters, people, professions, horses, clothes, names, foods, wines and singers of the two cities, until eventually he asks for food. He recites a long poem on the kind of food he would like to eat, and when told that he is too demanding, adds further kinds of food to the list, describing how they are prepared. After he has eaten, he plays chess and makes full use of his repertoire of rude remarks while so doing, commenting on every move made by his opponent. Next he begins to satirise Baghdad, enumerating terms relating to swimming, boats and ships, as well as sailors' expressions in the process, and goes on to praise the people of Iṣfahān in a reversal of the first *mufākhara*. Next he turns to the players of mandoline (*ṭumbūrī*) and lute (*'awwād*) and flirts with the singing girl, reciting amorous verses to her and dirty verses to two men who approach her. He then farts in her presence and, when reprimanded by her, recites verses on farting in a manner reminiscent of the *ḍarrāṭūn* at the Abbasid court.[44] The guests eventually get tired of Abū 'l-Qāsim's fooling around and decide to get him drunk. He notices their intentions and starts cursing every single one of them. After being scolded for his rudeness, he asks the singer to sing and starts dancing and reciting verses until he falls to the ground. He curses the singer, using musical terms and a long poem of impudence. At last he falls into a drunken stupor. When he gets up the next morning at the call of prayer, he starts reproving the guests for their impudence, and calls upon them to repent. He once more recites verses from the Qur'ān and pious verses in praise of Ḥusayn with which he started his performance. He then puts on his garment as before and leaves the house.

The very title of *Ḥikāyat Abī 'l-Qāsim al-Baghdādī* suggests that the work is a repertoire of theatrical scenes played in tenth-century Baghdad, put together by the author to mock Shi'ite piety and depict everyday life in Baghdad. That *ḥikāya* meant impersonation or mime to him is clear from a passage in which he describes 'Abū 'Abd Allāh al-Marzubānī ... rolling around in the dust, ranging and roaming, snorting and fuming, biting his fingertips, kicking with his legs and slapping his face a thousand times all the while. When he performed this mime (*kharaja fī 'l-ḥikāya*), he was like 'Abd al-Razzāq the madman at al-Ṭāq Gate'.[45] Besides, he actually compares his work with that of the mimic (*ḥākiya*) mentioned by al-Jāḥiẓ, saying that they are similar.[46] Unlike the mimics who performed to the accompaniment of song, al-Jāḥiẓ' impersonator did not engage in silent mimicry, but rather told a story in the course of which he would imitate people's behaviour and accent. This is precisely how Abū 'l-Muṭahhar's *ḥikāya* could have been performed. The author also defines his work as a *risāla* (treatise), a *qiṣṣa* (tale), a *ḥadīth* (story) and a *samar* (conversation at an evening gathering),[47] requesting the reader or audience to listen to the verse by Ibn al-Ḥajjāj declaring (*basīṭ* meter) ' Sir! All my talk is nightly chat / Be free to listen to this nightly chat from me' ([*Yā*] *sayyidī wa-ḥadīthī kulluhu samarun / ufrugh li-tasma' minnī dhālika 'l-samara*).[48]

In fact there is much evidence to suggest that *Ḥikāyat Abī 'l-Qāsim* is a play composed for recitation by a live actor (or actors), or at least a collection of theatrical scenes seen or read by the author and put together by him to form a burlesque.

First, we may note that Abū 'l-Qāsim, the protagonist, is described as someone mimed or alternatively as a mimic. The senseless sentence in which he is characterised as a *maḥallī*, 'a local person', is clearly the result of one of the many copying errors in which the book abounds.[49] *Maḥallī* should be emended to *maḥkī* or *muḥākī*: 'this impersonated person/impersonator was known as Abū 'l-Qāsim ... al-Baghdādī'.[50] Abū 'l-Qāsim is also said to have 'acquired the manners of entertainers (*makhānīth*) and monkey-trainers (*qarrādīn*) and used to reach the arts of the astrologers and jugglers (*al-zarrāqīn wa-'l-musha'bidhīn*)';[51] and he twice refers to one of the guests at the party as 'our master, the mimic' (*sayyidunā al-mumayyis*).[52]

Second, the text is constructed as a continuous dialogue between Abū 'l-Qāsim and the guests at the party, with Abū 'l-Qāsim doing most of the talking. In this respect the *Ḥikāya* resembles the 'Trial of the Caliphs'. In both cases the action is focused on a single actor who approaches members of the audience or has subsidiary actors brought to him so that he can talk to them: the subsidiary actors say little or nothing. In neither case is there any suggestion that the actors dressed up, though they commonly did so in other *ḥikāyāt*; and in both cases there was scope for improvisation.

The text of *Ḥikāyat Abī 'l-Qāsim* actually alludes to improvisation on several occasions. When Abū 'l-Qāsim asks the host about the name of the visitors at the beginning of the *Ḥikāya*, the text states that Abū 'l-Qāsim 'would say, for instance (*mathalan*) ... [such and such]';[53] he was free to vary the statement. Elsewhere we are told that such and such food and other things 'might be brought to him',[54] which again suggests that he was meant to improvise in the fashion familiar from *commedia dell' arte*, in which the actor knows the general plot in advance, but is free to extemporise. It also informs us that props were used. All this could be taken to mean that the episodes contained in the work were meant to be enacted by a single *ḥākiya*..

Third, the text is full of *maskhara* elements of the type we have met already. Thus Abū 'l-Qāsim recites that 'today is the day of my buffoonery and of my dancing and acting/playing' (*al-yawma yawmu mujūnī/wa-yawmu raqsī wa-la'bī*),[55] though in keeping with his chameleon-like character he is also made to deny that he is a buffoon himself.[56] The jokes he tells are typical of those associated with impersonation too. A characteristic example is his jokes about slave girls:[57]

> Another [entertainer] said, 'I saw a black slave girl, plump and fat, in a street in Baghdad. I told my friend that nobody in the world makes more farts than a black woman. She answered quickly, 'In your beard, old man!' Another one related, 'I inspected a pretty slave girl. I hesitated in buying her because she was lame. She said, 'if you want to buy a camel in order to go on pilgrimage, then I am no use to you. But if you want a slave girl for enjoyment, lameness does not stand in your way'.

Finally, it should be noted that the *Ḥikāyat Abī 'l-Qāsim al-Baghdādī* incorporates dialogue material which is attested as early as the reign of al-Mutawakkil (d. 247/861) and which is also found in the *Maqāma Dināriyya* of al-Hamadhānī (d. 1007), in the *Nathr al-Durr* of al-Ābī (d. 421/1030) and in a shadow play by Ibn Dāniyāl (d. 710/1310–11).

The first attestation of this material is in a report by a postmaster by the name of Ibn al-Kalbī in the reign of al-Mutawakkil:

> To al-Mutawakkil:
>
> Yesterday, the (man) known as Ibn al-Maghribī the commander crossed the bridge drunk. He snored and snorted, prattled, roared and rumbled, and did bub bub with his mouth. He crossed the path to the water and rushed forth saying: 'I am a rhinoceros! So beware of me!' (*anā 'l-karkadan fa'rifūnī*).[58]

According to al-Ābī, the sentence *anā 'l-karkadan fa'rifūnī* is part of a dialogue between four *shuṭṭār* characters (urban rowdies) called Ṣaḥnāt, Ḥarmala, Ghazzūn and Ṭafshiyya, who were rivals for the favor of a beardless youth (*amrad*). Ṣaḥnāt, the first *shāṭir*, speaking in prose rhymed couplets says: *anā 'l-jamalu 'l-hā'ij, anā 'l-karkadannu 'l-mu'ālij, anā 'l-fīlu 'l-mughtalim, anā 'l-dahru al-muṣṭalim* … ('I am the rutting camel, I am the surging rhinoceros, I am the elephant seized by sexual desire, I am the exterminating time …').[59] Al-Hamadhānī divided this dialogue between Abū 'l-Fatḥ and a beggar in his *al-Maqāma al-Dīnāriyya*.[60] On the other hand, in *Ḥikāyat Abī 'l-Qāsim* the four dialogues are given in a different sequence and transformed into a monologue; and the sentence *anā 'l-karkadan al-mu'ālij* ('I am the surging rhinoceros') is missing. But this is probably due to careless redaction in the manuscript. For the previous sentence, *anā 'l-jamal al-hā'ij*, with which *anā 'l-karkadan al-mu'ālij* rhymes, is there,[61] and one paragraph starts with the words *wā-laka ta'rifunī* ('woe to you, beware of me!').[62] At all events, the drunken commander was clearly familiar with material later taken up by Abū 'l-Qāsim and others. Whether he had heard it recited or actually seen it enacted cannot be established, though al-Ābī's division of the dialogue between four characters (*shuṭṭār*) suggests that such material was in fact used for dramatic performance. The fact that dialogue material from the time of al-Mutawakkil is to be found in *Ḥikāyat Abī 'l-Qāsim al-Baghdādī*, al-Hamadhānī,[63] al-Ābī and Ibn Dāniyal alike, certainly suggests that they all made use of oral dialogue from live plays. Moreover, if the play of the Ṣūfī from the time of the caliph al-Mahdī was the nucleus of al-Jāḥiẓ's *Risāla fī Banī Umayya* is right, then we have another evidence that Arabic live plays influenced highbrow literature.

All in all there is therefore reason to suppose that *Ḥikāyat Abī 'l-Qāsim* was not only meant to depict the repertoire of buffoons and mimes, or to give a realistic presentation of Baghdadi society, but also to provide material for dramatic performances. Bits of it were certainly used by later dramatists.[64] In Ibn Dāniyal's shadow play *Bābat Ṭayf al-Khayāl* ('The Play of the Phantom') the protagonist, al-Amīr Wiṣāl, presents himself with the following passage:[65]

> I butt more than a ram and stink worse than a monster. I steal swifter than slumber and I am more of a sodomite than Abū Nuwās. I grew up among ... I am the disgrace of the faultfinder and the sins of the sinner. I am the boxing fist of the stoker and a wink in the eye of a pimp. I slap more than the palm of a baker ... I am a nightly entertainer and a gambler. I am a mocker,[67] a slanderer, a biter, a carper and blamer, a creeper (at night to rape youths sleeping in the same house or *khān*), a riotous person, a threatener, a devotee and an assassin.

This is clearly based on Abū 'l-Muṭahhar's presentation of Abū 'l-Qāsim in his *Ḥikāya*:[68]

> This impersonated person/impersonator was known as Abū 'l-Qāsim ... He was a nightly entertainer and a gambler, a sodomite [engaging in sexual intercourse] from behind, a boisterous man, a mocker, a slanderer, a blamer, an abuser and a faultfinder, a riotous person and a defamator ... worse than the mud of fishmongers and more stinking than the smell of tanners. He grew up among (rowdies of Banū Sāsān such as) Dakkūl, Daqqīsh, Qammūr and Zankalāsh. He trusts in and draws out. He is the disgrace of the faultfinder and the sins of sinners. He is the boxing fist of a stoker.

The author of *Ḥikāyat Abī 'l-Qāsim* tells us that he used to be closely associated with Abū 'l-Qāsim and heard both pleasant and vulgar expressions from him which he collected in one *ḥikāya.*[69] In this *ḥikāya,* he says, his work became like that of al-Jāḥiẓ' *ḥākiya.* Apparently Abū 'l-Qāsim did not perform all the *ḥikāya* at one time, but rather used bits suitable to various occasions. The author-redactor unified them in a single *ḥikāya* to be recited or acted by an actor who was free to improvise as he saw fit in response to the reaction of the audience.

Notes

1. Cf. Ibn Manẓūr, *Lisān al-'Arab,* s.v. (where the meaning is only given as 'imitation'); Lane, *Lexicon,* s.v. (where it is only given as 'story, narration and tale'); A.-'A. Abdel-Maguid, *The Modern Arabic Short Story* (Cairo, n.d. [1956?]), pp. 14–18.
2. C. Pellat, 'Ḥikāya' in EI[2]
3. Al-Jāḥiẓ, *Rasā'il al-Jāḥiẓ* (Cairo, 1933), p. 68.
4. Id. *al-Bayān wa-'l-Tabyīn* (Cairo, 1288/1968), vol. I, pp. 69f.
5. al-Shābushtī, *Diyārāt,* pp. 12f. On Ibn Ḥamdūn's family, see Yāqūt, *Mu'jam al-Udabā',* vol. II, pp. 204–18; on Jaḥza al-Barmakī, see ibid, pp. 241–88.
6. al-Musabbiḥī, *Akhbār Miṣr,* pp. 18f.
7. al-Sha'rānī, *al-Ṭabaqāt al-Kubrā* (Cairo, n.d.), pp. 123f.
8. Mattā b. Yūnis in Badawī, *Fann,* pp. 86, 88–92, 98, etc.
9. Ibn Sīnā in Badawī, *Fann,* pp. 173, 175, 176, 180, 184, 191, 194, 197, 198.
10. Ibn Abī Uṣaybi'a, *Kitāb 'Uyūn al-Anbā' fī Ṭabaqāt al-Aṭibbā'* (Cairo, 1299/1882), vol. I, p. 26, where incompetent physicians are compared with 'the figures (*ashbāḥ*) which actors (*aṣḥāb al-ḥikāya*) present in order to entertain people. They are but masks (*ṣuwar*) without reality'. Cf. Hippokrates, *al-Waṣiyya* in F. Sezgin, *Geschichte des arabischen Schrifttums* (Leiden, 1970), vol. III, p. 39; id., *Oeuvres Complètes d'Hippocrate,* ed. and tr. E. Littré (Amsterdam, 1962), vol. IV, pp. 638 (Greek), 639 (French). For the term *shabaḥ,* pl. *ashbāḥ* see al-Ghazūlī, *Maṭāli' al-Budūr fī Manāzil al-Surūr* (Cairo, 1299/1881f), vol. I, p. 230; al-Rāghib al-Iṣfahānī, *Muḥāḍarāt al-Udabā,* vol. I, p.442.
11. Maimonides, *Commentaire,* vol. I, p. 189, 1. 35. The text is in Arabic in Hebrew characters.
12. Above, Ch. 1, p. 8.
13. Cf. Pellat, 'Ḥikāya', col. 369a.
14. Cf. above, Ch. 2, p. 34.
15. Ibn Abī 'Awn, *al-Ajwiba al-Muskita,* ed. Muḥammad 'Abd al-Qādir Aḥmad (Cairo, 1985), p. 133 (my thanks to J. Sadan for supplying me with a copy of this book); al-Shābushtī, *Diyārāt,* p. 188, n. 16 (where the editor cites Iraqi Museum, MS no. 744, fol. 31b; I was unable to get a microfilm of this manuscript). On Ibrahim Ibn Abī 'Awn, see EI[2], s.v.

16. al-Shābushtī, *Diyārāt*, p. 188; cf. p. 185 where the verb *ḥākā* is used instead of *khayāl*.
17. Ibn 'Āṣim al-Qaysī, *Ḥadā'iq*, fol. 12b (corresponding to id., *Hada'iq al-Azhār*, MS Bibliothèque Nationale, arabe 3528, fol. 10b; my thanks to Prof. J. Sadan for pointing out this passage to me.
18. Ibn al-Athīr, *Kāmil*, vol. VII. pp. 55f. On 'Abbāda, see above, Ch. 2, n. 5.
19. The text wrongly has *kātib* for *kalb*.
20. al-Iṣfahānī, *Aghānī*, vol. XI, pp. 338f; also quoted by Yāqūt, *Udabā'*, vol. II, pp. 220–24, where al-Khalanjī's name has been changed to al-Khalījī.
21. Cf. Ch. 7, pp. 134f (Ibn al-Ḥājj, al-Sha'rānī).
22. Ibn 'Abd Rabbih, *'Iqd*, vol. VI, pp. 152f; also reproduced in A. al-Yamanī al-Shirwānī, *Ḥadīqat al-Afrāḥ*, (Būlāq, 1282/1865), p. 185, where the verb *taḥammaqa* (pretended to be a fool) in *'Iqd*, is changed into *tajannana* (pretended to be mad).
23. al-Jāḥiẓ, *Rasā'il al-Jāḥiẓ*, pp. 292–300. The comparison between the two works is in Appendix I. For a similar *ḥikāya* based upon dialogue, see al-Naysābūrī, *'Uqalā' al-Majānin* pp. 183ff.
24. A. Miquel, *La Littérature Arabe* (Paris, 1969), p. 81; cf. also R. Blachère and P. Mansou, *Al-Hamadhānī-choix de maqāmāt* (Paris, 1957), pp. 4, 7–13; and Sadan, 'Kings', Pt. I, pp. 23, 37.
25. A curious statement: 'Uthmān is supposed to have mixed good and bad in the twelve years of this reign, the first six being good and the last six bad, cf. al-Jāḥiẓ, *Risāla ... fī Banī Umayya*, in id. *Rasā'il al-Jāḥiẓ*, p. 292, where he says: *wa-sitt sinīn min khilāfat 'Uthmān* ('and six years out of the caliphate of 'Uthmān').
26. According to al-Jāḥiẓ, *Radā'il al-Jāḥiẓ*, p. 294, he is Ḥujr b. 'Adiyy.
27. Compare the woman who rides a palm-leaf stalk in one of Ibn Sūdūn's *maqāmāt* Ch. 4, p. 77. See also our suggestion that the riding on a reed might be a Shamanic influence on the Muslim World in Ch. 2, p. 34.
28. Cf. N. Molé, *Les Mystiques Musulmans* (Paris, 1965), pp. 72f.
29. Compare Abū Ḥamza the Khārijite on the early caliphs in P. Crone and M. Hinds, *God's Caliph, Religious Authority in the First Centuries of Islam* (Cambridge, 1986), pp. 129–32. On the possibility of Shamanic influences on this play, see Ch. 2, pp. 34.
30. See *E.I.2* art. Bishr b. Ghiyāth.
31. Ibn al-Ḥājj, *Madkhal*, vol. II, p. 52.
32. al-Ṭahṭāwī, *Talkhīṣ*, p. 166.
33. Mez, *Abulḳāsim ein baghdāder Sittenbild*. On Abū 'l-Muṭahhar, see also al-Bākharzī, *Dumyat al-Qaṣr* (Cairo, 1968), vol. I, pp. 434–6 (under Abū 'l-Muṭahhar al-Iṣfahānī). On the *Ḥikāya*, see also F. Gabrieli, 'Sulla Ḥikāyat Abī 'l-Qāsim di Abī 'l-Muṭahhar al-Azdī', *Rivista degli Studi Orientali XX* (1942), pp. 33–45.
34. 'A. al-Shāljī (ed.), *al-Risāla al-Baghdādiyya* (Beirut, 1400/1980). Al-Shāljī was influenced by M. Jawād, 'Ḥikāyat Abī 'l-Qāsim al-Baghdādī, hal allafahā Abū Ḥayyān al-Tawḥīdī?', *al-'Irfān* (Ṣaydā) XLII, nos. 5–6, March 1955, pp. 561–6.

35. Mez, *Sittenbild*, pp. 6, 61–6, 134, 142–5. Other poets cited are Abū Nuwās (p. 14), Ibn al-Rūmī (p. 99), al-Buḥturī (p. 50), Kushājim (p. 101), and Ibn al-Muʿtazz (pp. 27, 106).
36. Mez, *Sittenbild*, pp. 78–87; cf. al-Tawḥīdī, *Imtāʿ*, vol. II, pp. 165–83.
37. Cf. Ibid, p. 166 (Ibn Fahm al-Ṣūfī); Mez, *Sittenbild*, pp. 78 (where Ibn Fahm's reaction to singing is attributed to Abū ʿAbd Allāh al-Marzubānī), p. 81 (where Ibn Fahm reappears as Ibn al-Mutayyam al-Ṣūfī).
38. al-Tawḥīdī, *Imtāʿ*, vol. II, pp. 59f; al-Ābī, *Nathr*, vol. III, pp. 295, 300–4; Mez, *Sittenbild*, pp. 137–40.
39. Ibn al-Ḥajjāj in *Tadhkirat Ibn Ḥamdūn*, MS British Library, Or. 3179, fol. 321b; al-Thaʿālibī, *Yatīma*, vol. III, pp. 35–8; Mez, *Sittenbild*, pp. 142f.
40. Ibid. p. 1.
41. Ibid. p. 19.
42. Ibid. p. 137; cf. I. Ḥamāda, *Khayāl al-Ẓill* (Cairo, 1963), pp. 154f.
43. Ibid. p. 21.
44. On *ḍarrāṭūn* cf. Ch. 4, pp. 68–9; Sadan, *Adab*, pp. 29–49; cf. also al-Rāghib al-Iṣfahānī, *Muḥāḍarāt al-Udabāʾ*, vol. I, p. 442.
45. Mez, *Sittenbild*, p. 78; cf. Abū Ḥayyān al-Tawḥīdī, *Imtaʿ*, vol. II, p. 166. For *kharaja fī 'l-ḥikāya* in the sense of performing a live play, see Ch. 7, pp. 131–8.
46. Mez, *Sittenbild*, pp. 1f. He adds that his *ḥikāya* depicts one whole day, or a night and a day: are we to take it that he was familiar with Aristotle's finding that tragedy 'tries, as far as possible, to keep within a single revolution of the sun, or only slightly to exceed it' (Dorsch, *Classical Literary Criticism*, p. 38)?
47. Mez, *Sittenbild*, pp. 1f (*risāla*), 4 (*qiṣṣa, ḥadīth*), 3 (*samar*), cf. pp. 3, 146 (*ḥikāya*). On the definition of these terms, see Pellat, 'Ḥikāya'; Abdel-Maguid, *Short Story*, pp. 14–18.
48. Mez, *Sittenbild*, p. 3.
49. Ibid., p. 6. It is clear that the play took place in Iṣfahān (cf. ibid., p. 21, where Abū 'l-Qāsim addresses the guests as 'O people of Iṣfahān'); but Abū 'l-Qāsim was a Baghdadi and thus not a local person. Al-Shāljī emends *al-maḥallī* to *al-mujallī*, explaining it as *al-mujallī min al-sabq*, 'the winner in the race' (ibid., pp. 10, 46); but this does not fit the context.
50. The emendation *al-maḥkī* was suggested by M. H. al-Aʿrajī, *Fann al-Tamthīl 'inda 'l-'Arab* (Baghdad, 1978), p. 75. I suggested *al-muḥākī* in my 'Live Theatre in Medieval Islam', pp. 606f (cf. al-Masʿūdī, *Murūj*, vol. VIII, p. 109, where a Khalawayh al-Muḥākī is mentioned); but I think that al-Aʿrajī's suggestion is sounder.
51. Mez, *Sittenbild*, p. 4.
52. Ibid., 16. *Mumayyis* is probably a corruption of *muyammis*, attested in David ben Abraham al-Fāsī (cf. Ch. 1, n. 56); cf. also Dozy, *Supplément*, vol. II, p. 631, col. 1, though al-Shāljī explains it as pimp (*qawwād*) on the basis of the continuation of the statement *sayyidunā mumayyis aw-maṭrūḥ, mā lī uṭawwil al-qiṣṣa, sayyidunā qawwād*, ct. ibid., p. 78n and Mez, *Sittenbild*, p. 16. Neither

mumayyis nor *maṭrūḥ* figures in Aḥmad al-Tīfāshī (d. 651/1253), '*Fī Awṣāf al-Qawwādīn wa-'l-Qawwādāt wa-mā jā'a fīhim min Nawādir al-Ash'ār*', in his *Nuzhat al-Albāb fīmā lā yūjad fī kitāb*, MS Bibliothèque Nationale, arabe 3055, fols 10a–20b, which deals with pimps. In Dozy, *Supplément*, vol. II, p. 32, col. 2, the word *muṭarraḥ* means merry and joyful.
53. Mez, *Sittenbild*, p. 6.
54. Ibid., pp. 6, 100, 104.
55. Ibid., p. 134.
56. Ibid., pp. 75f.; cf. pp. xv, xviii, where Mez describes this *ḥikāya* as mimesis and burlesque.
57. Ibid., pp. 75f; cf. Bar-Hebraeus, *Laughable Stories*, p. 105 (Syriac), 129 (English); Bosworth, *Underworld*,, p. 20.
58. al-Ḥuṣrī, *Dhayl*, p. 99.
59. al-Ābī, *Nathr*, vol. III, p. 300, l. 14.
60. al-Hamadhānī, *Maqāmāt*, ed. M. 'Abduh, 2nd edn (Beirut, 1908), No. 43, pp. 224–30.
61. Mez, *Sittenbild*, p. 137, l. 23.
62. Mez, *Sittenbild*, p. 139.
63. al-Hamadhānī, *Maqāmāt*, no. 43, pp. 224–30; Mez, *Sittenbild*, pp. 137–40.
64. Note also that the shadow play *al-'Āshiq wa-'l-Ma'shūq* is called a *ḥikāya* as well as a *faṣl* (Wetzstein, *Die Liebenden*, p. 132).
65. I. Ḥamāda, *Khayāl al-Ẓill*, pp. 154f.
66. reading *asraq* for *ashraf*.
67. reading *ṭannāz* for *ṭaffāz*.
68. Mez, *Sittenbild*, p. 3.
69. Ibid., p. 1.

6

Ḥikāya and Literary Genres: *Maqāma* and *Risāla*

From prior discussions it has become clear that the *ḥikāya* was a play performed by actors, sometimes dressed in accordance with the requirements of the 'dramatis personae' and sometimes using props as well. The *ḥikāya* was well developed before the emergence of the shadow play. It is not clear whether any *ḥikāya* or *khayāl*, as it came to be known, was actually staged by shadow play presenters or whether the latter relied exclusively on new plays composed for them. The sources do not enable us to say whether a play composed as *ḥikāya* or *Khayāl* might be adopted for the shadow play.[1] However, as we have seen, certain paragraphs in *Ḥikāyat Abī 'l-Qāsim al-Baghdādī* are found both in al-Hamadhānī's *al-Maqāma al-Dīnāriyya* and in Ibn Dāniyāl's *Bābat Ṭayf al-Khayāl*. In fact Ibn Dāniyāl hints in his poetry that live actors and shadow play presenters used to perform side by side in the taverns he frequented;[2] and he himself a composer of shadow plays for 'Alī b. Mawlāhum al-Kayālī, complains that his wife used to force him to take his child with him to perform dances of live plays with him (*uraqqiṣuhu bi-anwā'i 'l-khayāli*).[3] It is thus clear that there was interaction between the two genres.

The *ḥikāya* was also well developed before the emergence of the *maqāma* and *risāla*, both of which rely on dialogue for their dramatic effect, and it greatly influenced these genres. Previous scholars have not devoted much attention to its role in the development of medieval Arabic literature, but that it did play such a role is clear. Many writers and scholars attended performances at the Abbasid court of plays such as the *ḥikāya* of 'Abbāda al-Mukhannath (performed in the presence of al-Mutawakkil and his boon-companions, who included well-known authors) and 'Alluwayh's *Ḥikāyat al-Khalanjī*, of which we are explicitly told that it became famous.[4] The fact that al-Tawḥīdī compared the artificial behaviour of al-Ṣāḥib b. 'Abbād (d. 995) with that of a *samāja* actor impersonating prostitutes shows that these performances made an impression on the literary circles of the Abbasid period.

The *maqāma*

The *maqāma* elaborated by Badīʿ al-Zamān al-Hamadhānī (969-1007) is a short and ornate 'picaresque' work in rhymed prose, couched in the first person singular.[5] It usually contains a narrative element consisting of an amusing or surprising, real or true to life scene, and it is formulated in the present tense. In every *maqāma* there is a narrator (*rāwī*) called ʿĪsā Ibn Hishām, and a hero, Abū 'l-Fatḥ al-Iskandarī, who generally appears as a disguised beggar (*mukaddī*) trying to earn his living by his wits, his linguistic virtuosity and rhetorical talent. Nearly every *maqāma* begins with the sentence *ḥaddathanā ʿĪsā Ibn Hishām, qāla* ... (ʿĪsā Ibn Hishām narrated to us, saying ...) suggesting a parody of *ḥadīth* and other genres which use the *isnād* (sc. the chain of authorities on which the Islamic traditon is based);[6] and nearly everyone ends with the narrator's realisation that the hero is, in fact, the same Abū'l-Fatḥ al-Iskandarī, disguised in various roles. Each *maqāma* contains a separate episode in whch the narrator meets the disguised hero, there being no connection between them except for the haphazard wanderings of narrator and hero. There is no serious developing plot, narrative thread or full characterisation. However, the purpose of the *maqāma* would appear to have been not just exhibition of rhetorical skills, and admonition, but also imitation of the dialogue of the *ḥikāya* in the sense of play.

There is good evidence to suggest that the *ḥākiya* was taken over as a narrative *maqāma.* Pellat observed that 'in the formation of the (*maḳāma*) it is in fact possible to discern a certain influence from earlier literature relating to the adventures of some marginal elements of society .... To this influence there should be no doubt be added that of mime (*ḥākiya*), since the *maḳāma* contains an undeniable theatrical element, at least in the makeup of the hero and the posture of the narrator'.[7] Pellat also remarks that 'from the 4th/10th century onwards elements of mimicry appear in the *maqāma* genre, which the literary efforts of Badīʿ al-Zamān and his successors separated from the *ḥikāya* proper'.[8]

Egyptian scholars such as ʿAbd al-Ḥamīd Yūnis went beyond Pellat in saying that 'the *maqāma* has its origin in dramatic literature composed as early as the pre-Islamic period. The form was derived from 'standing' (*qiyām*) in an assembly place (*dār al-nadwa*) ... and, in fact, it consisted of one direct and continuous acting performance by a single actor'.[9]

ʿAlī al-Rāʿī confirmed Yūnis's opinion in his interesting book on the development of comedy in Egypt, adducing al-Hamadhānī's *Maqāma al-Maḍīriyya* as an example of this kind of dramatic art. Al-Rāʿī proved that it has a dramatic structure by dividing up the dialogue between Abū'Fatḥ and the merchant. He also emphasised

Figure 6 An illustration of *al-Maqāma al-Baghdādiyya*, no. 13. Abū Zayd, the protagonist of *Maqāmāt al-Ḥarīrī* disguised as an old woman accompanied by thin, sickly children. This illustration might reveal the way in which the *ḥākiyas* or *khayālīs* used to disguise themselves to perform their repertoires. (*Maqāmāt*, Bibliothéque Nationale Paris, MS Arabe 5847, f. 35 r.)

the elaborate dramatic structure in al-Ḥarīrī's *al-Maqāma al-Baghdādiyya*, in which Abū 'l-Fatḥ disguises himself as an old woman with hungry children.[10] All this confirms our assumption that the *maqāma* proper is, in fact, a written composition imitating the dialogue and structure of the *ḥikāya*.[11] It places the *ḥākiya* (impersonator) 'on stage' as an anti-hero, not of the middle class, but rather from the underworld.[12] This, as well as the element of mimicry, was noted by Bosworth in his commentary on the lead character of *Maqāmāt Badī' al-Zamān*, Abū'l-Fatḥ al-Iskandarī: 'He poses in various guises in order to get money. Indeed, he boasts openly at the end of the *Maqāma of Qazwīn* of his ability to assume any guise (just like the *ḥākiya*).[13]

That the dramatic dialogue and structure of the *maqāma* is an imitation of the *ḥikāya* or *khayāl* and debates (*munāẓarāt*) of the Abbasid period can be seen in a debate (*munāẓara*) between Badī' al-Zamān al-Hamadhānī and Abū Bakr al-Khwārizmī (326–88/935–93) in Nishapur at the investigation of Abū 'Alī the *naqīb* of the descendents of the Prophet, in 382/992.[14] The young Hamadhānī challenged the older al-Khwārizmī to a debate on poetry and prose based on improvisation (*badīha*). This *munāẓara* was based on quick and sharp retorts. One threatened to slap the other. It ended with the guests falling asleep. Later on, al-Hamadhānī apologised to al-Khwārizmī and repented of his deed. The structure of the debate is reminiscent of that of many *maqāmāt, munāẓarāt, munādamāt, ḥikāyāt* and *khayāl al-ẓill* plays.[15]

Moreover, when al-Ḥarīrī defended his *Maqāmāt* against the accusation that they were false stories forbidden by Islamic law, he argued that they were useful compositions of the category of fables (*ḥikāyāt*) put in the mouth of animals and objects, known in Arabic literature as *munāẓarāt* and *mufākharāt* (rivalry and vain glory), as well as the stories of *Kalīla wa-Dimna*. Such *ḥikāyāt*, according to al-Ḥarīrī, were recited or performed by *ruwāt* (story-tellers):[16]

> But yet, whoever scans matters with the eye of intelligence, and makes good his insight into principles will rank these Assemblies in the order of useful writings, and class them with the fables that relate to brutes and lifeless objects. Now none was ever heard of whose hearing shrank from such tales, or who held as sinful those who related them at ordinary times. Moreover ... What fault is there in one who composes stories for instruction not for display, and whose purpose in them is the education and not the fablings?

Another indication that drama was used as a model for the *maqāma* is the fact that, as mentioned before, dialogue material from the time of al-Mutawakkil, probably taken from a *ḥikāya* or *khayāl*, reappears in the *Ḥikāyat Abī'l-Qāsim al-Baghdādī*, the

Maqāmāt of al-Hamadhānī, the *Nathr al-Durr* of al-Ābī and Ibn Dāniyāl's *Bābat Ṭayf al-Khayāl.*[17] Themes such as the judge, the Banū Sāsān, villagers, curses of rogues, etc., are common in the *maqāmāt* and other dramatic genres, especially the theatrical plays of the *khayāl* or *ḥikāya.* This would seem to indicate that the *maqāma* can be used as evidence of the repertoire, structure, themes, plots, dialogue and characters of the *ḥikāya* and *khayāl* plays, of which no written text is extant, due to their oral and improvised character, apart from *Ḥikāyat Abī 'l-Qāsim al-Baghdādī* and some summaries. (This observation only applies to the *maqāma* proper, not to all compositions bearing the name *maqāma,* as we shall see later.) It may be concluded that contrary to what some scholars, notably Horovitz, claimed, the *maqāma* is an indigenous Arabic genre which only has Hellenistic roots in so far as it is indebted to the *ḥikāya.*[18] The *maqāma* was composed for mimetic declamation and used a harangue style with a prodigious store of sophisticated rhetoric and eloquent turn of phrase. These characteristics endowed the *maqāma* with the seriousness Muslims sought and admired in Arabic literature. It overshadowed all other oral genres – especially the *ḥikāya* – and the *maqāma* was spared the improvisation typical of the old oral genres, which tended toward colloquialism and weak style, properties which Muslim writers despised.

That it was written composition is evident from its brevity, its tendency to harangue, its use of extensive rhymed prose, pun, alliteration, and the composition of verses and/or treatises containing letters with and without dots and with antithetical meanings if read in reverse. These characteristics could not have come about without a written art. In fact, a well-known anecdote about al-Ḥarīrī makes it clear that the *maqāma* is written and not just improvised. When examined in order to prove his ability to compose this highly rhetorical and sophisticated genre, he was placed alone in a room with pen and paper.[19]

The recording of dramatic literature for reading or recitation occurred sometime during the third/ninth century if not earlier.[20] When the term *ḥikāya* had acquired the meaning of a 'written' story, the term *khayāl* replaced it to describe a dramatic performance with dialogue and props (to be discussed in the next chapter). A transitional stage is evident in al-Shābushtī's use of the two terms. In his discussion of 'Abbāda's plays before al-Ma'mūn he used the term *ḥākā*; but in his account of his encounter with Di'bil (d. 246/860) several years later he uses the term *khayāl.*[21]

Later, a new type of *maqāma* using dialogue in ungrammatical Arabic developed. Al-Hamadhānī wrote serious *maqāmāt,* as the thirteen-century Aḥmad b. Aḥmad al-Rāzī al-Ḥanafī remarked, but 'I permit (the author) to incline towards joking (*muṭāyaba*) and to abandon seriousness for jesting and fun'.[22] The most representative work of the new type is *al-Maqāma al-Mukhtaṣara fī 'l-Khamsīn Mara*, 'The Abridged Assembly about Fifty Women', by the fourteenth-century Muḥammad b. Mawlāhum al-Khayālī, which consists of debates between exponents of different crafts and uses technical terms for punning.[23] It may be compared with the *maqāmāt* dealing with rivalries between flowers or objects.[24] About fifty women representing different professions – those of singer, dancer, seamstress, actress (*khayāliyya*), and so forth – are introduced. Each woman gives a short speech, using the terminology of her own profession to make punning retorts to the woman before her. The genre dealing with craftsmen was developed after the fourth/tenth century according to Sadan.[25] There are only vague indications that such *maqāmāt* were enacted in public, but it does seem that 'The Foolish Assemblies' (*al-Maqāmāt al-Habbāliyya*), written in ungrammatical Arabic, were performed by Ibn Sūdūn in public places with the audience forming a circle around him as part of his buffoonery (*maskhara*);[26] and the 'Assembly about Fifty Women' must have been performed too. Many scholars, notably al-Rā'ī and Sadan, assume that the *maqāmāt* were narrated rather then performed, in so far as they were not read silently, the mimetic element being limited to gestures and changing tones of voice by the narrator;[27] this was how 'proper' *maqāmāt* were presented, and it is also how stories were told by the Turkish *meddāḥ*[28] and *mukallit* and the Arab *ḥakawātī*.[29] But the 'Assembly about Fifty Women' was composed by a professional actor (*khayālī*) who explicitly declared that he intended it as 'something that will stay behind among my friends after my death' (*khalafan ba'dī 'inda 'l-aṣḥāb*) so that 'those who succeed me (*man ba'dī*) will ask God to have mercy on me'.[30] The friends and successors to whom he refers were presumably colleagues and successors within his profession, in which case he must have written the work for theatrical performance. In fact, the work employs extensive dialogue, and the performance for which it was intended cannot have been a shadow play. It begins with a request by the performer that the audience *listen* to him, and he introduces himself as Muḥammad b. Mawlāhum, the actor, not as the shadow play presenter, and he adds that 'everyone declaims my narratives and speeches' (*wa-kullu wāḥidin yuḥaddithu ḥadīthī wa-maqālī*).[31] It is also the actress (*khayāliyya*) from among the fifty women who invites the other 'dramatis personae' to dance and who uses the verb associated with live performance – *kharaja* – in various senses.

That the vulgar *maqāmāt* lent themselves to theatrical performance is clear from the fact that at least one of them was integrated in a shadow play. According to Ibn Iyās, Ibn Dāniyāl composed a *maqāma* on the banning of taverns, ḥashīsh, wine and brothels by sultan Baybars,[32] and this *maqāma* reappears in a slightly shortened version in the introduction to his *Bābat Ṭayf al-Khayāl*, where it is put in the mouth of Ṭayf al-Khayāl himself.[33] In fact, Ibn Dāniyāl also borrowed from the *Ḥikāyat Abī 'l-Qāsim al-Baghdādī* here, for Amīr Wiṣāl introduces himself with a speech based on the introduction to that work.[34] Ṭayf al-Khayāl responds to Amīr Wiṣāl's speech by calling him 'the beauty of assemblies' (*jamāl al-maqāmāt*),[35] while Amīr Wiṣāl has previously greeted 'those who attended my assembly'.[36] These two statements put in the mouth of Amīr Wiṣāl might indicate that the author of this shadow play, Ibn Dāniyāl, considers the introduction of *Ḥikāyat Abī 'l-Qāsim* which he integrated in this shadow play, a *maqāma*.

It is worth noting that in Ottoman Turkey there was a close link between the shadow play *Karagöz* and the live play *Orta Oyunu*, the Turkish *commedia dell' arte*, especially from the seventeenth century onwards. Such evidence as we have suggest that the same was the case in the Arabic-speaking world, though the paucity of plays of either kind makes it difficult to clinch the argument.[37]

The *risāla*

The *risāla* is another genre which developed as an offshoot of the *ḥikāya* in the fifth/eleventh century. The great similarity in contents between the play of the ṣūfī in the reign of al-Mahdī and al-Jāḥiẓ's *risāla fī Banī Umayya*, can be considered as the first step in this process. It is also based on an extensive use of dialogue, as may be seen in *Risālat al-Tawābi' wa-'l-Zawābi'* ('The Treatise of Familiar Spirits and Demons'), also called *Shajarat al-Fukāha* ('The Tree of Humor'), by Ibn Shuhayd al-Andalusī (322–426/922–1034),[38] and in *Risālat al-Ghufrān*, by Abū 'l-'Alā' al-Ma'arrī (363–449/979–1059).[39] Ibn Shuhayd used his dialogue for literary criticism to prove his ability as a poet and writer as well as 'exposing and criticising the defects of the age'.[40] Al-Ma'arrī employed his dialogue for theological criticism as well. Both works resemble the *maqāma* in their embellished style, punning, rhymed prose and extensive use of dialogue.

According to Pellat, 'Ibn Shuhayd wrote the *Risālat al-Tawābi' wa-'l-Zawābi'* in his youth as a kind of school exercise after the manner of celebrated poets and writers of the past in order to show his own ability in prose and poetry, as requested by a *kātib*';[41] but even so, there are many indications that the *ḥikāya* and *khayāl* was taken as a narrative model for this *risāla*. It adopted the dramatic dialogue as its model, as did the *maqāma*. Ibn Shuhayd was, as a matter of fact, close to the inner circles of jesting poets and writers dedicted to buffoonery and entertainment.[42] He is described by contemporaries as a *baṭṭāl* (buffoon)[43] and expert in *hazl* (comedy) and *nawādir* (anecdote),[44] in short as an expert in the repertoire of the *ḥākiya*. In his writings he employs metaphors derived from live theatre.[45] He was also a close friend of the famous poet and writer Abū'l-Qāsim Ibn al-Iflīlī, whom he describes as the best performer of 'The Play of the Jew', suggesting that many actors had tried their hand at this play:[46]

> What is amazing in his (al-Iflīlī's) case is that the treatises and poems of every secretary who served the rulers and every poet who celebrated them in our country are memorized for recitation (*ruwiyat*) except for those of Abū'l-Qāsim (Ibn al-Iflīlī), so that he became a teacher for that purpose. He hinted, at times, that some of his poems and treatises should be memorised, but none of his students would obey him. 'The deprived is always deprived of everything.' However, if [only] he would buy raisins for the pupils of the mosques, and walnut rind to dye the lips of the prostitutes of the inns (*kharājiyyāt al-khānāt*),[47] and teach them his works, then they would take in his fees and bribes and perform (*rawā*) his poems and treatises. (They) would sing them on open roads, in the marshes and on the dunghills, in the same way that they are wont to sing their poems and recitations of follies. In this way his works would become famous. People would see and recognise them .... and, he observed, some of our children ... related that when he hobbled about, slightly advancing, then retreating, with staff in hand and sack on shoulder, he was the most skilful person at performing the play of the Jew (*ikhrāj la'bat al-Yahūdī*)

Ibn Shuhayd here mocks Ibn al-Iflīlī and expresses his amazement that only Ibn al-Iflīlī of all the ruler's secretaries could find no student or woman singers to memorise his poems for recitation. He is even too mean to bribe them. This sentence may imply that Ibn Shuhayd, who was vizier and boon companion to ʿAbd al-Raḥmān b. Hishām in 414/1023 and to Hishām III al-Muʿtadd from 418/1027 to 422/1031,[48] had first-rate young men and women to memorize his poems and treatises for recitation. By contrast, Ibn al-Iflīlī would recite his own works when he could not find anyone else to do so.

It is possible that Ibn al-Iflīlī's work was intended to be not just recited, but actually staged. Ibn Dāniyāl uses the verb *rawā* in sense of performing a shadow play.[49] Does Ibn Shuhayd also refer to a performance by his use of the word *riwāya* ? There were certainly many kinds of dramatic entertainment in Andalusia. Al-Shaqundī enumerates among the varous theatrical skills of the dancers of the city of Ubbada in Andalusia 'sword play, juggling, staging the villagers, sleight-of-hand tricks and masquerades';[50] and Ibn al-Iflīlī was himself a performer of 'the Play of the Jew', as has been seen.[51]

There is also other evidence that Ibn Shuhayd was familiar with *ḥikāyas* in the sense of plays. Thus his father, Abū Marwān ʿAbd al-Malik b. Aḥmad, was an expert in performance with dance, reciting poetry and making gestures (*ishārāt*) at the same time. Even in his old age when he was ill and unable to walk because of his gout, he was brought on a stretcher to join in such performance. Al-Maqqarī described such a dancing session:[52]

> Their joy surged and they were transported by rapture and they danced. Then they danced in turn until Abū Marwān's turn came. The vizier Abū ʿAbd Allāh Ibn ʿAbbās supported him and he danced while leaning on him, improvising and making gestures towards al-Manṣūr, overwhelmed by drunkenness.

Abū Marwān's dancing while improvising poetry and/or prose accompanied by gestures and with other attendants of the party dancing, singly or in groups, may indicate that they performed scenes from plays (*ḥikāya, khayāl*).[53] It makes no sense that they should have dragged an old man suffering from gout laid on a stretcher to simply dance caprice.

On the one hand, then, there is good evidence that Ibn Shuhayd was familiar with live plays. On the other hand, there is great similarity between his *Risāla* and Ibn Dāniyāl's shadow play *Bābat Ṭayf al-Khayāl* in respect of the way in which the characters are called forward, perform their roles, speak their dialogue and exit. There can thus be little doubt that his *risāla* adopted the *ḥikāya* as a model for its structure. Whether it was actually meant to be performed is another matter. Ibn Shuhayd asks his friend, Abū Bakr, to *listen* to his *risāla* ,[54] but this does not, of course, necessarily mean that it was performed rather than merely recited. Still, in Abbasid Iraq, as we have seen, ʿAlluwayh composed a *ḥikāya* ridiculing the judge al-Khalanjī and gave it to actors to perform[55] and Ibn al-Iflīlī may similarly have given compositions of his to be performed by *kharājiyyāt al-khānāt* in al-Andalus. But concrete evidence for the performance of Ibn Shuhayd's *Risāla* is absent. If it actually was performed, both the supernatural scene of his flight with the Jinni on horseback and the mule and swan who recite poetry and prose would make his work more suitable for a shadow play than for a live performance.

Al-Maʿarrī's *Risālat al-Ghufrān,* written some five to seven years later,[56] contains elements borrowed from Ibn Shuhayd's *Risālat al-Tawābiʿ wa-'l-Zawābiʿ* (notably the supernatural event and the dialogue with poets and writers of former generations), and it may well be that he used Ibn Shuhayd's dramatic work as a model for his narrative.

There is at any rate no doubt that al-Maʿarrī was familiar with dramatic literature. According to Yāqūt, he composed a work entitled *Saj' al-Ḥamā'im* ('The Cooing of Pigeons'), which dealt with arguments for and against asceticism and used the device of putting words into the mouths of four pigeons.[57] What is interesting in Yāqūt's information is that al-Ma'arrī composed this work at the request of a *rayyis* [58] Yāqūt gives no indication who the *rayyis* or *ra'īs* was or the reason he ordered it for. Was he a notable who had a shadow play presenter (as did Saladin) or who had *samājas* (as did al-Mu'taḍid)? Or should the word *ra'īs* be understood as 'leader of a troup of actors or shadow play presenters'? 'Alī Ibn Mawlāhum al-Khayālī for whom Ibn Dāniyāl composed three shadow plays, was *rayyis* of a troup of presenters, while al-Rayyis Muḥammad Fattāt al-'Anbar (d. 1518) and his successor Burraywa were *ru'asā' al-muḥabbazīn,* leaders of troupes of actors.[59]

Al-Ma'arrī also used dialogue and the device of putting words into the mouths of animals in the work of *Khuṭab al-Khayl* ('Sermons of Horses'), and probably also in his *Kitāb al-Ṣāhil wa-'l-Shāḥij* (The Book of Horse and Mule).[60] Such animal fables were regarded by the Ikhwān al-Ṣafā, al-Ḥarīrī and Ibn al-Fāriḍ as a useful literary genre. They took the form of *munāẓarāt, mufākharāt* and *muḥawarāt* (rivalry, vainglory and debates), and they were also considered *ḥikāyāt* (stories, or plays?) to be recited (*turwā*) by narrators (or possibly actors).

There is no way of telling whether al-Ma'arrī's *rasā'il* written in dramatic dialogue were taken up by actors or shadow play presenters, but they were probably too highbrow for medieval actors, who were fond of frivolous and impudent literature, of scatology, or of light and amusing literature like al-Tawḥīdī's *al-Imtā' wa-'l-Mu'ānasa.*[61] Even so, the fact that al-Ma'arrī was acquainted with dramatic literature strengthens the conjecture that he used Ibn Shuhayd's *Risālat al-Tawābi' wa-'l-Zawābi'* as a structural model for his *Risālat al-Ghufrān.* Its dramatic structure has attracted the attention fo 'Ā'isha Bint 'Abd al-Raḥmān (Bint al-Shāṭi'). who argues that it is a dramatic text (*naṣṣ masraḥī*) on the grounds that if one omits the explanation of difficult words and arranges the text in dialogue form, the result is a play. However, she emphasises that al-Ma'arri did not intend his *Risāla* to be performed, arguing that 'this was an art which was unknown in his time', and that the text is at all events unsuitable for theatrical performance 'due to its complicated subject and literary style'.[62] As we have seen, theatrical performances were in fact known in his time, but the art was too low brow for al-Ma'arrī. The reason why he made use of the genre is probably that he wanted its humorous and sarcastic effect, though its sheer popularity at the time may also have been a factor.

The influence of theatre is also evident in other works by al-Ma'arrī. P. Cachia has analysed the thirty poems on armour

(*Dir'iyyāt*) at the end of *Siqṭ al-Zand* , and he concludes that each poem is actually part of a continuous monologue of a single individual in different stages of life. Some of the poems are of the genre *mufākhara* (vainglory) and others of *munāẓara* (rivalry). But Cachia, like Ṭaha Ḥusayn, could not ascertain the purpose of these dramatic poems.[63] In fact, the dominant idea behind the *Dir'iyyāt* is that the armour which may save the life of a young fighter does not protect him from old age and death. The sword, in these poems, represents death and the armour is a symbol of long life and safety. But life is such that armour cannot protect man from old age and death.

The fluidity of the genres

Some modern scholars deny that *ḥikāya* and *khayāl* (to which I shall come back in the next chapter), are dramatic literature written for theatrical performances.[65] As mentioned already, Sadan denies this characteristic even to the colloquial *maqāmāt* such as Muḥammad Ibn Mawlāhum al-Khayālī's *al-Maqāma al-Mukhtaṣara,* in which 'a group of artisans and other tradesmen was supposedly asked to give literary performances (employing) vocabulary of the genre in question ...'. He agrees that these compositions are 'a literary phenomenon which *verges* on drama', but he insists that 'they approach the boundary which defines genuine drama *without* crossing it to fall under a dramatic category'.[66]

However, it is doubtful whether all the Arabic dramatic literature was recorded; and what was recorded is not necessarily extant. Above all, the distinction between literature with a dramatic quality on the one hand and compositons destined for actual performance on the other is not easily made. The terms *ḥikāya, khayāl, bāba, khayāl al-ẓill, maqāma, risāla, samar* and *qiṣṣa* are used interchangeably. In our discussions above we saw that Abū 'l-Muṭahhar al-Azdī uses the terms, *ḥikāya, samar, risāla* and *qiṣṣa* synonymously.[67] Ibn Dāniyāl called his shadow plays '*bāba, khayāl al-ẓill* and *khayāl.*'[68] Muḥammad Ibn Mawlāhum al-Khayālī and al-Bilbaysī called their works *maqāmas, munādama, kalām* and *ḥadīth* (discussion) under the collective title of *Majmū' min Ḥikāyāt.*[69] The anonymous author of the shadow play *al-'Āshiq wa-'l-Ma'shūq* called his play alternatively a *faṣl, ḥikāya* and *khayāl al-ẓill* .[70] The Egyptian poet 'Adb al- Bāqī al-Isḥāqī (d. 1660) called his live theatrical play *khayāl* and used the term *munādama* as a synonym,[71] while Ya'qūb Ṣanū' called his plays *muḥāwara, la'ba* and *munādama* .[72] Clearly, all these genres overlap. Thus *al-Maqāma al-Mukhtaṣara* shares numerous motifs with al-Bilbaysī and Ibn Dāniyāl, and to a certain extent also with Ibn Shuhayd and al-Ma'arrī, notably roaming around, finding a friend (or a Jinni in Ibn Shuhayd's *Risāla*) to take the narrator to the gathering of artisans (in the case of Ibn Shuhayd and al-Ma'arrī who discussed literature and poetry, the protagonists are taken to the poets and writers in Paradise and Hell (al-Ma'arrī), or to the Jinnis of these poets and writers in their valley).[73] The dialogue is in professional terminology. Finally, all these compositions end with repentance and forgiveness of the sins of the protagonists, and only in *Risālat al-Ghufrān* the poets and writers who were in Paradise are asked by the protagonist why God forgave their sins.[74] Hard and fast distinctions between narratives, with a dramatic structure, and texts meant for actual performance are thus hard to make. The question is whether the intention of al-Ma'arrī and other writers of dramatic literature was to show that the recognition of God's existence, for which poets and writers of lore were granted forgiveness and purified from their sins, is the Muslim equivalent to the Greek *katharsis* of the drama? Arabic drama may not be drama in terms of Greek or European criteria, but then why should such criteria be applied to it? Though there is a superficial similarity between the Catharsis of Greek theatre and the repentence of sins in Muslim dramatic literature, to evaluate the one in terms of the other would be to fail to do justice to either.

Let us review the similarities between the various genres. The *Ḥikāyat Abī 'l-Qāsim, Risālat al-Tawābi' wa-'l-Zawābi', Risālat al-Ghufrān, Bābat 'Ajīb wa-Gharīb,* the *maqāmāt* of Muḥammad Ibn Mawlāhum and al-Bilbaysī are all similar in structure. The opening lines present the reasons for their composition. These reasons are always either an external request from a certain person (as in *al-Ghufrān, 'Ajīb wa-Gharīb* and *Maqāmat al-Ṭuraf min Munādamāt Arbāb al-Ḥiraf* (c. 1345, by Muḥammad al-Bilbaysī) or an internal impulse (as in the case of *Ḥikāyat Abī 'l-Qāsim* and *al-Maqāma al-Mukhtaṣara* by Ibn Mawlāhum). This is invariably followed by the wandering around of the narrator and his meeting with artisans, professionals, poets, writers or their demons. In the *Ḥikāyat Abī 'l-Qāsim*, which is crude in structure, the narrator explains that Abū 'l-Qāsim will ask the profession of so-and-so and comment on the profession. Descriptions are also given of singers, food, swimming and chess besides the professions of the members of the party. In *'Ajīb wa-Gharīb* the monkey and bear trainers, the juggler, etc. describe their professions using the specialist terms of their trade. In all these compositions (apart from *Risālat al-Ghufrān*, in which the characters are asked what merits have caused God to forgive them), the artisans and tradesmen repent and their sins are forgiven. In fact the *Risālat al-Ghufrān* is the most elaborate, rhetorical and sophisticated composition in which the verbal exchanges include philosophical and dramatic dialogues surpassing those of the fables in *Rasā'il Ikhwān al-Safā*.[75]

Unlike Abū Ḥayyān al-Tawḥīdī's work and Ibn al-Ḥajjāj's poetry which can be traced in *Ḥikāyat Abī 'l-Qāsim*,[76] there is no trace of al-Ma'arrī's dramatic dialogues in any *ḥikāya* or shadow play available, and it seems that al-Ma'arrī's sophisticated ways were not favoured by the actors and shadow play presenters of the medieval Arab world. However, what can be said definitely is that the *ḥikāya* imposed its structure on the high literary genres of *maqāma* and *risāla* which were written in classical Arabic. The *maqāma* in colloquial Arabic, on the other hand, may have been plays written for theatrical performance. The use of the terms *maqāma* and *risāla* as synonyms for *ḥikāya* and *khayāl* in these plays seems to point to such a conclusion. The highbrow *maqāmāt* and *risālas*, including the dialogue epistles of *Rasā'il Ikhwān al-Ṣafā* were deliberately composed as 'dramatic literature', for didactic purposes, but were not necessarily intended for performance.

According to Sadan, al-Jāḥiẓ's 'Epistle on the Crafts of the Masters' (*Risāla fī ṣinā'at al-Quwwād*) was the first composition to 'put into the mouths of practitioners of various professions pronouncements on the same topic, concerning which they had been requested by the author to demonstrate their literary powers'.[77] It is not possible to prove any influence from Aristotle's *Poetics* in this epistle, though al-Jāḥiẓ was one of Aristotle's admirers. However, the influence of Aristotle may perhaps, and that of al-Jāḥiẓ may certainly, be found in the introduction of Abū 'l-Muṭahhar al-Azdī to his *Ḥikāyat Abī 'l-Qāsim*.[78]

If it has been established that Arabs developed a dramatic art of their own, why did they not pay more attention to Greek writers on theatre? Why were only a few Arabic theatrical terms used by translators and commentators of Aristotle's *Poetics*? Why were the terms 'comedy' and 'tragedy' borrowed from the Greek (via Syriac) by Ibn Sīnī as *qūmūdhyā* and *trāghūdhyā* and rendered by others as *madīḥ* (panegyric) for tragedy and *hijā'* (satire) for comedy, both of which terms are borrowed from poetry?

The answer to these questions may lie in the fact that theatre was considered by the Muslim *'ulamā'* and serious writers and poets as low and popular arts unworthy of serious attention.[79] They were considered *sukhf* (scurrilous material), *mujūn* (impudence) and sometimes even *junūn* (folly). Pious Muslim rulers and *'ulamā'* prohibited all sorts of entertainment. The aim of Muslim commentators of Aristotle's *Poetics* was primarily to understand Aristotle's method of criticism and to apply his method to their own poetry. They were comparing serious Greek poetry and serious Arab poetry, mainly pre-Islamic. Ibn Sīnā (d. 1030) expresses his hope, at the end of his summary of the *Poetics*, that Arabs may write a study of Arabic poetry using Aristotle's methodology by saying:[80]

> This is a summary of the part of the book *Poetics* by Aristotle found in this country, a good extent of which we were unable to find. It is not unlikely that we should endeavour to formulate a discussion of great scientific and elaborate exposition from the general art of the *Poetics* and the art of the poetry current in our time. We now have to limit ourselves to this extent since the aim of our objective is to make an enquiry on the sciences whch may be to our advantage.

When Ibn Rushd (d. 1198) uses the term *madīḥ* (panegyrical poetry) for comedy, it may well be out of a desire to apply Aristotle's methodology to Arabic poetry, not due to ignorance of the theatrical arts and their terminology.[81] Ḥazim al-Qarṭājannī (608/1211–683-5/1286–8) admitted in his book *Minhāj al-Bulaghā' wa-Sirāj al-Udabā* that he composed his work to fulfil the aspiration Ibn Sīnā expressed at the end of his summary of the *Poetics*.[82] In discussing the differences between Greek and Arab poetry, Ḥāzim al-Qarṭājannī commented that Greek poetry is limited to certain themes. Each theme is written in a certain metre and deals mainly with legends (*khurāfāt*).[83] He continued by saying that:

> the Greek poets would invent things upon which they would set their poetic imaginations and they made this an aspect of their speech. They presumed things which did not happen at all and used them as a model for what happens, and they built upon them legends such as those old women relate to children at night, fables of things which cannot possibly happen.

He concludes with the statement that 'Ibn Sīnā condemned (*dhamma*) this kind of poetry and said: 'There is no need for poetic imagination of the simple fables (*khurāfāt basīṭa*) which are but invented narratives.' He also said: 'This (type of poetry) does not suit all temperaments.'[84]

Still, Ibn Sīnā does use Arabic theatrical terms current in his time, such as *wajh al-maskhara* (the mask of the comedian), *samāja* (a man with a mask), *muḥāwara wa-munāẓara* (performance of dramatic dialogue), *al-akhdh bi-'l-wujūh* (acting, mimicry), *al-muḥākāt wa-'l-takhyīl* (imitation and representation), *al-hazl wa-'l-taṭānuz* (comic play) and more.[85]

The above discussion can be summarised as follows:

1. The *ḥikāya* (the tenth century's *khayāl*) served as a model for the narrative of the *maqāma* and *khayāl al-ẓill*. The *maqāma* with its prodigious store of sophisticated rhetoric and eloquent phrases overshadowed all other oral and written genres in medieval Arabic literature. It is a written genre intended for silent reading or for recitation before an audience.
2. In time the term *maqāma* was also used for ungrammatical compositons intended for theatrical performance.

3. There are various indications that Ibn Shuhayd's *Risālat al-Tawābi'* was intended for recitation, if not for performance. However, the supernatural plot makes it more suitable for use as a shadow play than for live acting.
4. From the eleventh century onwards the terms *khayāl, maqāma, risāla, ḥikāya, muḥāwara, munāẓara* and *ḥadīth* were applied to dramatic literature intended for either recitation or live actors. These terms did not denote distinct and separate genres. All encompassed reading, recitation and performance.
5. These terms were most probably given to compositions according to their length and level of style. The *khayāl* and shadow play were distinguished by their ungrammatical style and impudent contents (*sukhf wa-mujūn*). It could be a long or short composition. The *maqāma* was a short composition written in highly rhetorical and eloquent style, with few characters. The *risāla* was a long composition with a highly eloquent style and great number of characters.
6. Maestros (*rayyis,* p. *rua'sā'*) of troops of actors (*khayālī* or *mukhāyil*) would compose live plays or shadow plays for themselves, as did 'Alluwayh and Muḥammad b. Mawlāhum al-Khayālī, or ask playwrights to write for them (as did 'Alī b. Mawlāhum al-Khayālī too: he asked Ibn Dāniyāl to compose three shadow plays for him). Some playwrights composed plays based on frivolous verses, *maqāmas* and *risālas* written by other writers (such as Abū 'l-Muṭahhar al-Azdī in *Ḥikāyat Abī 'l-Qāsim*)
7. The verb *rawā* (to tell, relate) is also used by Ibn Dāniyāl in the sense of presenting a shadow play.
8. Ibn Sīnā was aware of the indigenous theatre, which was well known in his time, and used some of its teminology in his Arabic version of Aristotle's *Poetics.* On the other hand, Ibn Rushd, who tried to apply Aristotle's method of poetic criticism to Arabic poetry, used the terms *hijā'* for comedy and *madīḥ* for tragedy.

Notes

1. See my 'Shadow Play', p. 59.
2. See my 'Shadow Play', p. 56 and nn. 36m, 38.
3. Cf. Ch. 7, n. 98.
4. Cf. Ch. 5 nn. 20, 22.
5. For my own definition of the *maqāma* , see S. Moreh, 'The Arabic Novel between Arabic and European Influences during the Nineteenth Century', in my *Studies in Modern Arabic Prose and Poetry* (Leiden, 1988), p. 108.
6. Cf. J. T. Monroe, *The Art of Badī' al-Zamān al-Hamadhānī as Picaresque Narrative* (Beirut, 1983), pp. 20ff.

7. C. Pellat, 'Maḳāma', *EI2.*
8. Pellat, 'Ḥikāya'. On elements of mimicry in the *maqāma*, see also Horovitz, *Spuren*, pp. 21–3.
9. 'A. Ḥ. Yūnis, *Kitāb Khayāl al-Ẓill* (Cairo, 1965), p. 60.
10. 'A. al-Rā'ī, *Funūn al-Kūmīdiya min Khayāl al- Ẓill ilā Najīb al-Rīhānī* (Cairo, 1971), pp. 14–21; cf. al-Hamadhānī, *Maqāmāt*, (Beirut, 1908), no. 22, pp. 109–23; al-Ḥarīrī, *Maqāmāt* (Cairo, n.d.), no. 13, p. 120. See Figure 6, an illustration of *maqāma* no. 13 *al-Maqāma al-Baghdādiyya*, p. 106.
11. On drama as the structural model of the novel, see Z. Levy, *Jerome Antagonistes, Les Structures Dramatiques et les Procédures Narratives de la Porte Etroite* (Paris, 1984), pp. x–xiv.
12. Bosworth, *Underworld,* p. 99; cf. Monroe, *Art,* pp. 20–38.
13. Bosworth, *Underworld,* p. 99.
14. Ibn Khallikān, *Wafayāt al-A'yān* (Beirut, 1968–71), vol. IV, pp. 400–03,
15. Yāqūt, *Udabā'*, vol. I, pp. 174–83; cf. E. K. Rowson 'Religion and Politics in the Career of Badī al-Zamān al-Hamadhānī, *Journal of the American Oriental Society* CVII (1987), pp. 653–73. Cf. also Yāqūt, *Udabā'*, vol. II, p. 166, on debates at the Abbasid court, and Z. Mubārak, *al-Nathr al-Fannī fī 'l-Qarn al-Rābi'* (Cairo, 1934), vol. II, pp. 328–50, on this particular one.
16. a-Ḥarīrī, *Maqāmāt*, p. 9; id., *The Assemblies of al-Ḥarīrī*, tr. T. Chenery (London, 1867), vol. I, p. 107.
17. Ch. 5, n. 58 –63.
18. Horovitz, *Spuren*, p. 15.
19. Ibn Khallikān, *Wafayāt*, vol. IV, p. 65.
20. Pellat, *Ḥikāya, EI2*, p. 367, col. 1.
21. Cf. Ch. 5, n. 5–6.
22. Ahmad al-Hanafi, *Maqāmāt al-Ḥanafī wa-Ibn Nāqiyā wa-ghayrihimā* (Istanbul, 1331–1913), p. 4.
23. Muḥammad Ibn Mawlāhum al-Khayālī, *al-Maqāma al-Mukhtaṣara fī 'l-Khamsīn Mara*, MS British Library, Add. 19411, fols 89a–104a. My thanks to Professor J. Sadan for pointing out this manuscript to me; we are preparing a joint edition of this part of it and we shall revert to the question of authorship, which is not yet entirely certain. The manuscript contains several *maqāmāt* by this and other authors, cf. *Catalogus Codicum Manuscriptorum Orientalium qui in Museo Britannico Asservantur* (London, 1871), vol. III, pp. 514f.
24. On *munāẓara*, see E. Wagner, 'Die arabische Rangstreitsdichtung und ihrer Einordnung in die allgemeine Literaturgeschichte', *Abhandlungen der Akademie der Wissenschaften und Literatur* (Mainz, 1962), geistes- und sozialwissenschaftliche Klasse, no. 1.
25. Sadan, 'Kings', part 1, pp. 5–49; ibid., part 2, pp. 89–120,
26. Cf, Ibn al-'Imād, *Shadharāt*, vol. VII, pp. 307f; Ch. 4, no. 64.
27. al-Rā'ī, *Funūn al-Kūmīdyā*, pp. 10f, and Sadan, 'Kings', part 1, p. 8.
28. And, *Culture*, pp. 110ff; id. *Theatre*, pp. 28ff; O. Spies, *Türkisches Puppentheater* (Emsdetten, Westf., Lechte, c. 1959), vol. I, p. 36;

Menzel, *Meddāh* ; J. M. Landau, *Studies in the Arab Theatre and Cinema* (Philadelphia, 1958), p. 3.

29. 'A. -Ḥ. Yūnis, 'al-Shā'ir wa-'l-Rabāba', in *al-Majalla*, vol. IV, no. 38, February 1960, pp. 22–9; Landau, *Studies* , p. 3; F. Khūrshīd, *al-Siyar al-Sha'biyya* , pp. 48f; Prüfer, 'Drama', p. 872, col. 2.
30. al-Khayālī, *Maqāma* , fol. 89a.
31. Ibid., fol. 90a, lines 7f. there was a family of actors called al-Khayālī in Iraq of the 1940s, cf. S. Moreh, 'The Jewish Theatre in Iraq in the first Half of the Twentieth Century' (in Hebrew), *Pe'amim Studies in the Cultural Heritage of Oriental Jewry* XXIII (1985), p. 85.
32. Ibn Iyās, *Badā'i'* , vol. I, part 1, p. 326, l. 16. Badawi, *Early Arabic Drama*, p. 6 has misunderstood this passage. Ibn Iyās is not referring to Ibn Dāniyāl's *Bābat Ṭayf al-Khayāl* as a *Maqāma* , but saying that he composed a *maqama* on this particular incident.
33. Ḥamāda, *Khayāl al-Ẓill*, pp. 150–4.
34. Ibid. pp. 154f; Mez, *Sittenbild* , pp. 3, 11.
35. Ḥamāda, *Khayāl al-Ẓill* , p. 155, l. 11.
36. Ibid., p. 154, l. 13.
37. And, *Theatre* , p. 39.
38. Cf. C. Pellat, *Ibn Shuhayd al-Andalusī, Ḥayyātuh wa-Āthāruh* (Amman, 1965). The *Risāla* was composed in 423/1032; on its title as *Shajarat al-Fukāha,* see al-Ḥamīdī, *Jadhwat al-Muqtabis* (Cairo, n.d.), p. 305; Ibn Bassām, *Dhakhīra* , vol. I, part i, p. 245, n. 4.
39. Cf. 'Ā'isha 'Abd al-Raḥmān (Bint al-Shāṭi'), *al-Ghufrān li-Abī 'l-'Alā' al-Ma'arrī, Dirāsa Naqdiyya* (Cairo, 1968), p. 8f, the *Ghufrān* is here dated c. 424/1033.
40. Ibn Shuhayd al-Andalusī *Risālat al-Tawābi' wa-'l-Zawābi'* (Los Angeles, 1971), p. 40 of the editorial introduction.
41. Pellat, private communication.
42. Ibn Bassām, *Dhakhīra* , vol. I, part i, p. 196.
43. Ibid., p. 50.
44. Ibid., p. 192.
45. Ibid., p. 192.
46. Ibid., pp. 241f; cf. ch. 2, n. 24; Ch. 7, n. 65.
47. Iḥsān 'Abbās suggests that *kharājiyyāt al-khānāt* means 'women (sc. prostitutes) who dwell in inns and pay taxes', connecting *kharājiyyāt* with *kharāj* (Ibn Bassām, *Khakhīra* , vol. I, part i, p. 242n). On actresses as prostitutes, see Ch. 7, n. 33.
48. Pellat, *Ibn Shuhayd* , pp. 42–52.
49. Ḥamāda, *Khayāl* , p. 144, l. 8.
50. Cf. Ch. 7, n. 61.
51. Cf. above, n. 47.
52. al-Maqqarī, *Nafḥ al-Ṭīb,* ed. R. Dozy *et al.,* vol. ii, pp. 176f; cf. Pellat, *Ibn Shuhayd* p. 23.
53. Cf. the dancing of Ibn al-Iflīlī, above, n. 46; and cf. Ch. 7, n. 41–3 where scenes of live play (*khayāl*) are performed with dancing.
54. Ibn Shuhayd, *Risāla* , p. 51; (ed. Buṭrus al-Bustānī (Beirut, 1967), p. 88); Ibn Bassām, *Dhakhīra* , vol. I, part i, p. 246.
55. Cf. Ch. 5, n. 20.

56. Ibn Shuhayd, *Risāla*, p. 17.
57. Yāqūt, *Udabā'*, vol. III, p. 151.
58. Ibid. l. 5.
59. For *rayyis* in the sense of leader of a troupe of shadow play presenters, see Ḥamāda, *Khayāl*, pp. 144, 230; for the same word in the sense of leader of a troupe of actors, see Ch. 8, nn. 1f.
60. Yāqūt, *Udabā'*, vol. III, pp. 158, 160. See also Abū al-'Alā' al-Ma'arrī, *Risālat al-Ṣāhil wa-'l-Shāḥij*, ed. 'Āisha 'Abd al Raḥmān (Cairo 1975); 'Alī 'Uqla 'Arsān al-*Ẓawāhir al-Masraḥiyya 'ind al-'Arab* (Damascus, 1985), pp. 402–13, where he reprinted this *Risāla* as a play.
61. See Ch. 5, n. 46.
62. 'Ā'isha 'Abd 'l- Raḥmān, Qirā'a *Jadīda fī Risālat al-Ghufrān* (Cairo, 1970), p. 188.
63. P. Cachia, 'The Dramatic Monologues of al-Ma'arrī', *Journal of Arabic Literature* I (1970) pp. 129–36; Ṭaha Ḥusayn is discussed at p. 132f.
64. Cf. Preface, n. 1.
65. Cf. G. Jacob, *Geschichte des Schattentheaters im Morgen- und Abendland* (Osnabrück, 1972), pp. 26f, 93f; Prüfer, 'Drama', p. 873, col. 2, p. 878, col. 1; Badawi, *Early Arabic Drama*, p. 5f.
66. Sadan, 'Kings', Part 1, p. 8.
67. Cf. Ch. 5, nn. 47f.
68. Ḥamāda *Khayāl al-Ẓill*, pp. 143ff.
69. al-Khayālī, *Maqāma*, ff. 1a, 63a–64a, 89a.
70. Wetzstein, *Liebenden*, p. 132.
71. 'Abd al-Bāqī al-Isḥāqī, *Misṭara Khayāl*, fol. 142a, quoted in Appendix I.
72. Cf. N. 'Ānūs, *Masraḥ Ya'qūb Ṣanū'* (Cairo, 1984), pp. 83–128, where the titles of Ṣanū''s plays are given as *la'ba tiyātriyya, muḥāwara, mukhāṭaba, muḥādatha* and *ḥadīth*.
73. Cf. above, nn. 38f.
74. Cf. L. E. Goodman, 'Hamadhānī, Schadenfreude and Salvation through Sin', *Journal of Arabic Literature* XIX (1988), pp. 27–39.
75. Khayr al-Dīn al-Ziriklī (ed.) *Rasā'il Ikhwān al-Ṣafā* (Cairo, 1928), vol. II, pp. 173–317.
76. Cf. Ch. 5, *Ḥikāyat Abī 'l-Qāsim al-Baghdādī*, p. 94f.
77. Sadan, 'Kings', part 1, p. 11; cf. al-Jāḥiẓ, 'Risāla fī Ṣinā'at al-Quwwād' in *Rasā'il al-Jāḥiẓ*, pp. 260–5.
78. Mez, *Sittenbild*, pp. 1f; cf. Ch. 5, n. 46.
79. See the verses of Ibn Nubāta (d. 768/1366) where he accused other poets that their foolish and patched up poems (borrowed from other poets), are like *bābāt* (scenes of live plays and of shadow plays), *Dīwān Ibn Nubāta* (Cairo, 1905), p. 71.
80. Ibn Sīnā in Badawī, *Fann*, p. 198.
81. Badawī, *Early Arabic Drama*, pp. 3f, misunderstood this point.
82. Ḥāzim al-Qarṭājannī, *Minhāj al-Bulaghā' wa-Sirāj al-Udabā*, (Tunis, 1966), pp. 1, 68f.
83. Ibid., p. 68.

84. Ibid., p. 78; cf. Ibn Sīnā in Badawī, *Fann*, p. 184.
85. Ibid., pp. 168, 173f, 175f, 180, 184, 191, 194, 197f.

7

Khayāl as Live Theatre

Khayāl without *Ẓill*

Scholars of Muslim shadow plays have generally regarded the term *khayāl* (or *khiyāl*) as a shortened form of *khayāl al-ẓill*, shadow play. Even those who realised that the two terms stood for different types of performances had little idea of what *khayāl* meant in medieval literary and historical works.[1]

In Arabic lexicography the noun *khayāl* means 'figure' or 'phamtom': the *Lisān al-'Arab*, for example, defines it as *al-shakhṣ wa 'l-ṭayf*.[2] In its most prosaic sense it is a stick dressed in cloth so as to look like a man, that is a scare-crow used to frighten away birds and other animals;[3] the word occurs in this sense in the *Naqā'iḍ* ('scare-crow to frighten away wolves from the sheep').[4] In its least prosaic sense it is a phanton of the lover seen at night or in a dream (mainly in the form *ṭayf al-khayāl*). But it also meant 'statue', 'shadow', 'reflection' and 'fantasy'.[5] Medieval poets and playwrights used the term in all its many shades of meaning in their search for original and effective puns.

To the commentators on the *Naqā'iḍ*, from Abū 'Ubayda (d. 207/809) to Abū 'Abdallāh al-Yazīdī (d. 310/923), the word *khayāl* was synonymous with *kurraj* under a laughing-stock (*lu'ba*), or in other words with a figure used in live performances. Jarīr compared al-Farazdaq in his finery with a laughing-stock upon a *kurraj*,[6] and the commentators explained the term *kurraj* as *al-khayāl alladhī yal'ab bihi 'l-mukhannathūn* ('the figure with which *mukhannathūn* play'), *la'ba yal'abuhā 'l-mukhannathūn* ('a play which *mukhannathūn* play') and *al-kurraj alladhī yal'ab bihi al-mukhannathūn fī ḥikāyātihim* ('the *kurraj* with which *mukhannathūn* play in their impersonations').[7] Here, then, *khayāl*, and *kurraj* are implements of *la'ba* (play) and *ḥikāya* (impersonation).

In the *Kitāb al-Manāẓir* of Ibn al-Haytham (d. 430/1039), on the other hand, *khayāl* are figures moved by a shadow-player: *wa-ayḍan fa-inna 'l-baṣara idhā adraka 'l-khayāl alladhī yaẓharu min khalf al-izār, wa-kāna dhālika 'l-khayālu ashkhāṣan yuḥarrikuhā 'l-mukhayyil fa-taẓharu aẓlāluhā 'alā 'l-jidār alladhī warā' al-izār wa-'alā 'l-izār nafsih.* ('moreover, when the sight perceives the figures behind the screen, these figures being images which the presenter moves so that their shadows appear upon the wall behind the screen and upon the screen itself').[8] Though this is evidently a description of a shadow play, Ibn al-Haytham did not use the combined term *khayāl al-ẓill*, but it appears in the work of his Andalusian contemporary, Ibn Ḥazm (d. 456/1064). Ibn Ḥazm compared this world to a shadow play in which images are mounted on a wooden wheel revolving rapidly, so that one group of images (*tamāthīl*) disappears as another appears: thus too one generation follows another in this world.[9] (The technique described by Ibn Ḥazm may represent one of the earliest in the development of the art.) The combined term reappears also in the time of Saladin (1139–91),[10] and it becomes common thereafter. By the eleventh century, the term *khayāl* had thus come to be paired with *al-ẓill* (shadow). The combination was adopted to describe a new type of entertainment originating in the Far East,[11] and it is generally assumed that *khayāl* only acquired the meaning of 'play' as part of this expression. But this is not correct.

Khayāl was used in the sense of play or live performance, not just the implements associated therewith, before it came to be appropriated by the shadow play. In the story of the Jewish magician of 35/655, for example, *khayālāt* means mimes or illusion tricks.[12] Elsewhere, *Khayāl* is synonymous with *ḥikāya*, a term it tended to replace as *ḥikāya* became a written genre. The anecdote related now of Jarīr and now of Di'bil illustrates the interchangeability of these two words. According to Ibrāhīm b. Abī 'Awn, a *mukhannath* declared that if Jarīr satirised him, he 'would produce Jarīr's mother in a *ḥikāya*';[13] according to al-Shābushtī, 'Abbāda al-Mukhannath similarly told Di'bil that if he satirised him, he would produce his mother in a *khayāl*, and according to Ibn 'Āṣim al-Qaysī, Di'bil said that 'I shall produce your mother in a *la'ba*'.[14] Gurguis 'Awwād, the editor of al-Shābushtī's *Diyārāt*, took *khayāl* to mean *khayāl al-ẓill* and believed al-Shābushtī's message to be the oldest attestation of shadow plays in the Islamic world.[15] But it is obvious that *khayāl* is here synonymous with *ḥikāya* and *la'ba* and that all three terms stand for live theatrical performances.

Khayāl also means live theatrical performance in al-Maqrīzī's account (cited from al-Musabbiḥī) of the pilgrimage to Joseph's prison in Egypt, which we have encountered before:

> [The commander of the Faithful, 'Alī b. al-Ḥākim bi-Amr Allāh] stayed there for two days and two nights until the performing actors (*al-ramādiyya al-khārijūn*) returned to prison with the (sugar) statues, comic figures, *ḥikāyāt* and *samājāt* ....

> For two weeks the market people remained, roving the streets with *khayāl*, *samājāt* and (sugar) statues.... They passed through the streets with *ḥikāyāt*, *samājāt* and (sugar) statues.[16]

This passage has attracted the attention of many European Orientalists. Quatremère translated *khayāl* as 'ombres chinoises', a translation also adopted by Wiet.[17] Mez, who rendered the *samājāt* and *ḥikāyāt* of this passage as 'Schauspiele' and 'Mimereien', held *khayāl* to have been shadow plays.[18] But Jacob (who rendered *samājāt* as 'obscenities'), adduced a verse from *A Thousand and One Nights*: 'you go with one (coloured) beard and return with another (of different colour) / as if you were one of the performers of *khayāl*'. He paraphrased a performer of *khayāl* as an actor, and suggested the translation 'Phantasiegebilde, wohl Theater' for *khayāl* in al-Maqrīzī's passage, rightly noting that *khayāl* only means shadow theatre in conjunction with *ẓill*.[19] Inostrantsev likewise suggested that *khayāl* means figures and/or performances.[20] But Menzel still found the term puzzling: 'The word *khayāl* cannot be unequivocally associated with shadow play in every context unless it occurs in a complete form: *ẓill-i-khayāl* or *khayāl al-ẓill*. For me, the particular word *khayāl* has been the greatest cause of confusion. Unfortunately the use of the word *khayāl* in the Arabic, Persian and Turkish literature has surely not been sufficiently studied.'[21] As both Jacob and Inostrantsev pointed out, however, *khayāl* here stands for live performance.

Neither Jacob nor Inostrantsev, however, noticed that al-Maqrīzī's passage's clearly uses *khayāl* synonymously with *ḥikāya*. The Arabic text is reproduced on p. 53 of this book. In line 5 of the passage given there, al-Maqrīzī uses the phrase *bi 'l-khayāl wa-'l-samājāt wa-'l-tamāthīl*, and in line 9 he repeats it, this time saying *bi 'l-ḥikāyāt wa-'l-samājāt wa-'l-tamāthīl*; and both versions in their turn are clearly repetitions in slightly varied form of *bi 'l-tamāthīl wa-'l-maḍāḥik wa-'l-ḥikāyāt wa-'l-samājāt*, used in line 3. In other words, *khayāl* in al-Maqrīzī's passage has the same meaning as it does in the anecdote told of Jarīr and Di'bil.

That *khayāl* was synonymous with *ḥikāya*, and with *tamthīl* too, is also clear from the Arabic translations of and commentaries on Aristotle's *Poetics*. Thus Mattā b. Yūnis (d. 328/940) paraphrased Aristotle's *mimesis* as *tashbīh wa-'l-muḥākāt* and *al-tashbīh wa'l-ḥikāya*, while al-Fārābī (d. 339/950) adopted *tashbīh wa'l-tamthīl*; but Ibn Sīnā (d. 428/1037) used the expression *yukhayyilūn wa-yuḥākūn* and *al-muḥākāt wa-'l-takhyīl*.[22] The fact that Mattā b. Yūnis translated the *Poetics* in the first half of the tenth century suggests that *muḥākāt*, which is also used by al-Jāḥiẓ in the ninth century, was the earliest term for impersonation and that *khayāl* replaced it in the course of the tenth century.

Several other passages confirm that *khayāl* on its own was different from *khayāl al-ẓill*. In the *Thamarāt al-Awrāq* of Ibn Ḥijja al-Ḥamawī (768-838/1366-1434), for example, we find the following observation:

وهذا يشبه قول القاضي الفاضل وقد اخرج له السلطان الملك الناصر صلاح الدين من القصر من يُغانِي الخيال اعني خيال الظل ليفرّجَه عليه ، فقام الفاضل عند الشروع في عمله . . .

> This is similar to the response of al-Qāḍī al-Fāḍil when the sultan al-Malik al-Nāṣir Ṣalāh al-Dīn [sc. Saladin] produced from his palace a performer of *khayāl* for him, I mean *khayāl al-ẓill*, in order to entertain him. Al-Qāḍī al-Fāḍil got up when they started the performance.

Quatremère failed to notice the qualification and omitted it in his French translation: 'celui qui s'occupe des ombres chinoises'.[24] But if the terms *khayāl* and *khayāl al-ẓill* had been synonymous, the author would not have found it necessary to specify which type of *khayāl* he had in mind.

Another example is found in Ibn Iyās (d. 930/1524): *akhadha ma'ahu fī ṭarīq al-Ḥijāz jamā'a min arbāb al-malāhī wa-'l-mukhāyiln min ṣunnā' khayāl al-ẓill*, 'he [sc. al-Malik al-Ashraf Sha'bān, in 768/1366] took with him on his way to the Ḥijāz a troupe of entertainers and *mukhāyilūn* who performed shadow plays'.[25] If there had not been several types of *mukhāyilūn*, the author would not have found it necessary to specify which kind of *mukhāyilūn* they were.

Yet another example is found in Ibn Khallikān's description of the *mawlid* celebrated by al-Malik al-Mu'aẓẓam Muẓaffar al-Dīn, governor of Arbil, in 586/1172f. For this *mawlid*, which was every year attended by scholars and poets from all over the Muslim world, Muẓaffar al-Dīn prepared twenty pavilions, each of which contained 'a choir of singers (*maghānī*), a troupe of *arbāb al-khayāl* and a group of musicians (*malāhī*) .... During the whole period all business was suspended and people's only occupation was to amuse themselves ... every day, after the afternoon (*'aṣr*) prayer, Muẓaffar al-Dīn went forth and stopped at each pavilion successively, listening to the music and amusing himself by looking at their plays (*wa-yatafarraju 'alā khayālihim*) or whatever else might be going on.'[26] Both Quatremère and von Grunebaum took the *arbāb al-khayāl* to be shadow play presenters.[27] But the *khayāl* plays were performed during the day,[28] and as Lane rightly notes, *khayāl al-ẓill* can only be performed at night: 'The puppet show of 'Kara Gyooz' has been introduced into Egypt by the Turks, in whose language the puppets are made to speak .... They are conducted in the manner of the

'Chinese shadows' and therefore only exhibited at night'.[29] Clearly, we have here another example of *khayāl* in the sense of live performance.

If shadow plays could only be performed at night, then the *arbāb al-khayāl* mentioned by al-Maqrīzī, as performing during the day in 740/1339f together with musicians (*malāhī*) must also have been live players.[30] The *khayāl al-'Arab* mentioned by Ibn Taghrī Birdī with reference to the year 871/1446f was probably a play by or about bedouin, but hardly a shadow play and at any rate not a form of bedouin sport, as Popper suggested in his glossary.[31]

Maimonides in his *Mishna Commentary* speaks clearly about the actress called in Hebrew *yotset ha-ḥuts* (lit. the woman who goes out), who performs *khayāl*. He explains that such an actress performs with masks and acts plays, and that she puts on a gown made of fine net fabric which is unsuitable for wearing, but she uses it for comical purposes, as many *khayyālūn* (sic)[32] used to do in his time. In an another passage, he called the play of such an actress or prostitute who wears net fabric on her head when going out to perform in several houses in the same street, that she uses it *li-'l-li'b fī 'l-khayāl* ('for performance of live play').[33]

We are not told much about the manner in which performers of *ḥikāyāt* or *khayāl* did their acting. Al-Kutubī (d. 769/1367) and al-Ṣafadī (d. 764/1363) have an anecdote about Ibn Dāniyāl (d. 710/1311), the author of the earliest shadow plays preserved in Arabic,[34] in which the verb *khāyala* means to improvise an exchange of sharp retorts or making fun of somebody. 'The physician Shams al-Dīn Ibn Dāniyāl had a shop in Bāb al-Futūḥ in which he used to treat eyes. Once I passed by him along with a group of his friends. One of them said, "come, let us make fun of the doctor" (*nukhāyilu 'alā 'l-ḥakīm*). I said to them, "don't compete with him; for sure, you will be disgraced". But they did not heed (me), and said, "O physician, do you need sticks?", meaning that his patients become blind and need sticks. He promptly replied, "no, only if some of you would lead (blind people) for the sake of God". They passed by ashamed.'[35] If one of the meanings of *khāyala* was to engage in sharp retorts, the actor known as *mukhāyil* or *khayālī* might perhaps also engage in such retorts in addition to, or as part of, performing plays.

There are several references to actors dressing up. Thus, as has been seen, the poem from *A Thousand and One Nights* cited by Jacob refers to *ṣunnā' al-khayāl* who change beards. Al-Maqrīzī's account of the judge Shams al-Dīn Muḥammad al-Harawī (d. 828/1424) implies that they would also change clothes. This man, he says, changed his attire (*ziyy*) every time he was appointed to a new post. Once he had worn a non-Arab costume; when he was appointed chief judge, he put on a wide-sleeved *jubba*, enlarged his turban and let its ends hang between his shoulders; when he was appointed secretary, he donned the attire of secretaries, narrowed his sleeves and changed his turban to a smaller, rounder and ridged version without the loose ends; but when he was once more appointed chief judge, he changed back again: 'in his various changes of attire he resembled the slapstick comedians (*ṣafā'ita* [*sic* = *ṣafā'ina*] *min al-mukhāyilīn*) who amuse a frivolous and impudent audience;.[36] This is clearly a reference to live actors changing costume, not to shadow play presenters; possibly, it was to distinguish between the two that he added the term *al-ṣafā'ina.*[37]

That actors used different kinds of costumes can perhaps also be inferred from an incident in the palace of the caliph al-Mu'taḍid (279-89/892-902). Ibn al-Athīr relates that in 284/897 a person appeared in the palace of this caliph and stabbed a eunuch who went to see who he was, whereupon he disappeared in the orchard. He was looked for in vain and thought to be a *jinn* or a ghost.[38] Though he reappeared several times, his identity was discovered only after the death of al-Muktafī (d. 295/908). According to Ibn Taghrī Birdī, 'he was a servant boy who was in love with one of the slave girls in the palace. Al-Mu'taḍid used to forbid servant boys to enter the harem once they had attained puberty. Outside the harem was a big orchard. This servant acquired a white beard. He appeared once in the form of a monk and sometimes in the attire of a soldier with a sword in his hand. He put on several beards of different shapes and colours. When the slave girl would come out with other maidens to look for him, he would retire in private with her among the trees. If searched for, he would enter among the trees, take off the beard, the hooded cloak and the sword, hide them and leave the sword drawn in his hand [sic] as if he were one of those searching for him ... (later he) was deported to Tarsus, and the maiden revealed his story'.[39] It seems unlikely that a young palace servant should have been able to acquire so many different outfits, not to mention so many different kinds of coloured beards, without such outfits having been available in the palace itself. We know from other sources that al-Mu'taḍid and his wife Qaṭr al-Nadā used to celebrate Nawrūz with *samājāt* and *ṣafā'ina,*[40] or in other words with actors of the same type, in part, as those mentioned by al-Maqrīzī in his account of the judge. It is thus hard not to infer that the palace servant had acquired access to costumes used by the *ṣafā'ina* (or, as al-Maqrīzī put it, *al-ṣafā'ina min al-mukhāyilīn*) for professional purposes.

Dressing up is also attested in the *Madkhal* of the North African Ibn al-Ḥājj (compiled in 732/1331):

وانظر . . . الى ما جرّت اليه بدعة هذه اللبسة التي جعلوها علامة
على الفقه . . . وهو ان بعض المخايلين من اهل اللهو واللعب اذا
عملوا الخيال بحضرة بعض العوام وغيرهم في بعض الاوقات يخرجون
في اثناء لَعْبهم لَعْبة يسمونها بابة القاضي ، فيلبسون زيّه من كبر
العمامة وسعة الاكمام وطولها وطول الطيلسان ، فيرقصون به
ويذكرون عليه فواحش كثيرة ينسبوها اليه فيكثر ضحك من هنا ك
ويسخرون به ويكثرون النقوط عليهم بسبب ذلك . . .

> And look ... at the consequences of the heresy of wearing such attire which people made as a symbol of the legist ... that is when actors (*mukhāyilūn*) from among the class of entertainers perform theatrical plays (*khayāl*) in the presence of the common people and others, they sometimes produce in the course of their acting a play called the 'Scene of the Judge' (*la'bat al-qāḍī*). They put on his attire, with his large turban, long wide sleeves and long garment (*ṭaylasān*). They dance, wearing this attire and give voice to many rude remarks which they attribute to him. The laughter of the audience grows. They (join in) the mockery of him and lavish money on them [the actors] for this reason.[41]

This is clearly yet another example (if more are needed) of *khayāl* in the sense of live theatre rather than shadow play, but the main interest of the passage lies in the striking similarity between the manner in which the 'Play of the Judge' and 'Abbāda al-Mukhannath's satire of 'Alī b. Abī Ṭālib were performed.[42] In both cases the actors were dressed to look like the persons they represented, but in neither case did they actually *represent* them; on the contrary, the actors would utter rude remarks against them: the remarks were put in the mouths of the persons they impersonated, but they were criticisms of the persons in question, not attempts to formulate their points of view or their manner of presenting them.[43]

Technical terms relating to *khayāl*

An alternative, and at first sight more obvious, translation of Ibn al-Ḥājj's passage would be the following:

> When actors form among the class of entertainers perform theatrical plays ... they sometimes produce in the course of their acting a doll. (*yukhrijūna fī athnā' li'bihim lu'ba*) which they call *Bābat al-qāḍī* and which they dress in his [the judge's] attire .... Then they dance with it, giving voice to many rude remarks which they attribute to him.

However, there are good reasons why the first translation should be preferred.

la'ba

The term *l'bat* has here been rendered as *la'ba*, play, rather than *lu'ba*, doll. For one thing, the text has *fa-yulbisūna ziyyahu*, which can only mean 'they put on his attire'; if a doll has been intended, the text would have had to say *fa-yulbisūnahā ziyyahu*, 'they dress it in his attire'. For another thing the term *la'ba* is well-attested in the sense of play. Above we met a *La'bat al-Yahūdī.*[44] Numerous shadow plays are also known as *la'bat* thus *La'bat al-Laymūn* ('The Play of the Lemon'), *La'bat al-Ḥammām* ('The Play of the Bathhouse'), *La'bat al-Marākib fī 'l-Baḥr* ('The Play of the Ships on the Sea'),[45] *Li'b al-Timsāḥ* ('Crocodile Play'), *La'bat al-Ḥūta* ('The Play of the Fish').[46] These plays were all from Tunisia, and Ibn al-Ḥājj was a North African from Fez.[47] As we have seen, *la'ba* also means play in al-Ṭahṭāwī and Ṣanua's works.[48]

khayālī

From the thirteenth century, poets composed verses on various crafts and professions, concentrating mainly on those dealing with entertainment, such as those of the dancer, the musicians and the *khayālī* or *mukhāyil*, *khayyāl* and *mukhayyil* of both sexes. It is difficult to tell, in these cases, whether an actor or a presenter of shadow plays is meant, since these words are applied to both. The best indication that an actor is meant is the poet's describing his appearance; the shadow player is hidden behind his curtain.[49]

The following verses of al-'Ādilī 'l-Ṭūsī (d. c.654/1256) are a rare example of describing the beauty of an actress (*mukhayyila*) wearing a shirt, with her black hair decorated with jewellery, elegantly performing her play with dancing[50] (*ṭawīl* metre).

وقال في جارية مخيّلة [طويل]:

مُخَيِّلَةٌ مِثْلُ الخَيَالِ إِذَا سَرَى   مَتَى مَا تَرِدْ إِتْمَامَةً مِنْهُ يَنْقُصُ
عَلَيْهَا قَمِيصٌ يُطْلِعُ البَدْرَ طَوْقُه   عَلَاهُ ظَلَامٌ بِالنُّجُومِ مُفَصَّصُ
فَحُورِيَّةٌ إِنْسِيَّةٌ حِينَ تُجْتَلَى   وَجِنِّيَّةٌ مِنْ خِفَّةٍ حِينَ تَرْقُصُ

He (al-'Ādilī 'l-Ṭūsī) said describing a maiden actress:

> An actress is like a roving phantom at night, whenever you ask it for fulfilment, the more it diminishes. / She wears a shirt whose collar reveals (her face)as a full moon, upon which darkness is decorated with stars. / A human houri when she appears, and a fairy when she performs (her play) by dance. /

In verses describing young actors the poets depict the player's first beard ('*idhār*), his dancing and his body. If, on the other hand, a shadow player is meant, poets introduce items of the appropriate equipment, the lamp, the screen, or the figures, etc.

ikhrāj

The expression *yukhrijūna* has here been translated as 'they produce (a play)' rather than 'they get out (a doll)'. In defence of this translation I adduce the following table, in which all the medieval attestations of *akhraja* in a theatrical context known to me are arranged in the chronological order of the authors with indication of the context in which the term is used:

(1) Ibn Abī 'Awn, (d. 934):
in hajānī akhrajtu ummahu fī 'l-ḥikāya (if he satirises me, I shall produce (*akhrajtu*) his mother in a *ḥikāya*.[51]

(2) Mattā b. Yūnis, (d. 940):
khārij al-qayna (the play proper).

Mattā b. Yūnis, in his translation of Aristotle's *Poetics* from Syriac to Arabic, translated the term 'play proper' as *khārij al-qayna.* 'Abd al-Rahmān Badawī, in his edition of this translation, commented in a note: *kadhā! bi-ma'nā al-masraḥiyya* ('sic, in the sense of drama').[52] In view of the attestations of the term *akhraja*, given below, it may be suggested that *khārij al-qayna* means performing of drama.

(3) Ibn 'Abd Rabbih, (d. 940):
yakhruju wa-yakhrujūn (He sets out for performance and (the audience) set out with him).[53]

(4) Ibn al-Dāya, (d. 951):
wa-akhraja ḥikāyatahu fī tazammutih wa-kalāmih (he impersonated him in his gravity and manner of speech).

(5) Abū 'l-Muṭahhar al-Azdī (wrote *ca.* 1010):
kharaja fī 'l-ḥikāya ka'annahu 'Abd al-Razzāq al-majnūn (in his performance of this mime he was like 'Abd al-Razzāq, the madman).[55]

(6) Abū 'l-Faraj al-Iṣfahānī, (d. 967):
wa-'amila lahu 'Alluwayh ḥikāyatan a'ṭāhā li-'l-zaffānīn wa-'l-mukhannathīn fa-akhrajūhu fīhā ('Alluwayh composed a play, which he handed over to the dancers and actors, and they impersonated him in it).[56]

(7) Al-Shābushtī, (d. 998):
la-ukhrijanna ummaka fī 'l-khayāl (I shall produce your mother in an impersonation).[57]

(8) Ibn al-Zubayr, (d. eleventh century):
Qatr al Nadā ... made *samājāt* ... and thirty servant girls were produced (*ukhrija*) from the palace to perform a dance or a play with the *ṣafā'ina.*[58]

(9) Al-Musabbiḥī, (d. 1029), quoted by al-Maqrīzī:
ilā an'āda al-ramādiyya al-khārijūn ilā 'l-sijn bi-'l-tamātīl wa-'l-maḍāḥik wa-'l-ḥikāyāt ... (until the performing actors returned to the prison (of Joseph) with statues, comic figures, mimes, and masked actors).[59]

(10) Abū Ḥayyān al-Tawḥīdī, (d. 1010):
yuḥākī 'l-mūmisāt wa-yakhruju fī aṣḥāb al-samājāt (He impersonates prostitutes and acts in the manner of masked actors.[60]

Al-Tawḥīdī describes the personality of Ibn al-'Amīd who tries to hide his real character behind a curtain of artificial behaviour, resembling a pantomime. This phrase is amongst the rare examples in which a *samāja's* performance is described.

(11) Al-Shaqundī, (d. 1129):
ikhrāj al-qarawī wa-'l-murābiṭ wa-'l-mutawajjih (staging the villager, sleight-of-hand tricks and masquerade.[61]

Al-Shaqundī here enumerates the skills of the dancers of Ubbada. According to Monroe, whose translation I have reproduced, *ikhrāj al-qarawī* is something done with female dances to musical accompaniment and in a jongleur milieu. It must therefore be the name of a dance.[62] But given the technical meaning of *akhraja, ikhrāj al-qarawī* may well mean 'staging the play of the villager'. Indeed, there may be a reference to the same play in Ibn Quzmān's *zajal* no. 12: *qarawīkum wāqif / al-malā'ib huzzu,* 'your villager is waiting / enliven the stage',[63] though Monroe, whose translation I have once more adopted, thinks that the villager here too is a character in a particular kind of dance rather than a character in a live play.[64] I shall come back to this *zajal* later in this chapter (pp. 141–2).

(12) Ibn Shuhayd (d. 1147), quoted by Ibn Bassām.
They relate that when he [sc. Ibn al-Iflīlī] hobbled about, slightly advancing, then retreating, staff in hand and sack on shoulder, he was the most skillful of persons at *ikhrāj l'bat al-yahūdī.*[65]

Monroe transliterates the last three words of this passage *ikhrāj lu'bat al-yahūdī* and translates it as 'staging the Jewish puppet'.[66] But the text clearly states that Ibn al-Iflīlī himself acted the part of the Jew. It was *in the course* of hobbling about with a staff in his hand and a sack on his back that he displayed his skill at *ikhrāj l'bat al-yahūdī,* and it is hardly to be presumed that he could manipulate puppets at the same time. On the contrary, we must take it that the staff and the sack were props and that the hobbling was part of the impersonation. The similarity between Ibn al-Iflīlī's play and the image of the Jew in Turkish shadow puppet productions, remarked on by

Monroe, only goes to show that there was close connection between live acting and the production of shadow plays (or simply that the image was widespread and longlived).[67] The phrase should be transliterated *ikhrāj la'bat al-yahūdī*, and the correct translation is 'acting the play of the Jew'.

(13) Umayya b. 'Abd al-'Azīz al-Andalusī (d. 1133):
yukhriju lahu wujūhan muḍhika (he would perform for him with comic masks).[68]
Here the association of the verb *yukhriju* with *wujūh* leaves no doubt that we have to do with an actor. Both Ibn Sīnā and Ibn Rushd use the term *al-akhdh bi-'l-wujūh*, 'using masks', as the Arabic equivalent of 'play' in their comments on Aristotle's *Poetics*, obviously because Greek actors used masks;[69] and Ibn Sīnā translates 'actors' (Greek *hypokrites*) as *al-munāfiqūn al-ākhidhūn bi-'l-wujūh.*[70]

(14) Maimonides (Mūsā b. Maymūn) (d. 1204):
Yotṣet ha-ḥūts: allatī tukhriju 'l-wujūha wa-'l-al'āba, fa-hiya talbasu hādhā 'l-thawba 'l-mushawwaha alladhī lā yaṣluḥu li-l-libāsi kay yuḍḥaka minhā, wa-kathīran mā yaf'alu 'l-khayyālūn (sic) dhālika. (lit. The woman who goes out = actress): She is the one who performs with masks and (acts) plays. She puts on this ugly cloth which is not fit for wearing, in order to be made fun of. In fact, *khayyālūn* do such things frequently.[71]

In his commentary on the *Mishna*, written in Arabic in Hebrew characters, Maimonides explains the meaning of the gown (*ḥalūq*) of *yotset ha-ḥuts* (of the woman who goes out) which is made like a net. Maimonides says that this woman is not a 'prostitute', as commentators generally think, but rather an actress who acts with masks and performs plays, wearing a funny gown or shirt. The importance of this passage is that it shows clearly that the verb *akhraja* is connected with live plays (*al'āb,* sin. *la'b, li'b,* la'ib) and not with dolls (*lu'ab,* sin. *lu'ba*), and that such live plays are performed either with masks or without. Moreover, the *khayāliyyūn* (live actors) perform in the same manner, i.e. they wear funny clothes in their performances. In a former example given by Maimonides we learn that the *mithāl* and *muḥākāt* (theatrical performances and plays) are performed with shield also.[72]

(15) Ibn Abī Uṣaybi'a (d. 1269):
kāna muḥibban li-'l-sharābi mudminan lahu wa-yu'ānī 'l-khayāl; kāna idhā ṭariba yakhruju fī 'l-khayāl wa-yughannī lahu (he was fond of wine, addicted to it, and dealt with *khayāl*; when moved with joy, he would perform a play and sing to his performance).[73]
This passage refers to Abū 'l-Ḥakam al-Andalusī (d. 549/1154), a

distinguished physician and frivolous poet who was fond of entertainment and dissipation (*lahw wa-khalāʿa*). He composed poetry for the purpose of 'play and buffoonery' (*liʿb wa-mujūn*), or in other words poetry of the kind also composed by Ibn al-Ḥajjāj, the scurrilous poet quoted by Abū 'l-Muṭahhar in his *Ḥikāyat Abī 'l-Qāsim al-Baghdādī,* by the tenth-century al-Aḥnaf al-ʿUkbarī and Ibn Sukkara al-Hāshimī, Ibn Dāniyāl (d. 1311), Ibn Sūdūn (d. 1407-64) and many other poets involved in entertainment and theatrical performance. Ibn Abī Uṣaybi's adds a specimen of what he would sing when playing a *khayāl*: 'hunter of the bee, the (time of) action has arrived / get up and set out early in the morning, bring the honey'

(16) In Muḥammad b. Mawlāhūm al-Khayālī's *al-Maqāma al-Mukhtaṣara fī 'l-Khamsīn Marah,* the actress (*khayāliyya*) gives the following speech in colloquial Arabic in which she puns on the word *akhraja* and its derivatives as part of the vocabulary of her profession:

قالت الخياليّة : عهدناكم ظراف كأنكم أم قاوشتي وضرّتها وقت يتقايسوا ، اخرجوا من دي البابة وادخلوا في غيرها يا خوارج ، قوموا اشغلوا الطابق برقصة قبل ما نصبّح ، وانشدت شعر [كان وكان] :

إنّ الخروج لي اصلح من الدخول بيناتكم فكل من هو داخل
بينا تكم مخروج

The actress said: 'I am used to your being as witty as Umm Qawishtī and her husband's second wife when they quarrel. End the performance of this play (ukhrujū min di 'l-bāba) and get into another, O you outsiders! Get out and fill the room with dance before morning comes upon us.' And she recites: 'To get out is better for me / than to get into your midst. / Everyone who mingles with you is expelled.'[74]

(17) Ibn al-Ḥājj (d. 1336):

They produce in the course of their acting (*liʿb*) a play (*laʿba*) called 'The Scene of the Judge' (*bābat al-qāḍī*).[75]

Ibn al-Ḥājj adduced this play as an example of how some judges disgrace themselves and their colleagues by their corrupt behaviour, which induces actors to mock the entire rank of judges in the Muslim world.

(18) Ibn ʿĀṣim al-Qaysī (d. 1426):

Akhrajtu ummaka fī 'l-laʿba (I would stage your mother in a play).[76]

(19) ʿAbd al-Wahhāb al-Shaʿrānī (d. 1565):

Its status [sc. that of the soul] is comparable to that of the buffoon of the female singers when he performs a scene from a play representing a judge or a scholar (*khalbūṣ al-maghānī idhā kharaja fī bābat al-khayāl fī ṣifat qāḍin aw ʿālim.* The audience mock him and laugh at him. But they should not approve of his behaviour; rather, they should be of the opinion that he deserves harsh punishment.[77]

Al-Shaʿrānī here adds important data on theatrical performances in the sixteenth century. The buffoon is called *khalbūs* (a male servant of female singers);[78] he is performing a live play (*khayāl*), which is referred to as a *bāba*, 'scene', and the object of mockery is once more judges and religious scholars.

(20) ʿAbd al-Wahhāb al-Shaʿrānī.

In his *Tabaqāt* al-Shaʿrānī relates a miracle accomplished by a Ṣūfī mendicant. 'I have seen a jurist who rebuked a mendicant for his practice of the theatrical trade along with itinerant actors (*ṣanʿata 'l-khayāl maʿa 'l-mukhabbiṭīn* [*sic* = *muḥabbazīn*]) The mendicant performed a play (*akhraja ... bāban fī 'l-khayāl*) for the jurist and made him sit on a seat. The elephant came, and the mendicant wound its trunk and threw it on the ground so that it died. The next morning the same thing happened to the jurist, and they buried him in the evening'.[79]

The Ṣūfī here was possibly a *malāmatī* who had joined itinerant actors in order to humiliate himself. At all events, he performed a play, and his miraculous killing of the (illusory?) elephant somehow caused the jurist to die. In the previous passage al-Shaʿrānī used the phrase *kharaja fī bābat al-khayāl*, 'he performed a scene of a play'. The phrase used here, *akhraja bāban fī 'l-khayāl*, must mean 'he produced a scene of a play'.

(21) Ibn Ḥijja al-Ḥamawī (d. 1434):

akhraja min al-qaṣr man yuʿānī 'l-khayāl, aʿnī khayāl al-ẓill (he produced a player from his palace dealing with *khayāl*, I mean *khayāl al-ẓill*).[80]

In this passage, referring to Saladin, *akhraja* is clearly non-technical. It is one of three cases in which this verb is used in connection with shadow plays. In the first it simply means 'appears', sc. on the screen: 'a figure called *al-waṣṣāf* appears (*yakhruju*)'.[81] In the second the terms *khurūj* and *dukhūl* are used to denote 'starting and ending a shadow play'.[82]

It is clear from these examples that *kharaja* in a theatrical context means 'to go out to perform' and thus simply 'to perform' (cf. nos 3, 16, 19). Correspondingly, *akhraja* means 'to make somebody (go out to) perform' (cf. nos 8, 21). The expression *akhrajtu ummaka fī 'l-ḥikāya* literally means 'I shall make your mother (go out to) perform in a mime', or, differently put, 'I shall impersonate her' (nos 1, 7, 18). Similarly, *ikhrāj al-qarawī/al-yahūdī* means impersonating a villager/Jew (nos 11, 12), while the more general expression *akhraja la'batan/bāban* means to produce a play (nos 14, 19, 20). *Kharaja* takes the preposition *fī* (*kharaja fī 'l-ḥikāya, kharaja fī bābat al-khayāl*, etc, cf. nos 5, 10, 15, 19), while *akhraja* takes a direct object (cf. nos 4, 6, 7, 11, 13, 14, 17, 20).

Both forms of the verb are largely or wholly used in connection with live plays. the root is indeed used in connection with shadow plays in no. 21, but only in its ordinary, not in its technical sense. Staging a shadow play is usually described with other words. Ibn Iyās called the players of shadow play *ṣunnā' khayāl al-ẓill* and spoke of someone who *ṣana'a khayāl al-ẓill*, 'performed a shadow play'.[83] He uses the same verb in his description of a shadow play performed before the Ottoman sultan Selim I (who conquered Egypt in 1517 and hanged the last Mamluk sultan, Ṭūmān Bāy): *inna 'l-mukhāyil ṣana'a ṣifat Bāb Zuwayla wa-ṣifat al-sulṭān Ṭūmān Bāy lammā shuniqa 'alayhi*, 'the player made the figure of Bāb Zuwayla and the figure of sultan Ṭumān Bay when he was hanged at the gate (of Zuwayla)'.[84] Al-Sakhāwī (d. 903/1497) uses the verb *fa'ala* in his account of how the sultan burned the shadow play figures in 855/1415: *wa-kataba 'alayhim qasā'im fī 'adam al-'awda li-fi'lihi*, 'he made them sign an undertaking that they should not stage it at all'.[85] Ibn Taghrī Birdī also uses this verb.[86] In the *zajal* of Dāwūd al-Manāwī *'amila al-khayāl* is used,[87] while al-Wajīh al-Mināwī has *aratnā khayāl al-ẓill*, 'she showed us a shadow play'.[88] *Akhraja* would thus appear to be reserved for live plays.[89]

To go back now to Ibn al-Ḥājj, it should be clear that *yukhrijuna ... la'bat yusammūnahā bābat al-qāḍī* is unlikely to mean 'they produce a doll (*lu'ba*) which they call *Bābat al-qāḍī*' (an odd name for a doll), as opposed to 'they stage a play (*la'ba*) which they call the "Scene of the Judge", the translation adopted in the previous section and again in the list above, no. 17. It is true that there is no precise parallel to the expression *akhraja la'batan* in our list, but the phrases *akḥraja ḥikāyatahu* (no. 4) and *tukhrij 'l-wujūha wa-'l-al'āba* (*sin. la'ba*) (no. 14) are closely parallel.

Bāba

Ibn al-Ḥājj's actors called their play *bābat al-qāḍī*, using a term of which there are other attestations in our list (cf. nos 19, 20). In all three cases it clearly means a scene, synonymously with *faṣl*, a term employed already by 'Abbāda al-Mukhannath (d. 250/864)[90] and attested with great regularity thereafter. *Bāba* is attested in the work of the scurrilous poet Ibn al-Ḥajjāj (d. 391/1001), though only in the sense of 'type': he refers to his own poetry as *ẓarīfun min bābat al-*

ẓurafā' ('elegant, of the category of the elegant people').[91] In the sense of 'scene' it is not directly attested until Ibn al-Ḥājj, or in other words the fourteenth century, but there is indirect evidence which takes it back to the twelfth.

In the *Shifā'* of al-Khafājī (d. 977/1569f) there is mention of a *bāba* by a certain Ja'far the Dancer. "*Bāba* means 'type' (*naw'*), and accordingly they call the shadow play *bāba*. There is an example in the verses of Ibn 'Abd al-Ẓāhir [d. 962/1554]: 'beware of ignoring Ja'far / the *khayālī* and his friends. The Nile of your Egypt has a different Ja'far / which *yakhruju fī bāba*'. *Bāba* is a scene in a play (*wa-bāba iḥdā bābāt al-khayāl*), either in Ja'far the dancer's *khayāl* or in *Khayāl al-izār* [curtain play = shadow play]. Ja'far is the name of the inventor of the play performed by dancing.'[92]

Ja'far al-Rāqiṣ, then, was an actor (*khayālī*) and performer of a play (*yakhruju fī bāba*, compare the list above, no. 15; the verse is a pun: the Nile also *yakhruju fī Bāba*, sc. overflows in the month of Bāba.) Modern scholars such as Aḥmad Taymūr and Ibrāhīm Ḥamāda have taken him to be a shadow player,'[93] but this cannot be right. In the first place, the verb *kharaja* is associated with live plays rather than shadow plays, as we have seen. In the second place, al-Khafājī tells us that Ja'far's performance involved dancing. Dancing was of course also an element in shadow theatre. In Ibn Dāniyāl's *Bābat Ṭayf al-Khayāl*, for example, we are told that Ṭayf al-Khayāl 'dances in accordance with the custom of the play' (*yarquṣu 'alā 'ādat al-khayāl*)[94], and Ṭayf al-Khayāl himself recites, 'before I perform my dance in this play (*wa-min qabli raqṣī bi-hādhā 'l-khayāl*) ... I have to praise the Lord'.[95] But in the shadow play it was the puppet that danced, not the *khayālī* himself. Ja'far was however both a *khayālī* and a dancer, so his dancing must have been part of a live performance. In other words, his *bāba* must have been a play of the same type as that of the villager performed by the dancers of Ubbada (above, no. 11), the *bābat al-qāḍī* described by Ibn al-Ḥājj, which also involved dancing, and the *khayāl* referred to by Ibn Dāniyāl in his complaint about his wife: *tuḥammilunīhi lā ḥamalathu kay-mā / uraqqiṣuhu bi-anwā'i 'l-khayāli*, 'she makes me carry him [sc. his son], may she not (live to) carry him, / in order that I dance with him in all kinds of plays'.[96] Finally, it should be noted that al-Khafājī explicitly distinguishes Ja'far's play from *khayāl al-izār* (wrongly given as *khayāl al-izād* in both editions of the text)[97]; and Ibn Dāniyāl likewise distinguishes the performance of the dancing *khayālī* from that of a *khayāl al-izār: innī 'mru'un ahwā 'l-khayāliyya fī raqṣin / wa-lā ahwā khāyal al-izār* (*sarī'* metre), 'I am a man who loves the actor / who dances, and I do not love shadow play'.[98] In short, there can be no doubt that Ja'far al-Rāqiṣ was a performer of live plays.

We know that Ja'far al-Rāqiṣ was a friend of the poet Sibṭ Ibn al-

Ta'āwīdhī (518-83/1124-87),[99] so he must have been active in the twelfth century, a period for which there is other evidence for theatrical dancing too: the Persian drawings described by Ettinghausen of unmasked actors who perform by dancing also date from the twelfth century.[100] Al-Khafājī's, claim that he was the actual inventor of plays involving dancing should not be taken seriously, for dancers participated along with *mukhannathūn* in the performance of the play about the judge al-Khalanjī by the ninth-century 'Alluwayh;[101] and a twelfth-century Egyptian invention could hardly have got into Persian drawings of the same century or reached Spain by 1129, the death-date of al-Shaqundī, to whom we own our knowledge of the play of the villager performed by the dancers of Ubbada. Ja'far may well have invented a particular kind of play associated with dancing which became popular in Iraq, but dancing and clearly been associated with live theatre long before his time. In fact, it must have been thanks to this association that dancing came to be a standard ingredient of shadow plays too.

However, there is no reason to dispute the claim that Ja'far al-Rāqiṣ was associated with works of the type called *bāba*. By the twelfth century, then, the term *bāba* was current in the sense of 'scene'; and in this sense it was clearly used, not just in the context of shadow theatre, but also in that of live plays.

The plays and their actors

The list given above gives us the names of some plays: 'the Play of the Jew' (no. 12), 'The Play of the Villager' (no. 11), 'the Play of Umm Qāwishtī and her Husband's Second Wife' (? of no. 16), and 'The Play of the Judge' (no. 17, cf. no. 20). But there must obviously have been countless more. Most plays seem only to have involved one actor: nos 1 (=7, 18), 10-15, 20-1. But several actors are attested for six (nos 3, 6, 8, 9, 16, 17). Actresses only appear in three (nos 11, 14, 16), and only once together with men (no 16).

On the size of audiences we have practically no information. Shams al-Dīn al-Jazarī (751-832/1350-1429) relates that in the year 737/1336f about seven hundred *ḥarāfisha*, or members of the riff-raff, watched an actor performing a play (*khayālī ya'mal al-khayāl*) in which he ridiculed them (*'amila lahum nawba yumaṣkhir bihim*); they complained to the governor of Damascus, who gave orders for the actor to be deported.[102] But whether the size of this audience was typical is impossible to say.

We owe practically all our information to medieval historians who were not themselves involved with theatre and whose brief accounts are given incidentally. Only one author gives us a first-hand description of the environment in which actors lived, that is Ibn Dāniyāl, whose poetry is full of references to life in medieval taverns, the variety of performances given in them, the types of food, drink and *ḥashīsh* one could enjoy there, the prostitutes, Banū Sāsān and other people who frequented them, and the quarrels in which they abounded.

In one of his poems Ibn Dāniyāl describes Satan's sadness at the abolition of alcoholic beverages in the reign of sultan Ḥusām al-Dīn Lājīn (696/1296f) and throws in references to the wine merchant, the *ḥashīsh* smoker, the drunk negro, the pimp, the masturbator and the *khayālī*, the singer and the flautist ('among them a *khayālī*, a singer and a flautist who came with the group'.[103] In another poem he describes his visit to a tavern (*ḥān*) with his friends, their singing and performance of impromptu sketches there, their getting drunk, taking up with prostitutes and their quarrels; and here too he refers to acting: 'we were as if driven to a tavern / with a frivolous group of my kind; one is singing, another is making gestures with the palm of his hand (? *yubashliq*) / and yet another is performing a scene and a play (*wa-hādhā fī bābatin wa-khayāli*)'.[104] In one poem, as has been seen, he curses his wife for forcing him to carry his son with him to dance in various kinds of plays;[105] and in another he confesses that he loves young men (literally 'the first of beards', *'idhār*), because he loves the dancing actor rather than the shadow play:[106] apparently, dancing actors were young and handsome.

Ibn Dāniyāl also mentions actors called *ṣafā'ina min al-mukhāyilīn*, 'slapstick comedians from among the *khayāl* players',[108] while al-Jazarī knew of a *khayālī* who performed for *ḥarāfish*:[109] Ibn Dāniyāl's expression is thus likely to refer to actors who performed for the riff-raff. He describes them as smokers of *ḥashīsh*, lazy, fond of dancing and of staging scenes (? *al-raqṣ wa-'l-mashāhid*).[110] According to al-Badrī, who discussed the nicknames of *ḥashīsh* among the different nations and professions of the Muslim world, *ḥashīsh* in the parlance of actors was *al-batin* whereas it was *bunduq* in the parlance of the riff-raff (*wa-in kunta min al-mukhāyila fa-'smihā 'l-batin ... wa-'smihā bayna 'l-ḥarāfisha bunduqa*).[111]

Theatre was thus associated with immorality and indecency, as Muslim scholars were well aware. Ibn Taghrī Birdī speaks with derision of a son of a Christian convert to Islam called 'Alī b. Ramaḍān (d. 871/1466) whose house was called an inn (*khān*) on account of the many musicians and mean people (*arbāb al-malāhī wa-'l-aṭrāf*) who frequented it without modesty or shame. On the day of his death a *khayāl al-'Arab* was performed for Mamluks and children because the deceased had been fond of entertainment. Ibn Taghrī Birdī comments with a rhetorical question: 'and you know what *khayāl al-'Arab* implies [in the way of immorality]?'[112]

Khayāl in al-Andalus

In Muslim Spain there does not appear to have been any development of theatrical terms comparable to that which can be observed in the eastern part of the Arab world. The terms *la'ba* and *khayāl* for live play, and *la''āb* for actor, seem to have been used from the beginning right up to the expulsion of the Muslims from Spain; terms such as *ḥākiya, samāja, ṣafā'ina* and *muḥabbaẓūn* would appear to have been unknown, though this may simply be due to the fact that the sources pay little attention to theatrical activities. At all events, there is some compensation for the general paucity of information in Pedro de Alcala's dictionary *Vocabulista en letra castellana,* published in Granada 1505. In this work we find the terms *tamthīl* and *mumaththil,* translated as *representacio* and *representador* ('acting' and 'actor'), both of which terms are still used in the modern Arab world; *shā'ir* for *representador de comedias* and *de tragedias; la''āb* for mime or buffoon (*representador de momos),* synonymous with *la''āb al-khiyāl,* or *momo contrahazedors;* and *kabīr la''āb al-khiyāl* for leader of a troupe of actors (*momo contrahazedora;* and *kabīr la''āb al-Khiyāl* for leader of a troupe of actors (*momo principal*), (*La''āb* is also given in the sense of *teatral cosa de teatro); mal'ab* for theatre (*teatro de hazia Juegos*); and *mulay'ab* for puppet theatre (*teatro pequeñio*).[113]

Pedro de Alcala, then, leaves no doubt that there was live theatre in Spain. In fact, four items of the list given above (pp. 000–00), refer to live theatre in al-Andalus (nos 11–13, 18), and there is a brief reference to it in Ibn Bassām's *Dhakhīra,* too. Here we are given a description of a man who stretched out ropes in his house *Ka'annahu yurīdu an yukhrija khayālan,*[114] 'as if he wanted to stage a play', and who proceeded to hang sacks, gowns, trousers, head-cloths, veils and other kinds of clothing on them. As has been seen, performers of *khayāl.* used different kinds of clothing and other props such as beards and (in the 'Play of the Jew') sacks. It is thus reasonable to assume that the ropes associated with *khayāl* were meant for the actors to hang their costumes and other articles on them.

Ibn Quzmān's *zajal* (no 12) can give us an idea of the repertoire of actors in al-Andalus. In fact this *zajal* has aroused controversies among eminent Orientalists such as García Gómez, Monroe and Corriente.[115] According to Monroe, Ibn Quzmān (d. 1160) is here 'simulating the voice of a jongleur who is directing a popular performance of some kind. As the mimetic poem develops, Ibn Quzmān turns to address different group of participants, among them, his musical consort, stage assistants, dancers, singers, actors, property men, and two white dogs ... Ibn Quzmān also refers to a 'villager', to a judge, to a male dancer named Qurra, and to three dancing girls named Zuhra, Maryam, and 'Aysha. He further mentions a group of Arabs, a camel, a warrior, a wounded sheikh, and the latter's retainer, who bears a fly-whisk. All these characters are jumbled togeher in seeming confusion, thereby contributing to the apparent obscurity of the poem.'[116] Monroe concludes that the shadow play and puppet show provide the closest analogy to the spectacle described here.[117] Corriente, on the other hand, suggests that Ibn Quzmān is directing his words to a troupe of actors and actresses performing live plays.[118] Because of the importance of this *zajal* to the present study I reproduce Monroe's translation here with some emendations based on the Arabic text provided by Corriente.[119] The metre is *majzū' al-madīd al-mabtūr* (*fā'ilātun fa'lun*), as Corriente noted, and the italics are my corrections.

0 Greetings to you, greetings to you
        I'll be soon with you!
1 Prepare the kettledrum
        and take the framedrum in hand,
   Hurry, hurry, the castanets,[120]
        let no one be remiss in playing them!
   And if a tambourine were available,
        the addition would be excellent.
   and the reed, my friends,
        the reed, will revive you.
2 Cover *Qurro* for me.[121]
        in an *inclined veil.*[122]
   Let him wear a taffeta robe
        with a full *embroidered flag.*[123]
   Let there be amulets upon him
        like those that come from Babylon.
   Don't nap, by God,
        for I know you well!
3 Your [*actor in the role of the*] 'Villager' is waiting.[124]
        enliven the stage!
   Whoever gets out of tune,
        slap him on the nape of the neck!
   Zuhra, Maryam, 'Aysha,
        where are you? Get moving!
   Ululate *O little whores*[125] with him who leads you.
4 Make for the judge
        a seat out of cushions.
   For he must be honored,
        being of my class.
   What a fellow, enchanter!

Indeed, he is my joy!
Let me count your number,[126] [I protect you] by God's name!
where is Qunbar among you?
5 *To find that* the sword is ready
and the sashes are coming,
Along with a white turban
and a red *veil.*[127]
Let me have a warcry from the Arabs;
they must appear.
Prepare your she-camel,
prepare *your Hebrew man.*[128]
6 What do you think of this warrior,
and the little *decrepit old-man.*[129]
Beside whom is an attendant with a fly-whisk,
by God he is excused[130] (for his grief).
What about his lament as he *elegises,*[181]
and his drivel as he weeps?
Thus indeed he makes his exit,
after having appeared before you.
7 Here comes big magic:
Whoever does not go to sleep, will get sick.
Shoo, white dog!
Shoo, white dog!
Curl up your tails
and go to sleep in your kennel
For when morning comes,
I'm taking you hunting.
8 I love all of you,
by the Prophet, love me in return.
Without you, I'm unhappy,
so are you, without me.
If anything should befall me,
mourn for me, all of you.
And if anything should befall you,
(I will mourn for you).

In my understanding of this *zajal,* which is close to Corriente's, the entire poem is put in the mouth of what Pedro de Alcala called a *kabīr la''āb al-khiyāl* or *momo principal,* that is to say a leader of a troupe of actors (a *rayyis* is the terminology of the Mashriq). He starts by greeting the audience and then gives order for music to be played. He proceeds to order one Qurra or Qorro to be dressed up and equipped with a flag and amulets (stanza 2). This Qorro was presumably an actor or, as Monroe states, a dancer, though Corriente offers a different suggestion.[132]

The speaker next tells his troupe to get moving 'your villager is waiting, enliven the stage'. The villager here must be an actor playing the role of villager, a possibility considered by Corriente too, though, following Dozy, he also thought that *qarawī* might mean 'sleight-of-hand'.[133] We have already met an Andalusian play about a villager: it was performed by the dancers of Ubbada (cf. no. 11 of the list on p. 132). So it makes sense to assume that Ibn Quzmān is here referring to a play on the same theme.

Next Zuhra, Maryam and 'Aysha are told to get moving, presumably actresses and/or dancing girls, as Monroe says, though whether they were supposed to dance in the play of the villagers or in some other scene is left unclear. At all events, orders are given for a seat to be made for a judge, possibly a member of the audience: we are told that he must be honoured because he is 'of my class' (*min jinsī*). But it could also be an ironic reference to an actor playing a judge, plays on that theme being well attested in the eastern part of the Arab world, as has been seen 'Let me count your number', the speaker continues, presumably referring to the members of the troupe rather than the audience, for he goes on to ask where Qunbar is, and this person was doubtless another actor. Qunbar may have been his name or he may have played the role of one Qunbar; either way, the stanza suggests that he dressed up for his part.

The speaker proceeds to demand 'a war-cry from the Arabs; they must appear'. This sounds like a call for yet another scene to be staged. In fifteenth-century Egypt we hear of a *khayāl al-'Arab*[134] and it seems likely that Ibn Quzmān is here referring to a comparable performance in this line. But whereas the Egyptian *khayal al-'Arab* was an independent play, the Arab scene in Ibn Quzmān should perhaps be envisaged as part of the play of the Hebrew which follows. 'Prepare your she-camel, prepare your Hebrew man', the speaker says, presumably once more referring to a person in a play. Corriente, who favours this possibility, takes the successive mention of Arabs, a she-camel, a Hebrew and (in stanza 6) an old man grieving to suggest that the play of the Hebrew was about Joseph and his brothers. At all events, the play of the Hebrew does not seem to have had anything to do with the play of the Jew. (cf. no 12 in the list, p. 132).

'Here comes big magic', the speaker continues, which could be taken to suggest that the performance ended with a display of juggling and illusion tricks. He concludes with a declaration of love for 'all of you', possibly meaning the audience, possibly the actors and possibly both.

Ibn Quzmān's *zajal* clearly implies that Andalusian actors performed what one might call 'variety shows', or in other words performances in which theatrical scenes alternated with dances, juggling, illusion tricks and other kinds of entertainment to the accompaniment of music, much as they do in modern circuses. This seems to have been the case elsewhere in the medieval Muslim word as well, for Ibn al-Ḥājj states that actors would produce the 'Scene of the Judge' *in the course* of their acting, implying that they produced other spectacles as well (cf. no 17, p. 134)and al-Maqrīzī's account of the judge al-Harawī implies that actors would appear and reappear in different costumes in the course of a single performance. Andalusian theatre also seems to have been indebted to the eastern part of the Arab world for some of its themes, though figures such as Qurra, Qunbar, the villager and the Hebrew have not so far been attested outside Spain.

In a personal letter of November 10, 1984, Professor Corriente writes:[135]

> I have not come across any other evidence of live theatrical plays in al-Andalus in Arabic literature [apart from Ibn Quzmān's *zajal*, no 12]. But in Spanish medieval authors such as Juan Ruiz ... one can find some information about similar troupes of acting jongleurs, including Moslem women, generally supposed to be only dancers and/or singers, that might have occasionally performed in Moslem lands or given rise to Moslem counterparts, when the social circumstances and relaxations of religious pressures allowed so. In Ibn Quzman ... I have found evidence of jingle-hooded buffoons and jesters, typically associated with early medieval theatre in Christian lands, which leads me to believe that al-Andalus did know elementary forms of theatre, like the *moralité* in France, patterned after European models and performed together with juggling and other circus acts. In this sense it is not at all surpising that the act alluded to in Ibn Quzmān seems to be based upon the Biblical story of Joseph in Egypt, if I am correct in my guessing, in an almost perfect match with the religious character of early medieval theatre.

Monroe's investigation of literary parallels to Ibn Quzmān in Spanish Christian literature also suggests that there is a connection between Muslim and Christian theatre in Spain:[136]

> F. Antonio de Bances y Candamo [wrote in 1690] states that throughout the province of Toledo a type of mime was often performed at popular festivals. According to BC, this genre constitutes the original form of the Spanish *comedia.* He adds that the drama to be performed was first written down in the form of a 'desalifiado romance ... en forma de relación' (i.e., a narrative ballad). The latter was then sung by a 'músico', and as he mentioned the characters in his song, the latter would

> appear on the stage wearing masks. they did not speak, but rather, by means of acts and gestures, they performed what the musician was simultaneously singing. It seems that the kind of tales represented usually involved heroic episodes. BC ends his description of the *danzas castellanas* with an account of one particular mime of this type which was performed in Esquivias (the home town of Cervantes' wife), and for which he himself composed the required ballad ...

There is an interesting parallel to these performances in the play in which ʿAbbāda al-Mukhannath mocked ʿAlī b. Abī Ṭālib. Here too the text of the play was sung by singers while the actor merely impersonated. There were several singers rather than a single one in this particular case, and ʿAbbāda did not wear a mask, as opposed to a pillow in imitation of ʿAlī's paunch; but the division of labour between the performers was clearly the same. The sources do not enable us to say how common this division of labour was in the eastern part of the Muslim world: when ʿAlluwayh composed a *ḥikāya* about the judge al-Khalanjī, handing it to dancers and *mukhannathūn,* the words were perhaps also declaimed to the accompaniment of silent miming and dancing.[137] But at all events, Pedro de Alcala's vocabulary can be taken to suggest that it was common in al-Andalus. As has been seen, he distinguishes between the *representador de momos* and the *representador de comedias/tragedias*: the former, given in Arabic as *laʿʿāb* was obviously a mime; but the identity of the latter, given in Arabic as *shāʿir*, 'poet' is anything but obvious at first sight: he was hardly a poet of the ordinary kind. On the other hand, it makes excellent sense that he should have been a declaimer of comic and tragic tales mimed by *representadores de momos.*

This is not of course to say that all performances in al-Andalus were of this type. But if the above interpretation of the information is correct, it is by no means obvious that Muslim theatre in al-Andalus as heavily influenced by Christian theatre as Corriente suggests. Basically, Muslim theatre in Spain had its roots in the Muslim East, as the technical terminology, the manner of performance and the dramatic themes make clear, Christian theatre may well have contributed to the development of theatre in Muslim Spain, but the influence of Muslim theatre on its Christian counterpart was hardly less important: in the case of the Toledan *danzas castellanas* discussed by Monroe, it is the Christian plays that appear to be patterned after Muslim models rather than the other way round. However, this is a topic on which much further research is needed.

Notes

1. See for example Prüfer, 'Drama', col. 1; Ḥamāda, *Khayāl*, p. 108.
2. Ibn Manẓūr, *Lisān*, vol. XI, col. 130b; cf. also Lane, *Lexicon*, s.v; Seybold, *Glossarium*, p. 195.
3. Ibn Manẓūr, *Lisān*, vol. XI, col. 231a. It is also called a *la'īn* (al-Ālūsī, *Bulūgh*, vol. III, pp. 26f; Aḥmad Taymūr, *Khayāl al-Ẓill wa-'l-Lu'ab wa-'l-Tamāthīl al-Muṣawwara 'inda 'l-'Arab* (Cairo, 1376/1957), p. 36).
4. Bevan, *Naḳā'iḍ*, vol. III, p. 362.
5. Cf. W. Heinrichs, *Arabische Dichtung und Griechische Poetik* (Beirut, 1969), p. 149 ('the words *khayāl* and *takhyīl* ... serve as an equivalent of the Greek word fantazia'), cf. Aḥmad Ibn Abyūrdī, *Rawḍ al-Jinān*, MS Staatsbibliothek Berlin, shelf no. We. 1087, fol. 129b, where *khayāl* in optics means fantasy.
6. Bevan, *Naḳā'iḍ* vol. II, p. 650, poem no. 64; cf. above, ch. 2, n. 71.
7. Ibid. vol. I, p. 246; vol II, pp. 624, 844.
8. Ibn al-Haytham, *Kitāb al-Manāẓir* (Kuwait, 1983), p. 408. (My thanks to the editor for sending me a copy of the passage.)
9. Ibn Ḥazm, *Kitāb al-Akhlāq wa-'l-Siyar* (Beirut, 1961), p. 28; also quoted in J. T. Monroe, 'Prolegomena to the Study of Ibn Quzmān: the Poet as Jongleur' in *The Hispanic Ballad Today: History, Comparativism, Critical Bibliography* (Madrid, 1979), pp. 98f.
10. Ibn Ḥijja al-Ḥamawī, *Thamarāt al-Awrāq* (Cairo, 1314/1896f), vol. I, p. 35; al-Ghazūlī, *Maṭāli'*, vol. I, pp. 78f.
11. V. H. Mair, *Tun-huag Popular Narratives* (Cambridge, 1980), pp. 18f.
12. See Ch. 1, n. 64
13. See Ch. 5, n. 15
14. See Ch. 5, n. 16–7
15. G. 'Awwād, 'Ṭayf al-Khayāl', in *al-Thaqāfa* no. 216 (Cairo, 16 February 1943, pp. 15f, with reference to al-Shābushtī, *Diyārāt*, p. 188.
16. See the references given above, Ch. 3, n. 40.
17. M. Quatremère (tr.), *Histoire des Sultans Mamlouks de l'Égypte* (Paris, 1837); Wiet in al-Maqrīzī, *Khiṭaṭ*, vol. XLIX, p. 10n.
18. A. Mez, *Die Renaissance des Islams* (Heidelberg, 1922), p. 309.
19. G. Jacob, *Schattentheater*, p. 24; cf. *Alf Layla wa-Layla*, ed. MacNaughten, vol. II, pp. 217–18, ed. M. Habicht, vol. VII, p. 270 (Night, no. 571). Lane wrongly took the beard-changing performers to be 'puppet-men' (cf. E. W. Lane (tr.), *The Arabian Nights' Entertainments* (London, 1928), vol. II, p. 321.
20. Inostrantsev, 'K upominaniyu *khayāl* 'a', pp. 165–6.
21. Menzel, *Meddāḥ* p. 14.
22. Mattā b. Yūnis in Badawī, *Fann*, pp. 86, 88–92, 98, etc; al-Fārābī, ibid., pp. 155f; Ibn Sīnā, ibid., pp. 163, 170 (cf. my 'Shadow Play', pp. 46–61); Ibn Rushd, Ibid., pp. 203f. 209.

23. Ibn Ḥijja, *Thamarāt*, vol. I, p. 35; id., *Thamarāt* printed in the margin of al-Ibshīhī, *Mustaṭraf*, vol. I, p. 48; al-Ghazūlī, *Maṭāli'*, vol. I, pp. 78f.
24. Quatremère, *Histoire*, vol. I, pp. 152f, n. 27.
25. Ibn Iyās, *Badā'i'*, vol. I, part i, p. 174; G. Wiet (tr.), *Journal d'un Bourgeois du Caire* (Cairo, 1960), pp. 186f.
26. Ibn Khallikān, *Wafayāt al-A'yān*, vol. IV, p. 118.
27. Quatremére, *Histoire*, vol. I, p. 152, n. 27; G. von Grunebaum, *Muḥammadan Festivals* (Leiden, 1958), pp. 72f. Contrary to what Quatremère states in his note, the term used by Ibn Khallikān is *arbāb al-khayāl*, not *aṣḥāb al-khayāl* (cf. Ibn Khallikān, *Wafayāt al-A'yān wa-Anbā' Abnā' al-Zamān*, MS Bibliothèque Nationale, arabe 2050, fol. 237a: this is the manuscript that Quatremère used, under its former number of arabe 730); cf. id. *Wafayāt*, vol. IV, p. 118.
28. Cf. P. Shinar, 'Traditional and Reformist *Mawlid* Celebrations in the Maghrib' in M. Rosen-Ayalon (ed.), *Studies in Memory of Gaston Wiet* (Jerusalem, 1977), p. 374, where it is rightly noted that Muẓaffar al-Dīn's celebration 'took place by day and ended before nightfall'.
29. Lane, *Manners and Customs*, p. 397; cf. also Taymur, *Khayāl al-Ẓill*, p. 19; And, *Theatre*, pp. 32, 130.
30. al-Maqrīzī, *Sūlūk* vol. II, p. 480.
31. Ibn Taghrī Birdī, *Ḥāwadith*, vol. VIII, part iii, p. 537 and glossary, p. 671.
32. Maimonides, *Commentaire*, vol. I, p. 221, I. 32. See also n. 71 below.
33. Maimonides, *Commentaire*, vol. I, p. 141, I. 1.
34. On whom, see *EI2*, s.v.; M. M. Badawī, 'Medieval Arabic Drama: Ibn Daniyal', *Journal of Arabic Theatre* XIII (1982), pp. 83–107.
35. al-Kutubī, *Fawāt al-Wafayāt*, vol. II, p. 384; al-Ṣafadī, *Kitāb al-Wāfī bi-'l-Wafayāt* (Damascus, 1953), vol. III, pp. 51f.
36. al-Maqrīzī, *Sulūk*, vol. IV, pp. 670–1. On *ṣafā'ina*, see Ch. 3 and 4 of this book.
37. Cf. al-Maqrīzī, *Sulūk*, vol. II, part 1, pp. 480–2; cf. also vol. II, part 3, p. 916 and vol. III, part 1, p. 273.
38. Ibn al-Athīr, *Kāmil*, vol. VII, p. 477.
39. Ibn Taghrī Birdī, *Nujūm*, vol. III, p. 114.
40. Ibn al-Zubayr, *Dhakhā'ir*, p. 38 (discussed above, Ch. 3).
41. Ibn al-Ḥājj, *Madkhal*, p. 146.
42. Ch. 5, n. 18. It was not only Muslim actors who were present in medieval Egypt, Coptic actors were also active, see al-Maqrizi, *Khiṭaṭ*, Būlāq edn, vol. I, p. 488 where *mukhāyil al-Qubūṭ* (actor of the Copts) is mentioned.
43. Cf. And, *Theatre*, p. 41: 'The actor does not lose his identity as an actor' .... The audience does not regard him as pretending to be a real person, but as an actor.'
44. Ch. 6, n. 38.
45. 42. Taymūr, *Khayāl al-Ẓill* pp. 25–19; cf. also Landau, *Studies*, pp.

271, 275.
46. Levy, *Lá'bät Elḥôtä*, pp. 119–24.
47. Cf. *EI2*, sv. 'Ibn al-Ḥadjdj'.
48. Above, Ch. 2, n. 38–41.
49. See my 'Shadow Play', pp. 59f.
50. See al-Ṭūsī, *Kitāb Alf Jāriya* MS Naz. Bib. Vienna A.F. 115 (Flügel, 387), f. 214b; Sadan, 'Kings', part 2, pp. 110f., and Brockelmann, *Geschichte der Arabischen Literatur*, vol. I, p. 352, and id. *GAL.*, Suppl. I, p. 501. Cf. Maimonides, *Commentaire*, vol. I, pp. 195, 221, where there is a description of the shirt (*qamīṣ*) and the hairnet of fine fabric (Ar, *shabaka*, Heb. *sbakha*) used by the actresses in their plays with the hobby-horse.
51. Ch. 5, n. 15.
52. Mattā b. Yūnis in Badawī, *Fann*, p. 116 and Badawī in the note thereto.
53. Ibn 'Abd Rabbih, *'Iqd*, vol. VI, pp. 152–4.
54. Ch. 4, n. 27.
55. Mez, *Sittenbild*, p. 78; cf. Abū Ḥayyān al-Tawḥīdī, *Imtā'*, vol. II, p. 166.
56. Ch. 5, n. 20.
57. Ch. 5, n. 16.
58. Ibn al-Zubayr, *Dhakhā'ir*, p. 38 (cf. Ch. 3, *Samāja*, pp. 48–9. Cp. al-Shābushtī, *Diyārāt*, p. 178, where twenty slave girls are produced (*ukhrija*) in order to sing and dance to al-Ma'mūn, who subsequently *akhraja* another slave girl to sing to him. No impersonation was involved, however.
59. Cf. Ch. 3, n. 41.
60. al-Tawḥīdī, *Imtā'*, vol. I, p. 59
61. Thus the translation by Monroe, 'Prolegomena', pp. 87f. For the original, see al-Shaqundī, *Risāla fī Faḍl al-Andalus wa-Ahlihā*, p. 58; or id., *Elogio des Islam Español* (*Risāla fī Faḍl al-Andalus*) (Madrid, 1934), p. 107. See also al-Maqqarī, *Nafḥ al-Ṭīb*, vol. II, pp. 146f.
62. Monroe, 'Prolegomena', p. 88.
63. Cf. below, n. 120.
64. Monroe, 'Prolegomena', p. 88; cf. above, n. 59.
65. Ibn Bassām, *Dhakhīra*, cf. Ch. 6, n. 38.
66. Monroe, 'Prolegomena', p. 99.
67. Cf. Monroe, 'Prolegomena', pp 99–100.
68. Umayya b. 'Abd al-'Azīz, *al-Risāla al-Miṣriyya*, p. 34.
69. Badawī, *Fann*, p. 17, 124, 173, 175f, 184, 191, 209, 211, 215.
70. Ibn Sīnā in Badawī, *Fann*. p. 194.
71. See Maimonides, *Commentaire* vol.I, p. 221, I. 32 and above n. 32. Maimonides transliterates the term *khayāliyyūn* into *khayyālūn*, see I. Freidlaender, *Arabisch-Deutsches Lexikon*, p. 40.
72. See Ch. 5, n. 10.
73. Ibn Abī Uṣaybi'a, *'Uyūn* vol. II, pp. 144f.
74. al-Khayālī, *Maqāma*, fol. 93b. For the terms *khurūj* and *dukhūl* in the sense of ending and starting a play, see the reference given

below, n. 81 (where a shadow-play rather than a live performance is involved: some terms were clearly common to the two genres).

75. Above, n. 41.
76. Cf. Ch. 5, n. 17.
77. al-Sha'rānī, *Laṭā'if al-Minan* (Cairo, 1321/1903), vol. II, p. 172.
78. Cf. Lane, *Manners*, p. 507.
79. al-Sha'rānī, *Ṭabaqāt*, p. 127, l. 3.
80. Cf. above, n. 23.
81. Ibn al-'Arabī, *al-Futūḥāt al-Makkiyya* (Cairo, n.d.), vol. III, p. 68. On the *waṣṣāf*, see Wetzstein, *Die Liebenden*, pp. 78f.
82. P. Kahle, 'Das Krokodilspiel (*Li'b al-Timsāḥ*). Ein aegyptisches Schattenspiel', *Nachrichten der königlischen Gesellschaft der Wissenschaften zu Göttingen* (Göttingen, 1915), phil.-hist. Klasse, p. 306, st. 2, v. 3.
83. Cf. above, n. 25; cf. also Ibn Iyās, *Tārīkh*, vol. II, fol. 210b (*lā aḥad min al-nās yaṣna' khayāl al-ẓill ... ba'da 'l-'ishā'*); id., *Badā'i'*, vol. V, p. 283 (similarly).
84. Ibn Iyās, *Tārīkh*, vol. II, fol. 169b; id., *Badā'i'*, vol. V, p. 192.
85. al-Sakhāwī, *al-Tibr al-Masbūk* (Cairo, n.d.), p. 353.
86. Ibn Taghrī Birdī, *Ḥawādith*, vol. VIII, p. 144.
87. P. Kahle, *Zur Geschichte des arabischen Schattentheaters in Aegypten* (Leipzig, 1909), p. 39; also quoted by M. Z. al-'Anānī, 'Ḥawla Khayāl al-Ẓill fī Miṣr', *al-Kātib* XVIII, no. 202 (January 1978), p. 36n.
88. al-Minawī in al-Nawājī, *Ḥalbat al-Kumayt* (Cairo, 1938), p. 204; id. in al-Ṣafadī, *Kitāb al-Ghayth al-Musjam fī Sharḥ Lāmiyyat al-'Ajam* Cairo, 1305/1887), vol. II, p. 247.
89. Cf. my 'Shadow Play', pp. 59f.
90. Ibn al-Athīr, *Kāmil*, vol. VII, p. 55.
91. Cf. al-Tha'ālibī, *Yatīma*, vol. III, p. 31.
92. al-Khafājī, *Shifā' al-Ghalīl fīmā fī Kalām al-'Arab min al-Dakhīl* (Cairo, 1371/1952), p. 73. Both this edition and that by Muḥammad Badr al-Dīn al-Na'sānī (Cairo, 1325/1907) has *khayāl al-izād* for *khayāl al-izār*, which must be a mistake, cf. my 'Shadow Play', pp. 47f, 52f; cf. also Ibn Sa'īd al-Maghribī, *al-Mughrib fī Ḥulā 'l-Maghrib* (Leiden, 1896), vol. IV, p. 121 (the *izār* of the *khayālī*); Ibn Iyās, *Badā'i'*, vol. I, p. 374 (*mizwarat al-khayālī*).
93. Taymūr, *Khayāl al-Ẓill*, p. 21; Ḥamāda, *Khayāl*, p. 46.
94. Ibn Dāniyāl, *Bābat Ṭayf al-Khayāl*, in Ḥamāda, *Khayāl*, p. 147, l. 5.
95. Ibid., l. 12.
96. Ibn Dāniyāl, *al-Mukhtār min Shi'r Ibn Dāniyāl* (Mosul, 1399/1979), p. 175 (no. 118: 15).
97. Cf. above, n. 88.
98. Ibn Dāniyāl, *Shi'r*, p. 213 (no. 175: 1f).
99. Sibṭ Ibn al-Ta'āwīdhī, *Dīwān* (Cairo, 1903), p. 369 (no. 242).

100. Ettinghausen, 'Dance', pp. 215f.
101. Cf. Ch. 5.
102. al-Jazarī, *Tārīkh al-Jazarī*, MS Dār al-Kutub al-Miṣriyya, (no number is given), quoted by H. Zayyāt, 'Lughat al-Ḥaḍāra fī 'l-Islām' *al-Mashriq* LXIII (July–Oct., 1969), p. 466f.
103. Ibn Dāniyāl, *Shi'r*, pp. 119–21 (no. 71: 29).
104. Ibid., pp. 137–9 (no. 87: 10f).
105. Ibid., p. 175 (no. 118: 15).
106. See the reference given above, n. 94.
107. Ibn Dāniyāl, *Babāt Ṭayf al-Khayāl* in Ḥamāda, *Khayāl*, p. 149.
108. Above, n. 36.
109. Cf. above, no. 98.
110. Ibn Dāniyāl, *Babāt Ṭayf al-Khayāl*, in Ḥamāda, *Khayāl*, p. 149, P. 1.
111. Taqiy al-Dīn al-Badrī, *Kitāb Rāḥat al-Arwāḥ fī 'l-Ḥashīsh wa-'l-Rāḥ*, MS Bibliothèque Nationale, arabe 3552, fols 9a–b.
112. Ibn Taghrī Birdī, *Ḥawādith*, vol. VIII, p. 537 (on the year 871/ 1466) and glossary, p. XXXI.
111. Alcala, *Vocabulista*, pp. Fiii, Jii; cf. Dozy, *Supplément*, vol I, p. 418, col. 2; vol. II, p. 535, col. 1, F. Corriente, in *Léxico Árabe Andalusī Segūn P. de Alcalā* (Medrid, 1988), p. 63b explains the term *li'āb al-khiyāl* as identical with *khayāl al-Ẓill*.
112. Ibn Bassām, *Dhakhīra*, vol. I, part ii, p. 677.
113. Cf. E. Garcia Gómez, *Todo Ben Quzmān* (Madrid, 1972), vol. I, pp. 64–7, and the works of Monroe and Corriente cited in the following notes.
114. Monroe, 'Prolegomena', p. 80.
115. Monroe, 'Prolegomena', pp. 97–101.
116. F. Coriente, *Grammática, métrica y texto del cancionero hispanoárabe de ABAN Quzmān* (Madrid, 1980), p. 91.
117. Corriente, *Grammática*, pp. 90–95.
118. Thus Monroe, 'Prolegomena', p. 114 (for *shīz*).
119. Monroe, 'Prolegomena', p. 78, has *qurra*.
120. Monroe, 'Prolegomena', p. 79, has 'full border' (for *'alāmin kāmil*).
122. Cf. the discussion above, p. 132 and notes 59–62.
125. Monroe, 'Prolegomena', pp. 79, 88f, has *fa-ḥaybash* for Corriente's *quḥaybash* (in Grammatica) and translates it as 'in unison'.
126. Ibid., p. 79, has *arākum* for Corriente's *arā kam?*.
127. Ibid., p. 80, prefers 'kerchief' for *khimār*.
128. *'Ibrīkum* in Corriente, *Grammatica*, but *'abrīkum* in Monroe, 'Prolegomena', p. 79, where it is translated as 'to enter'. [??]
129. Ibid., p. 80, reads *shuwaykh manḥūr*, 'the little wounded shaykh'.
130. Differently ibid., p. 80.
131. 'He mourns' (for *yarthī*) in Monroe, 'Prolegomena', p. 80.
132. Corriente, *Grammática*, p. 91n, where it is suggested that *qurra* might be *corro, ayy al-mal'ab aw jawqat al-jawārī al-murannimāt*

(*corro*, that is, the theatre or the choir of the singing maids).

133. Corriente, *Grammática*, p. 94.
134. Cf. above, n. 39.
135. Corriente, private correspondence.
136. Monroe, 'Prolegomena', pp. 100f.
137. Ibid., p. 105. Cf. above n. 41–42.

8

The Last Phase of Arabic Theatre

Muḥabbaẓūn and *Awlād Rābiya*

In the process of the development of Arabic theatre a new term, *muḥabbaẓ* or *muḥabbiẓ* (sometimes *muḥabbaḍ*) appeared. It was applied to live performers only, not to performers of *khayāl al-ẓill*, as is clear from Ibn Iyās.

Ibn Iyās relates in his *Badā'i' al-Zuhūr* that during the month of Jumādā II. 924/May-June, 1518, 'the *rayyis* Muḥammad Fattāt al-'Anbar, the *rayyis* of the *muḥabbazūn* died. He was master in the art of *khayāl* . He even surpassed Burraywa in this art'.[1] In another passage Ibn Iyās says, with reference to the events of Rabī 'I, 904/ Oct.-Nov. 1498, that the sultan al-Malik al-Nāṣir 'sent someone to bring Abū 'l-Khayr with the equipment of shadow play, the troupe of Arab singers (*maghānī 'l-'Arab*) and Burraywa, the *rayyis al-muḥabbaẓīn*'.[2] Wiet translated the *rayyis al-muḥabbiẓīn* of the first passage as 'un maitre de la composition des pieces de théâtre d'ombres' and that of the second passage as 'Barrīwah, le chef des bouffons';[3] Of these two translations, the latter is clearly the better. Ibn Iyās explicitly states in his first passage that a *rayyis al-muḥabbaẓīn* was a master in the art of *khayāl* (not *khayāl al-ẓill*); and in the second he distinguishes between Abū'l-Khayr, the shadow play presenter who came with the equipment of his art, and Burraywah, the leader of the *muḥabbaẓūn* were practitioners of live acting.

The term *muḥabbaẓ* would appear to be older than the sixteenth century. Ibn Dāniyāl's *Bābat Ṭayf al-Khayāl* the Amīr Wiṣāl, one of the characters of the shadow play, introduces himself as 'the *muḥabbaẓ* of Satan', adding that 'I bite worse than a snake and carry more than a scale beam'.[4] But whatever the date of its origin, it was still current in the time of al-Jabartī. 'They distributed [the taxes] among tax contractors, members of guilds, and even among snake charmers, monkey-keepers and *muḥabbaẓūn*'', he remarks in one passage.[5] 'In al-Azbakiyya gathered all sorts of performers (*arbāb al-malā'ib*) such as itinerant singers (*mughazlikin*), acrobats

Figure 7 Turkish itinerant actors (*Orta oyunu* in Arabic *muḥabbaẓūn*) performing a play involving a woman. The performance is accompanied by musicians, with *naqqāra, duff* and *mizmār*. (*Surname - i Vehbi, Ahmed III*, 1703 - 30. After Metin And., *Osmali Şenlikerine Türk Sanatlari* (Ankara, 1982). Courtesy of Professor Metin And)

(*junbādhiyya*), *ḥababẓiyya,* snake charmers, monkey keepers, male and female dancers (*barāmka*), he remarks in another, with reference to the wedding of Ismā'īl Pāsha in 1813:[6] *ḥababẓiyya* was presumably another term for *muḥabbaẓūn.* In his account of the mosque of 'Amr b. al-'Ās, written about 1212/1797, he enumerates much the same kind of entertainers, though this time without explicit mention of the *muḥabbaẓun* : 'in its courtyard entertainers (*arbāb al-malāhī*) used to meet, such as snake charmers (*ḥuwāt*), monkey-keepers (*qirdātiyya*), performers (*ahl al-malā'ib*) and female dancers known as *ghawāzī*'.[7] The *muḥabbaẓun* were clearly included in the guild of *arbāb al-malāhī* or *arbāb al-malā'ib* (terms also used by Ibn Dāniyāl and Ibn Iyās).

There are several European accounts of theatrical performances in the Arab world from the eighteenth century onwards. With one exception, none of them uses the term *muḥabbaẓūn* or any other Arabic term for 'actor'; but the performers must in fact have been *muḥabbaẓūn* and other *arbāb al-malā'ib* of the kind mentioned by al-Jabartī, and they are in fact explicitly named as such by Lane.

The earliest account is that by Alexander Russell, whose description of the performances of buffoons in Aleppo, quoted in Chapter 4, relates to about 1750.[8] Some twenty years later Niebuhr watched a dramatic performance in Cairo. 'There was in Cairo a numerous company of players, Maḥometans, Christians and Jews, who play in the Arabic language', he said, adding that a few Europeans had the chance to see 'an Egyptian play'. The players 'played their pieces, wherever they were invited, for a moderate hire. They exhibited in the open air. The court of the house was their theatre; and a screen concealed them from the audience as they changed their dresses'. The company he watched was invited to the house of an Italian, but the Europeans were not amused by either the music or the players, mainly because the play was long and stereotyped. 'The principal character was a female; but was acted by a man in a woman's dress, who had much to do to hide his beard. The heroine enticed all travellers into her tent, and, after robbing them of their purses, caused them to be beaten off. She had already plundered a good many, when a young merchant, weary of this insipid repetition, expressed aloud his disapproval of the piece.' The play was stopped in the middle.[9]

In *Courrier de l'Egypte* of 1798 we learn of an Arab comedy performed in the presence of French generals. 'Mu'allem Ya'coub, commandant général des legions qobtes, a donné le 19 de ce mois au Général en Chef, aux généraux et principaux officiers de l'armée, un magnifique dîner qui a été suivi de la représentation d'un comédie arabe.'[10] The editor did not comment on the standard of the performance.

Another European traveller, G. Belzoni, watched two plays in Cairo in 1815, both of them performed at wedding feasts. 'When the dancing was at an end, a sort of play was performed, the intent of which was to exhibit life and manners, as we do in our theatres.' The subject of the first play was a Hadgee, who wants to go to Mecca, and applies to a camel-driver, to procure a camel for him. The driver imposes on him, by not letting him see the seller of the camel, and putting a higher price on it than is really asked, giving so much less to the seller than he received from the purchaser. A camel is produced at last, made up by two men covered with a cloth, as if ready to depart for Mecca. The Hadgee mounts on the camel, but finds it so bad, that he refuses to take it, and demands his money back again. A scuffle takes place, when by chance, the seller of the camel appears and finds that the camel in question is not that which he sold to the driver for the Hadgee. Thus it turns out, that the driver was not satisfied with imposing both on the buyer and seller in the price, but had also kept the good camel for himself. and produced a bad one to the Hadgee. In consequence he received a good drubbing, and runs off. Simple as this story appears yet it was so interesting to the audience, that it seemed as if nothing could please them better, as it taught them to be on their guard against dealers in camels, etc.[11]

The second play was a ridicule of Europeans. This subject was popular with monkey-trainers, who would dress their monkeys like Europeans,[12] and also with playwrights such as Yaʿqūb Ṣanūʿ, whose *al-Sawwāḥ wa-'l-Ḥammār* ('The Tourist and the Donkey-driver') also pokes fun at Europeans.[13] Belzoni's play featured:

> a European traveller, who served as a sort of clown. He is in the dress of a Frank; and, on his travels, comes to the house of an Arab, who, though poor, wishes to have the appearance of being rich. Accordingly he gives orders to his wife, to kill a sheep immediately. She pretends to obey; but returns in a few minutes, saying that the flock has strayed away, and it would be the loss of too much time to fetch one. The host then orders four fowls to be killed but these cannot be caught. A third time, he sends his wife for pigeons; but the pigeons are all out of their holes, and at last the traveller is treated only with sour milk and dhourra bread, the only provision in the house ....[14]

In the mid-nineteenth century (1857?) the Prussian consul in Damascus, J. G. Wetzstein, attended some similar plays, as mentioned before.[15] But the fullest account of *muḥabbaẓūn,* this time with explicit mention of their name, is that by E. W. Lane (1801-76), who did not like their plays, but who described their activities with his usual attention to detail and summarises one of their plays, performed before Muḥammad ʿAlī in about 1834:[16]

The Egyptians are often amused by players of low and ridiculous farces, who are called 'Moḥabbaẓeen'. these frequently perform at the festivals prior to weddings and circumcisions, at the houses of the great; and sometimes attract rings of auditors and spectators in the public places in Cairo. Their performances are scarcely worthy of description; it is chiefly vulgar jests and indecent action, that they amuse and obtain applause. The actors are only men and boys; the part of a woman always being performed by a man or a boy in female attire. As a specimen of their plays, I shall give a short account of one which was acted before the Basha, a short time ago, at a festival celebrated in honour of the circumcision of one of his sons; on which occasion, as was usual, several sons of grandees were also circumcised. The *dramatis personae* were a Nāẓir (or governor of a district), a Sheykh Beled (or chief of a village), a servant of the latter, a Copt clerk, a Fellāḥ indebted to the government, his wife and five other persons, of whom two made their appearance first in the character of drummers, one as a hautboy-player, and the other two as dancers. After a little drumming and piping and dancing by these five, the Nāẓir and the rest of the performers enter the ring. The Nāẓir asks, 'How much does 'Awaḍ the son of Regeb owe?' The musicians and dancers, who now act as simple fellāheen, answer, 'Desire the Christian to look in the register'. The Christian clerk has a large *dawāyeh* (or ink-horn) in his girdle, and is dressed as a Copt, with a black turban. The Sheykh el-Beled asks him, 'How much is written against 'Awaḍ the son of Regeb?' The clerk answers, 'A thousand piaster'. 'How much', says the Sheykh, 'has he paid?' He is answered, 'Five piasters'. 'Man', says he, addressing the fellāḥ, 'why don't you bring the money?' The fellāḥ answers, 'I have not any'. 'You have not any?' exclaims the Sheykh: 'Throw him down'. An inflated piece of an intestine, resembling a large kurbāg, is brought; and with this the fellah is beaten. He roars out to the Nāzir, 'By the honour of thy horse's tail, O Bey! By the honour of thy wife's trousers, O Bey! By the honour of thy wife's head-band, O Bey!' After twenty such absurd appeals, his beating is finished, and he is taken away, and imprisoned. Presently hs wife comes to him, and asks him, 'How art thou?' He answers, 'Do me a kindness, my wife; take a little kishk and some eggs and some sha'eereeyeh, and go with them to the house of the Christian clerk, and appeal to his generosity to get me set at liberty'. She takes these, in three baskets, to the Christian's house, and asks the people there, 'Where is the M'allim Ḥannā, the clerk?' They answer, 'There he sits'. She says to him, 'O M'allim Ḥannā, do me the favour

> to receive these, and obtain the liberation of my husband'. 'Who is thy husband?' he asks. She answers, 'The fellāḥ who owes a thousand piasters'. 'Bring', says he, 'twenty or thirty piasters to bribe the Sheykh el-Beled.' She goes away and soon returns with the money in her hand, and gives it to the Sheykh el-Beled. 'What is this?' says the Sheykh. She answers, 'Take it as a bribe and liberate my husband'. He says, 'Very well; go to the Nāẓir'. she retires for a while, blackens the edges of her eyelids with koḥl, applies fresh red dye of the ḥennā to her hands and feet, and repairs to the Nāẓir. 'Good evening, my master', she says to him. 'What dost though want?' he asks again. She says, 'My husband is imprisoned and I appeal to thy generosity to liberate him'; and as she urges this request she smiles, and shows him that she does not ask this favour without being willing to grant him a recompense. He obtains this, takes the husband's part, and liberates him. – This farce was played before the Basha with the view of opening his eyes to the conduct of those persons to whom was committed the office of collecting the taxes.

Short farces of the type performed by *muḥabbaẓūn* continued to be performed in the Arab world long after the rise, from the mid-nineteenth century onwards of new comedies which imitated European theatre. Even after the establishment of Yaʻqūb Ṣanūʻ's Europeanised theatre in 1870, popular plays continued to be shown both inside and outside Cairo. C. D. Warner watched such a play on board a ship in the winter of 1874-5, an experience of which he left the following account:

> The sailors celebrate the finishing of the journey by a ceremony of state and dignity. The chief actor is Farrag, the wit of the crew. Suddenly he appears as the Governor of Wady Halfa, with horns on his head, face painted, and a long beard, hair sprinkled with flour, and dressed in a shaggy sheepskin. He has come on board to collect his taxes. He opens his court, with the sailors about him, holding a long marline-spike which he pretends to smoke as a chibook. His imitation of the town dignitaries along the river is very comical, and his remarks are greeted with roars of laughter. One of the crew acts as his bailiff and summons all the officers and servants of the boat before him, who are thrown down upon the deck and bastinadoed, and released on payment of backsheesh. The travellers also have to go before the court and pay a fine for passing through the governor's country. The govenor is treated with great deference till the end of the farce, when one of his attendants set fire to his beard, and another puts him out with a bucket of water.[17]

One play performed by actors of the *muḥabbaẓūn* type actually survives. Its title is *Misṭarat Khayāl, Munādamat Umm Mujbir*; it was written by 'Abd al-Bāqī al-Isḥāqī (d. 1660) in 1064/1654, included in his *Dīwān* and discovered by Dr. Muḥammad Zakariyyā 'Anānī, who published it in the Egyptian magazine *al-Kātib* with a comprehensive introduction on shadow plays in Egypt and a critical study of the author and his work.[18] The reader will find the full text of the play together with an English translation in Appendix II.

Dr. 'Anānī took al-Isḥāqī's work to be a shadow play, though there is no indication in either the title or the play itself to indicate that this is the case. Manuscripts of shadow plays generally include the term *khayāl al-ẓill* in the title (thus for example *Kitāb al-Rawḍ al-Waḍḍāḥ fi Tahānī 'l-Afrāḥ aw Ijtimā' al-Shaml fi Fann Khayāl al-Ẓill*;[19] but there is only *khayāl*, no *ẓill*, in the title of al-Isḥāqī's play. Dr. 'Anānī did notice that the conventional characters of shadow plays, such as *al-Miqaddim* (the introducer of the play, as pronounced in colloquial Egyptian), *al-ḥāziq* (the presenter) and *al-rikhim* (the clown) were missing; and he also observed that the title made use of the new term *misṭara* in lieu of the conventional *bābā*.[20] in view of this we may conclude that what Dr. 'Anānī published was a play composed for live performance. It is the only seventeenth-century play of the *khayāl* type to have survived, or at any rate to have been discovered.

The play is short, consisting of one act alone, versified and composed in colloquial Egyptian Arabic. It has five characters, among them *al-rayyis*, who here seems to be the captain of a boat rather than *rayyis al-muḥabbaẓīn*, since his assistant is *al-qilā'ī*, or sailing master. The author admits that he is composing poetry of jest or comedy (*hazl*) and scurrilous mockery (*huz' sakhīf*), and Dr. 'Anānī concludes that it has no serious message.[21] But in fact it would seem to express al-Isḥāqī's attitude towards life and God's creation. God makes all sorts of people, white and black, happy and miserable, beautiful and ugly. Ugly women full of defects are despised by men, and all their efforts to seduce them are of no avail. This too is the moral of the shadow play *al-'Āshiq wa-'l-Ma'shūq*. Dālī Farḥāt prefers death to marrying Umm Shukardum, the ugly spinster; but the message of *Misṭarat Khayāl* seems to go deeper. It is concerned with the eternal struggle between beauty and ugliness, old and new, past and present. The new always has its own freshness and strong appeal, while the old becomes obsolete and loses its role in life; yet old people keep clinging to the present, forcing themselves on their surroundings and trying to prove that they are more suitable, more experienced and more useful to both the present and the future, an endeavour in which they must necessarily fail.

Recently, another popular play was discovered by Dr. Ph.

Sadgrove, written in Algerian colloquial Arabic, literary poetry and prose, printed in lithograph in Algeria in 1847. It was published under the rhymed title *Nazāhat al-Mushtāq wa-Ghuṣṣat al-'Ushshāq fī Madīnat Ṭiryāq fī 'l-'Irāq* (The Entertainment of the Enamoured and the Agony of Lovers in the City of Ṭiryāq in Iraq) composed by the Algerian Jewish playwright Abraham Daninos.[22] This play is the first Arabic printed play known to us, and its popular theme and its Arabian Nights milieu serve as a link between medieval indigenous Arabic drama and modern Arabic drama modelled according to European tradition.

Daninos was not the first North African Jewish playwright to compose a play. He was preceded by Isaac ben Joseph Falyadj (or Palache), an Algerian Hebrew playwright who wrote at the beginning of the eighteenth century a play in Hebrew entitled *Naḥat Ruaḥ* (Contentment). J. Schermann who discovered this play in the Bodleian Library says that 'the play was actually presented before an audience, and (the instructions) even indicate in what manner the presentation was arranged'.[23] Schirmann concludes that there is a strong influence of a Dutch allegorical drama in Hebrew *Asirei Tiqwa* (The Prisoners of Hope) (Amsterdam, 1673) written by Joseph Penço de la Vega,[24] a Jewish Dutch playwright of Spanish origin.

It seems that these dramatic activities in Hebrew influenced North African Jewish writers in Arabic. During the nineteenth century an anonymous pamphlet entitled *Khalā'at Purim* (Purim or Feast of Lots Profligacy) (Tunis Vittorio Pinsi Press, n.d.) was published in Hebrew characters in Tunisian Judeo-Arabic dialect, and contains a versified short drama (*tiyatru*, Italian = *teatro*). Although Schermann was not able to get a copy of this play, yet he suggested that the term *teatro* given to it indicates an Italian influence.[25] The suggestion that there is an Italian influence on this play needs further investigation. This is because even if we presume that the term *misṭara khayāl* given by al-Isḥāqī to his versified play *Munādamat Umm Mujbir* is derived from the Italian term *mostra* (show),[26] this does not necessarily mean an Italian influence, since there is nothing in theme or plot of al-Isḥāqī's play to indicate any such influence.

It seems therefore that Daninos drama is a product of dramatic activities known at least since the beginning of the eighteenth century among the Jewish communities in North Africa where indigenous Arabic as well as Hebrew, Spanish and probably Italian traditions of drama were well-known.

As for the *Awlād Rābiya*, they only seem to be mentioned in a small number of works. 'Alī Mubārak (1823-93) compares European theatre with the performances of Egyptian entertainers in his novel *'Alam al-Dīn,* published in 1882. The vulgar language, indecent behaviour and crude jokes of these actors are described in terms reminiscent of Lane's account of *muḥabbaẓūn*; 'Alī Mubārak does not however call his actors *Muḥabbaẓūn,* but rather *Awlād Rābiya,*[27] a category in which he includes Ya'qūb Sanū according to the latter's confession in his play *Molyīr Miṣr,* Aḥmad Fahīm al-Fār, an Egyptian farcical actor of great renown, is likewise described as an *Ibn Rābiya* in an article by Prüfer written at the beginning of the twentieth century. Prüfer's description of his troupe, the farces they performed and the occasions on which they did so also suggests that *Awlād Rābiya* were actors of much the same type as the *muḥabbaẓūn* known to earlier authors.[28] But there is also evidence that they performed serious plays. Their ancestor, real or eponymous, was the actor Abū Rābiya, who used to perform tragic plays depicting the tyranny of Egyptian rulers according to 'Abd Allāh Nadīm, the Egyptian journalist and playwright. Abū Rābiya portrayed officials sending people to corvée in chains, killing others for a few pence, plundering farms, stealing cattle and dispensing arbitrary justice. He also dealt with men who neglected their families, entrusting their women to eunuchs or mamluks and only discovering the tragic consequences of their behaviour when it was to late.[29] His dates are uncertain, but Ya'qūb Ṣanū' spoke of him as 'the late Abū Rābiya' in 1878.[30]

Traditional and modern Arabic theatre

Arabic plays in the European style were most probably inspired by the modernisation movement of the Ottoman sultan 'Abd al-Majīd I (1839-61). The so-called 'French Theatre' or 'Crystal Palace' (designed by the Italian Giustiniani), which had been inaugurated in 1872, probably as the first European style theatre in the Ottoman empire and burnt down in 1831, was rebuilt in his reign;[31] and another theatre, Bosco's, was established in 1840.[32] In 1844 Bosco's was taken over by Mīkhā'īl Na'ūm and his brother, Syrian Christians under whose leadership a succession of Italian plays and operas were staged until this theatre too was closed down, in 1870.[33] Among the authors who were active in the transplantation of the European theatrical tradition was Mārūn Naqqāsh (1817-55), also a Syrian Christian, who wrote his first comedy (*al-Bakhīl,* 'The Miser') under the influence of Molière and who copied the form of the European platform in Beirut in 1847,[34] as well as Ḥabīb Ablā Māltī, yet another Syrian Christian, who composed his play *al-Aḥmaq al-Basīt,* 'The Naive and Stupid One', some time before 1855 in response to the cultural revolution initiated by sultan 'Abd al-Majīd.[35]

This kind of theatre became so popular that men 'paid all their earnings to attend it, leaving their families hungry; the government was forced to abolish it completely'.[36]

Mārūn Naqqāsh tried to imitate the European stage with such fidelity that he caused David Urquhart, who watched one of his first plays, to smile mockingly:

> They had seen in Europe footlights and prompter's box, and fancied it an essential point of theatricals to stick them on where they were not required. In like manner they introduced chairs for the Caliph and his Vizar, and cheval glasses for the ladies. As to costume there was the design at least of observing the proprieties; and, as regards the women, that is the boys dressed up as such, with perfect success. As there were no women on the stage, so there were none in the court, and not even at the windows which opened on the stage.[37]

Mārūn Naqqāsh endeavoured to show that his art was a European offspring, unprecedented in Arabic literature, and he gives no indication that he was influenced by the popular theatrical tradition of the Arab world in his lecture on the importance of theatre (published along with his plays in his brother's *Arzat Lubnān*).[38] Nor does Ḥabīb Ablā Māltī acknowledge popular influence. But neither of them can have been unaware of popular theatre; and in Mārūn Naqqāsh's case, popular plays were actually performed by way of light entertainment in the intervals of his own, or so at least on one occasion. Urquhart, who watched a performance of Naqqāsh's second play, 'Abū 'l-Ḥasan al-Mughaffal, or Hārūn al-Rashīd' in 1850, reports that in the interval between the second and the third act the audience was treated to a short farce which proved more successful than Naqqāsh's own play and which was clearly a *faṣl muḍḥik* of the type seen by Wetzstein in Damascus in 1857. Urquhart's account of it goes as follows:[39]

> It was a husband befooled by his wife, a very grave case, and the ex-Muftī judged it to be so; taking the most vivid interest in its progress, and repeatedly informing the one party of the proceedings of the other. In fact he identified himself with the action, somewhat in the fashion of the ancient chorus, bewailing or approving. The husband at last is undeceived, by observing from the window at the side the lady and her lover; while the Muftī from the *Stalle d'Orchestre* commented vigorously on the guilty nature of the proceedings of the one, and the extreme imbecility of the other. The roars of laughter which these cross-purposes produced conferred on the farce unbounded success, which all were agreed to attribute to the actor whose part the author had not inserted.

As for Ya'qūb Ṣanū',[40] on the other hand, there are several indications that he was aware of traditional Egyptian theatre. In the preface of his play *Mūlyīr Miṣr wa-ma-yuqāsīh* ('The Molière of Egypt and his Suffering'),[41] he speaks of 'revealing the truth about Arabic theatre',[42] and the play itself is concerned, among other things, with the criticism he had attracted for his use of colloquial Egyptian and the strike which his actor and actresses had started in demand of salaries comparable with those received by their counterparts at the two new theatres in Cairo built by the khedive Ismā'īl, the Opera and the Comédie Française. Apparently Isṭifān, one of the loyal actors, coped with it by threatening to hire traditional actors of the *muḥabbaẓūn* or *awlād Rābiya* type: in the play in which the strike is discussed Isṭifān observes that 'these people think there are no actors in all Egypt except them', but that he has found 'twenty nice local actors (*'ishrīn li''ib min awlād al-balad al-liṭāf*), so we are not afraid of their intimidation'.[43] The characters in this play are all actors of the traditional types, introduced by Ṣanū' as 'Isṭifān, an actor good at imitating rogues' (*li''īb shāṭir fī taqlīd al-'iyyāq*) 'Ḥabīb, an actor expert at the imitation of merchants' (*li''īb māhir fī taqlīd al-tujjār*), 'Matrī, an actor famous for his imitation of peasants' (*li''īb mashhūr fī taqlīd al-fallāḥīn*, ''Abd al-Khāliq, a *khalbūṣ* and Ḥinayyin, imitator (*muqallid*) of Europeans'.[44] It may be added that Sanū was also familiar with the famous Abū Rābiya: in his *Riḥlat Abī Naẓẓāra*, he published a cartoon depicting Ismā'īl Pasha as Abū Rābiya standing on the stage and pulling the strings of marionettes representing Wilson and Nūbār (though there is no suggestion elsewhere that Abū Rābiya was a presenter of marionette plays rather than a live actor.[45]

Shadow plays, live performances by *muḥabbaẓūn* and *Awlād Rābiya*, and the plays of Ya'qūb Ṣanū' were all presented in colloquial Arabic in-so-far as they were presented in Arabic at all: according to Lane, shadow plays in Egypt were performed in Turkish.[46] All tended to use misunderstandings, beatings, imitation of non-Arab accents, indecent jokes and other farcical elements to provoke laughter. In addition to watching numerous Italian plays in Italy, Sanū' read Goldoni, Molière and Sheridan; and their influence is patent in his work.[47] But the reasons why these playwrights appealed so strongly to him may well have been that the element of comedy and farce in their works gave them an affinity with the theatrical tradition in which Sanū' had been brought up.

> In spite of preparatory mimic and dramatic elements in their literature, the Arabs have never found their way to actual drama. At all events, there seems to be no positive proof of the existence of an early Arabic stage. If occasionally we meet with the word *hiyāl* or *hayāl*, it means, in all probability, nothing more than the already mentioned *taqlīd*, the mimicry of comi-

> cal personal characteristics, or the presentation of short, loosely connected scenes and not a theatrical piece. The complete lack of all dramatic texts, the absence even of description of any dramatic representation, would be, when one considers the numerous chronicles of medieval Arabic amusements, an altogether too remarkable omission to be regarded as possible, had there been a stage.

Prüfer is here voicing a widespread view and, like many other scholars, holds Islam to be the main reason for the apparent failure of the Muslim world to develop a dramatic art.[48] But drama did exist in the Arab world; we do have dramatic texts; and we do have descriptions of dramatic representation. The problem is not why drama was absent, but why it was present without developing into a high art; and whatever the explanation for this fact may turn out to be, it is hardly to be found in Islam, let alone in 'the Arab mentality'. There is nothing in Islam as such to preclude dramatic development of intrinsically Islamic themes. On the contrary, one of the plays encountered in this book was spawned by the Qur'ānic injunction of *al-amr bi-'l-ma'rūf wa-'l-nahy 'an al-munkar,* and the emergence of the Shi'ite passion play likewise shows that the faith was perfectly compatible with religious drama. Nor was there anything about Islam as such to preclude dramatic development of non-Islamic, un-Islamic or even anti-Islamic themes. On the contrary, many of the plays we have encountered were extremely irreverent, while most of their authors were exponents of *sukhf* and *mujūn,* some of whom went so far as to declare Satan to be the head of their guild. As for 'the Arab mentality', few scholars these days regard it as a serious concept. Here, then, is a problem for further research. But there is no doubt that the medieval Arab world was far richer in theatrical culture than has so far been assumed.

Notes

1. Ibn Iyās, *Badā'i',* vol. III, p. 341.
2. Ibid., p. 401.
3. Wiet, *Journal,* vol. II, pp. 329, 443.
4. Ibn Dāniyāl in Ḥamāda, *Khayāl,* p. 154; the translation offered by P. E. Kahle, 'The Arabic Shadow Play in Medieval Egypt', *Journal of the Pakistan Historical Society* (1945), p. 105, suggests that Kahle read *mukhabbiṭ* for *muḥabbaẓ*.
5. al-Jabartī, *'Ajā'ib,* vol. III, p. 107. For *mughazlikin* as 'itinerant singers' (*chanteur ambulant*), see E. Fagnan, *Additions aux dictionnaires arabes* (Alger, 1923), p. 126. My thanks due to Dr. Ph. Sadgrove for his help.
6. Ibid., p. 198.
7. Ibid., p. 33.
8. Cf. Ch. 4, n. 75.

9. Niebuhr, *Travels Through Arabia, and Other Countries in the East,* tr. R. Heron (Edinburgh, 1792), vol. I, pp. 143f; cf. also *Description de l'Égypte,* 2nd ed. (Paris, 1826), vol. XVIII, pp. 172f.
10. *Courrier de l' Égypte,* no. 102 ('le 24 pluviose, IXe année de la République'), 1798. On French theatre in Cairo during the French occupation, see ibid., nos. 95, 98, 102. For the French text of the *Courrier* with an Arabic translation, see S.-D. al-Bustānī, *Ṣuḥuf Bunarbārteh fī Miṣr, 1798-1801* (Cairo, 1971).
11. G. Belzoni, *Narratives of the Operations and Recent Discoveries in Egypt and Nubia* (London, 1820), p. 19.
12. Niebuhr, *Travels,* vol. I, pp. 145f; cf. also M. Villoteau, *De l' État Actuel de l'Art Musical en Egypte* (Paris, 1812), p. 94.
13. Cf. Najm, *Masraḥ,* vol. III, pp. 75f; I. L. Gendzier, *The Practical Visions of Ya'qūb Ṣanū* (Harvard, 1966), P. 37.
14. Belzoni, *Narratives,* pp. 19f.
15. Cf. Ch. 3, pp. 56–7.
16. Lane, *Manners and Customs,* pp. 395-7; cf. also p. 173.
17. C. D. Warner, *My Winter on the Nile* (Hartford, 1904), pp. 314f.
18. M. Z. 'Anānī, 'Ḥawla Khayāl al-Ẓill fī Miṣr'
19. Cf. 'A. Abū Shanab, *Masraḥ 'Arabī Qadīm 'Karakūz'* (Damascus, n.d.).
20. 'Anānī, 'Ḥawla Khayāl al-Ẓill', p. 11. On the meaning of *misṭara,* see Appendix II.
21. 'Anānī, 'Ḥawla Khayāl al-Ẓill', p. 11.
22. Dr. Ph. Sadgrove discovered this play in the Bibliothèque of the Ecole des Langues Orientales (Institute National des Langues et Civilisation Oriental) (Shelf mark Mel 8.-95, Acquisitions no. Ar 2482). Dr. Sadgrove and the writer of this book are going to publish this play in a book entitled *The Pioneers of Nineteenth Century Modern Arabic Theatre*.
23. See J. Schirmann, 'Evidence of the Performance of a Hebrew Play in Algeria', *Tarbiz,* A Quarterly for Jewish Studies, Jerusalem, vol. XXXIV, 1965, pp. 272-78, and p. V in the English Summaries. Cf. A. Neubauer, *Catalogue of the Hebrew Manuscripts in the Bodleian Collection* (Oxford, 1888), vol. I, pp. 411-15, MS. no. 1194.
24. Schirmann, 'Evidence', p. 277. Cf. E. Silberschlag, *From Reneaissance to Renaissance* (New York, 1977), vol. II, p. 297.
25. Schirmann, 'Evidence', p. 275, n. 9. Cf. M. Steinschneider, *Die Arabische Literatur der Juden* (Frankfurt a. M., 1902), p. 271, no. 231.
26. See p. 158 note 18 above, and art. 'Teatro' in *Enciclopedia Italiana* (Rome, 1937), vol. XXXIII, p. 365.
27. 'A. Mubārak, *'Alam al-Dīn,* pp. 397-440; on *Awlād Rābiya,* see also A. Amīn, *Qāmūs al-'Adāt wa-'l-Taqālīd wa-'l-Ta'ābīr al-Miṣriyya* (Cairo, 1953), p. 9, where they are described as a family.
28. Prüfer, 'Drama'. Since Prüfer wrote, Landau has discovered five plays written by Aḥmad Fahīm al-Fār in the collection entitled *Kashf al-Sitār 'an Baladiyyāt Aḥmad al-Fār al-Ma'rūf bi-'bn Rābiya* (Leiden University Library, MS. Or. 14521 = Ar. 4380; the full title

is given at fol. 51a). The colophon gives the date as 9 Dhū 'l-Ḥijja, 1327/December 23, 1909, which suggests that actors of the *Awlād Rābiya* type were still performing in Cairo in the early twentieth century (cf. J. M. Landau, 'Popular Arabic Plays, 1909', *Journal of Arabic Literature* XVII (1986), pp. 120-5).
29. Nadīm, *Sulāfa,* vol. II, p 63.
30. Cf. Amīn, *Qāmūs,* p. 378.
31. And, *Theatre,* pp. 66f. 111f; cf. also *EI2,* s.v. ''Abd al-Madjīd I'.
32. And, *Theatre,* pp. 66, 112.
33. Ibid., pp. 66f. 111f.
34. See N. Naqqāsh, *Arzat Lubnān* (Beirut, 1869), p. 388; M. Y. Najm (ed.), *al-Masraḥiyya fī 'l-Adab al-'Arabī al-Ḥadīth,* pp. 42f; Landau, *Studies,* pp. 56ff.
35. Ḥabīb Ablā Mālṭī, *al-Aḥmaq al-Basīṭ,* MS Staatsbibliothek Berlin, shelf no. Sachau 23 (cf. Ahlwardt, *Verzeichnisse,* vol. VII, p. 230, no. 818). This manuscript was copied in 1855, but it is imposssible to say whether the play was composed before or after Mārūn Naqqāsh's *Bakhīl* (composed in 1848). Ḥabīb Ablā Mālṭi does not mention Mārūn Naqqāsh in his introduction. He does however explicitly say that his comedy was written under the inspiration of 'Abd al-Majīd's cultural revival. (Another manuscript of Mālṭī's comedy, copied by Wetzstein in 1857, is kept in 'Nachlass Wetzstein' in the same library.)
36. See M. S. al-Qāsimī, *Qāmūs al-Ṣinā'āt al-Shāmiyya (Dictionnaire des Métiers Damascaine* (Paris, 1960), vol. II, pp. 470f, s.v. *'mumaththil al-riwāyāt* (article no. 397).
37. Urquhart, *The Lebanon: Mount Souria, a History and Diary* (London, 1860), vol. II, p. 179.
38. See n. 29 above.
39. Urquhart, *Lebanon,* p. 180.
40. On Ya'qūb Ṣanū, see the interesting book by 'Ānūs, *Masraḥ Ya'qūb Ṣanū',* pp. 149–96; S. Moreh, 'Ya'qūb Ṣanū', 'His Religious Identity and Work in the Theatre and Journalism, according to the Family Archive' in S. Shamir (ed.), *The Jews in Egypt* (Boulder and London, 1987). His name, incidentally was not Sannū', as some Egyptian writers transliterate it: *Sanū'* (modern Hebrew Sanuwa') means modest. Many members of the Ṣanū' family live in Israel.
41. First published in Beirut 1912; reprinted in Najm, *al-Masraḥ al-'Arabī* vol. III, pp. 189–222.
42. Ṣanū', *Mulyīr Miṣr* in Najm, *al-Masraḥ al- 'Arabī,* vol. III, p. 189.
43. Ibid. p. 204.
44. Ibid. p. 195. On *khalbūṣ* see above Ch. 6, p. 135; Lane, *Manners,* p. 507; Villoteau, *Art Musical, p. 93.*
45. Ya'qūb Ṣanū, *Riḥlat Abī Naẓẓāra Zarqā 'l-Walī min Miṣr* (Paris, 1876), p. 28.
46. Lane, *Manners,* p. 397.
47. Ānūs, *Masraḥ Ya'qūb Ṣanū'* p. 28–30.
48. Prüfer, 'Drama', p. 873, col. 1.

49. Ibn Dāniyāl, *Bābat Ṭayf al-Khayāl* in Ḥamāda, *Khayāl al-Ẓill*, p. 151 (*māta yā qawm shaykhunā Iblīs*, 'O people, our *shaykh* Iblīs, has died'); cf. also above n. 4 ('The *muḥabbaẓ* of Satan'); Ibn Iyās, *Badā'i'*, vol. I, part i, pp. 326f.

Appendix I: The Trial of the Caliphs

The text is taken from Ibn ʿAbd Rabbih, *Kitāb al-ʿIqd al-Farīd*, edited by A. Amīn, A. al-Zayn and I. al-Abyārī (Cairo, 1940-65), vol. V, pp. 152-4. It is translated and discussed in Chapter 5, pp. 91ff.

سمعتُ ابا عبد الرحمن بِشرًا يقول : كان في زمن المهدي رجل صوفيّ ،
وكان عاقلاً عالمًا ورعًا فتحمّق[1] ليجد السبيل الى الامر بالمعروف والنهي
عن المنكر[2] وكان يركب قصبة في كل جمعة يومين: الاثنين والخميس فإذا
ركب في هذين اليومين فليس لمعلم على صبيانه حكم ولا طاعة . فيخرج
ويخرج معه الرجال والنساء والصبيان ، فيصعد تلاً وينادي بأعلى صوته :
ما فعل النبيون والمرسلون ، أليسوا في اعلى علّيّين ؟ فيقولون : نعم .
قال : هاتوا أبا بكر الصدّيق . فأخذ غلام فأجلس بين يديه ، فيقول :
جزاك الله خيرًا يا ابا بكر عن الرعية ، فقد عدلت وقمت بالقسط وخلفت
محمدًا عليه الصلاة والسلام فأحسنتَ الخلافة ، ووصلتَ حبل الدين بعد
حلّ وتنازع ، ونزعت فيه الى اوثق عروة واحسن ثقة ، اذهبوا به الى
اعلى علّيّين . ثم ينادي : هاتوا عمر ! فأجلس بين يديه غلام ، فقال :
جزاك الله خيرًا ابا حفص عن الاسلام ، قد فتحت الفتوح ، ووسّعت الفيء
وسلكت سبيل الصالحين وعدلت في الرعيّة وقسمت بالسوية ، اذهبوا /
به الى أعلى علّيّين بحذاء ابي بكر . ثم يقول : هاتوا عثمان . فأتي
بغلام فأجلس بين يديه ، فيقول له : خلطت في تلك السّت السنين[3] ،
ولكن الله تعالى يقول : " خَلَطُوا عَمَلاً صَالِحًا وآخَرَ سَيّئًا عَسَى اللّهَ
أنْ يَتُوبَ عَلَيْهِمْ[4] " وعسى من الله موجبة . ثم يقول : إذهبوا به الى
صاحبيه في اعلى علّيّين . ثم يقول : هاتوا علي بن ابي طالب . فأجلس
غلام بين يديه . فيقول : جزاك الله عن الامة خيرًا أبا الحسن ، فأنت
الوصيّ ووليّ النبي ، بسطت العدل ، وزهدت في الدنيا ، واعتزلت الفيء ،
فلم تَخمِشْ فيه بناب ولا ظفر ، وأنت ابو الذريّة المباركة ، وزوج
الزكيّة الطاهرة ، اذهبوا به الى اعلى علّيّين من الفردوس . ثم يقول :
هاتوا معاوية ، فأجلس بين يديه صبي فقال له : انت القاتل عمّار بن
ياسر وخزيمة بن ثابت ذا الشهادتين وحجر بن الادبر[5] الكندي الذي
اخلقت وجهَهُ العبادةُ ، وأنت الذي جعل الخلافة ملكًا[6] واستأثر
بالفيء وحكم بالهوى واستنصر بالظلمة وأنت أول من غيّر سُنّة
رسول الله صلّى الله عليه وسلّم ونقض أحكامه[7] وقام بالبغي . اذهبوا به

فأوقفوه مع الظلمة ، ثمّ قال : هاتوا يزيد . فأجلس بين يديه غلام . فقال له : يا قوّاد ، أنت الذي قتلت أهل الحرّة وابحت المدينة ثلاثة أيّام[9]، وانتهكت حرم رسول الله صلّى الله عليه وسلّم وآويت الملحدين وبؤت باللعنة على لسان رسول الله صلّى الله عليه وسلّم وتمثّلت بشعر الجاهليّة :

لَيْتَ أشْياخِي بِبَدْرٍ شَهِدُوا جَزَعَ الخَزْرَجِ مِنْ وَقْعِ الأسَلْ[10]

وقتلت حسينًا وحملت بنات رسول الله صلّى الله عليه وسلّم على حقائب الإبل[11]، اذهبوا به الى الدرك الاسفل من النار. ولا يزال يذكر واليًا بعد والٍ حتى بلغ الى عمر بن عبد العزيز ، فقال : هاتوا عمر. فأتي بغلام فأجلس بين يديه فقال: جزاك الله يا عمر خيرًا عن الاسلام ، فقد احييت العدل بعد موته وألنت القلوب القاسية وقام بك عمود الدين على ساق، بعد شقاق ونفاق ، اذهبوا به / فالحقوه بالصدّيقين. ثم ذكر من كان بعده من الخلفاء الى ان بلغ دولة بني العباس فسكت فقيل له : هذا ابو العباس امير المؤمنين ، قال : بلغ امرنا الى بني هاشم ، ارفعوا حساب هؤلاء جملة واقذفوا بهم في النار جميعًا .

Notes

١- الشرواني ، حدائق الافراح (بولاق ، ١٢٨٢/١٨٦٥) ، ص ١٨٥ : تَجَنّن.

٢- قرآن ، آية ١٠٤ ، سورة ٣، آية ١١٠، سورة ٩، آية ١١٣، سورة ٧٢.

٣- قارن : "رسالة الجاحظ في بني امية "، في كتاب : **رسائل الجاحظ** ، جمعها ونشرها حسن السندوبي (مصر ، ١٣٥٢/١٩٣٣) ، ص ٢٩٢ : وست سنين من خلافة عثمان رضي الله عنه ،كانوا على التوحيد والاخلاص المحض .

٤- قرآن، آية ١٠٢ ، سورة ٩ .

٥- في رسالة الجاحظ ، ص ٢٩٤ : حجر بن عدي .

٦- في رسالة الجاحظ ، ص ٢٩٤ : تحولت فيه الامامة ملكًا كسرويًا والخلافة منصبًا قيصريًا .

٧- في رسالة الجاحظ ، ص ٢٩٤ : والاستئثار بالفيء واختيار الولاة على الهوى .

٨- في رسالة الجاحظ ، ص ٢٩٤ : حتى ردّ قضية رسول الله صلى الله عليه وسلم ردًّا مكشوفًا وجحد حكمه جحدًا ظاهرًا في ولد الفراش وما يجب للعاهر .

٩- في رسالة الجاحظ ، ص ٢٩٤ : ثم غزو مكة ورمي الكعبة واستباحة المدينة .

١٠ـ في رسالة الجاحظ ، ص ٢٩٤ : ولو ثبت ايضًا على يزيد انه تمثل بقول ابن الزبعرى :

لَيْتَ اشياخِي بِبَدْرٍ شَهِدُوا … جَزَعَ الخزرَجِ مِنْ وَقْعِ الأَسَلْ
لاسْتَطارُوا واسْتَهلّوا فَرحًا … ثمّ قالُوا يا يَزيدُ لا تسل
قَدْ قَتَلْنَا الغُرّ من ساداتِهِمْ … وعَدَلْناهُ ببَدْرٍ فاعْتَدَلْ

١١ـ في رسالة الجاحظ ، ص ٢٩٥ : وحمل بنات رسول الله صلى الله عليه وسلم حواسر على الاقتاب العارية والابل الصعاب .

Appendix II: MISṬARAT KHAYĀL

f. 142a

*

وقلتُ وقد سُيلتُ في نظم مسطرة خَيال ، منادمة أم مجبر ، وهي بين اربعَة : الرايس والقلاعي والوَلد وام مجبر ، يقول الريس :

سبحان من خلق ذا العالم * ذا أبيَض وهذا اسودْ
وَاشقى من ارَاد من خلقو * وآخرِ في البرايا اسعدْ
وِ آخر اتحفو بالزلفى * وقدْ رُوا على الناس شيّدْ
وَاختص الملاح بالالطاف * من حورٍ في الجمال اوولدان
وَاختص القباح يَا عارف * بالبوَار وكثر النقصَان

المديح

وامتدح اجلّ الانبيا [1] * وَازكاهم وَاعلى وَاعلى [2]
خير الخلق طه الهادي * مدحو كررُوا لي يحلى
فلو أنّ الاقلام اجمع * يكتبوا جميع مَا يُملْى
لم يحصوا القليلِ من فضله * لو افنوِا البيَان بالتبيان
عليه صَلِ ربّي وَآله * وصحبُو وَاهل الايمان

الريس

كان لي في البَرايا زوجا * تسمّى أم مجبر حوبه
عجُوزا فزِورا جرِدا * من فوِق كل وِجنه قوبِه[3] f. 142b
صرت منِ نفسْها محرُوق * وَفي صُغر سِنّيِ شيبَه
بخرا وَسعا محروقه * تفوق فيِ السوَاد الغربان
ذلتني وَاحنت[4] قدري * وقد صيّرتني حيران

الريّس ايضًا

تزحف لي وَأنا في نوِمي * اقوم من نفَسْها مَطرْوب
تقصد بالقما حبا لعَشى * ماذا الا مقدّر مَكتوب
اسفقها تزيد سعلتها * وتجعر تريد الملعوِب
لمّا ضايقتني ناديت * ان تموتِ وَقلبي وَلهَان
ماتت وانقضت مدتها * وراحت سَقر والنيران

يقول[5] لريّس ايضًا

بدّلني إلهي طفلا [6] * دعجات العيُونِ معشوقه [7]
تخطر بالقوام الاهيف [8] * بَيْضا ناعما مَمشْوقه
احمدك [9] إلهي واشكر * منِ بعد العجوز اللوقه
بدّلت الحزن بالفرحة * وصيّرت قلبي نشوان
يا الله لا عدمت احسَانك * حين ابعدت عني الاحزان

يقول القلاعي للريّس[10]

نهنيك بل نهني صحابك * ونهني جميع الحضّار
خلّق بالزعافر بيتك * وخلّق لحيطان الدار
اتبرمك واحسن للناس * واسقِ الجمع قرقف عقار
وابدل الحزن بالفرحة * وقرب لربك قربان
المرا القد يما جاتك * تلمك سحر بالاحضان

يقول الريّس للقلاعي f. 143a

الله لا يجيب تعريصك [11] * يا من رَام بلقشوِا[12] الخونه /
تقول لي العجُوز اجاتك * وَهي في التراب مدفونه
بيدِي قبرها وَارَيتو * ليش هي المِيته مجنونه
بعد الدفن ترجع تحيا * بعد درجَها في الاكفان
من تسعين سنة في الصحرا * عليها تكر الازمان

تقول ام مجبر

اسم الله عليّا والله * يخلي شباب الشبّه
أنا اصدق من الّي قال لك * إنّي متّ أو في التربه
من قال لك وانا في العصما[13] * تاخذ لك شُلَيْقا قحبه
انظر يا حبيب ما احسَني * أفوق القمر في النقصان
ما لي من شبيه في ندي * ولا في سَرَايت السلطان

يقول الريس

الله يقطع الّي[14] جابك * وَالّي[15] باللقا لي خبّر
وَابنك ذا الكتيف المرِيول * هذا النحس الامخط مجبر
يا ايشم عجايز ربي * يا ام كـ ... ناشف مُشعر[16]
يا غرلا وعوجا لوقا * جيتي بالكذب والبهتان
ان لم ترجعي في قشرَه * قطعتك اربْ في الخلجان

تقول ام مجبر

سلمك وسَلم قدّك * وعقلك وسلّم ذاتك
يا قطي ويا قطقوطي * ليش[17] تهجر لحسن مراتك
وهيّا مليحا زينا * بكثر الدلال قد جاتك
لي تسعين سنا في الصحرا * اقطع القفار والوديان
وبك لمّ ربي شمْلي * بالله قم لشفري عريَان

يقول الريس /

تعَالوا انظروا ذي الشوها * اللوقا العجُوز الغبره f. 143b
وانظروا الى كوشتها * وانياب اكتسوا بالخضره
لا كان رَبنا لي جابك * ولا رَدّ خلفك سَفره
انتي من بقا يا قوم نوح * والآ عاد وتلك الازمان
قولي لي من اين جيتيني[18] * ومن هو أبُوكِ والاخوان

تقول ام مجبر

يا سيدي ابويا بحلق * وأخويا المعلم كيلون[19]
واسم امي شهيّة[20] واسمي * شهله[21] من نواحي طيْلون[22]
ومجبر بنيي وحدي * اذّي خلف ظهري مغبُون
هات لي ذي القحَيبا امراتك * انظرها هنا بالاعيان
ان كان[24] هي مليحة مثلي * اقلبْني وَشيل[25] السيقان

يقول الريس

قومي يا مليحه سُرّعه * يا زيني وقرّة عَيْني
وامشي في الحجُول والاقراط * وزيلي بخطوك شيني
ومسّيْ[٢٦] على ذي القشره * عسى تنكشط من عيني
ناد يها بلطفك ساعه * واطفي بالبشاشه النيران
قولي يَا عَجُوز تتمسي * بالخير والكرامه والشان

تقول المليحه

يا سيدي انا في الخدمه * ما عندي كلام يَا بعدي
يا روحي ويا روح ناسي * يا مالك فوادي وحدي
لكني[٢٧] خاف أتوجّه * لها عن هنا أو احدي
تجعلني فطور تاكلني * ذي غوله وأمّ الغيلان
او تنفخ عليّا أسقط * نقعها حنش أو تعبان /

تقول المليحه ايضًا f. 144a

قوامي الرشيق المايس * منِ مرّ النسيم يتألم
ويجرح ويولم خدي * اذِي بالمحاسن يرْقم
لما أنظرالى ذي الشوها * تمرضني وجفني يسقم

والحبرالبديع الشاعر * يجنّد[٢٨] في مَدحي او زان
والجمان[٢٩] وغالي الجوهر * ينظم من دموع الاجفان

تقول ام مجبر

يا سيدي انا احسَن منها * وقلب نهُودي تعرف
وشاهد لكافي والسين[٣٠] * لما أن ترى لو تقرف[٣١]
اشجع[٣٢] وشيل الساقين * ان شاالله تموت او تضعف
وِادخل زين وباقي الكاره * تبقى في النفايس وحلان
وَان طلبت تقلب اقلب * تنسى طفلتك والمردان

الاستشهاد

وأنا هو الاديب الماهر * صافي الفكر عبد الباقي
في جدي وهزلي نظمي * في درج المعالي راقي
جريال الادب في حاني * وانا هو المدير وَالساقي
وانثر الدررحين انظم * واحليه بذوب العقيان
والهُزْء السخيف من صوغي * ازينو بوزن الأوزان

*
There is a possibility that this term is derived from the Italian term *Mostra* (show).

١ـ هذا الصدر من البيت ساقط من مقال محمد زكريا عناني "حول خيال الظل في مصر" ، الكاتب ، السنة ١٨ ، العدد ٢٠٣ ، فبراير ١٩٧٨ ، ص ١٢.

٢ـ جعل عناني هذا العجز صدرًا للبيت التالي وغيّر الكلمتين الاخيرتين فيه الى : " واغلا واعطى " ولا تجيز القافية استعمال كلمة "أعطى".

٣ـ عند عناني " قوية " والقافية لا تجيزها .

٤ـ عند عناني " وأحسنت " والمعنى لا يستقيم بها ، ولعل الصواب "اخسّت".

٥- " يقول " ساقطة عند عناني .
٦- عند عناني : طفلة .
٧- عناني : معشوقة .
٨- عناني : الاليف .

٩- عناني : احمد .
١٠-عناني : الريس للقلاعي .
١١-عناني : تعريضك .
١٢-عناني : بلقسو .

١٣- عناني : العصمة .
١٤- عناني : اللي .
١٥- عناني : اللي .
١٦- اسقط عناني الكلمات الثلاث الاخيرة عمدًا.
١٧- في الاصل : ليس .
١٨- عناني : جئتيني .

١٩- عناني : كيلوا ن .
٢٠ - عناني : ضهية.
٢١- عناني : شملة .
٢٢- عناني : شملة

٢٣- عناني : كلمة "خلف " مكررة .
٢٤- عناني : كانت .
٢٥- عناني : " اقلبني وشيل " ، ساقطة عمدًا .
٢٥أ- عناني : بخطوطك .

٢٦- عناني : وامشي .
٢٧- عناني : لكن .
٢٨- عناني : يزيد .
٢٩- عناني : والجمال .

٣٠- اسقط عناني كلمة " السين " عمدًا .
٣١- كذا في الاصل، وعند عناني : " لو تعترف ".
٣٢- في الاصل : وا سجع .

'Abd al-Bāqī al-Isḥāqī's play *Misṭarat Khayāl Munādama Umm Mujbir*, 'A Sample Play, the Companionship of Umm Mujbir', is found in his *Dīwan Sulāf al-Anshā' fi 'l-Shi'r wa-'l-Inshā'*, MS Bibliothèque Nationale, Paris, arabe 4852, fols 142-4a, and published by A. Z. 'Anānī in his 'Ḥawla Khayāl al-Ẓill fi Miṣr, ma'a Naṣṣ Yunshar li-awwal Marra', *al-Kātib* XVIII, no. 23, February 1978, pp. 6-14. The text presented here is based on the manuscript (my thanks to the authorities of the Bibliothèque Nationale for sending me a microfilm); where 'Ananī's readings differ, they are given in the notes.

[The play is] between four [characters]: al-Rayyis (Captain), al-Qilā'ī (Sailing Master), al-Walad (the boy) [who does not in fact play any part and should be replaced by al-Malīḥa (the Beautiful girl)] and Umm Mujbir. 142a

The Rayyis says:
Glory be to Him who created this world
Some white and some black.
He made miserable those of his creatures He wished
And others He made happy.
To others He presented high position
And established their power over men.
He gave His special favours to those who are
As beautiful as houries, or as young men of Paradise.
And he singled out the ugly one
For unacceptability, and gave many defects,
How knowing He was.

Praise (to Muḥammad):
I praise the most illustrious prophet,
The purest of them and the dearest and the highest is
the best of the creations Ṭaha (Muḥammad) who guided us.
Repeat to me his praises, how sweet they are [to my ears].
If all pens were to write
of all that is dictated
They would only enumerate a small part of his virtues
Even if they are to cover the whole field of rhetorics,
in showing his virtues.
May my Lord bless him and his family
And companions and all believers.

al-Rayyis:
I had a troublesome wife in this world,
Called Umm Mujbir
Old hump-backed and bald

On each cheek tetters./
How her breath burnt me 142b
And although I was young I got white hair.
Her breath smelled bad, wide and black as if burnt
Blacker than any crow.
She humiliated me and lowered my esteem
And made me completely confused.

al-Rayyis once more:
She creeps up to me while I am asleep
I get up startled by her breath
She wants me to give her something for her 'supper'
That is only fated and decreed.
I give her a dig, her coughs increase
She screams wanting 'the game'
When she harassed me, I called out
In my desperation that she might die.
She died and passed away
She went to hell and its fires.

al-Rayyis continues:
God gave me a soft woman
Beloved, with wide black eyes.
Walking gracefully with her slender figure
Fair, soft and slender waisted
I praise God and thank Him [for her]
After that old lisping woman.
She changed my grief into joy,
And intoxicated my heart.
O God may I never forget your goodness
To me, when you dispelled my sorrows.

The Qilā'ī says to the Rayyis:
We congratulate you, or rather congratulate your friends,
And all the audience.
May your house be perfumed with saffron,
And perfumed the walls of the house.
Be generous and charitable to the people
And give all pure old wine to drink.
Turn sorrow into joy,
And make an offering to your Lord.
Here the former woman came to you,
Embracing you early in the morning.

The Rayyis says to the Qilā'ī:

May God not reply to your importuning,
 You who want to betray me with his mocking. /
You tell me that the old woman came to me, 143a
 While she is buried in the earth.
With my two hands I covered her grave,
 You think that the dead woman was beset by the *jinn*?
Coming back to life after being buried,
 And wrapped with her shroud?
For ninety years the ages have rolled
 Over her in the desert.

Umm Mujbir says:
 God bless me, may God
 Preserve the young girl's youth.
 I am more truthful than him who told you
 I have died or I was in my grave.
 Who told you while I was still your wife
 To take a quarrelsome harlot.
 Look my darling how beautiful I am,
 More beautiful than the moon on the wane.
 There is no like of me to rival with me,
 Even in the sultan's palace.

The Rayyis says:
 May God destroy who brought you forth,
 and those who revealed the news [of your coming].
 Your thick headed, slobbering son,
 That snotty ill-starred Mujbir.
 O most nauseating old woman [created] by my Lord,
 O you with a dry and hairy vulva
 O uncircumcised, twisted, lisper,
 You came with lies and falsehood
 If you don't return to your shroud,
 I'll cut you to pieces in the gulfs.

Umm Mujbir says:
 May God preserve you and preserve your esteem,
 And your mind, and may he preserve your person.
 O my cat! O my pussy-cat,
 Why do you shun your wife's beauty?
 She is beautiful, good,
 Who has come to you so coquettishly.
 I spent ninety years in the desert,
 Travelling through the wilderness and the valleys.
 And my Lord has brought me together with you,

By God get up and strip my labium.

The Rayyis says:/ 143b
Come, and see this deformed,
Lisping, dishevelled old woman.
See how fat she is,
And her teeth are coated with green.
I wish that God had not brought you to me,
And had never made your return safe from your journey.
You are a remainder of the people of Noah,
Or ʿĀd and those bygone ages.
Tell me where you have come from,
Who are your father and brothers?

Umm Mujbir says:
My Lord, my father is Baḥlaq,
And my brother is Kaylūn.
My mother is called Shahiyya, and my name is
Shahla from the region Ṭaylūn.
And Mujbir is my only son,
Here he is offspring cheated [of his inheritance].
Bring me that harlot wife of yours,
To see her here with my eyes.
If she is as beautiful as me...
Put me on my back and raise my legs.

The Rayyis says:
Come beautiful one, quickly,
My adornment and delight of my eyes.
Walk with your anklets and earrings,
And dispel my sorrows with your pace.
Walk forward to this shell of a woman,
Perhaps she will disappear from my eye.
Talk to her for a while,
And put out the fires with your cheerfulness.
Say, old woman, good evening,
You are honoured and how important you are!

The beautiful girl says:
My lord I am at your service!
I have nothing to add. O you who will survive me [by God's will].
O my soul and the soul of my heart
O possessor of my heart alone!
I am afraid to approach her from here,

Or to take the first steps.
She will make me her breeakfast, and eat me!
She is a ghoul and a mother of ghouls.
When she blows upon me I fall down.
Her poison is that of a viper or snake. /

The beautiful girl continues: 144a
My splendid swaying body,
Would be hurt even by the blowing of the breeze.
It wounds and hurts my cheeks,
Here it is decorated with beauty.
When I look at this hideous woman,
She makes me and my eyelids ill.
The wonderful scholar the poet
Adds meters in praise of me.
The tears of my eyelids,
Make a necklace of beauty and precious jewels.

Umm Mujbir says:
O my lord! I am more beautiful
Than her, and you know the heart under my breast.
And sufficiency as a witness is my Kāf and Sīn (vulva) when you see it
If you would only confess.
I can be bold and lift my leg,
May she die or get weak.
Thrust in well and (you know the) rest of the business
You'll get stuck in precious things.
If you wish to turn me over, I turn over,
Then you forget your girl and all the beardless young men.

Conclusion:
I am the skillful, pure minded man of letters ʿAbd al-Bāqī.
Whether I am serious or comical, my verse is
High on the ladder of rhetorics.
The wine of literature in in my tavern,
And I am the one who hands it around
And pours it out.
I scatter pearls when I compose my verse,
And embellish them with melted pure gold.
Ridiculous mockery is among my versification,
Which I decorate with metrification.

Bibliography

1. Books

Abdel-Meguid, A. -A., *The Modern Arabic Short Story* (Cairo, [1956?]).
Al-Ābī, Manṣūr b. al-Ḥusayn, *Nathr al-Durr*. vol. VII. ed. 'U. Bū-Ghanīmī. (Tunis, 1983).
Al-Ābī, Manṣūr b. al-Ḥusayn, *Nathr al-Durr*. vol. III, ed. 'Alī Qurna and 'A. M. al-Bujāwī (Cairo, 1984).
Abū 'l-Fidā, *Historia Anteislamica Arabica*, ed. H. O. Fleischer (Leipzig, 1831).
Abū 'l-Fidā, *Tārīkh Abī 'l-Fidā* (Cairo, n.d.).
Abul-Naga, Atia, *Recherche sur les termes de théâtre et leur traduction en Arabe moderne* (Alger, SNED, n.d.)
Abū Shanab, 'A., *Masraḥ 'Arabī Qadīm 'Karakūz'* (Damascus, n.d.).
Al-'Adawī, M. Qiṭṭa, *Alf Layla wa-Layla* (Būlāq, 1279-80/1862–3).
Ahlwardt, W., *Die Handschriften-Verzeichnisse der Königlichen Bibliothek zu Berlin, Verzeichniss der arabischen Handschriften* (Berlin, 1893).
Ahsan, M. M., *Social Life Under the Abbasids 170–289 H/ 786–902 A.D.* (London and New York, 1979).
'Ā'isha 'Abd al-Raḥmān, (Bint al-Shāti'), *al-Ghufrān li-Abī 'l-'Alā' al-Ma'arrī, Dirāsa Naqdiyya*. 3rd edn. (Cairo, 1968).
'Ā'isha 'Abd al-Raḥmān, *Qirā'a Jadīda fī Risālat al-Ghufrān* (Cairo, 1970).
Al-'Alawjī, 'Abd al-Ḥamīd *Min Turāthinā 'l-Sha'bī* (Baghdad, 1966).
de Alcalá, Pedro, *Vocabulista aravigo en lietra castellana* (Granada), 1505).
Alf Layla wa-Layla, See: al-'Adawī, Habicht, Lane, MacNaughten.
Al-Ālūsī, Maḥmūd Shukrī, *Bulūgh al-Arab fī Ma'rifat Aḥwāl al-'Arab* (Baghdad, 1314/1896f).
Amīn, A., *Qāmūs al-'Ādāt wa-'l-Taqālīd wa-'l-Ta'ābīr al-Miṣriyya* (Cairo, 1953).
'Anbar, 'A. -R., *Al-Masraḥiyya bayn al-Naẓariyya wa-'l-Taṭbīq* (Cairo, 1966).
And, M., *Culture, Performance and Communication in Turkey* (Tokyo, 1987).
And, M., *A History of Theatre and Popular Entertainment in Turkey* (Ankara, 1963–64).
And, M., *Osmanli Şenliklerinde Türk Sanatlari* (Ankara, 1982).
And, M., *A Pictorial History of Turkish Dancing* (Ankara, 1976)
And, M., *Karagoz, Theatre d'Ombres Turc* (Ankara, 1977).
'Ānūs, N., *Masraḥ Ya'qūb Ṣanū'* (Cairo, 1984).
al-A'rajī M. H., *Fann al-Tamthīl 'inda 'l-'Arab* (Baghdad, 1978).

'Arsān, 'Alī 'Uqla, *al-Ẓawāhir al-Masraḥiyya 'ind al-'Arab* (Damascus, 1985), 3rd edn.

Aristotle, *Fann al-Shi'r*, see 'A. -R. Badawī.

Asad, N. -D., *al-Qiyān wa-'l-Ghinā' fī 'l-'Aṣr al-Jāhilī* (Cairo, 1968).

'Āshūr, 'A. -F., *al-Mujtama' al-Miṣrī fī 'Aṣr Salāṭīn al-Mamālīk* (Cairo, 1962).

al-'Asqalānī, Ibn Ḥajar, *al-Iṣāba fī Ma'rifat al-Ṣaḥāba*, ed. 'A. M. al-Bujāwī. (Cairo, 1323/1905).

al-'Asqalānī, Ibn Ḥajar, *Fatḥ al-Bārī bi-Sharḥ Ṣaḥīḥ al-Bukhārī* (Cairo, 1325/ 1907).

Athanasius, *The Canons of Athanasius of Alexandria, the Arabic and Coptic versions* ed. and tr. Riedel and W. E. Crum (London-Oxford, 1904).

Ayalon, D., *Gunpowder and Firearms in the Mamluk Kingdom* (London, 1956).

'Azīza, Muḥammad, *Formes traditionelles du spectacle* (Tunis, 1975).

'Azīza, Muḥammad, *al-Islām wa-'l-Masraḥ* (Cairo, 1971).

The Babylonian Talmud, Seder Nezikin. 'Abodah Zarah, tr. A. Mishcon and A. Cohen (London, 1935).

The Babylonian Talmud, tr. H. Freeman (London, 1938).

Badawī, 'Abd al-Raḥman (ed.), *Fann al-Shi'r ma'a 'l-Tarjama al-'Arabiyya al-Qadīma wa-Shurūḥ al-Fārābī wa-Ibn Sīnā wa-Ibn Rushd* (Beirut, 1973).

Badawī, M. M., *Early Arabic Drama* (Cambridge, 1988).

al-Badrī, 'Abdallah b. Muḥammad, *Nuzhat al-Anām fī Maḥāsin al-Shām*. (Cairo, 1341 / 1922f).

Baer, G., *Egyptian Guilds in Modern Times* (Jerusalem, 1964).

al-Bākharzī, *Dumyat al-Qaṣr* (Cairo, 1968).

al-Balādhurī, *Ansāb al-Ashrāf*, ed. S. D. Goitein (Jerusalem, 1936).

al-Balawī, 'Abdallah al-Madīnī, *Sīrat Aḥmad b. Ṭūlūn*, ed. M. Kurd 'Alī, (Damascus, 1358/1939).

al-Baqlī, M. Q. *al-Awzān al-Mūsīqiyya fī Azjāl Ibn Sūdūn* (Cairo, 1976).

Bar Hebraeus, G. J., *The Laughable Stories, the Syriac Text* ed. and tr. E.A.W. Budge. (London, 1897).

Basset, René, *Le Syntaxaire Arabe Jacobite (Mois de Tout et de Babeh) in Patrologia Orientalis*, ed. R. Graffin and F. Nasu (Paris, 1907).

Baybars, Aḥmad Samīr, *al-Masraḥ al-'Arabī fī 'l-Qarn al-Tāsi' 'Ashar* (Cairo, 1985).

Beck, H. G., *Geschichte der byzantinischen Volksliteratur* (Munich, 1971).

Belzoni, G., *Narratives of the Operations and Recent Discoveries in Egypt and Nubia*. (London, 1820).

Bevan, A. A., (ed.) *The Nakā'iḍ of Jarīr and al-Farazdak* (Leiden, 1905–9).

al-Bīrūnī, *Taḥqīq mā li-'l-Hind min Maqūla Maqbūla fī-'l-'Aql aw-Mardhūla* (Ḥaydar Ābād al-Dakan, 1958).

Blachère, R. and Mansou, P., *Al-Hamadhānī-Choix de Maqāmāt* (Paris, 1957).

Bosworth, C. E., *The Medieval Islamic Underworld; the Banū Sāsān in Arabic Society and Literature* (Leiden, 1976).

Boyce, M., *A History of Zoroastrianism* (Leiden and Cologne, 1975-82).

Brockelmann, C., *Geschichte der arabischen Litteratur* (Leiden, 1943–49).

Brockelmann, C., *Mitteltürkischer Wortschatz* (Leipzig, 1938).

Brown, P., *The World of Late Antiquity* (London, 1971).

Bruns, K. G., and E. Schau, E. (eds. and trs.,) *Syrisch-römisches Rechtsbuch aus dem fünften Jahrhundert* (Leipzig, 1880; reprinted 1961).

al-Budayrī, Aḥmad, *Ḥawādith Dimashq al-Yawmiyya,* ed. M. S. al-Qāsimī ([Cairo], 1959).

al-Bukhārī, *The Translation of the Meanings of Ṣaḥīh al-Bukhārī,* Arabic-English by Muḥammad Muḥsin Khān (Gujranwala, 1971).

al-Bustānī, Sa'īd, *Riwāyat Dhāt al-Khidr* (Alexandria, 1904), 2nd edn.

al-Bustānī, Ṣ. -D., *Ṣuḥuf Bunabartah fī Miṣr 1798–1801* (Cairo, 1971).

Canova, Giovanni, *Egitto 1, epica i suoni Musica di Tradizione Orale* (Rome, 1982), with a record.

Catalogus Codicum Manuscriptorum Orientalium Qui in Museo Britannico Asservantur (London, 1871), vol. III.

Chelkowski, P. J. (ed.) *Ta'ziyeh, Ritual and Drama in Iran* (New York, 1979).

Christensen, A., *L'Iran sous les sassanides,* (Copenhagen, 1944), 2nd edn.

Crone, P., *Roman, Provincial and Islamic Law* (Cambridge, 1987).

Crone P. and Hinds M., *God's Caliph, Religious Authority in the First Centuries of Islam* (Cambridge, 1986).

Corriente, F., *Grammática, Métrica y texto del cancionero hispanoárabe de ABAN Quzman* (Madrid, 1980).

Corriente, F., *Léxico Ārabe Andalusī Según P. de Alcalá* (Madrid, 1988).

Chenery, T. (tr.), *The Assemblies of al-Ḥariri* (London, 1867).

Daninos, A., *Nazāhat al-Mushtāq wa-Ghuṣṣat al-'Ushshāq fī Madīnat Ṭiryāq fī 'l-'Irāq* (Algeria, 1847).

al-Dasūqī, 'Umar, *al-Malik Awdīb* (Oedipus Rex) (Cairo, 1944).

al-Dasūqī, 'Umar, *al-Masraḥiyya, Nash'atuhā wa-Uṣūluhā* (Cairo, 1957).

Dorsch, T. S. (tr.), *Classical Literary Criticism. Aristotle on the Art of Poetry...* (London, 1965).

Downey, G., *A History of Antioch from Seleucus to the Arab Conquest* (Princeton, 1961).

Dozy, R. and W. H. Engelmann, *Glossaire des mots espagnols et portugais derives de l'arabe,* (Amsterdam, 1915), 2nd edn.

Dozy, R., (ed.), *Historia Abbadidarum, Praemisis Screiptorum Arabum de ea Dynastia Locis Nuno...* (Leiden, 1846).

Dozy, R., (ed.), *Supplement aux dictionnaires arabes* (Leiden, 1967).

Eliade, M., *Shamanism, Archaic Technique of Ecstasy* (Princeton, 1974).

Encyclopedia Judaica, s.v. 'Theater', (Jerusalem, 1971), vol. 15, cols 1049–50.

al-Fākihī, *Akhbār Makka,* ed. F. Wüstenfeld (Leipzig, 1858–61), vol. II, pp. 9–10.

al-Fasi, David ben Avraham, *Kitāb Jāmi' al-Alfāẓ,* ed. S. L. Skoss (New Haven, 1936–45), vols I and II.

Friedlaender, I., *Arabisch-Deutsches Lexikon zum Sprachgebrauch des Maimonides* (Frankfurt a. M., 1902).

Gendzier, I. L., *The Practical Visions of Ya'qūb Ṣanū'* (Cambridge, Mass., 1966).

Gerlach, S., *Tage-buch* (Frankfurt a. M., 1674).

al-Ghazālī, *Iḥyā' 'Ulūm al-Dīn* (Cairo, 1352/1933).

al-Ghazūlī, *Naṭāli' al-Budūr fī Manāzil al-Surūr* (Cairo, 1299/1881f.)

al-Ghazzī, M., *al-Marāḥ fi-'l-Muzāḥ,* ed. A 'Ubayd (Damascus, 1349/ 1930).

Gibb, H. A. R. and Bowen H., *Islamic Society and the West* (London, 1950–57).

Gomez, E. G., *Todo Ben Quzmān* (Madrid, 1972).

Graber, O., *The Illustrations of the Maqāmāt* (Chicago and London, 1984).
von Grunebaum, G. E., *Muhammadan Festivals* (New York, 1951).
al-Ḥakīm, Tawfīq, *al-Malik Awdīb* [*Oedipus Rex*] (Cairo, 1944).
al-Ḥakīm, Tawfīq, *Qālabunā 'l-Masraḥī* (Cairo, 1949).
al-Ḥalwānī, Muḥammad Khayr, *al-'Arab wa-Adab al-Yūnān* (Ḥalab, 1969).
Ḥamāda, I., *Khayāl al-Ẓill wa-Tamthīliyyāt Ibn Dāniyāl* (Cairo, 1963).
al-Hamadhānī, *Maqāmāt,* ed. M. 'Abduh, second edition. (Beirut, 1908).
al-Hamadhānī, *al-Maqāmāt,* ed. Fārūq Sa'd (Beirut, n.d.).
al-Ḥamīdī, *Jadhwat al-Muqtabis,* ed. Muḥammad b. Yāwīt al-Tanjī. (Cairo, n.d.).
al-Ḥanafī, Aḥmad, *Maqāmāt al-Ḥanafī wa-Ibn Nāqiya wa-ghayrihimā* (Istanbul, 1331/1913).
al-Ḥarīrī, *Maqāmāt* (Cairo, n.d.).
al-Ḥarīrī, *The Assemblies of al-Hariri,* tr. T. Chenery (London, 1867), vol. I.
al-Ḥarīrī, *Les Seances de Ḥarīrī,* ed. Silvestre de Sacy (Paris, 1837).
Ḥassān Ibn Thābit, *Dīwān of Ḥassān ibn Thābit,* ed. W. N. 'Arafat. London, 1971).
Ḥassān Ibn Thābit, *Dīwān,* ed. H. Hirschfeld. (London and Leiden, 1910).
Hattox, R. S., *Coffee and Coffeehouses. The Origins of a Social Beverage in the Medieval Near East* (Seatle- London, 1985).
Haythamī, Ibn Ḥajar. *Kitāb Kaff al-Ru'ā' 'an Muḥarramāt al-lahw wa-'l-Samā',* printed in the margin of Ibn Ḥajar al-Haythamī, *Kitāb al-Zawājir 'an Iqtirāf al-Kabā'ir.* (Cairo, 1322/1904f.).
Heffening, W. and Kirfel W. (eds.), *Studien zur Geschichte und Kultur des Nahen und Fernen Ostens* (Leiden, 1935).
Heinrichs, W., *Arabische Dichtung und Griechische Poetik* (Beirut, 1969).
Hilāl, Muḥammad Ghunaymī, *al-Adab al-Muqāran,* 3rd edn. (Cairo, 1962).
al-Ḥimyarī, *Ṣifat Jazīrat al-'Arab,* ed. and tr. E. Levi-Provencal. (Cairo, 1937).
Hippocrates, *Oeuvres completes d'Hippocrate* ed. and tr. E. Littre, (Amsterdam, 1962).
Hoenerbach, W., *Das Nordafrikanische Schattentheater* (Mainz, 1959).
Hoenerbach, W., *Studien zum 'Mauren und Christen' - Festspiel Andalusien* (Ortslisten, Texte und Dokumente) (Walldorf-Hessen, 1975).
Horovitz, H. G. (ed.), *Mekhilta d'Rabbi Ishmael* (Jerusalem, 1960).
Horovitz, J., *Spuren griechischer Mimen im Orient.* (Berlin, 1905).
al-Ḥuṣrī al-Qayrawānī, *Dhayl Zahr al-Ādāb* (Cairo, 1353/1934).
al-Ḥuṣrī al-Qayrawānī, *Jam' al-Jawāhir fī-'l-Mulaḥ wa-'l-Nawādir,* ed. 'A. M. al-Bujāwī (Cairo, 1353/1934).
Ḥusayn, Ṭaha, *Fī 'l-Adab al-Jāhilī* (Cairo, 1927).
Ḥusayn, Ṭaha, *Ḥadīth al-Arbi'ā'* (Cairo, 1937).
Ibn 'Abd al-'Azīz, Abū 'l-Salt b. Umayya. *al-Risāla al-Miṣriyya* in 'Abd al-Salām Hārūn (ed.), *Nawādir al-Makhṭūṭāt.* (Cairo, 1951).
Ibn 'Abd Rabbih, *al-Iqd al-Farīd,* ed. A. Amīn, I. Abyārī and 'A. -S. Hārūn (Cairo, 1368/1949).
Ibn 'Abdūn, 'Risāla fī 'l-Qaḍā' wa-'l'Ḥisba', in E. Levi-Provencal (ed.), *Thalāth Rasā'il Andalusiyya fī Adab al-Ḥisba wa-'l-Muḥtasib.* (Cairo, 1955).
Ibn Abī 'Awn, *al-Ajwiba al-Muskita* ed. Muḥammad 'Abd al-Qādir Aḥmad. (Cairo, 1985).
Ibn Abī 'l-Ḥadīd. *Sharḥ Nahj al-Balāgha* (Cairo, 1959).

Ibn Abī Uṣaybiʿa, *Kitāb ʿUyūn al-Anbā' fī Ṭabaqāt al-Aṭibbā'* (Cairo, 1299/1882).
Ibn al-ʿArabī, Muḥyī al-Dīn, *al-Futūḥāt al-Makkiyya* (Cairo, n.d.).
Ibn ʿAsākir, *Tārīkh Madīnat Dimashq,* vol. XX ed. Shukrī Faysal, Rūḥiyya al-Naḥḥās and Riyāḍ Murād (Dimashq, 1981).
Ibn ʿAsākir, *Tahdhīb Tārīkh Dimashq al-Kabīr,* ed. ʿAbd al-Qādir Badran (Dimashq, 1351/1932-33).
Ibn al-Athīr, *al-Kāmil fī 'l-Tā'rīkh,* ed. C. J. Tornberg. (Leiden, 1851-76).
Ibn al-Athīr, *al-Kāmil fī-'l-Tā'rīkh* (Beirut, 1965).
Ibn Bassām al-Shantarīnī, *al-Dhakhīra fī Maḥāsin Ahl al-Jazīra,* ed. I. ʿAbbās. (Beirut, 1979).
Ibn Dāniyāl, *Bābat Ṭayf al-Khayāl, Bābat ʿAjīb wa-Gharīb, Bābat al-Mutayyam,* in Ḥamāda, *Khayāl al-Ẓill wa-Tamthīliyyāt Ibn Dāniyāl* (Cairo, 1963).
Ibn Dāniyāl, *al-Mukhtār min Shiʿr Ibn Dāniyāl.* Selected by Khalīl b. Aybak al-Ṣafadī, ed. M. Nāyif al-Daylamī (Mosul, 1399/1979).
Ibn al-Dāya, Aḥmad b. Yūsuf. *Kitāb al-Mukāfa'a wa-Ḥusn al-ʿUqba* ed. Maḥmūd Muḥammad Shākir (Cairo, 1940).
Ibn Durayd, *Kitāb al-Ishtiqāq,* ed. F. Wüstenfeld. (Gottingen, 1854).
Ibn al-Ḥājj M. b. M. al-ʿAbdarī, *al-Madkhal* (Cairo, 1348/1929).
Ibn Ḥanbal, Aḥmad, *al-Musnad* (Cairo, 1313/1895f).
Ibn al-Haytham, al-Ḥasan, *Kitāb al-Manāẓir,* ed. ʿAbd al-Ḥamīd Ṣabra (Kuwait, 1983).
Ibn Ḥazm, *Kitāb al-Akhlāq wa-'l-Siyar,* ed. and tr. N. Tomiche. (Beirut, 1961).
Ibn Ḥijja al-Ḥamawī, *Thamarāt al-Awrāq* (Cairo, 1314/1896f).
Ibn al-Ikhwa, M. b. M., *Kitāb Maʿālim al-qurbā fī Aḥkām al-Ḥisba* (Cairo, 1976.
Ibn al-ʿImād, *Shadharāt al-Dhahab fī Akhbār man Dhahab* (Cairo, 1351/1932).
Ibn Iyās, *Badā'iʿ al-Zuhūr fī Waqā'iʿ al-Duhūr,* ed. M. M. Ziyāda (Wiesbaden, 1960-1984).
Ibn Janāḥ, *The Book of Hebrew Roots,* ed. C. Neubauer. (Oxford, 1875).
Ibn al-Jawzī, ʿA. -R., *Akhbar al-Ḥamqā wa-'l-Mughaffalīn* (Damascus, 1345/1926).
Ibn al-Jawzī, *al-Muntaẓam fī Tārīkh al-Mulūk wa-'l-Umam* (Hoydarabad al-Dakan, 1359/1940).
Ibn al-Jawzī, *Talbīs Iblīs,* ed. K. L. -D. ʿAlī, (Beirut, 1368/1948f).
Ibn Khaldūn, *Muqaddimat Ibn Khaldūn,* ed. M. Quatremère under the title *Prolégomènes d'Ebn-Khaldoun,* (Paris, 1858).
Ibn Khaldūn, *Muqaddima,* tr., F. Rosenthal (New York, 1958).
Ibn Khallikān, *Wafayāt al-Aʿyān,* ed. I. ʿAbbās (Beirut, 1968-71), vols. I-VII.
Ibn Manẓūr, *Lisān al-ʿArab* (Beirut, 1955-6).
Ibn al-Muʿtazz, *Dīwān,* ed. B. Lewin. (Istanbul, 1945).
Ibn al-Nadīm, M. b. I., *The Fihrist of al-Nadīm: a Tenth-Century Survey of Muslim Culture,* tr., Bayard Dodge (New York and London, 1970), vols I and II.
Ibn al-Nadīm, M. b. I., *Kitāb al-Fihrist,* ed. G. Flügel (Leipzig, 1872).
Ibn Nubātā, *Dīwān Ibn Nubātā* (Cairo, 1905).
Ibn Saʿd, *al-Ṭabaqāt al-Kubrā,* ed. Z. M. Manṣūr (al-Madina, 1408/1987-8), Suppl. Vol.
Ibn Saʿīd al-Maghribī. *al-Mughrib fī Ḥulā 'l-Maghrib* (Leiden, 1898).
Ibn Shuhayd al-Andalusī, *Risālat al-Tawābiʿ wa-'l-Zawābiʿ,* ed. and tr. J. T. Monroe (Los Angeles, 1971).

Ibn Sīda al-Marsī, Abū 'l-Hasan 'Alī b. Ismā'īl al-Andalusī. *Kitāb al-Mukhaṣṣaṣ* (Būlāq, 1320/1920f).
Ibn Sūdūn, 'A., *Kitāb Nuzhat al-Nufūs wa-Muḍḍik al-'Abūs* (Cairo, 1280/1863f).
Ibn al-Ta'āwīdhī, Sibṭ, *Dīwān*, ed. D. S. Margoliouth (Cairo, 1903).
Ibn Taghrī Birdī, *Ḥawādith al-Duhūr*, ed. W. Popper (Berkley and Los Angeles, 1930f).
Ibn Taghrī Birdī, *al-Nujūm al-Zāhira* (Cairo, n.d.).
Ibn al-Ṭiqṭaqā, *al-Fakhrī*, ed. H. Derenbourg (Paris, 1895).
Ibn Ṭūlūn, Shams al-Dīn Muḥammad, *Mufākahat al-Khullān fī Ḥawādith al-Zamān*. ed. M. M. Ziyāda (Cairo, 1381/1962).
Ibn al-Zubayr, al-Rashīd, *Kitāb al-Dhakhā'ir wa-'l-Tuḥaf*, ed. M. Ḥamīd Allah (Kuwait, 1959).
al-Ibshīhī, *al-Mustaṭraf min kull Fann Mustaẓraf* (Cairo, 1379/1959-60).
al-Idrīsī, *Description de l'Afrique et de l'Espagne*, ed. R.P.A. Dozy and M. J. de Goeje. (Amsterdam, 1866; repr. 1969).
al-Iṣfahānī, al-Rāghib, *Muḥāḍarāt al-Udabā'*, ed. I. Zaydān. (Beirut, n.d.).
al-Iṣfahānī, al-Rāghib, *Muḥāḍarāt al-Udabā' wa-Muḥāwarāt al-Shu'arā' al-Bulaghā'* (Cairo, 1287/1870f.), vol. I, (Cairo, 1968), vol. II.
al-Iṣfahānī, Abū-'l-Faraj, *Maqātil al-Tālibiyyīn*, ed. A. Ṣaqr (Cairo, 1949).
al-Iṣfahānī, Abū-'l-Faraj, *Kitāb al-Aghānī* (Būlāq, 1285), XX vols. (Cairo, 1927–74), XXI vols.
al-Jabartī, 'Abd al-Raḥman, *'Ajā'ib al-Āthār fī 'l-Tarājim wa-l-Akhbār* (Būlāq, 1297/1880), vols. 1-IV.
Jacob, G., *Geschichte des Schattentheaters im Morgen- und Abendland* (Osnabrück, 1972).
Jacobson, H., *The Exagoge of Ezechiel* (Cambridge, 1983).
al-Jāḥiẓ, *al-Bayān wa-'l-Tabyīn*, ed. 'A.-S. M. Hārūn, third edition (Cairo, 1388/1968).
al-Jāḥiẓ, (attrib.), *Kitāb al-Tāj fī Akhlāq al-Mulūk*, ed. F. 'Aṭawī (Beirut, 1970).
al-Jāḥiẓ, *Rasā'il al-Jāḥiẓ*, ed. H. al-Sandūbī (Cairo, 1933).
al-Jammāl, Aḥmad S., *al-Adab al-'Āmmī fī Miṣr fī al-'Aṣr al-Mamlūkī* (Cairo, 1966).
Jarīr b. 'Aṭiyya, *Dīwān*, ed. Muḥammad al-Ṣāwī (Cairo, 1935).
Jastrow, M., *A Dictionary of the Targumim* (New York, 1950).
al-Jawālīqī, *al-Mu'arrab*, ed. E. Sachau (Leipzig, 1867).
John of Ephesus, *Lives of the Eastern Saints*, Syriac text ed. and tr. E. W. Brooks, in *Patrologia Orientalis* (Paris, 1924), vol. XIX.
Joshua the Stylite, *Chronicle*, ed. and tr. W. Wright (Cambridge, 1882).
Kahle, P., *Das Krokodilspiel* (*Li'b al-Timsāḥ*). *Ein aegyptisches Schattenspiel*, (Göttingen, 1915).
Kahle, P., *Zur Geschichte des arabischen Schattentheaters in Ägypten* (Leipzig, 1909).
Kamāl al-Dīn, Muḥammad, *al-'Arab wa-'l-Masraḥ* (Cairo, 1975).
Kayāl, Munīr, *Ramaḍān wa-Taqālīduh al-Dimashqiyya* (Damascus, n.d.).
Al-Khafājī, Shihāb al-Dīn Aḥmad, *Kitāb Shifā' al-Ghalīl fīmā fī Kalām al-'Arab min al-Dakhīl* (Cairo, 1325/1907).
al-Khayyāṭ, Jalāl, *al-Uṣūl al-Drāmiyya fī-'l-Shi'r al-'Arabī* (Baghdad, 1982).

al-Khozai, M. A., *The Development of the Early Arabic Drama (1847-1900)* (London, 1984).

Khūrshīd, Fārūq, *al-Siyar al-Sha'biyya* (Cairo, 1978).

al-Kindī, *The Governors and Judges of Egypt or Kitāb el-'Umarā' (el-Wulāt) wa Kitāb el-Quḍāh of el Kindī, Together with an Appendix Derived mostly from Raf' el-Iṣr by Ibn Ḥajar,* ed. R. Guest (Leiden, 1912).

Kutscher, Y., *Millim ve-Toldoteihen* (*Words and their History*) (Jerusalem, 1965).

al-Kutubī, Ibn Shākir, *Fawāt al-Wafayāt* (Būlāq, 1283/1866f), vol. I; ed. M. M. -D. 'Abd al-Ḥamīd. (Cairo, 1951), vol. II.

Laistner, M. L. W., *Christianity and Pagan Culture in the Later Roman Empire* (Cornell, 1951).

Landau, J. M., *Studies in the Arab Theater and Cinema* (Philadelphia, 1958).

Lane, E. W., (tr.), *The Arabian Nights' Entertainments* (London, 1928), vol. II.

Lane, E. W., *An Arabic-English Lexicon* (London 1869-93).

Lane, E. W., *The Manners and Customs of the Modern Egyptians* (London and New York), (London, 1954).

Lassy, I., *The Muḥarram Mysteries among the Azerbeijan Turks Of Caucasia* (Helsinki, 1916).

Levy, Z., *Jerome Antagonistes. Les Structures dramatiques et les procedures narratives de la Porte Etroite* (Paris, 1984).

Liebermann, S., *Greek in Jewish Palestine: Studies in the Life and Manners of Jewish Palestine in the II-IV Centuries CE* (New York, 1942).

Link, J., *Die Geschichte der Schauspieler nach einem syrischen Manuskript der königlichen Bibliothek in Berlin* (Berlin, 1904).

Littré, E. (ed. and tr.) *Oeuvres complètes d'Hippocrate* (Amsterdam, 1962), vol. IV.

MacNaughten, W. H. (ed.), *Alf Layla wa-layla* (Calcutta and London, 1839), vol. I.

Maimonides, *Commentaire sur la Mischnah, Seder Tohorot,* ed. J. Derenbourg (Berlin, 1887).

Maimonides, *Mishna 'im Perush Rabbenu Moshe ben Maymon* (*Mishna Commentary*), ed. J. Qafih (Jerusalem, 1968), vols. IV-V.

Mair, V. H., *Tun-huang Popular Narratives* (Cambridge, 1980?).

Malīḥ, Waṣfī, *Tārīkh al-Masraḥ al-Sūrī* (Damascus, 1984).

Mandūr, M., *al-Adab wa-Funūnuh* (Cairo, 1963).

Mandūr, M., *al-Masraḥ* (Cairo, 1963), 2nd edn.

Mandūr, M., *Masraḥiyyāt Shawqī* (Cairo, 1955).

Mandūr, M., *al-Thaqāfah wa-Ajhizatuhā* (Cairo, 1962).

Mansi, J. D., (ed.), *Sacrorum Conciliorum ... Collectio,* (Graz, 1960).

Mansou, P., and Blachère R., *al-Hamadhani-choix de maqamat* (Paris, 1957).

al-Maqqarī, *Nafḥ al-Ṭīb,* ed. R. Dozy *et al.* (Leiden, 1855-61), vol. II, and ed. Iḥsān 'Abbās (Beirut, 1962), 2nd edn., vol. II.

al-Maqqarī, *Annalectes sur l'histoire et la Litterature des arabes d'Espagne* (Leiden, 1856-61).

al-Maqrīzī, *al-Mawā'iẓ wa-'l-I'tibār fī Dhikr al-Khiṭaṭ wa-'l-Āathār* (Būlāq, 1270/1854). ed. G. Wiet, (Cairo, 1911-23).

al-Maqrīzī, *Al-Sulūk li-Ma'rifat Duwal al-Mulūk,* ed. Sa'īd 'Abd al-Fattāḥ 'Āshūr (Cairo, 1936-1972).

al-Maqrīzī, *Histoire des Sultans mamlouks des l'Egypte* (tr.) M., Quatremère, (Paris, 1837).
Marzolph, U., *Der Weise Mar Buhlūl* (Wiesbaden, 1983).
al-Mas'ūdī, 'A. b. al-Ḥ., *Murūj al-Dhahab* (*Les Prairies d'Or*), ed. and tr. C. Barbier de Meynard and A. J. B. Pavet de Courteille (Paris, 1861-77).
al-Mas'ūdī, 'A. b. al-Ḥ., *Murūj al-Dhahab wa-Ma'ādin al-Jawhar* ed. Ch. Pellat (Beirut, 1973-74).
Mateos, J., *Leyla-Sapra* (Rome, 1959).
Menzel, Th., *Meddāḥ Schattentheater und Orta Ojunu* (Prague, 1941).
Mez, A., (ed.), *Abulḳāsim, ein baghdader Sittenbild-Ḥikāyat Abī-'l-Qāsim al-Baghdādī* (Heidelberg, 1902).
Mez, A., (ed.), *Die Renaissance des Islams* (Heidelberg, 1922).
Midrash Rabba letter gimel and letters yud-zayn (Jerusalem, 1965), vols I and IV. Cf. *Midrash Rabbah,* translated under the editorship of Rabbi H. Freedman and Maurice Simon (London, 1939).
al-Mināwī, 'Abd al-Ra'ūf, *Kitāb al-Taysīr bi-Sharḥ al-Jāmi' al-Ṣaghīr* (Cairo, 1286/1869).
Miquel, A., *La Litterature Arabe* (Paris, 1969).
al-Miṣrī, Irīs Ḥabīb, *Qiṣṣat al-Kanīsa al-Qibṭiyya* (Cairo, 1953).
al-Mizzī, Ibn Yūsuf, *Tuḥfat al-Ashrāf fī Ma'rifat al-Aṭrāf* (Bombay, 1400/1980).
Molé, M., *Les Mystiques musulmans* (Paris, 1965).
Monroe, J. T., *The Art of Badī' al-Zamān al-Hamadhānī as Picaresque Narrative* (Beirut, 1983).
Montet, E., *La Religion et le Theatre en perse* (Paris, 1887).
Moosa, Matti, *The Origins of Modern Arabic Fiction* (Washington, 1983).
Mubārak, 'Alī. *'Alam al-Din* (Cairo, 1889).
Mubārak, Z., *al-Nathr al-Fannī fī 'l-Qarn al-Rābi'* (Cairo, 1934).
al-Muqaffa', Severus, *History of the Patriarchs of the Coptic Church of Alexandria,* ed. and tr. B. Evetts, in 'Patrologie Orientalis (Paris, 1907 and 1910), vols. I and IV.
al-Musabbiḥī, M., *Akhbār Misr,* ed. A. F. Sayyid and T. Bianquis (Cairo, 1978).
Muslim, *Ṣaḥīḥ,* ed. M. F. 'Abd al-Bāqī (Cairo, 1955).
al-Nadīm, 'Abdallah, *Sulāfat al-Nadīm* (Cairo, 1901).
Najm, M. Y., *al-Masraḥiyya fī 'l-Adab al-'Arabī al-Ḥadīth 1847–1914* (Beirut, 1956).
Naqqāsh, Mārūn, *al-Masraḥ al-'Arabī: Dirāsāt wa-Nuṣūṣ,* ed. M. Y. Najm (Beirut, 1963).
Naqqāsh, Mārūn, *Arzat Lubnān,* ed. Nīqūlā Naqqāsh (Beirut, 1869).
Nathan me-Romi, *Sefer ha-Arukh* (*Aruch Completum*), ed. A. Kohut (Vienna, 1926).
al-Nawājī, M. b. al-Ḥasan, *Ḥalbat al-Kumayt* (Cairo, 1938).
al-Naysābūrī, *'Uqlā' al-Majānīn,* ed. M. Baḥr al-'Ulūm (Najaf, 1387/1968).
Niebuhr, C., *Travels Through Arabia and Other Countries in the East,* tr. R. Heron (Edinburgh, 1792).
al-Nuwayrī, *Nihāyat al-Arab* (Cairo, 1923-1984).
Palladius, *The Paradise of the Holy Fathers,* tr. E. A. W. Budge (London, 1907); repr. (Oxford, 1934).

Payne Smith, R., *Thesaurus Syriacus* (Oxford, 1879-1901).
Pellat, Ch., *Ibn Shuhayd al-Andalusī, Ḥayātuh wa-Āthāruh* (Amman, 1965).
Pérés, H., *La Poésie andalouse en arabe classique au XIè siècle* (Paris, 1937).
Putintseva, T. A., *Tysiacha i odin god arabskogo teatra* (Moskow, 1977), tr. from Russian into Arabic T. al-Mu'adhin into *Alf 'Ām wa-'Ām 'Alā al-Masraḥ al-'Arabī* (Beirut, 1981).
Qamḥiyya, Jābir, *al-Taqlīdiyya wa-'l-Drāmiyya fī Maqāmāt al-Ḥarīrī* (Cairo, 1985).
Qarah 'Alī, M., *al-Ḍāḥikūn* (Beirut, 1980).
al-Qarṭājannī, Abū 'l-Ḥasan Ḥāzim, *Minhāj al-Bulaghā' wa-Sirāj al-Udabā'*, ed. M. H. Ibn al-Khūjah (Tunis, 1966).
Qāsim, Aḥmad Shawqī, *al-Masraḥ al-Islāmī* (Cairo, 1980).
al-Qāsimī, M. S., *Qāmūs al-Ṣinā'āt al-Shāmiyya* (*dictionnaire des metiers damascain*) (Paris, 1960).
al-Qazwīnī, *Kosmographie,* ed. F. Wüstenfeld (Göttingen, 1848).
al-Qazwīnī, *'Ajā'ib al-Makhlūqāt* (Leipzig, 1848), vol. I; (Wiesbaden, 1967) vol.II.
al-Qurṭubī, M. b., known as Ibn al-Ukhuvva, *Kitāb Ma'ālim al-Qurbā fī Aḥkām al-Ḥisba,* ed. M. M. Sha'bān and S. A. 'I. al-Muṭī'ī (Cairo, 1976).
al-Qurṭubī, Ibn 'Abd al-Barr, *al-Istī'āb fī Ma'rifat al-Aṣḥāb,* ed. 'A. M. al-Bujāwī (Cairo, 1970).
al-Rā'ī, 'A., *Funūn al-Kūmīdiya min Khayāl al-Ẓill ilā Najīb al-Rīḥānī* (Cairo, 1971).
al-Rā'ī, 'A., *al-Kūmīdya al-Murtajala fī 'l-Masraḥ al-Miṣrī* (Cairo, 1968).
Reich, H., *Der Mimus, ein literar-entwickelungs geschichtlicher Versuch* (Berlin, 1903).
Richardson, J., *Dictionary: Persia, Arabic and English* (London, 1906).
Riedel, W. and Crum, W. E. (eds and trs), *The Canons of Athanasius of Alexandria* (Oxford, 1904).
Roger, F. E., *La Terre Saincte* (Paris, 1646).
Rosenthal, F., *Humor in Early Islam* (Leiden, 1965: rpt. Westport, Conn., 1976).
Russel, A., *The Natural History of Aleppo,* ed. P. Russel. (London, 1794), 2nd edn, vol. I.
Ryden, L. (ed.), *Das Leben des heiligen Narren Symeon, von Leontius von Neapolis* (Uppsala, 1963).
Sadan, J., *al-Adab al-'Arabī al-Hāzil wa-Nawādir al-Thuqalā'* (Tel Aviv, 1983).
al-Ṣafadī, Kh. b. Aybak, *Kitāb al-Wāfī bi-'l-Wafayāt,* ed. S. Dedering (Damascus, 1953).
al-Ṣafadī, Kh. b. Aybak, *Kitāb al-Ghayth al-Musjam fī Sharḥ Lāmiyyat al-'Ajam* (Cairo, 1305/1887). vol. II.
al-Sakhāwī, *al-Tibr al-Masbūk* (Cairo, n.d.).
Samhouri, Z., *The Explorer* (Damascus, 1969).
Ṣanū', Ya'qūb, *al-Masraḥ al-'Arabī, Dirādsāt wa-Nuṣūs, Ya'qūb Ṣannū'* (sic.) (*Abū Naḍḍāra*), ed. M. Y. Najm (Beirut, 1963).
Ṣanū', Ya'qūb, *Riḥlat Abī Naẓẓāra Zarqā 'l-Walī min Miṣr* (Paris, 1876).
Segal, J. B., *Edessa, 'The Blessed City'* (Oxford, 1970).
Seybold, Ch. F., *Glossarium Latino-Arabicum* (Berlin, 1900).
Sezgin, F., *Geschichte des arabischen Schrifttums* (Leiden, 1970), vol. III.

al-Sha'rānī, *al-Ṭabaqāt al-Kubrā* (Cairo, n.d.),

al-Sha'rānī, *Laṭā'if al-Minan* (Cairo, 1321/1903).

al-Shābushtī, 'A. b. M., *Kitāb al-Diyārāt,* ed. G. 'Awwād, second edition (Baghdad, 1966).

al-Shak'a, Muṣṭafā, *Min Funūn al-Adab al-'Arabī* (Cairo, 1957).

al-Shāljī, 'A. (ed.), *al-Risāla al-Baghdādiyya li-Abī Ḥayyān al-Tawḥīdī* (Beirut, 1400/1980).

al-Shaqundī, *Elogio des Islam español* (*Risāla fī Faḍl al-Andalus*), ed. E. Garcia Gomez (Madrid, 1934).

al-Shaqundī, *Risāla fī Faḍl al-andalus in Faḍā'il al-Andalus wa-Ahlihā, li-Ibn Ḥazm, wa-Ibn Sa'īd wa-'l-Shaqundī,* ed. Ṣalāh al-Dīn al-Munajjid (Beirut, 1968).

al-Shāyib, Aḥmad, *Uṣul al-Naqd al-Adabī* (Cairo, 1946), 3rd edn.

Shidyāq, Aḥmad Fāris, *al-Wāsiṭa fī Ma'rifat Aḥwāl al-Maliṭā wa-Kashf al-Mukhabbā 'an Funūn Urubbā* (Constantinopole, 1299/1881f).

al-Shirbīnī, Yūsuf b. M., *K. Hazz al-Quḥūf fī Sharḥ Qaṣīdat Abī Shādūf* (Būlāq, 1282/1865).

al-Shirwānī, A. b. M. al-Yamanī, *Ḥadā'iq al-Afrāḥ fī Izāḥat al-Atrāḥ* (Būlāq, 1282/1865).

Sifakis, G. M., *Studies in the History of Hellenistic Drama* (London, 1967).

Silberschlag, E., *From Renaissance to Renaissance* (New York, 1977), 2 vols.

Speis, O., *Türkisches Puppentheater* (Wests., 1955).

Steingass, F., *A Comprehensive Persian-English Dictionary* (London, 1947).

Steinschneider, M., *Die arabische Litteratur der Juden* (Frankfurt a.M., 1902).

al-Suhaylī, 'Abd al-Raḥmān, *al-Rawḍ al-Unuf,* ed. 'A. R. al-Wakīl (Cairo, 1967-70).

al-Ṣūlī, Muḥammad b. Yaḥyā, *Ash'ār Awlād al-Khulafā',* ed. J. Heyworth-Dunne (Cairo, 1936).

al-Ṭabarī, *Annales,* ed. M. J. de Goeje *et al.* (Leiden, 1879-1901).

al-Ṭabarsī, *Makārim al-Akhlāq* (Cairo, 1304/1886).

al-Ṭahṭāwī, Rifā'a Rāfi', *Takhlīs al-Ibrīz fī Talkhīs Bārīz,* ed. M. 'Allām, A. A. Badawī and A. Lūqā (Cairo, 1958).

Talmud Babli, eds. A. Mishcon, A. Cohen and Talmud Bably (London, 1935 and New York, 1944)

Talmud Yemshalmi (New York,, 1948)

al-Tanūkhī, Abū 'Alī al-Muḥsin, *K. Jāmi' al-Tawārīkh al-Musammā bi-Kitāb Nishwār al-Muḥāḍara wa-Akhbār al-Mudhākara* (The Table Talk of a Mesopotamian Judge), ed. S. Margoliouth (Cairo, 1921).

al-Tanūkhī, Abū 'Alī al-Muḥsin, *Nishwār al-Muḥāḍara,* ed. 'A. al-Shāljī (Beirut, 1971).

al-Tanūkhī, Abū 'Alī al-Muḥsin, *al-Baṣā'ir wa-'l-Dhakha'ir,* ed. I. Kailānī (Damascus, 1964).

al-Tanūkhī, Abū 'Alī al-Muḥsin, *Kitāb al-Imtā' wa-'l-Mu'ānasa,* ed. A Amīn and A. al-Zīn (Cairo, 1939; reprinted Beirut, 1953).

Taymūr, Aḥmad, *Khayāl al-Ẓill wa-'l-Lu'ab wa-'l-Tamāthīl al-Muṣawwara 'inda 'l-'Arab* (Cairo, 1376/1957).

Tertullian, *Apology, De Spectaculis,* tr. T. R. Glover (London, 1931).

al-Tha'ālibī, *Yatīmat al-Dahr* (Cairo, 1399/1979).

Thévenot, *Voyage au Levant* (Paris, 1665).

Titley, N. M., *Sports and Pastimes, Scenes from Turkish, Persian and Mughal Paintings* (London, 1979).
Tomiche, Nada, *Histoire de la Littérature Romanesque de L'Egypte Moderne* (Paris, 1981).
Ullmann, M., *Wörterbuch der klassischen arabischen Sprache* (Wiesbaden, 1970).
Urquhart, D., *The Lebanon: (Mount Souria), a History and Diary* (London, 1860).
Villoteau, M., *De l'état actuel de l'art musical en Egypte* (Paris, 1812).
Warner, C. D., *My Winter on the Nile* (Hartford, 1904).
Wensinck, A. J. et al. (eds.), *Concordance et Indices de la Tradition Musulmane* (Leiden, 1967 ff.).
Wetzstein, J. G., (ed.), *Die Liebenden von Amasia, ein Damascener Schattenspiel* (Leipzig, 1906).
Wieneke, J., (ed.), *Ezechielis Judaici Poetae Alexandrini Fabulae Quae Inscribitur Exagoge Fragmenta* (Munster, 1931).
Wiet, G. (tr.) *Journal d'un Bourgeois du Caire, Chronique d'Ibn Iyas* (Cairo, 1960).
Wigram, W. A., *The Assyrians and their Neighbours* (London, 1929).
Wright, W., *A Grammar of the Arabic Language* (Cambridge, 1955).
al-Yāfi al-Yamānī, *Kitāb Rawḍ al-Rayāḥīn fī Ḥikāyāt al-Ṣāliḥīn* (Cairo, 1297/1880).
Yāqūt, *Mu'jam al-Udabā'*, ed. A. F. Rifā'ī (Cairo, 1936-38).
Yūnis, 'A. -H., *Kitāb Khayāl al-Ẓill* (Cairo, 1963).
Zaydān, Jurjī, *Mudhakkirāt Jurjī Zaydān*, ed. Ṣalāḥ al-Dīn al-Munajjid (Beirut, 1968).
al-Ziriklī, Khayr al-Dīn. (ed.) *Rasā'il Ikhwān al-Ṣafā* (Cairo, 1928).

2. *Articles*

'Anānī, M. Z., 'Ḥawla Khāyal al-Ẓill fī Miṣr ma'a Naṣṣ Yunshar li-Awwali Marra', *al-Kātib*, LXVIII, nos. 202-203, January-February 1978, pp. 6-14; 20-40.
Andersen, C., 'Altkristliche Kritik am Tanz – ein Ausschnitt aus dem Kampf der alten Kirche gegen heidnische Sitten' in H. Frohnes and W. Knorr (eds.), *Die Alte Kirche* (Munich, 1974).
'Awwād, G., 'Ṭayf al-Khayāl', in *al-Thaqāfa* (Cairo) no. 216, February 16, 1943, pp. 15 ff.
Badawi, M. M., 'Medieval Arabic Drama: Ibn Dāniyāl', *Journal of Arabic Literature*, XIII, 1982, pp. 83–107.
Brock, S., 'Syriac Dialogue Poems: Marginalia to a Recent Edition', *Le Museon*, XCVII, nos. 1–2, 1984, pp. 29–58.
Cachia, P., 'The Dramatic Monologues of al-Ma'arri', *Journal of Arabic Literature*, I, 1970, pp. 129–136
Cachia, P., 'The Theatrical Movement of the Arabs', *Middle Eastern Studies Association Bulletin*, XVI, no. 1, July 1982, pp. 9–23.
Canard, M., 'Le ceremonial fāṭimide et le ceremonial byzantin', *Byzantion*, XXI, 1951, pp. 355-95.
Cöln, F., 'Erste Abteilung: Texte und Uebersetzungen *al-Ṭibb al-Rūḥānī*, der Nomokanon Mikhā'ils von Malig', *Oriens Christianus 1907*, vol. VII.

Desparmet, J., 'Note sur les Mascarades chez les Indigenes de Blida', *Revue africaine* 52 (1908), pp. 265–271.

Esin, E., 'The Cultural Background of Afshīn Ḥaidar of Ushrusana in the Light of Recent Numismatic and Iconographic Data', in A. Dietrich (ed.), *Akten des VII. Kongresses für Arabistik und Islamwissenschaft* (Göttingen, 1976), pp. 126–45.

Ettinghausen, R., 'The Dance with Zoomorphic Masks and Other forms of Entertainment Seen in Islamic Art', in *Arabic and Islamic Studies in Honor of Hamilton A. R. Gibb*, ed. George Makdisi (Leiden, 1965), pp. 211-224.

Ettinghausen, R., 'Early Realism in Islamic Art', *Studi Orientalistici in onore di Giorgio Levi Della Vida* (Roma, 1956), I, 250–273.

Ezekiel, The Poet. *Encyclopaedia Judaica.2* (Jerusalem, 1971), vol. 15, cols. 1049-51).

Gabrieli, F., 'Sulla Ḥikāyat Abī 'l-Qāsim di Abī 'l-Muṭahhar al-Azdī', *Revista degli Studi Orientali* XX (1942), pp. 33–45.

Gaudefroy-Demombynes, M., 'Sur le cheval-jupon et al-jurraj' in *Melanges offerts à William Marcais* (Paris, 1950), pp. 155–160.

Goodman, L. E., 'Hamadhānī, Schadenfreude and Salvation through Sin', *Journal of Arabic Literature* XIX, 1988, pp. 27–39.

Ḥunayn, Idwār, 'Shawqī wa-'l-Masraḥ', *al-Mashriq*, xxxii (1934), pp. 563–577

Husain, S. M., 'The Poems of Surāqa b. Mirdās al-Bāriqī, an Umayyad Poet', *Journal of the Royal Asiatic Society*, (1936), p. 620.

Ibn Ṭūlūn al-Ḥanafī 'l-Ṣāliḥī, Dhakhā'ir al-Qaṣr fī Tarājim Nubalā' al-'Aṣr' in *Majallat al-Majma' al -'Ilmī* (Damascus) II, Pt. 4, April 1922, 148.

Inostrantseve, K., *'K upominaniyu Khayāl'a* v *arabskoy literature'* ('On the occurrence of *Khayal* in Arabic Literature'), *Zapiski vostonchogo otdel. Imp. Russk. Arkheol. Obšcestva* (St. Petersburg, 1907), XVII, p. 164ff.

Jabrī, Sh., 'Dimashq fi Māḍīhā 'l-Qarīb', *Majallat Majma' al-Lugha al-'Arabiyya bi-Dimashq*, XXXVI, Pt. 4 (October, 1961), pp. 529–538.

Jawād, M., 'Ḥikāyat Abī 'l-Qāsim al-Baghdādī hal allafahā Abū Ḥayyān al-Tawḥīdī?' *al-'Irfān* (Ṣaydā) XLII, nos. 5-6 (March 1955), pp. 561–6.

Kahle, P., 'The Arabic Shadow Play in Medieval Egypt (Old Texts and Old Figures)', *The Journal of the Pakistan Historical Society* (Karachi), April 1954, pp. 85–115.

Kahle, P., 'The Arabic Shadow Play in Egypt', *J. R. A. S.*, 1940, pp. 21–34.

Kahle, P., Muḥammad Ibn Dānijāl und sein zweites Arabisches Schattenspiel', in *Miscellanea Academica Berolinensis* (1950), pp. 155–167.

al-Kirmilī, Anastās, 'Al-Marfa' Aṣluh wa-Shuyū'uh 'inda 'l-Umam', *al-Mashriq* IX, (1 March 1906), no. 5, pp. 198f.

Kurd 'Alī, M., 'Ḥāḍir al-Andalus wa-Ghābiruhā', *Majallat al-Majma' al-'Ilmī al-'Arabī* (Damascus) II, 1922, p. 235.

La Piana, G., 'The Byzantine Theatre', *Speculum* XI (1936).

Landau, J. M., 'Popular Arabic Plays, 1909', *Journal of Arabic Literature* XVII, 1986, pp. 120–125.

Levy, Kurt, 'La'bat Elḥôta, Ein tunesisches Schattenspiel', in W. Heffenung and W. Kirfel (eds) *Studien zur Geschichte und Kultur des Nahen und Fernen Ostens.* Paul Kahle zum 60. (Leiden, 1935), pp. 119–124.

Macdonald, D. B., *Ḥikāya*, in *EI*.

Marzolph, U., 'Die Quellen der Ergötzlichen Erzahlungen des Bar Hebraeus', *Oriens Christianus* LXXVIII, 1984, p. 218 and LXXIX, 1985, pp. 81–125.

Monchicourt, Ch., 'La fete de l'Achoura', *Revue tunisienne* 17 (1919), pp. 278–301.

Monroe, J. T., 'Prolegomena to the Study of Ibn Quzmān: the Poet as Jongleur' in *The Hispanic Ballad Today: History, Comparativism, Critical Bibliography* (Madrid, 1979), pp. 77–129.

Moreh, S., 'The Arabic Novel between Arabic and European Influences during the Nineteenth Century', in *Studies in Modern Arabic Prose and Poetry* (Leiden, 1988), pp. 88–115.

Moreh, S., 'The Arabic Theatre in Egypt in the Eighteenth and Nineteenth Centuries', in *Etudes Arabes et Islamiques*, (Paris, 1975), Vol. III, pt. 2, pp. 109–113.

Moreh, S., 'The Jewish Theatre in Iraq in the First Half of the Twentieth Century' (in Hebrew), *Pe'amim Studies in the Cultural Heritage of Oriental Jewry* XXIII, (1985), pp. 64–98.

Moreh, S., 'Live Theatre in Medieval Islam' in M. Sharon (ed.) *Studies in Islamic History and Civilizations in Honour of Professor David Ayalon* (Jerusalem, - Leiden, 1986), pp. 565–611.

Moreh, S., 'The Meaning of the term *Kharja* of the Arabic Andalusian *Muwashshah*', in Y. Ben-Abou, (ed.) *Litterare Judaerum* in *Terra Hispanica* (Jerusalem, 1991).

Moreh, S., 'The Shadow Play (*Khayāl al-Ẓill*) in the Light of Arabic Literature', *Journal of Arabic Literature*, XVIII (1987), pp. 46–61.

Moreh, S., 'Ya'qūb Ṣanū', His Religious Identity and Work in the Theatre and Journalism, according to the Family Archive' in S. Shamir (ed.), *The Jews in Egypt* (Boulder and London, 1987), pp. pp. 111–129, 244–264.

Moss, C., 'Jacob of Serugh's Homilies on the Spectacles of the Theatre', *Le Museon* XLVIII 1935, pp. 87–112.

Musso, J. -C., 'Masques de l'Achoura en Grande Kabylie,' *Libyca* 18 (1970), 269–274.

Najm, M. Y., 'Ṣuwar min al-Tamthīl fī 'l-Ḥaḍāra al-'Arabiyya min al-Kurraj ḥattā 'l-Maqāmāt', *Āfāq 'Arabiyya* III, (Baghdad), no. 3, Nov. 1977, pp. 59–63.

Pascon, R., '*Pratiques animistes Interfermant avec le culte musulman,*' *Hesperis*, 42 (1955), 261–263.

Patel, J. 'The Navroz, its History and its Significance', *Journal of the K. R. Cama institute (Bombay)* XXXI, (1937), pp. 1–51.

Pellat, Ch. 'Ḥikāya' in *EI*².

Pellat, Ch. 'Maḳāma', in *EI*².

Peltier-Grobleron, J. et Bousquet, G. -H., 'Le carnaval de l'Achoura a Quarzazate (Maroc),' *Revue africaine*, 92 (1948), pp. 185–186.

Prüfer, C., 'Drama (Arabic)' in *Encyclopaedia of Religion and Ethics* (New York, 1914), vol. IV, pp. 872–878.

Rabate, M. -R., 'La mascarades de l'Aid el Kebir a Ouirgane (Haut-Atlas),' *Objets et Mondes* 7/3 (1961), pp. 165–184.

Rice, D. S., 'Deacon or Drink: Some Paintings from Samarra Re-examined, *Arabica* V (1958), pp. 15–33.

Rowson, E. K., 'Religion and Politics in the Career of Badī' al-Zamān al-Hamadhānī', *Journal of the American Oriental Society*, CVII (1987), pp. 653–673.

Sadan, J., 'The Nomad versus Sedentary Framework', *Fabula* (Gottingen), XV, (1974), pp. 59–86.

Sadan, J., 'Kings and Craftsmen, a Pattern of Contrasts', in *Studia Islamica*, Pt. i, LVI (1982), pp. 5–49; Pt. 2, LXII (1985), pp. 89–120.

Sadan, J., 'Vin- Fait de civilisation' in M. Rosen-Ayalon (ed.), *Studies in Memory of Gaston Wiet.* (Jerusalem, 1977), pp. 129–160.

Sadan, J., 'Wine, Woman and Seas : Some Images of Rulers in Medieval Arabic Literature', *Journal of Semitic Studies*, XXXIV (Spring 1989), pp. 133–152.

Schork, R. J., 'Dramatic Dimensions in Byzantine Hymns', *Studia Patristica* VIII (1966), pp. 271–279.

Schulthess, 'Über den Dichter al Nagasi und einige Zeitgenossen', *Zeitschrift der Deutschen Morgenländischen Gesellschaft*, LIV, 1900, pp. 421–74.

Segal, J. B., 'Ibn al-'Ibrī' in *EI*².

Segal, J. B., 'Mesopotamian Communities from Julian to the rise of Islam', *Proceedings of the British Academy*, XLI, 1955.

al-Shaykh al-Maghribī, 'al-Thaqāla wa 'l-Thuqalā', *Majallat al-Majma' al-'Ilmī bi-Dimashq*, XII, 1932.

Shiloah, A., 'Reflexions sur la danse artistique musulmane au moyen age', *Cahiers de civilisations medievale*, V (1962), pp. 463–474.

Shinar, P., 'Traditional and Reformist Mawlid Celebrations in the Maghrib' in M. Rosen-Ayalon (ed.), *Studies in Memory of Gaston Wiet* (Jerusalem, 1977), p. 371-413.

Theater, *Encyclopaedia Judaica* (Jerusalem, 1971), vol. 15, cols. 1049–51.

Thevenot, *The Travels of Monsieur de Thevenot into the Levant* (London, 1686).

Vandenberghe, B. H., 'Saint Chrysostome et les Spectacles', *Zeitschrift für Religions- und Geistesgeschichte* VII (1955), pp. 34–46.

Wagner, E., 'Die arabische Rangstreitsdichtung und ihre Einordnung in die allgemeine Literaturgeschichte', *Abhandlungen der Akademie der Wissenschaften und Literatur.* Mainz, geistes- und sozialwissenschaftliche Klasse, no. i, 1962.

Wetzstein, J. G., 'Sprachliches aus den Zeltlagern der syrischen Wüste', *ZDMG* XXII (1868).

Widengren, G. 'Harlekintracht und Mönchskutte, Clownhut und Derwischmütze. Eine gesellschafts-, religions- und trachtgeschichtliche Studie', *Orientalia Suecena* II, (Uppsala, 1953), pp. 41–87.

Wild, S., 'A Juggler's Programme in Medieval Islam' in R. Matran (ed.), *La Signification du bas moyen age dans l'histoire et la culture du monde arabe (Actes du 8me congres de l'Union Européenne des Arabisants et Islamisants, Aix-en-Provence 1976)* (Aix-en-Provence, n.d.)

Yūnis, 'Abd al-Ḥamīd, 'al-Shā'ir wa-'l-Rabāba', in *al-Majalla*, (February 1960) vol. IV, pp. 22–9.

Zayyāt, Ḥabīb, 'Lughat al-Ḥaḍāra fī al-Islām,' *al-Mashriq*, LXIII (July-Oct., 1969) pp. 466–67.

3. Manuscripts

Anon., *Durrat al-Zayn wa Qurrat al-'Ayn*, MS Bibliothèque Nationale, Paris, Ar. 3440.

Anon., *Kitāb Raqā'iq al-Ḥulal fī Daqā'iq al-Ḥiyal*, Bibliothèque Nationale, Paris, Ar. 3552.

Anon., *Kitāb yusammā al-Muntakhab bi-Fawāyid wa-Ḥikāyāt wa-La'ib*, MS. Cambridge Univ. Library, SM Qq. 164.

Anon., *Risāla fī Bayān Ḥurmat Istimā' Ṣawt al-Mizmār*... MS Staatsbibliothek Berlin, Shelf no. We. 1811.

al-Badrī, Taqiy al-Dīn, *Kitāb Rāḥat al-Arwāḥ fī 'l-Ḥashīsh wa-'l-Rāḥ*, Bibliothèque Nationale, Paris, Ar. 3552.

al-Dakdakjī, 'Abd al-Wahhāb, *Raf' al-Mushkilāt fī Ḥukm Ibāḥat al-Ālāt bi'l-Naghamāt al-Ṭayyibāt*, MS Staatsbibliothek Berlin, Shelf no. We. 1811a.

al-Ghazzī, Abū 'l-Barakāt Muḥammad, *al-Marāḥ fī 'l-Muzāḥ*, MS Staatsbibliothek Berlin, shelf no. We 1764 and ed. A. 'Ubayd (Damascus, 1349/1930).

al-Hakim, Darwish Rajab, *Defter der Abu Mustafa*, v. Jahre 1860, MS Staatsbibliothek Berlin, Nachlass Wetzstein, no. 31–43.

al-Ḥamawī, Ibn Ḥijja, see Ibn Ḥijja.

Ibn Abyurdī, Aḥmad, *Rawḍ al-Jinān*, MS Staatsbibliothek Berlin, Shelf No. We. 1087.

Ibn 'Āṣim al-Qaysī al-Andalusī, *Ḥadā'iq al-Azhār fī Mustaḥsan al-Ajwiba wa-'l-Afkār*, MS British Library, MS Or. 1378.

Ibn Ayyūb, Sharaf al-Din, *al-Tadhkira al-Ayyūbiyya*, MS. al-Maktaba al-Ẓāhiriyya, Damascus.

Ibn Ḥamdūn, *Tadhkirat Ibn Ḥamdūn*, British Library, MS. Or. 3179.

Ibn al-Ḥajjāj, *Dīwān*, MS British Library, Add. 7588.

Ibn Ḥijja al-Ḥamawī, *Thamarāt al-Awrāq*, MS. Bibliothèque Nationale, Paris, Ar. 3531.

Ibn Iyās, *al-Nujūm al-Zāhira*, MS. Bibliothèque Nationale, Paris Ar. 1783.

Ibn Iyās, *Tārīkh Ibn Iyās al-Kabīr*, MS Bibliothèque Nationale, Paris, Ar. 1823.

Ibn Khallikān, *Wafayāt al-A'yān wa-Anbā' Abnā' al-Zamān*, MS Bibliothèque Nationale, Paris, Ar. 2050.

Ibn Mawlāhum al-Khayālī, Muḥammad, *Al-Maqāma al-Mukhtaṣara fī 'l-Khamsīn Marah*, British Library MS., Add. 19411.

Ibn Sūdūn, *Dīwān Ibn Sūdūn*, MS Bibliothèque Nationale, Paris, Ar. 3220.

Ibn Taghrī Birdī, *al-Nujūm al-Zāhira fī Mulūk Miṣr wa-'l-Qāhira*, MS Bibliothèque Nationale, Paris, Ar. 1783.

Ibn Zūlāq, *Tārīkh Miṣr wa-Faḍā'iluhā*, MS Bibliothèque Nationale, Paris, Ar. 1820.

al-Isḥāqī, 'Abd al-Bāqī, *Misṭāra Khayāl, Munādamat Umm Mijbir*, MS Bibliothèque Nationale, Paris, Ar. 4852.

al-Khayālī, see: Ibn Mawlāhum.

Mālṭī, Ḥabīb Ablā. *al-Aḥmaq al-Basīṭ*, MS Staatsbibliothek Berlin, shelf no. Sachau 23.

Maqrīzī, *al-Sulūk*, MS. Bibliothèque Nationale, Paris, Ar. 1726.

al-Ṣafadī, Ṣalāḥ al-Dīn b. Aybak, *Al-Ḥusn al-Ṣarīḥ fī Mi'at Malīḥ* (Dār al-

Kutub al-Miṣriyya MS., Cairo).
Shafi' b. 'Alī 'Abbās al-Kātib, *K. Ḥusn al-Manāqib al-Sariyya al-Muntaza'a min al-Sīra al-Ẓāhiriyya*, MS. Bibliothèque Nationale, Paris, Ar. 1707.
al-Tanūkhī, *K. Jāmi' al-Tawārīkh al-Musammā bi-Kitāb al-Muḥāḍara wa-Akhbār al-Mudhākara*, MS. Bibliothèque Nationale, Paris, Ar. 3482.
al-Tīfāshī, Aḥmad, *Kitāb Nuzhat al-Albāb fīmā lā yūjad fī Kitāb*, MS Bibliothèque Nationale, Paris, Ar. 3055.
al-Tūnisī, Muḥammad b. Aḥmad, *Kitāb Faraḥ al-Asmā' bi-Rukhaṣ al-Samā'*, Staatsbibliothek Berlin, shelf no. We. 1505.
al-Ṭūsī, Abū 'l-Ḥasan 'Abd Allāh Daftar Khān al-'Ādilī, *Kitāb Alf Jāriya wa-Jāriya*, MS Vienna, Nat. Bib. A. F. 115 (Flugel, 387).

Index